"THE LAST THING I NEED IN MY LIFE AT THIS TIME IS A MAN WHO FLIRTS AS EASILY AS HE BREATHES."

"But you are attracted to me."

"Yes, I am."

The confession made Griff smile. He crossed the room to where she sat. He slowly ran his finger across her cheek.

"I've been wondering if your skin was as soft as it looked, but it's softer." He brushed his lips against her cheek. "Much softer."

Jessi was trembling like a virgin bride. His mouth left her jaw to journey to the sensitive parted corners of her own, then touched it with a kiss that closed her eyes and made her legs feel like pudding. Using the same feather-light pressure, he soundlessly cajoled and invited her to taste the passion he wished for them to share. His lips were a temptation she felt powerless to resist.

When he pulled her into his arms and kissed her fully, Jessi's whole world began to spin . . .

BEVERLY JENKINS

The Taming of Jessi Rose

AVON BOOKS
An Imprint of HarperCollinsPublishers

To Alex, because he is my light

This is a work of fiction. Names, characters, places, and incidents are products of the author's imagination or are used fictitiously and are not to be construed as real. Any resemblance to actual events, locales, organizations, or persons, living or dead, is entirely coincidental.

AVON BOOKS
An Imprint of HarperCollins*Publishers*
10 East 53rd Street
New York, New York 10022-5299

Copyright © 1999 by Beverly Jenkins
Inside back cover author photo by Glamour Shots
Library of Congress Catalog Card Number: 99-94811
ISBN: 0-380-79865-4
www.avonromance.com

First Avon Books paperback printing: October 1999

Avon Trademark Reg. U.S. Pat. Off. and in Other Countries, Marca Registrada, Hecho en U.S.A.
HarperCollins® is a trademark of HarperCollins Publishers Inc.

Printed in the U.S.A.

10 9 8 7 6

Prologue

Nebraska
Spring 1873

Ten-year-old Griffin Sloan knew his ma, Belinda, was dying. She'd been sick a long time and the end seemed near. Yesterday, she'd started coughing up blood. This morning, she'd been unable to get out of bed. It scared him seeing her this way, so still and worn-out looking, because he'd never known his ma to be sick a day in her life.

Ten years of age and almost a man, Griffin supposed he shouldn't be scared. After all, he'd been the only man in the house ever since his pa went to war for Mr. Lincoln and came back in a plain pine box. That was nearly eight years ago, according to his ma. After his death, she'd run a layover station for the railroads, serving meals and providing a place to stay for the occasional Black passengers other station managers on the line wouldn't house due to prejudice.

Things were fine for a while. Then everything changed, and Griffin held the railroad responsible.

The railroad bosses promised Belinda she would get the spanking new station they were planning on a newly constructed line of track, but the promises never came

1

to be. The station went to someone else, and since the new rail line no longer came their way, her station became unneeded.

She had no one to turn to, no family back east, no understanding neighbors to beg charity from. She tried farming for a while, but like many others on the plains, had neither the money nor the tools to make it go. Last year, Griffin began walking the five miles to the nearest farm to steal food so they wouldn't starve. The farm's owner, Ol' Man McIntosh, caught him in his corn field and hen house more than a few times and whipped him like a runaway slave, but Griffin had continued stealing whatever he could, whenever he could. Sometimes at night, as he lay on his thin pallet, he would hear his ma crying softly. He knew she thought he was asleep and wouldn't hear, but he did, and he prayed night after night to be bigger and stronger so he could make her life better, or for the Good Lord to send them a savior.

The prayers were never answered. She'd written to the railroads to see if they could offer her other employment, but her letters were never answered. Griffin's supply of stolen corn had almost gotten them through the winter, but when it ran out two months ago, they were reduced to eating the wallpaper on the thin drafty walls. Because of the lack of food, she'd wasted away and was terribly thin.

Seated beside her now, watching over her as she slept fitfully, he was afraid, not because he would be left alone, but because he loved her so very much.

The hacking coughs that were as much a part of her now as her heartbeat signaled she'd soon be opening her eyes. Mercifully, it had rained last night, and he'd been able to collect some of it in the bottom of an old wooden bucket. He dipped out a bit with a battered tin cup and offered her a small sip, but it only brought on more body-wracking coughs. Undaunted, Griffin wiped her cracked lips with a rain-dampened rag, then whispered, "Rest now, Ma."

Her voice had once been hail and hearty; now it was a rustling whisper. "Did you go for the doctor, Griffin?"

He couldn't tell her the man wouldn't come. No matter how hard Griffin had begged, he'd been turned away because the Sloans had no money. "Yeah, Ma," Griffin lied. "He's coming, should be here anytime now."

Tears were fuzzing up Griffin's eyes.

She looked into his face and raised her frail brown hand to gently cup his cheek. "I know the doctor's not coming and I know I'm dying."

He placed his hand atop hers. "No, Ma, you're going to be fine. You'll see."

"You've been a good son, Griffin. A *good* son. You're strong—smart, too. You'll do just fine without me. It might be tough in the beginning, but the Good Lord will watch after you and keep you safe."

Tears ran freely down his face now. He didn't want to be looked after; he wanted her to live.

"Go and get the Bible, son."

Griffin was reluctant to leave her side, but he knew how much stock she set in the Good Book.

When he returned, she whispered, "Read me Psalm 62."

Griffin leafed through the worn, well-read pages until he found the psalms, then began to read in a clear but soft voice. *"For God alone my soul waits in silence; from him comes my salvation."*

By the time he moved down to the seventh verse, his tears were so thick he could barely see, but he didn't falter. *"On God rests my deliverance and my honor; my mighty rock, my refuge is in God."*

When he looked up, she was dead.

*   *   *

It took Griffin six hours to dig his ma's grave. Only last night's rain kept it from being any longer. Digging with his hands and an old ax handle he and his ma once used for plowing, he finally managed to open the earth deep enough to protect her from predators both animal and human.

Going back in the house, he washed her up as best he could, then wrapped her in the tarp that covered the hole in the sod roof. It took all of his ten-year-old strength, but he managed to place her body in the grave, and with all the reverence of a loving son, covered her up with the mounded dirt.

Griffin sat by her grave site until the sun came up again, then went into the house. He had no personal belongings to gather; everything they'd owned had been sold over time for food. So he washed his face, picked up his mother's Bible, and struck out, walking west.

He had no idea where he was going or where he'd wind up, but he knew this: when he grew up and became a man, the railroad bosses would pay. They were responsible for his ma's death, and he swore on her grave he'd have his revenge.

Chapter 1

Blanco County, Texas
March 1888

After only a few hours of sleep, Jessi Rose Clayton was roughly awakened by her father. "Jessi Rose, wake up! Stampede!"

It was one of the most dreaded words in cattle ranching, and Jessi didn't need to hear it twice. Jumping out of bed while her father went off to rouse the others, the dark-skinned woman threw off her nightgown and pulled on her shirt, denims, and boots. Only then did she hear the storm. Outside the wind howled and the rain pelted the roof so hard it could've been rocks falling instead. The answering roll of thunder echoed ominously as Jessi ran down the hall to grab her slicker and hat from the peg by the door. She slammed the hat down on top of her short cropped hair and tied the strings tight.

Out on the porch, the wind blew with such tremendous force, it momentarily robbed her of her breath. Someone was calling her name. Peering through the downpour she spied Jeter Lewis, one of the ranch hands. He was mounted and holding the reins of her horse, Snake Eyes. Racing to join him, she mounted quickly, then galloped off fast in Jeter's wake. The wet wind

5

whipped at her fiercely. It was coming down so hard and the night was so black she couldn't see her horse's head.

She could hear the cows off in the distance, though. Steers didn't like storms, and this one looked to be one of the worst of the season. A flash of lightning momentarily turned the rain-filled night into an eerie day, giving her just the briefest glimpse of the fast-riding hands, the cows, and the chaos. The din of screaming steers, men shouting, and guns shooting competed with the noises of the storm. Jessi raced Snake Eyes up and down the edges of the fray, yelling and firing her pistol in the air. She and the others had to keep the herd from spreading out. She looked around for her father. He and Jeter were riding hard to the front of the line in an effort to turn the 500 storm-maddened steers back toward the open range and away from the house. If it stopped raining, the herd would eventually settle down, but if the storm didn't pass quickly, they could be in for a long night. As she continued her ride, yelling and shooting, she hoped her nine-year-old nephew, Jotham, hadn't decided to join in. A stampede was no place for a child.

Just then a particularly bright flash of lightning showed her father, Dexter, falling from his horse. ''No!'' she screamed, as she watched him disappear into the blackness of the stampeding herd. Fearing for his life, she spurred Snake Eyes forward, plunging into the lightning lit chaos of riders and fast-moving longhorns to get to his side. Thunder shook the ground and the flashes of lightning again turned night into day. She screamed for help from the hands as she rode but doubted anyone could hear her over the din.

When she finally reached the place where she thought he'd gone down, her years in the saddle showed in how quickly she dismounted. The downpour and the darkness made it difficult to spot him at first, but seconds later she was dragging him free of the stampede and kneeling in the mud by his side. Cold fear mixed with the cold rain, as she gently raised his head and pillowed him against her body. "Pa?"

A flash of lightning showed her that his eyes were closed. "Pa!"

She shook him gently. "Pa!"

"Jessi Rose?" His once booming voice could barely be heard.

She leaned down, trying to shelter him from the rain and to hear him. "I'm here, Pa. Are you okay, anything broken?"

"Damn coward bastards shot me in the back."

Her eyes widened. "What? Who?"

"One of Darcy's men. Clem Davis. Saw him over my shoulder in the lightning flash just as he was aiming."

She quickly scanned the night, but saw no one. "Hold on, Pa! We'll get the doc!"

"Too late," he whispered. He grabbed hold of Jessi's arm with all the strength he had remaining and said fiercely, "Don't give in. Don't let that bastard Darcy take the land."

Her fears rising, she vowed, "I won't, Pa." He was talking like he was going to die.

Frantically she looked around. He needed help. "Just hold on."

She and her father were now on the outskirts of the herd. Gunshots pierced the air as the expertly riding hands increased their efforts to end the stampede. As the rain continued to pour down, she screamed for someone to go for the doc.

The funeral was held the next day. Dexter Clayton was laid to rest deep in the soil of his own land. Only a few people came by to pay their respects, the others were too afraid. Reed Darcy's terror-filled campaign to take over all the land in their small corner of the county had resulted in burnings, beatings, and the deaths of anyone who stood in his way. He wanted to sell the land to the railroad just to feed his own greed.

The day after the funeral, Jessi rode the forty minutes into the small Black township of Vale. Filled with anger and grief over her father's murder, she ignored the curious looks of the folks who watched and whispered behind their hands about her as she passed. She raised her chin defiantly in response to the women who crossed the street rather than share the planked walk. Jessi's past association with the deadly outlaw known as Calico Bob made her a pariah here in the township. The citizens didn't care for her any more than she cared for them.

When she entered the sheriff's small office, the lawman Casper Hatcher, seated at his desk, looked up warily. "Afternoon, Jessi, what can I do for you?"

"Cap, I want an investigation into my father's death."

The aging and graying Hatcher went back to his paperwork. "Nothing to investigate."

"What do you mean, nothing to investigate? He was murdered."

A patronizing smile crossed his pale brown face. "Nobody murdered Dex. Probably you or one of your hands shot him by mistake." He then looked up. "At least, I hope it was by mistake."

Everyone in town knew Dexter Clayton had a stubborn streak as wide as the state of Texas, and over the years, he'd rubbed more than a few folks the wrong way, but Jessi wasn't buying it. Her father was one of the few men who'd openly opposed Reed Darcy, and he'd paid for it with his life. "He was shot in the *back.*"

"I know, but it was pretty stormy that night, right?"

"Yes."

"Weren't you all out shooting trying to turn that herd?"

"Yes, but—"

"See, there you go, an accident."

Jessi could feel her rage threatening to explode like cannon fire, and it grabbed her so hard her hands shook. "My father *saw* Darcy's man that night. It was Clem Davis."

"So I hear, but both Mr. Darcy and Clem say he wasn't there."

"So it's my father's word against theirs?"

"Exactly. And dead men can't testify."

Reed Darcy's hired guns had deliberately stampeded the herd that night, and then murdered her father—Jessi knew that as sure as her name. She also knew that she'd had no business seeking help here. Even though Hatcher and her father had been friends for many years, and he'd been very instrumental in Jessi's life when she was younger, Hatcher had been elected sheriff with Darcy money. The lawman now owed his loyalty to Darcy, not to the people he'd known most of his life. "So you aren't going to do anything?"

"Like I said before, no need to. I did see Mr. Darcy this morning and he says to tell you he won't hold a grudge against you for running him off your land, and that he's sorry for your loss. If there's anything he can do, just let him know."

Reed Darcy had shown up at the Clayton ranch after her father's funeral flanked by his son, Roscoe, and Roscoe's wife, Minerva, ostensibly to pay their respects. Jessi met them on the porch with a raised Winchester and ordered them off her land. Darcy, who was no fool, had acquiesced. Once word got around town about what she'd done, the incident had made Jessi Rose Clayton the talk of Vale once again, but she didn't care. "How can you call yourself an officer of the law?" she now asked Hatcher. "People you've known all your life have been burned out, run off, and terrorized by Darcy, while you sit here doing nothing!"

"Don't you sass me, girl," he warned, standing up. "If your pa had sold that land like he was asked to, he'd probably be alive."

"Oh, really?" she shot back coldly. "Are you saying his death was not an accident after all?"

She had him and he knew it.

Bristling, he snapped, "Get out of my office, Jessi Clayton. Now!"

Giving him a brittle smile that did not reach her eyes, she said, "I'm going, but know this, I am not selling my land to Darcy or anyone else!"

She stormed out, well aware that she would find no champion in Vale. She and her nephew Jotham were in this fight alone.

Kansas State Penitentiary
April 1888

"Get up, Blake! Visitor!"

A sleeping Griffin Sloan Blake stirred and slowly opened his eyes. He peered up at the armed guard looming over him in the pre-dawn darkness.

"There's nobody I want to see," he declared caustically and pulled the too-short moth-eaten blanket back over his big body. The cell was cold. The sun had yet to rise and the only heat available emanated from the sleeping bodies of the other fifteen prisoners crammed like cattle into the small fetid cell.

The guard jabbed him sharply in the back with the butt of the rifle. "Get up, damn you, I don't have all day!"

Griffin shot the man a malevolent look but got to his feet. Half awake, he ignored the angry curses of the other prisoners he inadvertently kicked or stepped on as he made his way to the door. Griffin couldn't imagine who would be coming to see him here, but he didn't ask. He'd know soon enough.

He was escorted to the warden's office and was surprised to see U.S. Deputy Marshal Dixon Wildhorse, a Black Seminole from Indian Territory, a good friend of Griffin's half-brother Jackson. He was Griffin's friend, too—as long as they didn't meet on opposite sides of the law.

"Hello, Dix. What brings you to this little patch of paradise?"

The big Seminole ignored Griffin's sarcasm and turned to the armed guard waiting in the doorway. "You can go. Lock me in if you think it's necessary."

The guard looked between the two, nodded to the lawman and closed the door. He did turn the key however.

Alone now, Dix asked, "Why didn't you write and let somebody know you were in here?"

Griffin scratched at the lice that'd taken up residence in his clothing in the six months since he'd been sentenced. A prisoner's personal hygiene was not high on the warden's list of concerns. "Who's there to write?"

"Me. Your brother."

"Why? So you could come and bust me out?"

The lawman ignored the crack. "The warden said they gave you seven years."

Griff shrugged. "Give or take a few months." He had been a handsome man at one time, but the red gold hair and the muscular physique were hard to discern beneath all the dirt, beard, and grime. Griffin knew that he smelled as bad as he looked "So, how is big brother? Last I heard he was still back east."

"No. He and I left Chicago together in '84. We took a wagon train of mail order brides to Kansas, then he headed down to Texas. He was going back to try and clear his name."

Griff thought his brother's quest would be a futile one. "Those rebs aren't ever going to admit Jack was framed, or that they killed Royce."

Royce was Royce Blake, a Texas preacher who'd pulled a twelve-year-old Griffin Sloan out of a whorehouse in Abilene and taken him home to be raised alongside his natural son, Jackson. Even though Royce and Griff rarely saw eye to eye, Griff had come to love and respect the old man. Years later, Royce's ambush death at the hands of a well-connected West Texas rancher had further hardened Griff's heart against the rich and powerful. "I wish big brother luck."

And he truly did. Even though he and Jack often argued about Griffin's profession, they'd had some good times growing up. He hadn't seen his half-brother in many years. "So why are you here, Dix?"

"To save your hide, maybe."

"You busting me out?" he asked with sarcasm in his voice and in his topaz eyes.

Dix didn't smile. "In a way."

Griffin studied the lawman. Dix would make an excellent poker player; his face rarely gave anything away, but since the Seminole didn't play cards, the attribute seemed wasted. "What does 'in a way' mean?"

"It means I have a job for you. Complete it satisfactorily and you could walk away a free man."

"Could?"

"Could," was the only commitment the marshal seemed ready to make.

"It wouldn't happen to involve robbing trains, now, would it?"

The lawman did not appear amused by Griff's flippant attitude. "You are about to lose seven years of your life in this hellhole. Robbing trains is the last thing you should be joking about."

Griff knew he was right. Robbing trains was why he'd

been sentenced here in the first place—that, and the woman who'd betrayed him to the Pinkertons six months ago. Were it not for his attraction to pretty women, Griff would undoubtedly be still robbing trains. "I admit it, you're right. But I had a damn good time while it lasted."

And he had. Keeping true to his vow to make the railroads pay for his mother's death, he'd robbed trains for nearly five years, from California to the Mississippi and back again, sampling as many willing women along the way as the days and nights allowed. He'd given a good portion of the money away to needy families facing desperate situations, but had kept enough to make sure he'd end his days comfortably. Prison had momentarily derailed those plans. "What do you want me to do?"

"Read this."

Wildhorse pulled a letter from his shirt pocket and handed it over.

Griff looked at the front. "It's addressed to you."

"I know, read it anyway."

It began:

Dear Sheriff Wildhorse,

How are you? This time I am not writing to ask for old wanted bulletins for my collection. This time I'm writing because me and my aunt Jessi need your help. Reed Darcy wants to take our land. He killed my grandfather. I know you are very busy in Indian Territory, but could you see your way clear to come down and arrest Darcy? Our sheriff is in his vest pocket and won't help. If you can't come, will you send one of your deputies? Please come soon.
Sincerely,
Jotham

Griff looked up and handed the note back. "Sounds like it was written by a child."

"It was. Jotham's ten or eleven now. My wife and I met him and his grandfather in Denver last year, and—"

Amazed, Griff interrupted him. "You have a wife?"

"Yep, name's Kate."

"Since when?"

"Since '84."

"No disrespect, Dix, but *you* married? That's unbelievable. What's she like?"

For the first time, Dixon Wildhorse smiled. "A handful. She's a crusading newspaperwoman, and it seems like I spend more time bailing her out of jail than chasing outlaws. She's amazing."

Wildhorse, married. Griff found *that* amazing. The marshal he knew had been married to only one thing: bringing lawbreakers to justice. If Griff ever got out of prison, he'd certainly have to make it a point to meet Mrs. Kate Wildhorse. Any woman who could take Dix's mind off of his duties, even for a moment, had to be very special indeed. "Okay go on, explain the letter."

"Kate and I met Joth and his grandfather in Denver last year. When the boy found out I was a lawman, he asked if he could have my old Wanted bulletins for his collection. He and I have been writing back and forth since then."

"The boy collects wanted posters."

"His daddy was Calico Bob."

Griff stared. He'd crossed paths with the notorious Calico Bob on only a few occasions, but had found him to be one of the most intelligent outlaws he had ever met. He was also one of the most deadly. Rumor had it that he'd shot and killed a man simply because he didn't care for the make of the man's shoes. One of the territorial judges had given Bob twenty-five years in the Ohio State Penitentiary for that irrational act. "This boy is Calico Bob's kid?"

"Yep."

"Never knew Bob had family. So what does this have to do with me?"

"I want you to go help Joth and his aunt."

Griff stared. "You're joshing, right."

The marshal's face said he was not.

"I'm no knight, Dix, and besides, the warden would never buy it."

"He already has."

Griff fought down the inner excitement that one phrase sparked. Would he really be able to walk free once more? "Why would he agree?"

"Because he's been asked to."

"By whom?"

"Judge Isaac Parker."

Griff was stunned. Every outlaw in the West knew Hanging Judge Parker. He ran the court down at Fort Smith, Arkansas. Usually, once Parker sentenced you, not even divine intervention could pry you loose. "Why send me?"

"Because you're smart and resourceful and you know how to stay alive. There's been a murder, you know."

"And?"

"It'll give you a chance to tweak some noses, legally."

"Meaning?"

"Railroad's involved."

For the first time in months, Griffin flashed the smile that had endeared him to women from the Mississippi to the Rio Grande. Maybe this was going to be a better scheme than he first thought. "Start at the beginning."

"Judge Parker and I found a nest of vipers a couple of years ago who were selling phony railroad stocks to old people back east. Actually, my wife Kate was the one who turned over the rocks. Anyway, we caught the man we thought was the brains of the outfit, Rupert

Smalls. However, it now seems we didn't catch the other head—Reed Darcy.''

''That's the man the boy mentioned in his letter—the one he says murdered his grandfather.''

''Correct. Judge Parker wants Darcy brought to justice, too, but as Joth said in the letter, the local sheriff's on Darcy's payroll.''

''Does Parker have jurisdiction this far south?''

''He says he does.''

Griff had no intention of questioning the mandate of Hanging Judge Parker. The only person who'd ever questioned Parker had been the President of the United States, and he'd done it only once. ''So why doesn't he send you or one of his other lawmen?''

''We don't have the men to spare on what may be a long investigation, and Kate and I are leaving for San Francisco in a month.''

''Why doesn't Parker get a Texas lawman?''

''He wants somebody loyal only to him. He doesn't want to find out later that the man he sent in is on the railroad's payroll.''

''Okay. Say I agree. What's to keep me from just taking my freedom and heading on down to Mexico, like I'd always planned?''

''Me,'' the lawman replied bluntly. ''I will find you. Even if it takes a decade. And when I do, that red head of yours will be silver by the time you see freedom again.''

Griff believed him, although if he had a head start, who knew if Dix could really make good on his threats?

As if he'd read Griffin's mind, Dix repeated, ''I will find you.''

Griff shrugged. To tell the truth, Griff didn't really want to do this—because of his mother and the circumstances leading up to her death, he had a soft spot in his heart for women and kids in distress, and it would give him another chance to give the railroad bosses fits, but this endeavor sounded like it might be complicated. Outside of robbing trains, he preferred to keep life as simple as possible.

"So, will you do it?"

"Do these Claytons know I'm coming?"

"No. Judge Parker would prefer you went in unannounced."

"I'm just supposed to waltz up to the door and say, 'I'm here to help?' "

"No, you're going to go in as an old friend of Bob's. The boy's aunt is a widow, but she was Bob's woman at one time, too, according to Parker's report, so you shouldn't have any trouble. Bob died about three months ago. Consumption. Judge wants you to take her his things; hopefully she'll be grateful enough give you a job or something. That way you can help her and still nose around for evidence on Darcy. If that doesn't work, the judge has a letter for you to give to her, asking for her help."

Griff still didn't know if he liked this, but it beat his present situation hands down. "Okay, what do I have to do?"

"Raise your right hand."

"Why?"

"Just do it."

Griff was skeptical, but slowly raised his right hand.

"Repeat after me. I, Griffin Blake, promise to uphold the law—"

"Wait a minute, I'm not saying that."

"If you want to walk out of here with me, you'll say it."

"What is it?"

"United States Marshal oath."

Griff's eyes widened. "Marshal oath? Are you loco?"

Dix stood silent, waiting.

"If word gets around that I'm a marshal, even a pretend one, I won't have a friend left once I get to Mexico."

This was exactly the type of complication he'd meant. He couldn't take a marshal oath. He'd be unable to show his handsome face anywhere, especially in the old haunts where outlaws gathered. Griffin looked over at Dix standing silent and unreadable.

"This is your chance to walk on the right side of life, Griffin."

"And suppose I don't *want* to?"

"Then you can stay here."

Griff shook his head. Everything kept coming back to the seven years. No one in his right mind would choose the hospitality of the Kansas State Penitentiary over freedom, so he raised his hand and repeated the oath.

"Now," Dix said, when they were done reciting, "here's your star."

"Keep it."

"I can't. It's yours. And here are a few more, just in case you decide to hire a deputy or two."

Griffin looked over at the marshal and said in all seriousness, "If I put on that star, hell's going to freeze over and plagues are going to break out all over the land. No."

"Take the stars, Griff."

"Dix, boils are going to pop out all over my body."

"Take the stars."

Griff took the stars, but he held them in his hands as if the metal were forge hot.

Dixon shook his head at Griff's antics. "Gather up your stuff and let's get out of here."

Griff looked down at the stars in his hands and knew this was going to get a whole lot more complicated before he saw Mexico and the many señoritas awaiting him there.

Chapter 2

The fat Texas moon outlined a man riding slowly up to the house. From the roof, Jessi Clayton kept one eye on him and the other on the black expanse of the horizon. Earlier today she ridden into town intending to telegraph the Texas Rangers' office in Austin about her father's murder, but she'd been denied access to the wire by the Vale telegraph agent. Because of that, she had a feeling she'd be paid a visit by Darcy's men tonight, and by being up here on the roof, she'd be able to see them before they could see her. Her nephew, Jotham, was inside awaiting their coming, too. Granted, an eleven-year-old boy had no business being up at this hour with a rifle in his hand, but he refused to let her face this alone. This was his land, too, he'd argued, and as Jessi had promised Dexter, he wouldn't give up the land without a fight. Life under siege was no way to raise a young manchild, and it ate at her heart every day, but for now, Jessi had no choice.

The rider was getting closer. He rode like someone who'd been in the saddle a long time. She hoped he had no intention of seeking shelter here, because she couldn't help him. Unknown visitors were the last thing she needed.

To her displeasure, she saw that he did seem to be

riding her way, so when he got within shooting range, she yelled out, "Hold it right there!"

He eased his mount to a halt.

"State your business," she commanded.

She couldn't see his features, but could see him peering around, trying to figure out where her voice was coming from.

"I'm looking for Calico Bob's woman," he replied.

The big house with its listing chimney and long neglected outbuildings were silhouetted against the night. Griff remembered Dix saying the Claytons had boasted of having quite a spread here. Too bad no one had taken care of it.

All of a sudden he saw a lone figure move on the roof. "Why are you looking for her?"

Against the moonlight, the shadowy form looked to be that of a kid, but the rifle trained on Griff was definitely full grown.

"Promised him I'd bring her his last effects. He's dead."

"When?"

"Three months ago. Prison doc said it was consumption."

"Were you in prison, too?"

"Yeah." Griff didn't bother to add that it hadn't been the same prison.

"Just dump his stuff on the ground and get."

This was not the reception he'd been anticipating. He thought Dix had said she'd be grateful. "I've been in the saddle for a month. I was hoping to bed down here, at least for the night."

"No."

"Where's Bob's woman?"

"You're looking at her. Now, leave his things and head out. I need to—grieve."

"I've been riding a long time—"

"I don't care."

Exasperated and tired, Griff called up, "Lady, you got no manners!"

"I know."

They'd reached a stalemate. Griff wondered how he could convince her to let him stay. He was too bone weary to ride another foot. He tried another tactic. "Bob won't rest easy knowing you turned me away."

"If Bob's dead, he's in hell. He won't be resting easy for eternity."

Griff was taken aback. She didn't sound like any grieving woman he'd ever met.

Her smoky voice floated on the night. "Look, mister. I don't have a place for you to stay, and I don't want to waste a cartridge convincing you to leave, because I may need it for them." She gestured toward the horizon. "I've got visitors coming, and they're not after tea."

Fluidly raising himself in the saddle, Griff turned in the direction her rifle indicated; there were three of them, riding hard in the direction of the house.

"Friends of yours?"

"No, and if you have any sense, you'll point that horse east and ride fast."

He swung his attention back to the woman on the roof. "You up there because you're hiding?"

"No," she answered bluntly. "I'm up here because I want the first shot."

He watched as she yelled down into the chimney, "They're coming, get ready!"

Griff wondered who she might be alerting, but saved the speculating for later. Right now, he had to convince her to let him stay and he didn't want the debate to last all night. He was too damned tired to be arguing, especially with a woman with bad manners. "Do you want an extra gun?"

"It's not your fight."

"I know, but maybe it'll earn me a place to bunk for the night."

Silence.

He could see her evaluating him, and then the riders. She didn't take long to decide. "Put your horse round back."

Griff did as she instructed and quickly reined the gelding around to the back of the house. Moments later he was back, asking, "Any particular place you want me to fire from?"

"It's up to you, just don't let fly before I do. I get first pickings."

"Yes, ma'am."

She faded back into the darkness behind the chimney. He shook his head at her sergeantly manner, then took up a spot to the left of the porch, all the while hoping her visitors would be dispatched quickly so he could get some sleep.

The men had halted their horses a ways away from the house and were now talking, debating the best approach, Griff thought, or maybe trying to figure out if the occupants were asleep. With the house so dark and quiet, it certainly appeared that way. Moments later, they began moving on horses reined to a walk. Griff noted that they were being cautious. After meeting the lady on the roof, he didn't blame them a bit.

One of the men dismounted. When his feet hit the ground, her first bullet struck the earth only a foot away from his boots. He jumped and froze all in one motion as she yelled out, "Get back on your horse!"

"Crazy woman! You could have shot me!"

"I could've killed you, but I don't want your dead carcass poisoning my land."

The silently watching Griff was impressed. Her offensive tactics had obviously caught them off guard. The men seemed confused and angry. It was quite obvious she didn't need his help; at least, not for the moment.

One of the men still mounted yelled up, "Mr. Darcy just sent us out here to make sure you were all right, Miss Jessi. Everybody knows about the problems you been having, with your cows being butchered and all. He's just being neighborly."

"And my name is Sam Houston," she called down sarcastically. "Tell Darcy I don't need his help, and tell him the next time he sends you boys over to be neighborly, I won't be so hospitable. Now, *get!*"

A rider replied cockily, "If we wanted to, we could burn this place to the ground."

"Not before I send you to hell you won't."

Griff wondered what in life had made this woman so rawhide tough.

She then declared, "I'm counting to ten. Either be gone or be dead."

She started counting real slow. "One!"

The angry man stood his ground for a while, but as the number reached five, he took hold of his horse's reins and mounted up.

Her voice chimed out eight, accompanied by the sound of her rifle being primed.

Darcy's men reined their horses around. "We'll be back," one threatened.

"I'll be waiting," she promised.

They rode off toward the horizon and disappeared into the night.

Griff stepped away from his hiding spot and looked up to the roof, where she stood against the moon. It bothered him that he still couldn't make out her fetures. As if assessing him too, she said nothing for a moment, then told him, "You can bunk on the porch. Pump's out back."

Griff nodded and went to his mount to fetch his gear.

*   *   *

When he awakened the next morning, the sun was already up, and there was a young light-skinned boy of about ten bent over him, staring down curiously through a pair of spectacles. Griffin held the watching pale brown eyes for a moment, then asked gruffly, "Can I help you, son?"

"You're Kansas Red!!"

Griff's eyes widened hearing the declaration. *Shit! So much for anonymity.* "No, I'm not," he denied, getting out from beneath the blanket. Dressed in his Union suit, he began a search for his pants.

"You are, too. Texas Red, Kansas Red, Oklahoma Red. You've got a lot of names."

"No, I don't." Griff dragged on his pants and wondered if anybody would miss this tall, thin kid if he suddenly disappeared.

The boy disagreed. "I'd know your face anywhere. Seen it a million times in Wanted bulletins."

"Well, you're wrong."

The kid folded his arms and stated flatly, "I am not."

Griff didn't see the lady of the house standing behind the screened front door until just then. He held her unreadable eyes, wondering how much she'd heard. As she stepped outside onto the porch, he got his first good look at her.

The fierce-talking woman on the roof last night had a face so uncommonly beautiful it was jaw dropping: rich chocolate skin, a lush, full mouth. She was of average height and Texas slim. She dressed like a ranch hand, though—a man's shirt, denims, worn boots. Her dark hair was cropped short like a young boy's and there were small gold circlets in her ears. Like most women of the race, it was impossible to gauge her age, but if the lines beneath her serious dark eyes were a true indication, she hadn't slept in weeks.

As if she'd let Griff look long enough, she turned her

attention to Griff's tormentor and asked, "Have you finished your breakfast?"

The kid, still staring Griff's way, shook his head no.

She told him gently, "Then you need to do that and
get to school."

Griff could almost touch the affection in her voice.
After last night's encounter, he'd not thought her capable of such softness.

The boy looked up at her and said, "Okay, but I'm
not wrong about him."

He gave Griff one last look, then went on inside.

After they were alone, she asked, "Is my nephew correct?"

"About what?" The minute the words came out of
his mouth he wanted to take them back. She was smarter
than that and so was he.

"Your identity," she replied.

Griff knelt to reroll his bedding. "Does it matter?"

"Yes. I like to know with whom I'm dealing."

"I served my time," he said, by way of explanation.

As if that was all she wanted to know, she stuck out
her hand like a man. "Name's Jessi Clayton. Thanks for
backing me last night."

"Griffin Blake." He shook her hand.

"There's coffee and food on the stove."

He found her dark beauty a fascinating contrast to her
manner, and her handshake as firm as any man's.

"Where are you headed?" she asked then.

"Nowhere in particular. Looking to make my way
down to Mexico eventually."

"Good luck then," she stated, in a voice that imparted
both dismissal and departure, then went back into the
house. She didn't ask at all about Bob's possessions.

Griff shook his head. He sensed it was not going to
be as easy to infiltrate her life as Dix and Judge Parker
assumed it would be. He also wondered what a beautiful

woman like her had been doing with a murderer like Calico Bob.

Griff went inside. As he wondered where she'd gone, he followed the smell of bacon to the back of the house and found the kitchen. At the table sat the boy.

Griff didn't say anything as he poured himself a cup of coffee.

The boy said, "My name's Jotham. Everybody calls me Joth."

Griff offered a small smile. "Pleased to meet you, Joth. I'm Griffin Blake."

"That your true name?"

"Yep. How'd you know about my other names?"

"I collect Wanted posters. Got maybe three of you."

"Why do you collect them?"

"My pa's Calico Bob, and it's the only way I know what he's been doing. I don't see him much. I heard you say last night that he was dead." He paused. "Is he really?"

Griff observed the boy. Had Joth been the person Jessi Clayton had called down to alert last night when Darcy's men had come calling? Since Griff had yet to meet anyone else in the household he could only assume it to be true. A boy had no business in the middle of this, but then, Joth had been the one to write to Dixon for help in the first place.

"Yes, son, he is."

He didn't think it was his place to be discussing something like this, but the boy had asked and Griff had been eleven once too—he wouldn't have wanted to be lied to.

"You ever met my pa?" the boy asked softly.

Griff studied Joth and wondered how the boy felt about the death. He sensed a sadness behind the spectacled eyes. "A couple of times, yeah, I did."

Evidently Joth had no intentions of revealing his true

feelings, at least not to Griffin because he then changed the subject. "You planning on staying around here a while?"

Griff took a sip of the strong coffee and found it good. "Maybe. I'm looking for a job."

"You could work for us, except we can't pay you. Aunt Jessi and I don't have a lot of money. We could sure use the help, though."

"With what?"

"Reed Darcy. He wants to take our land."

Jessi Clayton entered the kitchen then. Once again Griff noticed how beautiful she was. "Jotham, finish your breakfast. School's waiting. Please excuse my nephew, Mr. Blake, but he needs to get going."

Joth finished the last of his meal and took his plate to the sink. "Hope I'll see you later, Mr. Blake."

Griff looked over at Joth and into young eyes he'd seen before in a dream. He shook off the odd sensation even as he wondered how this boy figured into his life's path. "Same here, Joth."

Joth gathered up his slate and left the kitchen, and his aunt followed. While she was gone, Griff looked around. He saw only the bare essentials: table, chairs, a few lamps. There were no frilly curtains, no throw rugs on the kitchen's linoleum floor, none of the knickknacks women seemed to collect, but beneath each window stood a well-oiled rifle and a box of cartridges. The two kitchen windows that looked out on the front of the house were framed with heavy shutter doors. The back door had been outfitted the same way. Other windows had been boarded shut. There was a ladder leading to a hole in the roof and a big bucket beside it which he assumed had been positioned to catch the elements. The interior looked as if it had been stripped down and prepared for war. The place resembled more of a hideout than a home. He could almost feel the strength of the battle the woman and the boy were waging. According to Dix, Darcy's power and his hired guns had forced many of the people around here to sell him their land; he probably wasn't pleased about being defied by Joth's rawhide aunt.

She returned to the kitchen pulling on a pair of gloves. "I've fences to mend, Mr. Blake. I trust you won't rob me after I'm gone, and can see yourself out when you're done here?"

What a woman, he thought to himself. "Yes, ma'am."

"Again, good luck wherever you're headed."

"Thanks."

After she rode off, Griff washed up his dishes and the boy's too, and placed them on the sideboard to dry. He'd been on his own a long time and he always left the trail behind him clean. When he was done, he poured himself another cup of coffee and sat down to wait.

Jessi came back two hours later, smelling of horses and cattle, and hauling a mess of freshly caught fish. As soon as she saw him sitting in the kitchen, she asked, "Why're you still here?"

He shrugged. "Coffee's good."

"Did you drink it all?"

"Yep, but made more."

She dropped the fish in a barrel of water by the sink, then poured herself a cup. She took a wary sip, knowing very few men who could make a brew decent enough to drink. "Not as good as mine, but it'll do."

In response he gave her a smile that seemed to bring sunshine into the dreary light of the kitchen. That he was a handsome man of the race there was no denying. He had dark auburn hair, which he wore long and tied back with a piece of rawhide, reddish gold skin, and light topaz eyes. The red gold beard and mustache added a dangerous edge to his already arresting looks. He looked younger than Jessi's own thirty-two years but was a man who could probably pick and choose his women whenever he had a mind to. She also guessed that that magnificent smile probably fluttered female hearts whenever and wherever it appeared, but Jessi considered herself far past the age of fluttering. "You haven't answered my question."

He shrugged his lean shoulders. Griff instinctively knew he was going to have to tell her the truth. She was not your standard female; there'd be no pulling the wool over her eyes. "I was sent here."

Jessi stilled. "By whom?"

"Hanging Judge Parker and Deputy Marshal Dixon Wildhorse."

"Judge Parker up at Fort Smith?"

Griff nodded.

"Why on earth would Judge Parker send you here?"

"To help you with Darcy."

Jessi didn't understand. "Why?"

"Because you need it, and because Parker wants to put Darcy in jail."

"Then why doesn't he just send someone down here to arrest him?"

"The judge needs more evidence."

"And that's why you're here, to gather more evidence?"

"And to help protect you and the boy."

"Tell the judge thanks, but Joth and I don't have time to play Pinkertons."

"You don't have a choice."

"Of course I have a choice," she said over her cup.

"Not you don't, because neither do I."

She eyed him skeptically. "Meaning?"

"Meaning, if I don't help you, I have to go back to the Kansas Penitentiary."

Jessi stared. "What?"

So he explained it to her. Griff reasoned that if he confessed everything now, it would save them both a lot of arguing. He was wrong.

Jessi put down her cup. "They sent me a convicted criminal to help catch an unconvicted criminal?"

"That about sums it up."

"What were you in jail for?"

"Train robbing. Mayhem."

"Ever kill anyone?"

"Nope. Not real partial to guns."

Jessi felt frustration rising. "Then if they were going to send me someone for protection, don't you think it should've been a gunslinger?"

"I suppose, but you get me instead," he replied, flashing that smile again in the hopes that it would melt her heart as easily as it did most women's.

When she didn't smile in return, he offered tersely, "Could be worse. They could've sent you a riverboat gambler."

"This is not funny, Mr. Blake."

"Never said it was, but looks like we're stuck with one another."

Not if she could help it. Because of her ties to Calico Bob she'd met more outlaws than she ever wanted to remember, and not one of them cared a horse's shoe about life or property unless it was his own, and now she was being told by this stranger that she would have to bring another outlaw in home. "How do I know you're really who you say you are?"

Griff reached inside his double-breasted shirt and handed over the letter from Judge Parker.

A skeptical Jessi took the missive and read it. It introduced Deputy Marshal Griffin Blake and asked for her cooperation. "Why didn't you say this last night?"

"The judge and the marshal thought it might be better

if you didn't know who I was at first. Give you a chance to get used to me being around. They assumed you'd be grateful to me for bringing Bob's things and give me a job.''

''Just like that.''

''Just like that,'' he echoed.

''Well, the only thing I'm grateful to you for is the news that he's dead.'' She handed the letter back to him. "I don't need anything else from you.''

''Like I said before, you don't have a choice. I am not going back to Kansas. So where do I bunk?''

Jessi wondered if he were deaf. ''Listen to me,'' she told him, speaking slowly, as if he were a child. ''I do not want you here, I will not have you here. I do not need your help.''

''Sure you do. Look at this place. I've seen hideouts with more frills.''

''If you want frills, Mr. Blake, I'd advise you to look elsewhere. I run a ranch, not a fancy boardinghouse.''

''Then how about the boy? He shouldn't be growing up like this.''

His words hit a nerve, making her reply coldly, ''I don't need you to tell me about my nephew's life. I know how hard this is on him, and if I could change it, I would. Right now, we're too busy surviving.''

''Then take the judge's help, stubborn woman,'' he said, his own frustration rising. ''Even Joth can see you're up to your neck in white water.''

''Meaning?''

''I'm here because Joth wrote Marshal Wildhorse and asked for help.''

Jessi stared.

That got her attention. ''So, where do I bunk?''

''Joth wrote for help?''

''Smart boy, I would say.''

Jessi didn't know what to do or say now. Parts of her

desperately wanted to take the branch of hope being offered by Judge Parker, but the end of the stick was being held by a man who'd known Calico Bob, and Bob couldn't've been trusted to bring water to a dying child. Blake's assessment of Joth's life had touched a nerve though; she too, worried what effect this fight with Darcy might be having on him. Her nephew was at an age now where he should be out riding his pony, fishing, hunting lizards, and just enjoying life as she and her sister, Mildred, his mother, had done in their youth. But things were just too dangerous now, and with Darcy and his men always lurking, Jessi refused to let Joth out of her sight.

She would still be escorting him back and forth to school had he not begged her to stop treating him like a baby. But in a way, he was her baby. When her sister had died in childbirth, the recently widowed Jessi had given up her teaching position in New York to come home and raise him. When she was young, a severe case of the measles had left her sterile, so she would have no children of her own; Joth represented the only family she had left in this world, and she loved him as much as life.

"Look, Miss Clayton," Griff said, interrupting her thoughts. "If we can get the goods on Darcy, I'll be out of your hair and you'll be out of mine. Personally, I don't like these arrangements any more than you do. I rob trains. That's what I do best. Even though I don't like men who declare war on women with children, I'd much rather be in Mexico. But I can't get there until this mess is settled. So why don't we declare a truce for now and you tell me about Darcy?"

Jessi thought that a reasonable idea. Once he heard the story, maybe he'd hightail it on out of here.

She began with the town meeting Darcy had called to announce the railroad's desire to buy land in the area.

Blake asked, "Was there much opposition?"

"Not at first, because we thought we had a choice to sell or not. Some folks signed on, most didn't. A week or so later, Darcy announced that we *all* had to sell, or no one would get anything. That's when the trouble started. He pitted neighbor against neighbor—those who wished to sell against those who didn't. Many people still refused and were paid visits like the one I had last night. If that didn't intimidate you, Darcy's bank denied folks credit for seed and equipment and he called in mortgages. Most gave in. My pa didn't."

"So Darcy killed him?"

"His men did, but under his orders. He's too yellow to do his own killing."

"I'm disliking this Darcy more and more. In the letter Joth wrote to Wildhorse, he said the sheriff wouldn't help."

"Nope. He and my pa had been friends for years, but once Darcy placed him on his payroll, their relationship changed. After the killing, Sheriff Hatcher said my pa's death was an accident, probably caused by a stray bullet from our own guns."

"What did he mean?"

"There was a terrible storm that night and it caused a stampede. We were all shooting and riding trying to make the herd turn. To this day, I believe Darcy's men started that stampede. My father saw one of Darcy's men that night aiming a rifle his way right before he was shot in the back. He was picked off like a crow on a fence."

Jessi set aside the still painful memory, then took a good long look at her immediate future. She wasn't naive enough to believe she could carry on this war indefinitely; Darcy had money, men, and time on his side. He'd often boasted that all he had to do was wait her out, and unfortunately it was the truth. She had very little money, and even less food, and she faced desperate times ahead. Were she alone in this, she'd defy him until hell froze over, but she had Joth's future to consider. Blake's remark about the effects of this fight on Joth still resonated. Joth didn't deserve to live his life under siege any more than he deserved to have to fend for himself were something to happen to her. She was his only family, and she needed to start acting that way. "You ever worked cattle, Mr. Blake?"

"Nope."

Jessi wanted to throw up her hands. "Do you think you can learn?"

"That an invitation to stay?"

His topaz-colored eyes were glowing.

Jessi's eyes narrowed. "You've already said I don't have a choice. I'm just trying to determine whether you'll be totally useless around here, or just partially."

Griff winced. "Not too many men come courting around here, do they?"

"Meaning?" she answered coolly.

"When was the last time you smiled? You're as ornery as a she-cat with a thorn in her paw."

"I *am* a she-cat with a thorn in her paw, Mr. Blake. It's called Darcy. And now I have another thorn—you."

Griff grinned. "Oh, we're going to have fun, you and I."

"No, we're not," she contradicted him. "If you're planning on staying around here, there won't be time for fun. There's too much work to do."

Griff decided he liked bantering with her. He enjoyed the way her dark eyes flashed. "Does Darcy have to deliver your land by a certain date?"

"Yes, first of September is what I'm hearing."

"So you're expecting him to step up his campaign against you."

She nodded.

Griff sensed she was on the verge of accepting the

judge's plan, but it was hard to tell. Women were as much a part of Griff's life as robbing trains, and he prided himself on his knowledge of both; however, this one didn't seem to fit any of the patterns. She was beautiful enough to be mistress of a Mexican emperor, yet she didn't seem to be the least bit aware of her beauty. He could see how rough and chapped her hands were as she cradled her cup. Granted, she was fighting for her life here and had precious little time for tea parties and the like, but what was she like behind closed doors?

Jessi had come to a decision. "Okay, Blake, although I don't see how much help you can be if you're not real partial to guns and have never worked cows, I'm going to reserve judgment and let you stay. When it's over, I want you gone."

"Yes, ma'am," he replied, flashing that smile.

Jessi thought he looked mighty comfortable sitting at her kitchen table with his arms folded across his chest so confidently. His topaz eyes seemed to be glittering with amusement, or was it challenge?

"You're one stubborn woman, Miss Clayton."

"Thank you."

A smile played across his lips. "Ever met a man that could handle that stubbornness?"

She studied him closely for a moment, and felt the aura of him touch her in spite of herself, then said, "No."

"Well, I'm one of the stubbornest men I know."

"I'm sure that's something you're very proud of, Mr. Blake."

He chuckled.

"What's so funny?"

"Nothing, Miss Clayton."

"How old are you?" she asked. He looked to be fairly young. Too young.

"Be twenty-six in October, and you?"

"Thirty-two this past February."

She'd given him a straight answer, something he rarely received in reply to what some women considered to be a highly personal question. He didn't know why he was surprised, though; he already knew she didn't fit the mold.

Jessi had no decent place for him to bunk except in the house with her and Joth, so she showed him to her pa's room. She usually avoided the room. Even though Dexter Clayton had been dead over a year now, the space still held his spirit. Every time she entered, the grief would rise again, as would the memories of their bittersweet relationship.

They'd not gotten along well, she and her father. Standing between them had been her mother's adultery and subsequent tragic death, and the role Dexter Clayton had played in Jessi's own liaison with Calico Bob. "This was once my pa's room, but you're welcome to it, unless you prefer the porch."

Griff looked around the book-lined room. It was the first room he'd had to himself in quite some time. "No, this is fine—as long as you don't feel I'm crowding you."

"As long as you don't believe I'm going to be part of your pay, we'll do fine."

Griff smiled inwardly. *Tough as rawhide, and sharp as a bed of nails.*

She looked up at him and asked quite plainly, "Do you get my meaning?"

He nodded. "I do," adding, "I know I'm a stranger, and you're a woman alone, but you have my word: I'm no danger to you or the boy."

"The word of a train robber?"

"The word of an honorable train robber."

Jessi looked skeptical. "Stash your gear and I'll give

you a tour of the place. Joth won't be home for another two hours or so.''

Griff noted that she sat her horse like a man and rode with an easiness that denoted much experience. She conversed only sparingly as she showed him as much of the place as the time allowed. He saw broken down fences, burned range shacks, and some of the prettiest land he'd ever laid eyes on. There was fat pasture grass for her milling herd of lowing cattle, and a wide ribbon of crystal blue water that tasted cold and pure. He could see why Darcy and the railroads wanted this land, and why she was fighting to keep it.

She explained, ''My sister Mildred and I grew up here. For a long time we thought Papa owned the whole world.''

Griff wondered what she must have been like as a child. ''Where's Mildred now?''

''Dead. Childbirth.''

''I'm sorry,'' he said genuinely.

''Thanks,'' she replied. ''Joth and I are the only Claytons left.''

''Marshal Wildhorse said you were a widow.''

''I am. My husband's buried back east.''

Griff sensed he'd pried into her personal life enough for now. ''How'd those range shacks get burned?'' he asked, changing the subject.

''Darcy's men,'' she replied bitterly. ''They burned all six in the last month. Since there was nothing I could do to stop it, I just let them have their fun.''

''How many head do you have?''

''There were thousands five years ago, but at last count only a hundred or so are left. Darcy's men began butchering them the day after my father was gunned down.''

She reined her horse around. ''We need to head back.

I don't like Joth coming home to any empty house."

They arrived about thirty minutes before Joth did. The boy, now sporting a healthy black and blue shiner behind his spectacles, broke into a grin upon seeing Griff standing on the porch beside his Aunt Jessi. "You're staying?"

"For a short while."

"Hot dog!"

Jessi steered the conversation back to more mundane matters. "Where'd you get the black eye?"

"Russ McCoy called you a whore so I whupped him. Mr. Trent says I'm expelled for three days. Here's the note."

"Jotham!" she exclaimed, taking the note from his light brown hand. "How many times must I tell you to ignore people like Russ McCoy?"

"Aunt Jessi, he called you a whore and my mother a whore too. I *had* to whup him."

Jessi sighed tiredly. Joth had taken to defending her honor more and more lately. The proud Clayton blood flowed in his veins almost as fiercely as it did in her own. "Did Mr. Trent send work for you to do while you're expelled?"

"Yes."

"Then leave it on the mantel. Get started on your chores. No riding tonight."

"Yes, ma'am."

He went on into the house.

Griff wanted to suggest she go easy on the boy. After all, he'd just been defending his womenfolk, but Griff kept the observation to himself; he doubted she wanted to hear his opinion. He hadn't been sent here to offer her advice on raising her nephew.

"I'm going to go into town—take a look around and see about some supplies," he said instead.

She looked up from reading the teacher's reprimand. "Do you know the way?"

"Yep, rode through last night on my way here. I'll be back before dark."

Jessi almost told him about Darcy's decree forbidding any of Vale's merchants to sell to the Claytons, but decided to let him find out for himself. Instead she watched silently as he mounted up and rode off toward town.

After his departure, Jessi gutted the fish she'd caught for dinner and spent the rest of the afternoon talking to Joth, but her mind kept straying to the man Joth called "Oklahoma Red." From the Wanted posters Joth had brought for her to see, Jessi learned that the outlaw deputy marshal had been wanted all over the West for myriad misdeeds, but train robbing seemed to be his specialty. The cash bounty the railroads had placed on his head would've fed the Clayton household for years. Add to that the rewards offered by numerous banks, the army, and the post offices, and you had the makings of a small fortune.

One poster told of him escaping from a jail in Colorado with the help of two women. Jessi didn't doubt it. His handsomeness had probably drawn many a woman to commit a variety of crimes. Jessi didn't believe she'd have to worry about him turning his charm her way, though. He looked to be a man who preferred his women young and attractive. Since she was neither, that suited her just fine.

She wondered what would happen when the road got rockier? Would Blake stay, or turn tail? According to rumors, Darcy had until September to close the deal. If he couldn't deliver all the properties by then, the syndicate bosses were promising to move on. Four months . . . if she and Joth could hold out until then, life might return to something akin to normal. She still didn't think Blake would be much help, but if he did stay, maybe his past reputation alone would be enough to make Darcy think twice about increasing his efforts to force her out.

On Griff's initial ride through the town last night, it had been very late and he hadn't seen anyone. Now however, it was mid-afternoon and the place bustled with life. He rode down the street at a nonchalant pace. He saw that every building seemed to bear Darcy's name, from the bank to the general store to the funeral parlor. He spied the small, flat roof building with the words "Vale Sheriff" painted above the door. Beside it stood the rather impressive Darcy Hotel.

There were quite a few wagons and horses tied up to the posts lining the plank walks framing the dusty street. Even though he tried not to draw attention to himself, he could see the curious glances coming his way as he tied his big gelding to a post outside the general store. He wondered if anyone recognized his face.

Inside, the wide eyes of the middle aged clerk told the tale. The dark-skinned man sputtered, "Aren't you—?"

"Griffin Blake."

"No, Oklahoma Red."

Griff sighed. Why fight it? He'd hoped Joth would be the only one to know his true identity, but that did not appear to be the case. Word was bound to get out sooner or later, and he decided sooner suited him just fine. Maybe his reputation alone would make Darcy lower the guns drawn on the Claytons.

The clerk's greeting seemed to kindle the interest of some of the store's other patrons. Griff could both see and feel their eyes. One particular young woman, a brown-skinned beauty in a yellow silk dress that seemed far too costly for such a backwater town, made no effort to hide her smiling gaze. The well-dressed man on her arm viewed Griff coolly.

The clerk behind the counter asked, "What brings you to Vale?"

"Business."

"What type of business?"

"I need supplies."

Griff handed over his list and the clerk's eyes widened. "All this?"

Griff nodded beneath the brim of his hat.

The clerk began filling the large order, saying, "This is an awful lot of stuff for a traveling man. You plan on staying around a while?"

Griff knew the nosy clerk was fishing for answers. "Possibly."

Griff sensed the ear of everyone in the store waiting for more details. The clerk piled up tarps, a rain slicker, jerky, canteens and a blanket or two, while Griff took a stroll over to the firearms available for purchase. The Winchesters interested him the most. He saw two that would be needed additions to the Clayton defenses, so he walked them back to the counter. The clerk blinked. "You're not planning on robbing the bank here, are you, Kid?"

"If I were, do you think I'd tell you?" Griff asked softly.

The clerk sputtered, "No—no, of course not. Let me get the rest or your order, sir."

While the clerk totaled up the bill, Griff took a discreet look around and saw the other customers frozen in place, staring his way. He touched his hat politely at a few of the ladies, especially the one in yellow silk, before returning his attention to the clerk.

He and the clerk were just about done when the scent of gardenias floated across his senses. Griff turned to see Miss Yellow Silk and her escort standing nearby. Mr. Escort did not seem pleased, but spoke, "My wife insisted we come over and introduce ourselves. I'm Roscoe Darcy. This is my wife, Minerva." His voice was a bit slurred. Griff wondered if he'd been drinking.

"Pleased to meet you, Mr. and Mrs. Darcy. Are you the Darcys on all the buildings?"

Minerva replied with a smile, "They're named for my husband's father and grandfather." She then said, "My husband tells me you are a dangerous outlaw. What brings you to Vale?"

Griff didn't miss the steel behind the velvet voice. She would be one to watch. "Business."

"And you're staying where?"

"I'm out at the Clayton place."

The alarm that flashed across her face made Griff curious about her reaction.

"Jessi Clayton?" she choked out.

"Yes, ma'am."

"How do you know Jessi Clayton?"

"Through a friend."

"Outlaws say that about her all the time. Did you know that?"

Griff was a bit taken aback by Minerva's venomous tone. "Meaning what?"

"Jessi Clayton is a whore."

Griff found the description angering. He looked around at the other people in the store. They all dropped their eyes under his direct stare. He turned back to Minerva. "Is that how Miss Clayton is known around here?"

She trilled a little laugh. "Of course. The good women in this town cross the street rather than walk near her."

Griff looked at Roscoe Darcy. He wouldn't meet Griff's eyes either.

Minerva then informed him, "You're keeping company with a fairly sordid woman, Mr. Blake. Her mother was an adulteress, her sister a whore. The Clayton women have bad blood I'm guessing, but let's change the subject. Are you in need of a job?''

''Someone around here hiring?''

''Yes, as a matter of fact. My father-in-law's always looking to employ skilled men such as yourself.''

I'll bet he is, Griff said to himself. It still angered him that Jessi Clayton would be looked upon with such derision. Even though he knew very little about her past, she'd impressed him with her fire and her determination. ''Thanks for the information, but I've already hired on someplace else.''

''Where, might I ask?''

''I work for Miss Clayton.''

Minerva managed to keep her alarm well hidden this time, but Griff knew the news had shaken her. When she composed herself, she turned to the clerk behind the counter and said, ''Mr. Thomas, you may as well reshelve his order. Everyone knows the Claytons and their people aren't welcome to trade here.''

Griff kept his face void of all emotion. ''Why not?''

''Jessi Clayton refuses to sell her land to the railroad.''

''If it's her land, it's her right.''

''Not when her stubbornness keeps everyone else from exercising their rights.''

''I don't understand,'' he lied.

''Every landowner in the valley stands to make a tidy profit selling his land to the railroads, but they *all* have to sell. The railroads want the land intact, not in pieces.''

''And Miss Clayton is the fly in the ointment?''

''Exactly.''

Griff turned and surveyed the store's other patrons. Were they all lined up against Jessi and Joth? Did they all call her a whore? If so, was it because she'd been

Calico Bob's woman? He then looked to the clerk, Thomas. The man appeared to be very uncomfortable. Griff wondered why. "Well, Mr. Thomas, guess I'll have to give all this gold to another merchant."

Griff took a small leather pouch from his shirt pocket and emptied the coins out onto the counter so the clerk could get a good look. Griff didn't miss the way Thomas's eyes widened. On his way to Vale, Griffin had stopped off in Denver to visit a pretty saloon girl named Sally who'd been graciously holding some of his stashed gold. Even though Griff had spent a good portion of it outfitting himself for the journey here, he still had small caches of railroad gold hidden with friends, mostly females all over the West.

Minerva said, "You'll have to go a long ways to find someone who'll take that gold, Mr. Blake. There isn't a merchant within miles who'll take Clayton money."

"I see," he said, noting the merchant's disappointed eyes as he put the coins back into the pouch. "Well, it's been real nice meeting you, Mr. and Mrs. Darcy."

"Same here," Minerva replied. "If you decide you do want a job, just come by the hotel and ask for me or my father-in-law."

"I'll keep that in mind." Griff promised. He touched the brim of his hat in departure and exited the store.

Jessi and Joth were just sitting down to dinner when he returned. The meal consisted of fish and fried corn-meal cakes. It was sparse fare, but after dining on nothing but prison slop for the past few months, Griff found the fish mouth-watering.

He looked up from his plate. "Met Roscoe and Minerva Darcy in town."

"A very pleasant encounter, no doubt," Jessi cracked.

"Quite. Especially the part where she ordered the

store clerk not to accept my gold for the supplies I was after.''

''That must've made Abe Thomas sick. He's as greedy as he is nosy.''

''Is everyone in town lined up on Darcy's side?''

''Mostly. Those who aren't keep quiet and pretend they are, especially if they've had their lives threatened. Still want to stay, Mr. Blake?''

He flashed her that smile and then went back to his meal.

After dinner, while Jessi cleaned up the kitchen, Joth spread his schoolwork on the table and grudgingly began the tasks assigned by his teacher, Mr. Trent. Griff stepped out onto the porch to have a smoke and to give them some privacy.

After being in a prison where noise reverberated night and day, he'd almost forgotten how silent and peaceful a sunset could be. Instead of the screams and cackles of the damned and demented, he could hear crickets and the wind in the trees. Here, night brought introspection and a sense of time passing, instead of worries over which prisoners would be found dead in the morning and whether one of the dead would be you.

Her light steps on the porch behind him broke his reverie. Without turning, he asked, ''Do you think we'll have visitors tonight?''

''I don't know. Sometimes they'll leave me alone for weeks at a time, and other times they're here every night.''

''Well, plan on sleeping tonight. I'll take the watch.''

''That isn't necessary. I can carry my share.''

He turned and looked into her tired but vibrant eyes. ''I'm sure you can, but when was the last time you had a full night's sleep?''

''A while,'' was all she would say.

He turned back to feast on the dying sun. ''A spread

this size must've had hands at one time. How many were there?''

''Ten full-time. During spring round-up we could call on as many as forty men. After my father was killed, Darcy ran most of them off. The rest I couldn't afford to pay anyway, after a while, so . . .'' She shrugged as if that were explanation enough.

''Anybody around we can hire?''

''Not for miles. Darcy has everyone scared, but even if they weren't, I can't pay them.''

He said nothing.

She asked, ''What do you wish to be called?''

''Griff is fine. Tomorrow I'll see about some hands.''

There was silence again for a moment, then she confessed, ''I still don't want you here.''

He turned and took a moment to observe her, once again drawn to her dark beauty. He knew if he told her about seeing Joth in his dreams many years ago, she'd think him loco, so he kept that to himself. ''I know, but I was a boy once and, when I needed help, there was no one around. No disrespect, but I'm here because of Joth, not you.''

''Touché, Mr. Blake. I'll take the second watch.''

She went back in the house, leaving him alone with his thoughts and the sunset.

Chapter 3

The next morning, Griff awakened to the ringing sound of an ax. Dawn had just arrived and he couldn't imagine why anybody in his right mind would be up at such an unholy hour. In prison the guards always woke the inmates as early as possible with as much noise as possible. The prisoners hated them for it, mostly because early rising was for farmers, not outlaws; outlaws rose late and went to bed late, preferably with a pretty girl. Griff swore, when he'd settled in Mexico, that he'd never to get up before noon. Snuggling back beneath the soft blanket, he drifted off once more.

Outside, Jessi put down her ax, tipped back her old beat-up hat, and wiped the sweat from her brow. The sun had been up over an hour, and so far no Blake. She wondered if her new hand knew there was work to be done, specifically, fence posts to cut. Marshal or no marshal, she had no intention of letting him laze around all day.

When she went inside and found the house as quiet as it had been when she began her day, she waltzed into his room, saying, "Mr. Blake, it is time to get up. There's work to do."

Cool as can be, Jessi marched over to the bed and snatched the covers back. She instantly regretted it. He was naked as the day he was born. Mortified, she blinked. She was so busy staring that it took her a moment to remember that no well-raised female ogled a naked man. She quickly spun around.

"Something wrong?" he chuckled from behind her back.

Embarrassed to the soles of her feet, she couldn't speak.

He lay back with his hands tucked behind his head. "That's what happens when you march around so hell bent on being in charge. Bet you'll never do that again, will you?" He found his eyes lingering over the sweet lines of her hips in the snug denims.

"No."

"Thought not."

Griff sat up. He didn't bother replacing the covers—he dared her to turn around. "I believe you owe me an apology."

Apologizing was not something Jessi did easily, but she tried. "I'm sorry. I should have knocked." Jessi dearly wanted to burn away the memory of his muscular red-gold nudity but found it impossible.

"Yes, you should've," he agreed, wishing he could see her face, because she appeared as shocked as a church lady in a brothel. "Now, I'm going to get up and get dressed, and unless you want to see what many ladies describe as the cutest butt this side of the Rio Grande, I'd advise you to march out of here the same way you marched in. *Comprendez*?"

With the sting of embarrassment still resonating in her cheeks, Jessi exited.

Struggling into his clothes, Griffin used the basin to rinse his mouth and throw some water on his face. *Damn woman*, he thought to himself. If she had someone in her bed at night besides that Winchester, she'd be too tired to be charging around at dawn, snatching the blankets off innocent folks. But that scenario was about as likely as him being named Mexico's next *El Presidente*. He sat on the bed to pull on his worn boots. Jessi Clayton was truly a unique and beautiful woman, but any rattler had a better disposition. He stood then and grabbed his gun belt. He'd truly enjoyed her reaction, however. Remembering her shocked dark eyes, he grinned. No, she'd never do that again.

Outside, she was still chopping wood when he strolled up.

She brought the ax down on the wood at her feet and it split in two. "If you've come out to tease me further, don't."

Griff wasn't loco. He knew better than to rile a rattler, especially one with an ax in her hand, but he couldn't resist. "You know, some painters consider the naked body a beautiful thing. What's your thinking on nudes, Miss Clayton?"

Embarrassed all over again, she said, "A gentleman would never ask a lady such a question."

"Maybe. But remember, *you* pulled the covers off *me*."

"I'm aware of that, Mr. Blake."

From beneath her hat, Jessi looked up into his eyes. In this early morning light they were the color of a mountain cat's and held the same challenging amusement she'd seen in them before. It was almost as if he knew something about her that she had yet to discover. Admittedly confused by whatever it was she was feeling, she changed the subject. "Around here, we start the day early, before it gets too hot. Coffee's on the stove in the kitchen."

"Changing the subject?"

"Yes."

"Well, maybe I'll get the chance to pull the covers off *you* one day."

Jessi felt her heartbeat increasing in response to his teasing tone. "I thought you said you weren't a danger to me, Mr. Blake."

"I'm not. I never pull back a woman's covers unless I'm asked."

"And I assume you're asked often?"

"Often enough."

She stooped to pick up the wood. After tossing it on the pile with the rest of the posts she'd cut, she dusted her gloved hands on the legs of her denims. "Well, I won't be asking, rest assured."

"You never know. Life doesn't always go as planned."

"You're right, but some things are very certain."

Griff smiled. He sensed the passion and power emanating from beneath Jessi's armor. "So, you never saw your husband in his birthday suit?"

"Mr. Blake, I am not answering any more of your forward questions!"

"Answer is no, then. Seems mighty strange to me, but there's a first time for everything."

Jessi shot him a look that would've sent any other man running for cover, but it only made him offer up that woman-melting grin again. Whistling, he left her and went back into the house.

A still amused Griff headed to the kitchen, where he poured coffee and watched a sleepy Joth enter moments later. The boy's smile of greeting bathed Griff in a way that seemed to warm his insides.

"Morning, Mr. Blake."

"Morning, Joth. Call me Griff, if you would."

The boy paused. "Aunt Jessi says I'm not supposed to call adults by their first names."

"She told you right, but I'm giving you permission. So no more Mr. Blake, okay?"

Joth smiled as he nodded and got himself some eggs from the skillet.

Griff liked the boy. The light brown skin proclaimed his mixed-race parentage. He was a bit tall for his age, but terribly thin. "What do you want to be when you grow up, Joth?" Griff asked, as Joth started in on his breakfast.

"I wanted to be an outlaw like my pa, but Aunt Jessi says that's not such a good idea. She says I'll either die young, wind up in prison, or swing from the end of a rope."

"She's pretty much right. Outlawing's not much of a life once you get old like me. You spend all of your time looking over your shoulder for bounty hunters or vigilantes or some younngun' who thinks he'll get his name in the paper for outdrawing you. Pick something out that has a future, like doctoring or ranching."

"Is that why you're going to Mexico, because you're tired of being an outlaw?"

"Yep. Prison made me see the errors of my ways, too."

Joth's eyes were wide. "How old are you?"

"Twenty-five."

"My pa was thirty-two, same age as Aunt Jessi."

Griff wondered how the boy felt about his pa's death. "Are you going to miss him?"

Joth shrugged his thin old shoulders. "I suppose. I didn't know him all that well—he only came around once a year or so. He and Aunt Jessi didn't get along."

Griff found that surprising. How could she be woman to a man she didn't like? The questions surrounding Miss Jessi Clayton were starting to stack up like corded wood. "So what are you going to do today, since you can't go to school?"

"Aunt Jessi's making me clean my room."

The desolate face made Griff smile. "You don't look real happy."

"I'd rather muck out the stables."

"That's because the stables are cleaner," Jessi cracked, entering the kitchen.

Her presence seemed to put the sun back in the boy's face. "Morning, Aunt Jessi."

She smiled. "Morning, Joth. Just about done?"

He looked down at his nearly empty plate. "Yes."

Jessi avoided looking at Blake's knowing expression. "Well, finish up and get going on your room. If you start early enough, you might be done by Thursday."

The boy's smile mirrored his aunt's. The two favored each other more than a bit.

After his breakfast was done, Joth went off to his room, leaving Jessi and Griff alone in the kitchen. She was sipping coffee. He was watching her, once again noting how chapped and raw her hands looked curled around the cup. They were not the hands of a woman who sat around all day.

Jessi forced herself to bring up a subject she thought needed discussing. "The Wanted bulletins say you have a way with the ladies."

Since Griff had no idea where this conversation was headed, especially in light of this morning's little incident, he shrugged. "It's not something I'll deny. I've always been partial to beautiful women."

Jessi sensed that he wasn't bragging; he truly enjoyed women, and they enjoyed him. Her traitorous memory once again revisited the sight of him all nude and bronzed. She hastily set it aside. "Well, I'd prefer you meet your women in town, not here. Joth shouldn't be exposed to such things."

"I agree."

Jessi had expected him to argue the point. It surprised her that he hadn't.

As if offering an explanation, he said, "I like your nephew, Miss Clayton. He's been raised well, I don't plan on messing that up."

Surprised again, Jessi confessed, "I say this in all honesty, Mr. Blake. I've met my share of outlaws, but I've never met one who cared at all about proper upbringing."

"Is that a compliment or a complaint?" His gaze was open, teasing.

"I believe you can take it as a compliment."

"Good. Then let me speak plainly as well. I've met my share of beautiful women, but I've never met one like you."

Jessi didn't know what to say at first. *Declaring* herself past the age of fluttering was one thing, but actually *being* past the age of fluttering was another breed of cow, she was finding. Tearing her attention away from the spell of his powerful eyes, she finally replied, "I'm a bit old for you. Save your sweet talk for the young ladies in town. They'll appreciate it more."

"A woman's just entering her prime at your age."

"Did Minerva tell you I was a whore?" Jessi asked plainly. "Is that what this flirting is about?"

Griff found her straightforwardness refreshing, but for now he ignored the first question. He was far more interested in the second. "Do you think I'm flirting with you?"

Jessi took one look into his tempter's eyes and replied without hesitation. "Yes, but I think it's just part of your nature. I doubt you really mean anything by it."

He responded with that grin. "Minerva told me some things, but they have nothing to do with this conversation, or anything else. I told you I'm no threat to you, and I mean that, but you are a beautiful woman."

"Well, regardless, I'm still too old for you."

''No, you're not, and whenever you want me to prove it, just say the word.''

Jessi blinked.

He stood then. ''I'm going into town and see if I can't rustle us up a few hands to help out around here.''

Jessi could see both mischief and manly knowing in his eyes. Somewhere deep down in her soul, doors she'd locked over a decade ago were opening on rusted hinges to this train robber's seductive power and she wasn't sure what to do about it.

When he rode off, she was still seated at the table wondering where this would all lead.

Griff rode into town. Word of his presence must've gotten around, because he received more than a few stares from more than a few people. He threw some of the gawkers off stride by nodding politely and smiling, especially at the ladies, as if he were the town's padre instead of a notorious outlaw.

He dismounted at the telegraph office, secured the reins of the gelding to the post, and went on inside. A small crowd of men were gathered around a big-bellied stove, talking and drinking coffee. Griff's entrance brought on an immediate silence.

''Morning, gentlemen.''

In reply, he was offered some cautious nods of greeting and a few mumbled ''Mornings.''

''Name's Griffin Blake. Who's the agent here?''

A short, balding man stood. ''Me. Name's Crenshaw Atkins. What can I do for you?''

''Like to send this telegram—or are the Clayton hands not allowed to use the wire, either?''

His challenging words made eyes widen all over the small room. A couple of the men gave him challenging looks in reply, but no one said anything.

Atkins hustled over to his post. "What's the message?"

Griff scribbled out what he wanted sent and to whom, then handed the slip of paper to the clerk. Atkins' eyes widened as he read the what Griff had written.

"But these men are—"

"Friends," Griff responded sagely. "Something a man can never have too many of. Is there a problem, Mr. Atkins?"

"No, no," the short bald clerk stammered. "I'll send these off right away."

One of the men by the stove said, "Reed Darcy's not going to like this, Atkins."

Griff turned slowly around and in response answered, "I'm not here to be liked, just to work for Miss Clayton."

"I'll tell him you said that," the man retorted.

"Please do," Griff responded.

Griff swore he saw Atkins smile, but the man's face was blank when he asked Griff, "Would you like to wait for verification from the agents on the other end?"

"Yep."

Atkins tapped out the message. Griffin wasn't sure where his friends, Neil July and Neil's twin brother, Two Shafts, were living at this particular moment, but was certain the telegraph agent down in their hometown of Brackettsville would get the word to them. The other man, a friend from Dallas named Vance Bigelow, would hopefully be easy to find as well.

Verification that Griff's messages had reached their destinations came back a few moments later. Both operators wired back that they'd pass Griff's information along.

Griff touched his hat in parting to the men sitting around the stove and headed out the door. By law, telegraph operators were not supposed to reveal their messages to anyone other than the recipient, but Griff knew that even before he walked the short distance to where the gelding stood tied and waiting, Atkins would have told everybody in the office that Blake was wiring for reinforcements. Griff just hoped they'd come.

As he rode down Vale's main street, Griff pondered the problem of supplies. The Clayton stores were very low, but with no one around willing to take Clayton money they couldn't be replenished. He wondered if the boss lady would mind him taking a trip over to Fort Worth? Surely Darcy's influence didn't reach that far. Once there he could buy everything they needed.

As he passed the Darcy Hotel, his thoughts returned to Jessi Clayton. She certainly didn't carry herself like any whores he'd ever known. She was way too serious, for one thing, and had given him no indication that she was free with her favors. This morning she seemed just as shocked by his nudity as any other properly raised woman. Had she really been Calico Bob's woman? The Jessi Clayton questions were stacking up again, but for the moment there didn't seem to by any solid answers.

Joth was still cleaning his room when Griff got back.

Griff stuck his head in the door and asked, "How're you coming?"

Joth looked up, glum. "If hogs can live in a sty, why can't I live like I want?"

"Mainly because you're not a hog," Griff quipped, giving him a look as he stared around the room. Hogs would certainly have felt comfortable, Griff had to admit. There were things everywhere: books and more books, stuffed in bookcases and stacked on the window seats. There were two telescopes, a microscope, and two saddles and their accompanying tack up on top of a barely visible desk resting against one wall. On the top of an equally barely discernible nightstand were jars of insects resting precariously atop a collection of glass-

framed mounted moths. "If you add one more thing to
this room, you're going to have to move your bed out."

"You sound like Aunt Jessi."

"Then forget I said that."

Joth grinned.

Griff grinned back.

The boy had more belongings than any other ten-year-
old Griff had ever met. In addition to the items he'd
noticed before, he saw mounds of clothes, boots, and a
fiddle with broken strings. There was a ball bat and la-
crosse sticks. There were even a pair of ice skates. What
amazed Griff most, however, were the walls plastered
with Wanted posters. There had to be a hundred or more.
Drawn by the sheer numbers, Griff waded over to the
nearest wall and just stared. There were notices for every
outlaw of color Griff had ever heard of and some he had
not. He saw one for the Black Seminole known as Charley Bowlegs, whose all-Indian gang had terrorized the
good citizens of Indian Territory a few years ago, but if
Griff remembered correctly, Charley had been caught,
sentenced by Judge Parker, and hanged back in '83.
Nailed up beside the Bowlegs warrant was one for Jackson Crow, a Choctaw wanted for the assassination of
Charles Wilson, a prominent Choctaw citizen. There
were at least five notices posted by Joth for the Black
outlaw Dick Glass, wanted in Indian Territory for everything from murder to whiskey running. Next to the Glass
poster, Joth had tacked up Glass's death notice, dated
June 11, 1885. Griff, not knowing Glass was dead, saw
that he had died in a shootout with a group of the Territory's Lighthorse policemen led by the well-known
lawman Sam Sixkiller. Griff had met Glass a couple of
times on his flights through Indian Territory and had
liked the man. Further down the wall, Griff came across
warrants for his old buddy, Isom Dart. The last time he
and Isom were together, they'd been sitting in a Colo-

rado saloon with a couple of lovely ladies on their re-
spective laps, toasting their friendship. Even though
Isom had a good ten years of age on Griff, they'd covered one another's backs on more than a few occasions.
At the time of their parting, Griff had been on his way
to California to relieve yet another railroad express car
of its gold, and Isom swore he planned on leaving the
life to settle down and be a farmer. Griff had laughed,
of course. Isom was notorious for getting religion and
then suddenly showing up to help Griff waylay a train.

"Where'd you get all these?" Griffin asked, still
amazed at the size of Joth's collection.

"From sheriffs and marshals I write to. It started out
as a school project Mr. Trent had us do on outlaws.
There's couple of my pa over there, and two of you over
there."

Griff went over and looked at his own. They were a
few years old. One was for his escape from the jail in
Colorado two years ago. He'd been helped in that by
the mayor's wife and the spinster daughter of the sheriff.
Both women had been very, *very* accommodating during
his week-long stay. Griff hoped they hadn't gotten in
too much trouble for the roles they'd played in his break-
out.

Griff turned his attention back to Joth and the room.
He was still amazed by the sheer volume of the boy's
possessions. "Did your Aunt Jessi buy all this stuff?"
Microscopes and telescopes were very expensive out
here in the West, as were books.

"She gave me some of the books, but most of the
other things are gifts from my Aunt Paris."

"Who's she?"

"She's a friend of Aunt Jessi's who lives back east.
Aunt Jessi says Aunt Paris has way more money than
she knows what to do with."

Griff chuckled. Looking at all Joth's possessions, he

thought Aunt Jessi must be right. "Have you been cleaning the whole time I've been gone?"

Joth shook his head solemnly as he began putting another handful of books upright in the bookcase.

"How about I see if I can wrangle you a reprieve from the governor?"

Joth's eyes widened with joy. "Would you? I've cleaned up a lot, I really have."

Griff doubted the boy's assessment as he surveyed the mountain of belongings still needing to be put in their places, but it was a beautiful day outside and it was begging to be enjoyed, even by a boy suspended from school.

"If I do get you pardoned, you'll have to promise me you'll make some real progress on this place once we get back. Deal?"

A grinning Joth came over and firmly shook Griff's outstretched hand. "Deal."

Griff found Jessi seated on a stool by the barn door, repairing the stitching on a saddle.

"Don't mean to bother you, Miss Clayton, but Joth and I would like to go riding, if that's okay with you."

"Where?" she asked, looking up from her task. Seeing him made her remember this morning all over again. She wondered how long it would take her to forget the beauty of his male body and its effects on her.

"I want him to give me a tour of the place."

"I already gave you one, remember?"

"I know, but I want him to show it to me from where he sits. Children see things different than adults do at times."

Jessi observed him for a moment, then said knowingly, "I think you're just trying to get Joth out of his chores."

Griff tried to keep his smile hidden but failed. "I just thought it being such a nice day and all—"

She waved a hand. "It's all right, Mr. Blake, we agree. I was just about to go in and tell him to take a break, so riding with you is fine."

"You're sure?"

"I'm sure, just don't be gone too long, because I can tell you without even going into his room that he has much left to do."

Griff wondered if her being embarrassed this morning had anything to do with her easy surrender now. Knowing better than to look a gift horse in the mouth, he didn't pursue the matter; instead, he touched his hat politely. "Then we'll see you later."

"Have a good time."

On the ride, Griff found he liked the boy more and more. Joth was much smarter than Griff had been at the same age. Joth knew about foreign countries, ancient history, and how to catch fish with his hands. As Joth knelt on the edge of the clear stream waiting to hand snag their lunch, he explained, "We had a Cheyenne brave work for us before Gramps was killed and he taught me how to spear fish, which is easy, but he also taught me how to fish with my hands."

Fascinated, Griff watched from where he stood nearby.

"You have to be real quiet, Griff."

"Okay."

"Then you have to let your hand become part of the stream."

Griff watched Joth stick his hand in the water and leave it there until the fish and other water dwellers began to swim around it, comfortable once more. Moments later, Joth snatched up a fat little fish and tossed it on the bank. "See?" he cried with a grin. "It's easy."

"Not bad," the impressed Griff admitted. "Next time, I'll try."

Joth caught a few more and didn't want any help scaling, gutting, or cooking the fish. "Aunt Jessi showed me how to do all this. Gramps, too, but mostly Aunt Jessi."

"You love her a lot, don't you?"

"More than Buttercup."

Griff laughed. Buttercup was Joth's palomino pony. "A woman's got to be mighty special to make a cowboy love her more than his horse."

Joth smiled, embarrassed.

Later, as they ate, Griff asked, "So, did you learn all that history you've been spouting from Mr. Trent at school?"

"Naw, from Aunt Jessi. She used to be a teacher back east before I was born."

Griff stared. He'd been handed another piece to fit into the Jessi Clayton puzzle, but had no idea where it went.

Before he could ask about it, however, Joth stood and looked across the rolling land. "Riders coming."

Griff stood by his side. There were two men on horseback and one man driving a large, fancy black carriage. One of the mounted riders was trailing a cow.

"It's Reed Darcy, and he's stealing our cows again!" Joth stalked over to his mount and pulled the rifle from his saddle's scabbard.

Watching him, Griff felt his eyes widen. As the determined boy fed cartridges into the gun, Griff held up his hands. "Whoa, there! What're you doing?"

"Protecting what's mine. I promised Gramps."

Griff could see that the boy's blood ran as fiercely as his Aunt Jessi's. "Well, how about we try and talk this out first? A firearm might not be necessary." Even though Griff had on a gunbelt, he hoped he wouldn't have to use the Colt it held.

"Reed Darcy doesn't talk," Joth replied firmly.

Griff waited silently.

"All right," Joth offered in surrender. "But if he shoots us, you're going to have to answer to Aunt Jessi, not me."

Griff grinned in spite of the tension. "I won't let him shoot us. Don't worry."

The men didn't seem to care that they'd been spotted. In fact, they rode right up to where Griff and Joth stood.

"That's a Clayton cow!" Joth declared accusingly, as the party reined their horses to a stop.

Griff placed a hand on the boy's shoulder to calm him a bit.

In the fancy black carriage sat a middle aged, brown-skinned man with pomaded hair. Dressed nattily in an expensive-looking dark suit and string tie, he had the girth of a man who lived well. He responded to Joth's angry accusation with a cold smile. "Now Joth, where are your manners? I'm sure your aunt taught you not to speak to adults unless you're spoken to first." The brittle black eyes assessed the boy. Then, as if deeming him unworthy of a further audience, the man pointedly ignored him and turned to Griff. "Afternoon, son. Who're you?"

"Name's Blake."

Darcy took a moment to look Griffin over. "Are you the man my son and his wife met in Abe's store yesterday?"

"Yes. And you are?"

"Reed Darcy. I own most of the land around here," he boasted.

Griffin was not impressed. "Is that a Clayton cow?"

"Not sure," Darcy lied easily. "The boys and I found it just sort of wandering around. But I'm having some friends over later in the week. I thought it would make a good barbecue candidate."

Griff assessed the two riders escorting Darcy, then asked coolly, "Is there a brand?"

"I didn't think to look," he said, eyeing Griff.

"Well, why don't we look now, just so there's no misunderstandings later?"

"How about we don't and I give you some advice instead? Nobody around here works for the Claytons. Bad for the health, if you catch my meaning."

"Oh, really?"

"Yep, and if you have any sense, you'll pack your gear and ride out."

Griff hated being told what to do, especially by a man in a fancy suit and tie. "Well, Mr. Darcy, I've never been one to have much sense, so I think I'll stick around. Besides, I especially like meeting men who pick fights with women and children."

Darcy's face flashed with anger. "You're a pretty up-pity cowboy."

"Thank you."

The two men assessed each other and neither appeared to like what they were seeing.

One of the riders, a tall lean man with bad teeth interrupted to ask Griff, "Don't I know you?"

Griff slowly turned his attention away from Darcy's angry face. "Maybe."

"Yeah, I do, but your name wasn't Blake."

The man paused a minute, staring intently, as if trying to place Griff, then declared, "You used to rob trains. Saw your picture in the paper in Omaha a few years back. Oklahoma Red!"

Griff executed a slight bow.

Darcy asked his employee, "He any good?"

Griff knew Darcy was asking about his prowess with a gun.

In answer, the man got down from his horse and untied the cow's rope from his saddle.

Darcy snapped, "What the hell are you doing?"

"No disrespect, Mr. Darcy, but maybe you want to

be in a pine box over a cow, but not me. Heard he and a couple of his friends took on a whole army of hired guns up in Montana. The army lost.''

He handed the rope over to Joth. ''Here you go, boy.''

Darcy appeared ready to explode. ''Have you lost your mind? I'm the one paying your salary, not the Claytons!''

''Not anymore. I quit. Him throwing in with the Claytons changes everything around here.''

Darcy looked first to Griffin and then to his now former ranch hand. ''My son says he's just a train robber, not a gunslinger.''

''Your son is wrong. It's been nice working for you, Mr. Darcy.'' The man turned his mount and galloped off toward town.

Reed Darcy appeared stunned. He looked to his remaining companion, who seemed to be viewing Griff with a lot less confidence than he had previously.

The man asked Griff, ''Are you really Oklahoma Red?''

''I've been called that, yes. Some folks call me Nevada Red, Omaha Red. I've got a lot of names, don't I, Joth?''

''Sure do,'' Joth chimed in with a smile. ''Do you know him, too, mister?''

''Uh, yeah. Mr. Darcy, maybe we should head on back.''

''You turning yellow, too?'' he barked.

''Not yellow. Just smart.'' He reined his horse around. ''You coming?''

It was easy to see that Darcy clearly had no idea what to do. This encounter had not played out as he'd planned. He was accustomed to having his orders carried out without question. ''There are two of us and only one of him,'' the wealthy land baron reminded the man.

''Makes no difference. My pappy always said never

provoke a rattler, and that, my friend, is a big one. See you back at the ranch.''

He rode off.

As the silence of the beautiful afternoon settled once again, Griff gave Reed Darcy a lazy smile and said, ''Well now. Looks like it's just you, me, and the boy.''

Darcy glared.

''You don't really want to lose your life over a cow, do you?''

Silence.

''I thought not,'' Griff replied, answering for him. ''So here's how it's gonna be—me and the boy are going to take this Clayton cow and head on back.''

''That cow's not going anywhere. My men may be afraid of you, but I'm not.''

The angry Darcy went for his gun, but it was way too late. Griff had already drawn his steel blue Colt and had the business end coolly pointed at the man's now very wide eyes.

Griff told him, ''If I shoot you, Miss Jessi's going to be real mad at me for letting your rotten carcass poison her land, and Lord knows we don't want to make the lady mad. So be a good boy and put that away. Better yet, just toss it over there on the ground—we wouldn't want anybody backshot by mistake, now, would we?''

Darcy seemed to swell with fury.

''Now.''

Reed Darcy must have seen the force in Griff's eyes, because he slowly but sullenly complied.

''Joth, go get it. Careful picking it up.''

Joth hustled over to retrieve the weapon and passed it to Griff, who placed the gun in his left hand, his eyes never wavering from his target. In a low voice filled with steel, he told Darcy, ''Now, let me give *you* some advice: stay off Clayton land. If I catch you or your hands out here again, I'm going to risk Miss Jessi's wrath and shoot you like the rustlers you are.''

Reed Darcy seethed. ''You'll pay for this!''

''Maybe, but it won't be today. Now, git.''

The furious and bested Darcy gave Griffin one last malevolent glare, then turned the carriage's team around and headed off.

Joth looked at Griff as if with new eyes and said simply, ''Wow!''

After they returned the cow to the herd, Joth and Griff headed home, and the very first thing Joth did when they reached the house was to run and tell his Aunt Jessi what had happened. Griff led his gelding and Joth's Buttercup around to the barn. Jessi found him inside.

''My nephew told me what happened.''

Griff looked down at her lush mouth as he pulled the saddle off the gelding. He wondered what it would be like to feel her kiss. ''Joth was in no danger, if that's what's worrying you.''

''No, it's not that, but I thought you said you weren't real partial to guns?''

''I'm not, but that doesn't mean I'm not good with one.''

''Joth says you're quite good.''

''Make you feel better about having me around?''

Jessi nodded. ''I won't lie. Yes, it does.''

Griff wondered if he'd ever become accustomed to her beauty. Her disposition and fondness for Winchesters notwithstanding, she was as tempting as an unguarded express car full of gold. But he reminded himself that he was supposed to be here on behalf of the judge, not sizing her up for his bed. To take his mind off things he had no business even contemplating, he said, ''Well, Darcy probably won't be having me over for dinner anytime soon.''

''Probably not,'' she replied with a knowing smile.

Jessi looked up at him and was reminded of how she'd seen him this morning—vividly, brilliantly nude. Once again she tried to set aside the unfamiliar rush of feelings the memories evoked. "He doesn't like being bested."

"He didn't look real happy when he left."

Silence prevailed for a few moments as the air between them thickened like fog. Jessi said genuinely, "Thanks for keeping Joth safe."

"Anytime."

They were assessing one another, each harboring their own thoughts. He wondered what she was thinking, and she wondered the same about him.

Griff finally broke the silence. "I wired some friends of mine. I'm hoping they'll start coming in in a week or so."

"More train robbers?" she asked.

He smiled. "Just a couple."

"Any of them ever worked cows?"

"Not that I know of, no."

Unable to hide her smile, Jessi shook her head.

"They're all fast learners, though," he added, coming to their defense. His voice softened suddenly. "I wondered how long it would take you to do that."

Jessi looked up into his power-filled eyes and felt his seductive spell slipping under her locked doors like intoxicating tendrils of smoke. "Do what?"

"Smile."

The tone of his voice stroked her like a hand. Her voice was soft, low. "Are you flirting again, Mr. Blake?"

"I believe I am." He thought she had a voice as smoky as a Mexican cantina.

"You're not supposed to flirt with your employer."

"Can't seem to help myself."

She grinned. "You're going to be a handful, aren't you?"

"Always have been—probably always will be. You'll get used to it."

Their gazes held. The air was charged.

Jessi looked away first. "Supper'll be done in a while."

He nodded.

Jessi hurried back to the house.

Alone in the barn, Griff smiled. Was she actually flirting back? He doubted she'd thought the short exchange as anything significant, but it certainly felt like a lot more than that to him. Her beauty and rawhide spirit were as intoxicating as fine tequila. The fact that it had taken him two days to get her to smile his way was pretty humbling for a man whose way with women was legendary, but the challenge she represented surpassed anything he'd ever come up against before. Because of his mission and his desire to head down to Mexico he knew he shouldn't be thinking about wanting her, but as he told her, he couldn't help himself.

Back in the house, Jessi tried to her best to concentrate on peeling the potatoes for supper, but her mind kept straying to Griffin Blake. What was it about him that caused her to smile up at him like a moonstruck girl after being in his presence less than three days? Jessi prided herself on her inner strength and her good sense, but with Griff around, her strength seemed to be fading and her good sense flying out of the window. She'd actually flirted with him back there in the barn, something she hadn't done with any man before, not even her late husband Evan.

Jessi paused. She hadn't thought about Evan in quite some time. She'd married him over a decade ago, more for convenience than anything else; he'd needed a wife to further his political aspirations, and she'd needed a husband in order to maintain her teaching position. At the time her school board had frowned on unmarried women teaching in their classrooms.

Although there had been nothing spectacular about their life together, she and Evan had gotten along reasonably well, only to have him succumb to pneumonia less than two years after the wedding day. When her father wrote to her a few weeks after Evan's death, asking that she come and help raise Joth after her sister died in childbirth, Jessi readily agreed because a part of her did grieve for Evan, and she hoped that going home would help her heal and get on with the business of living. For three years it did, until the day Calico Bob had ridden into town with his men to claim his young son and changed her life forever.

So now here she stood, over ten years later, peeling potatoes, sharing a house with another outlaw. But with the flirting Griffin she sensed a light she hadn't been touched by before; and if the truth be told, after experiencing so much darkness, a part of her wanted to run toward that blazing light and be bathed in it, but she doubted she could trust him. He was, after all, an outlaw and an avowed womanizer: two traits no woman in her right mind would ever want in a man. Surprised that she would even admit to being moved by Griffin Blake, she shook herself free of the disturbing thought and went back to peeling potatoes.

That night, after Joth went to bed, Jessi stepped out onto the porch to join Griff as he kept watch. "Nice night," she offered. The clear sky was filled with brilliantly twinkling stars and the moon was large. "Full moon like this is called a Comanche moon."

"My mother used to call it a courting moon."

Jessi looked down at him seated on the porch step near her feet. "I've never heard it called that."

"Where've you been?" he asked, in a voice soft with teasing. "Everybody's heard of a courting moon."

"I haven't."

"So now you're going to tell me you've never been courted?"

"Never been courted."

Griffin found that surprising and looked up at her in the moonlit darkness. "Not even by your husband?"

"No. It wasn't a love match. We married for convenience."

"Doesn't sound very romantic."

"It suited us, though. Marrying him allowed me to do the things I wanted to do in life, and it afforded him the same."

"No one's ever taken you for a ride in the moonlight or brought you flowers?"

She shook her head. "Nope. Evan asked me to marry him, told me all the reasons why I should say yes, and so I did. We were reasonably happy, I suppose."

"You suppose?"

"I've nothing to compare it with."

He thought about that a moment. "I guess that makes sense. Well, if I were courting you, I'd take you on rides in the moonlight, bring you flowers."

"Ah, but to what end? You don't impress me as the kind of man who'd settle down."

He shrugged. "I'm not. I'm not cut out for the marriage saddle."

Jessi had no problem believing that. Most of the outlaws she'd come in contact with were looking for nothing more than a fast tumble in the hay. She doubted he'd be any different. "You must've left a trail of broken hearts behind you, then."

"Not really. Most women know the score going in. That way, there are no tears when I pull up stakes and move on."

"My friend Paris believes that love finds everybody eventually."

"Do you believe her?"

"I don't know. It hasn't found me so far, and I doubt I want it to."

"Why not?"

Jessi was silent for awhile. "Being alone has its advantages. A woman doesn't have to bow to anyone's wishes but her own."

"Then we'd make a good pair, you and I."

"How so?"

"I don't want ties, and neither do you."

Jessi supposed he was right.

"Courting you would be a challenge, though."

Jessi looked at him. "Why?"

"Because I believe you'd enjoy it."

Jessi smiled in the dark. "You certainly are sure of yourself, Mr. Blake, but why court someone you know you aren't going to commit to?"

"For the joy and the passion of it."

"At least you're honest."

"I am, and as long as I am, no one gets hurt."

Jessi pondered that a moment, then heard herself asking without thought, "How would you court me?"

In response, he eased himself to his feet. Facing her now and only a heartbeat away, he said, "Slowly at first—then at whatever speed you'd like."

"You're very bold, Mr. Blake."

"Only as bold as you'd let me be, Miss Clayton."

They were standing so close, Jessi had to fight down the urge to touch his night shadowed cheek. They were as aware of each other as they were of the crickets singing softly against the night.

"How long were you married?" he asked quietly.

"Almost two years. Evan died of pneumonia."

"He ever kiss you?"

For a moment there was silence. "Occasionally, yes."

"A woman like you should be kissed thoroughly and often."

"Do you think so . . . ?"

"I know so . . ."

He slid a slow finger down her cheek and then lowered his mouth to hers. The kiss was as soft as the night. Jessi had only to stand there and let his whispery lips play cajolingly across her own. Nothing in life had prepared her for the sweet buffeting that claimed her, and when the kiss ended and he eased away, it took her a minute to open her eyes. "It this what you meant about courting me slowly?"

He nodded as he lazily traced the fullness of her bottom lip. "Yes. Every woman should be savored at least once in her life."

She'd never had a man touch her mouth so intimately before. Her lips, full from his kisses, felt as if they'd been infused with the sparkles of the starlight. The woman in her wanted more. "Kiss me again," she heard herself say softly.

He whispered his reply, "You're the boss . . ."

This kiss held more fire, more power. Jessi knew she was in the web of a man so expert he could make his living doing this, but she didn't care. She wanted to be filled by his light, be warmed by his lips moving so sensually over her own. He seemed reluctant to release her because he kept returning to steal slow, tender snatches from her lips.

"Is this enough?" he husked out, even as he brushed another series of kisses over her brow and her cheekbone.

Jessi's knees seemed to have melted away. All of her inner strength and good sense had been seared to ash by his overwhelming brilliance. Granted, calling a halt was not what she really wanted, but she had to reclaim herself or succumb totally. "Yes. I think we should stop . . ."

In reply to her soft words, he eased away and took a small step back.

Jessi had no idea what she was supposed to do with the yearning throbbing so heatedly inside herself, making her want more. Jessi knew she had to get off this porch or she would start begging for more. She forced herself to head toward the door. "Good night, Mr. Blake. Sleep well."

"You too."

As soon as she was inside, Griff put his head in his hands and asked himself, *"What the hell are you doing?"* Even though he knew he had absolutely no business pursuing Jessi Clayton, his manhood was hard as a length of railroad track, and it took all he had not to follow her inside and make love to her until they were both too sated to move. Nothing else mattered right now; not Reed Darcy, not Dixon Wildhorse, or the seven years awaiting him back at the Kansas State Penitentiary. What he and his body wanted revolved solely around the most tempting boss he'd ever worked for in his life.

He could hear her moving around inside the house as she prepared for bed. For a woman who was supposed to be both whore and widow, she kissed with all the experience of a virgin bride. He'd tasted a deep well of passion in the kisses she'd shared with him, but he'd also tasted an innocence he hadn't expected. In the past he'd always been very cavalier in his treatment of the women who attracted his attention, but he instinctively knew that Jessi Clayton was not the type of woman a man could simply love and leave; she would linger in a man's mind for a while, maybe for a lifetime. He'd always preferred cathouse ladies—memorable while they were under or atop you, but not for a lifetime. The only woman he carried constantly in his memory was the one he had buried when he was ten years old.

So what was he doing talking about courting Jessi

Clayton? Common sense dictated that he forget about wanting her and concentrate on what he'd come to Texas to do. But sometimes Griff chose not to pay attention to common sense, and now appeared to be one of those times.

As Jessi lay in bed, she spent a long time thinking back on Griffin Blake's kisses. They'd sent her soaring like a heroine in the pulp novels her friend Paris LaMarr had been so fond of. Although Paris had insisted that kisses from the right man could send you flying as high as an eagle, that had not been Jessi's experience—until now. Evan's kisses had been chaste and gentle. The few times they'd been intimate, he had been patient and respectful and made sure she didn't have to endure his needs any longer than necessary, because he knew she didn't enjoy the marriage bed.

Something told her it might be different with Griffin Blake. It was truly a scandalous thought, she admitted. Just being near him seemed to give birth to feelings she wasn't sure properly raised women were supposed to have. Her memories of the strength and beauty of his body had not dimmed, either. Thinking back on that sight in conjunction with his potent kisses made her dizzy. *What would it be like to lie with a man who enjoyed women?* she asked herself. Her lips still felt kiss-swollen, and the throbbing in her blood, although lessened, continued to echo like a faint drumbeat. The no-nonsense woman who usually directed her life scolded her for her musings and thought it better to dwell on a less volatile subject, and Jessi agreed.

Turning her pillow over in an effort to get more comfortable, Jessi found her thoughts turning to her father. What would he say about a man like Blake? She'd no idea if he was in heaven or hell, but she wondered what he would say about her battle to hold on to the land. In her heart, she knew none of her efforts would matter or be good enough. Even though she'd given everything to the land except her life, his will had declared Joth the sole heir. Not that she minded—she loved Joth very much. Jessi had been named her nephew's guardian and instructed to turn over the reins when the boy reached legal age. In exchange, she would be allowed to live out her life on the ranch if she chose, but he'd willed her nothing more.

Frankly, she hadn't even expected that; her father's opinion of her had been no secret. The pain associated with that realization flared once more. When she was younger, the knowledge that her father hadn't loved her had pierced her heart so badly she'd cried herself to sleep more nights than she cared to remember, but over the years the sharp edges had dulled. Now that hurt was just a dull ache sharing space with all the other heartaches she'd known.

The clock on her nightstand had once belonged to her late mother Violet, and it showed it to be almost 2 A.M., far past the time when she should've been asleep, but her thoughts kept swinging back to Blake. Having an extra set of eyes and hands on the place did make breathing a bit easier, even though he hadn't as yet done anything even resembling work. A voice in her head reminded her that he had run Darcy off her land yesterday, and that in itself should've earned him a bonus. She supposed she agreed with the assessment, but she refused to dwell any longer on his kisses. Her own uncharacteristic actions on the porch notwithstanding, Jessi was realistic: she was no more than a diversion for him. When he was done here, he'd ride out of her life and be gone like yesterday's sunrise.

Chapter 4

❧〜✺〜❧

The next morning, Jessi awakened to what sounded like someone walking on the roof. To make certain it hadn't just been her imagination, she sat up in bed and paused to listen. When the steps echoed again, she got up to investigate. Just in case the steps belonged to a trespasser, she grabbed her Winchester.

Dressed in the faded blue wrapper she'd pulled on over her thin cotton nightgown, she first went down the hall to check on Joth. His room was early morning silent and dappled by fingers of the dawn's faint light. He lay fast asleep, so she closed his door and withdrew quietly. She next stopped at Blake's door. When her soft knocks went unanswered, she gently turned the knob and peeked in. The silence of the room mirrored Joth's, but Blake's bed was empty.

Closing the door, Jessi assumed the footsteps on the roof were his, but she couldn't imagine what he could be doing up there, especially at this time of morning.

She climbed the ladder in the kitchen and found him seated with his back resting against the old chimney. His arms were folded across his plaid-shirted chest, and his eyes were focused out on the pink and gray sky of what promised to be a spectacular sunrise.

Upon seeing her, he gave her a smile any woman

76

would love having turned her way. It made Jessi remember last night's encounter all over again.

"Morning," he said in greeting.

"Good morning. What are you doing up here?"

The flat roof made it easy to maneuver, so she had no trouble walking. The early morning breeze gently teased the hems of her wrapper and gown, exposing the well-worn boots on her feet

"Watching the sky. I didn't get to see too many sunrises in the penitentiary."

"What's it like there?"

"Hellish. You break rocks from dawn to dusk, eat rancid army rations, and hope nobody kills you in the night."

Jessi could hear the bitterness in his tone.

"Coffee?" he asked, indicating the battered pot at his side.

Once she took a seat and settled her gown over her knees, she nodded and took the offered pot and a cup. She had a feeling he'd changed the subject purposefully. She didn't much blame him; after all, prison couldn't've been pleasant, but she *did* blame herself for making him dredge up such obviously garish memories.

"Sleep well?" he asked.

"Surprisingly, yes," she offered, as she sipped her coffee and gave thanks for a man who could brew a decent pot.

"Why surprisingly?"

"It took me a long time to fall asleep."

This time his smile was filled with mischief. "Me too."

She could feel her attraction to him uncoiling. "Do you always leave women sleepless?"

"It's happened a time or two."

"You don't believe in modesty, do you?"

"Can't be modest if you're robbing trains."

"Or if you're conquering women from the Mississippi to the Rio Grande."

He paused a minute and studied her face. "Does my reputation bother you?"

His expression was serious. He wanted an honest answer. "I'm not certain. I do wonder if you're just using me to pass the time until you move on."

"That's honest."

"Yes, it is. It's also the truth. As much as I enjoyed last night, I have a hard time, wondering whether you're just trying for another notch on your bedpost."

He reached out and slowly traced his finger across the dark skin of her cheekbone. The tenderness of the gesture seemed to touch her soul. "You'll never be just a notch . . ."

Leaning over he touched his lips to hers and Jessi fed herself on his kiss, then eased back. "And how many women have you said that to?"

He brushed his lips across her ear. "And meant it? Only one . . . *you.*"

Jessi pulled back and searched his face.

His gaze held amusement. "From that look I take it you don't believe me."

"Honestly?"

"Honestly."

"No, I don't."

He grinned. "You're hard on a man."

"I'm skeptical by nature."

He smiled and shook his head. "Women are supposed to be agreeable."

"You've had too many agreeable women in your life as it is, I'm thinking. A little disagreement is good."

"Is that why you made me wait three days to see you smile?"

"I didn't smile at you because I didn't like you."

"You like me better now, I take it?"

"You really don't expect me to answer that—surely you don't," she replied with a laugh.

"Why not?"

"I'm not adding one more breath of air to your already exaggerated view of yourself."

"Exaggerated?" he asked playfully.

"Exaggerated."

"Are you saying my kisses are exaggerated?"

Jessi went still.

"Well, Miss Skeptical, I'm waiting for your answer."

He had her and she knew it.

She turned her head to hide her smile. He reached out and gently coaxed her chin back around so she would look into his eyes. She answered him truthfully and softly, "No, your kisses are fine."

He slowly teased his thumb across her parted mouth, and once again the intimacy of the gesture rattled her and made her eyes slide shut.

"Are you sure . . . ?"

He was so close and his touch so vividly possessive, Jessi was having difficulty breathing, yet she managed to answer, "I'm sure . . ."

"Well, just so you don't forget later."

He kissed her so slowly and with such passion, she groaned softly in pleasurable response. Last night's kisses had been chaste in comparison to this heated, overwhelming rendition. He languidly branded her, enticed her; he tempted her to savor what only he could give. When he finally turned her loose, she swore the world was spinning.

From somewhere deep inside herself she managed to locate her will and slowly opened her eyes; his handsome satisfied-male smile was the very first thing she saw.

"You're much too good at this," she baldly admitted.

He chuckled softly. "Glad you think so. Now, finish

your coffee and quit distracting me, or we're going to miss the end of the sunrise.''

Jessi grinned. In the early morning light his humor-filled eyes were as faceted as a mountain cat's, and just like a cat he was toying with her, but in a way she thoroughly enjoyed. For the first time in a long time Jessi Rose Clayton did what she was told—she sat back and watched the sun and sipped at her now tepid coffee.

The crest of the sun broke through the pink and gray horizon in a blaze of colors so brilliant they were impossible to describe.

''That's a beautiful sky,'' he said, toasting the sight with his cup.

''Yes, it is.''

''If you could have three things in life, what would they be?'' he asked her suddenly.

Jessi found the question a bit surprising, but gave serious thought to her response. ''Let's see . . . I'd want this mess with Darcy settled, so Joth could enjoy the rest of his childhood. I'd get this roof fixed, so he and I don't drown every time it rains. And I'd go back to teaching.''

He turned to her. ''That's all you'd want for yourself?''

''Yes,'' she admitted truthfully. ''My needs are small. What about you, what would you wish for?''

''I'm not sure, but a different life, I think.''

''What kind of a different life?''

''One where I wouldn't have to be looking over my shoulder all the time.''

She studied him for a moment. ''A life on the right side of the law?''

He shrugged. ''Maybe.'' He then added, ''I can't see myself as a farmer, though.''

''Neither can I,'' she concurred.

''As a rancher, maybe.''

Suddenly Joth's head popped through the opening in

the roof. "What are you two doing up here?"

Jessi answered smiling, "Watching the sun come up. Good morning."

"Morning, Aunt Jessi. Morning, Griff."

"Morning, cowboy."

"Are you ready for breakfast?" she asked.

"Yep."

"I'll be right down."

He nodded and disappeared back down the hole.

Jessi realized she'd wanted to hear more about the change Blake wanted in his life, but the moment was lost.

As she got to her feet, he asked, "What do you need done around here today?"

"You're offering to work?"

He grinned. "I'm not as lazy as you might assume."

"You could've fooled me," she cracked teasingly.

"Be nice, or you won't get any more of my exaggerated kisses."

Jessi rolled her eyes. "The corral needs work."

"This roof could use some attention, too."

"I know, but we need more wood than I have on hand, and Darcy owns the only lumber mill around."

"We'll just have to work around him."

"I doubt he'll be very accommodating after your run-in with him yesterday."

"Probably not, but we can figure out something. In the meantime . . . thanks for watching the sunrise with me."

"My pleasure."

Jessi, Joth, and Griffin spent the early part of the day replacing some of the old posts and cross ties of the corral. Under Jessi's supervision, Joth used a rope tied to Buttercup's saddle to help free the rotten, weathered posts from their holes.

Griff was impressed at how well trained the little palomino pony was and how much affection Joth showed it as horse and rider worked in tandem. The pony stopped and held when Joth asked it to and pulled when Joth said to pull. Once the old wood was freed, Joth and Buttercup dragged it off to the barn.

As Joth and his pony made yet another trip to the barn, Jessi said with all seriousness. ''If anything ever happens to that horse, it would probably kill him. I think he loves Buttercup more than anything.''

''Except his Aunt Jessi.''

Jessi turned to face him.

''Told me so himself. I told him it takes a very special woman to make a cowboy love her more than his horse.''

''And you would know.''

''Not really, I've never been in love. Lust, yes; love, no.''

Griff wondered what she would say if he told her that last night, after he'd finally fallen asleep, he'd dreamt about them making wild and passionate love. The dream had been so vivid he'd wakened this morning as hard and as ready as though the dream were real. Looking over at her now, all he could think about were the dream-based memories of her riding sensuously astride him and how beautifully her breasts had filled his hands.

Jessi had never known a man whose eyes could make her feel as if her clothes were going to melt from her body, but that's exactly how she felt at this moment. ''Is there something wrong?''

''No, not really. Just thinking back on the dream I had about you last night. Pretty good dream, too, if you want to know the truth.''

Thinking this was just another form of his flirting, Jessi replied with a raised eyebrow, ''How many women have you roped with that old lariat?''

Griff's mustache lifted with his smile. "You don't believe me?"

"Remember my skeptical nature? I'm not a naive ingenue."

"No, you're not. You're a woman, there's a difference."

"And that difference is age."

"You're putting up barriers again, Jessi Clayton. You're not that much older."

"I know, but for you, I'll need all the barriers I can find."

He grinned and picked up another post.

As the work continued, Jessi couldn't help but wonder if he'd been telling her the truth about the dream. What had it been about? He'd said it had been a good dream. Had he dreamt about kissing her? Although neither of them made mention of this morning's rooftop interlude, the sweet memories lingered within Jessi, as did her desire to be kissed by him again.

Jessi hadn't cut all of the new posts the same size. Because of the inadvertent mistake, some of the new posts wouldn't fit into the old holes, so new ones had to be dug. The digging turned out to be the hardest work yet. Due to the lack of rain, the ground was as hard as rock.

"Where'd you get the wood for the posts?" Griff asked, as he stopped digging a moment to catch his breath.

"Joth and I cut down a few dead trees last fall. We used some of the wood for heat this winter. I figured what was left would come in handy for repairing the corral."

And she'd been right. She had just enough extra to replace most of the rotting wood, the rest of the corral fence repairs would have to wait until another time.

As early afternoon rolled in, Jessi left the men working while she went in to fix them all some lunch. She made sandwiches using the meat from the last ham in the cellar stores and some bread. It wasn't fancy fare, but they wouldn't go hungry.

As she went to the front door to call Joth and Blake inside, she paused at the screen door to watch them. They were stacking the last of the old wood. She couldn't hear their conversation, but she could see Joth smiling and talking and acting like the open, friendly young boy she'd always loved. He hadn't had much to smile about lately through no fault of his own, yet Blake seemed able to make that part of Joth come alive again and Joth seemed relaxed in his presence. Blake for his part did not act annoyed by the boy's attention and Jessi blessed him for that. She still didn't know if his being here would be of any value to the ranch, but so far, Joth looked to be benefiting, and that was more than enough for her now. She knew she would be remiss if she didn't keep an eye on Blake, however; he was, after all, an outlaw, and kisses or no kisses, badge or no badge, trying to make a house cat out of a mountain lion was much easier said than done.

As Jessi stepped out onto the porch, the sight of Sheriff Hatcher riding up made her stop. Her father and the Vale sheriff had been lifelong friends until Reed Darcy came between them. She wondered how the lawman slept at night, knowing he hadn't lifted a finger to find the ones responsible for the cowardly murder of his friends.

As Hatcher dismounted and tied his horse to the post in front of the porch, Jessi could see Griff and Joth put down their shovels to come and see what was going on.

"Afternoon, Jessi."

She didn't offer him any pleasantries. Even though he'd been dearly loved his whole life, he didn't deserve any. "What can I do for you, Sheriff?"

His jaw tightened at her unfriendly stance. "Came to see somebody named Blake. Heard he works for you?"

Jessi eyed Griff a moment, then turned her attention to her nephew. "Joth, your lunch is on the table. Go get washed up. I'll be in to join you shortly."

The boy gave the sheriff a wary look, then said, "Yes, Aunt Jessi."

Silence reigned until Joth disappeared around the side of the house.

Griff stepped up. "I'm Blake. How can I help, sheriff?"

Hatcher looked Griffin up and down. He didn't appear to care for what he was seeing. "You can stay the hell away from Reed Darcy to start."

Griffin could only assume Darcy had run back and tattled after their meeting the other day, but out of a sense of fairness, he vowed to listen to the sheriff anyway. "Explain."

"If I ever hear of you pulling a gun on him again, you'll go straight to jail."

"And what will Darcy get for drawing on me?"

"Mr. Darcy doesn't have the time to waste drawing on somebody like you."

"No? Well, he drew first, but he probably left that part out."

Hatcher seemed caught off guard for a moment, but it didn't take him long to recover. "Whatever happened, Darcy is not somebody you want to fool with."

"And neither am I," Griff pointed out firmly. "He was rustling, Sheriff. I was protecting ranch property."

"You keep getting in Darcy's way and *you're* going to need protecting."

"You think so?"

"I know so."

Griff began making a show of searching his pockets. "A friend of mine gave me a magic amulet a few weeks ago. He thought I should wear it to keep me safe. What did I do with it?''

Still patting the pockets of his pants and shirt Griffin looked up to Jessi standing on the porch and asked. ''Miss Clayton, do you know what I did with that amulet?''

With a completely straight face, Jessi replied, ''No, Mr. Blake, I don't. Maybe you should check your pockets again.''

''Good idea.''

Checking the pocket of his shirt again, Griff paused and then smiled. ''Here it is.''

When he withdrew the marshal star and held it up for Hatcher to see, Griff drawled coolly, ''Do you think this will protect me?''

Hatcher went stock still. ''Where'd you get that?''

''Friend of mine.''

Griffin pinned the star to his pocket. ''How's that look?''

Since Hatcher still seemed to be having problems with his speech, Griffin turned to Jessi. ''How's that look, Miss Clayton. Too flashy?''

''Some might think so, but I find it very stunning, Mr. Blake.''

They shared a grin.

The sheriff didn't appear amused by their antics. ''Who sent you here?''

''Deputy Marshal Dixon Wildhorse.''

''Never heard of him.''

''Probably not, but I'll bet you've heard of his boss, Hanging Judge Issac Parker, up at Fort Smith?''

Hatcher began to cough violently.

''I think he does,'' Griffin told Jessi.

''I'm guessing that, too,'' she said, amused. Jessi hadn't had this much fun in quite some time.

When Hatcher finally recovered from his fit of coughing, he barked, "I want to know everything, and I want to know it now, especially the parts about how you got out of that Kansas Penitentiary."

Griff had no intention of telling him any more than was necessary. "The judge pardoned me."

"Why?"

"Because he wants Reed Darcy to have my bed there instead. Judge Parker's had his eye on your friend for some time because the judge doesn't take kindly to men burning out their neighbors or shooting folks in the back."

"I had nothing to do with any of that!" Hatcher snapped angrily.

"Well, you'd better start having something to do with it, or your name's going to be right next to Darcy's on Judge Parker's list. How'd you know about my parole?"

"Darcy had me wire a few railroad friends of his up in Kansas to find out about you and they wired him back. They said you'd been paroled, but the warden couldn't tell them anything else."

Griffin found the situation highly ironic. How many outlaws had lawmen like Wildhorse and Judge Parker guarding their backs? "Sheriff, you can either honor that badge you're wearing and help me, or not. Either way, Darcy's going to be stopped."

The sheriff looked Griff up and down once more, then said with a brittle smile. "You're pretty damn sure of yourself, aren't you?"

"I've been told that a time or two."

"Well, Darcy ain't no train you're trying to rob, son. You're on your own."

Griff's jaw tightened. He'd hoped for the sheriff's help. "I think you're betting on the wrong horse, sheriff."

Hatcher turned to walk back to his mount. "Maybe, but *I'll* be alive to find out, you won't."

"Even if it means you spend the rest of your life in prison?"

The sheriff turned back and replied quietly, "I'm already in prison, son."

Hatcher got into the saddle, then looked over to Jessi, still standing on the porch. He told her, "Talk some sense into him, Jessi, before it's too late."

He touched his hat and rode off.

After the silence resettled, Jessi said. "I don't think he has much faith in your abilities, Marshal Blake."

"I don't think so, either."

After they finished lunch, they worked on the corral until the sun got too hot and they were forced to retire to the coolness of the house. Joth went to his room to work on his lessons. Jessi went to the kitchen to shell peas and start the bread for dinner. Griffin followed her in and as he walked behind her, feasted his eyes on the tempting sway of her lush denim-clad hips.

He took a seat at the table. "Mind if I sit awhile?"

"Nope," she told him as she grabbed the large wooden bowl that held the peas and joined him at the table.

"You know, the sheriff's visit did make me realize something, though."

"And that is?"

"I don't know the first thing about what I'm doing."

Jessi looked up. "I wondered when you'd get around to that, but I didn't think you'd admit it aloud."

"Me being so exaggerated and all," he came back sarcastically.

He sounded offended, but she ignored the tone. "Exactly."

"So you don't have any faith in my abilities, either?"

"I don't know anything about your abilities." She

paused. "Well, I know a bit about some of your abilities."

He smiled at that.

"But in reality I've known you less than a week. I don't have a true measure of what you're capable of. I do know Darcy, however, and he's been stampeding through folks' lives since before either of us were born. He's crafty, mean, and arrogant, and smart enough not to do his own killing."

She held his eyes. "I'm not saying you can't do what you came here to do. You obviously love a challenge."

He smiled at that too.

"But this challenge could cost you your life. Darcy's not going to surrender simply because you walk up and ask him to."

Jessi paused to observe him for a moment. Had she stepped on his manly pride with her words? "You're not one of those men who can't handle taking a woman's advice, are you?"

"I'm still deciding."

Gasping with mock offense, she threw a few peas at him.

He ducked, chuckling, "Hey, I was being honest. Now, tell me about the sheriff."

The light in Jessi eyes faded. "He and my father were best friends at one time. Grew up together. When Hatcher's wife Betsy became ill, the doctor visits and the medicines she needed cost more than he could afford. He sold his ranch to Darcy's bank because he needed the funds and then ran for sheriff with Darcy's blessings."

"When was this?"

"About five years ago. At first, Hatcher thought he was going to be a true sheriff. He'd fought on the side of the Union during the war, so he knew about honor, but Darcy stripped him of that. There were rumors that

Hatcher had to do what he was told or Darcy wouldn't pay for Betsy's treatments.''

"What happened to his wife?''

"She died. The doctors said some kind of cancer.''

"Did Hatcher love his wife?''

"As much as my father loved this land. He hasn't been the same since Betsy died. I thought he'd help avenge my father's murder, but he didn't.''

Jessi finished shelling the peas silently, then poured flour onto the tabletop and began combining the ingredients for the bread.

"How'd Darcy's family get to be in charge here?''

"Through his father.''

"Explain.''

"My grandfather, Thomas, and Reed Darcy's father, Vale, were given this land in '36 as a reward for their bravery during the Texas war for independence. They were both freedmen. My grandfather started this ranch after getting his title, and Vale started a town he named for himself.''

"Humble man.''

"Very,'' Jessi cracked. "Over time, more and more freedmen moved here and they brought their families and their businesses, and soon Vale was a real town. Vale Darcy died in '56. That's when Reed took over the reins.''

Griffin had heard about men of the race participating in the various Texas wars for independence, but had never been personally acquainted with one. He'd have to remember to ask her about her grandfather's role sometime. "Besides burning out his neighbors and declaring war on women and children, what's he like as a man?''

"You've met him. Pompous and arrogant. He's the richest person around, and he makes sure everyone knows it. Gives fancy parties; has all of his house furnishings shipped from back east.''

Jessi began to knead the dough with relish. Just thinking about Darcy made her blood rise, and she took it out on the bread.

Griff watched her pounding the dough and smiled to himself. She was all fire. ''I think that dough would yell surrender if it could.''

She stopped. ''I guess I am being a bit brutal.'' When she resumed, she worked the bread at a more normal pace.

Griff watched her silently for a while, noting the strength in her dark hands and how expertly she handled the task. ''Can't remember the last time I saw a woman making bread.''

''I've been making bread since my mother died.''

''How old were you?''

''Thirteen summers.''

After placing the bread in a big bowl to rise, Jessi covered it with a cloth, then rinsed her hands at the sink. Dipping herself a cup of water from the water jug by the sink, she told Blake, ''It's probably much cooler out on the back porch. How about we talk there?''

''An invitation?'' he teased.

Jessi did her best to hide the smile in her eyes. ''It's an invitation to talk, nothing more.''

''Pity,'' he replied without embarrassment.

Jessi decided that resisting him was going to be an all-day job. ''You flirt as easily as you breathe, I think.''

''And I think that deep down inside you're enjoying it.''

Jessi had to confess she *was* enjoying this highly-charged back-and-forth banter. It made her feel alive and, dare she say, sensual. Having him here awakened a part of herself she never knew existed. The path of life she'd been following since the death of her mother left little time to explore tenderness, frivolity, or feelings other than those fraught with pain and anger. Now life had put this man in her path and she didn't know what she was supposed to do with him or about him. "So are you going to come out to the porch or not?"

He stood slowly and gestured. "After you."

It was much cooler at the back of the house, just as she had hoped. She took a seat on the old rocker and he sat on the porch step.

"Where'd you grow up?" she asked, once they were comfortable and the silence of the Texas afternoon re-settled around them.

"Nebraska. Mother died when I was ten. Drifted awhile until a preacher man named Royce Blake hauled me out of a whorehouse in Abilene and took me home."

"A whorehouse? What were you doing there?"

"Worked there, ran errands for the girls and gamblers. Swept floors."

"How old were you?"

"Twelve, thirteen."

"Surely you weren't on your own all that time after your mother's passing?"

"Yep." Griff didn't want to think about those times.

"You had no other family?"

"None that I knew of."

Jessi realized Blake carried his own heartaches. Royce Blake must have been a very special man to take in a thirteen-year-old orphan. "Did Mr. Blake have other children?"

"One, a son named Jackson. He's a few years older than I am."

"Did you two get along?"

Griff grinned. "Yeah, we did, although we were noth-ing alike."

"Where is he now?"

"Here in Texas, last I heard. Probably in the Brazos

Valley. He was a sheriff down there after Lincoln's war, but when some rebs murdered Royce, Jackson had to leave or be lynched.''

"How long has it been since you've seen him?"

"Too long," he replied wistfully. "Going on six or seven years now."

Jessi could sense Blake's love for his brother in his tone. "What's he think about your way of life?"

A half smile curved his red gold mustache. "Hates it, of course. It's hard having a former lawman in the family when you're robbing trains, but he's always walked the straight and narrow, even when we were young. I was the wild one. In and out of scrapes the whole time."

Jessi bet he'd been a handful to raise.

"Now it's my turn to ask the questions," he said, looking up at her and marveling again at her dark beauty.

"I suppose that's only fair," she responded. "But no questions about Bob."

Griffin could see the firmness in her eyes. He nodded.

She looked away for a moment, her thoughts seemingly elsewhere, then she turned back. He could see pain in her eyes unveil itself briefly, then disappear. Someone had hurt her very badly, he sensed. "Joth said you were a teacher back east. I wanted to know where."

"At the Miss Paris LaMarr School for Young Women of Color, in upstate New York. I taught literature and the sciences," she replied, her voice brightening for a few moments. Then, as she began to relate more, the darkness returned. "When my sister died in childbirth, I came back to Texas to help my father raise Joth."

In reality, Jessi had raised Joth alone. Her father'd loved Joth, probably more than anyone else in the world, but he'd loved the land more. It left him little time for anything else.

"Did you enjoy teaching?"

"Very much. The young women were bright and eager to learn, and Paris was wealthy enough to equip the school with all the materials and supplies we needed. She and I became fast friends in the three years I was there. I miss her dearly."

"She's the one responsible for all that gear in Joth's room?"

"Yep. She's as rich as Cleopatra and because she has no children of her own, Joth is her beneficiary. He's still waiting to use those ice skates, even though he grew out of them a few years ago."

"Is the school still open?"

"As far as I know, yes, it is. "

Jessi wondered how Paris was faring. They'd written back and forth regularly over the past ten years, but in the last nine months Jessi hadn't had time to answer any of her friend's letters—she'd been too busy surviving. "Enough about me. How're you going to put Darcy in prison?"

"No idea. Now, if he were a train I wanted to rob, I'd do things like check out the arrival schedule and find out how many people are in the depot at night, what type of express car the train was running, how much gold it was carrying, and how secure it was."

"Darcy isn't a train," Jessi pointed out.

"No, he's not, but I'll still have study him if we're going to derail him."

"Train similes, Mr. Blake?"

He shrugged. "Hey, my boss is a very smart lady, I'm just trying to keep up."

She shook her head at his wit; she did enjoy his company. "So how would your friend Marshal Wildhorse start an investigation?"

"Probably by asking folks a bunch of questions."

"Sounds like a good place to start. I wonder if

Hatcher's going to tell Darcy the truth about why you're here?''

Griff shrugged. ''We'll have to wait and see.''

As the silence lengthened, Griff searched his mind for something, anything, to talk about. He didn't want her to leave and go back into the house. ''How'd your family come to be in Texas?''

''We Claytons are descendants of an African craftsman named Santo. He escaped from Louisiana and into Texas back in '03.''

'' '03? That was a long time ago.''

''Yes it was. After the French gave the United States Louisiana, Santo and many other Africans escaped across the Sabine River into Texas because the Spanish promised they'd be free here. Back then, the Spanish didn't care if we owned land or who we married or if we held office. In fact, my great-grandmother Lydia was African-Mexican. The story goes that Santo purchased her out of a Galveston brothel and that she was very fiery and beautiful.''

Jessi looked at his lazy silent smile and asked, ''What?''

''Nothing, just thinking that you could have been describing yourself when you said she was fiery and beautiful, but go on, I didn't mean to interrupt your *train* of thought.''

Jessi groaned in reaction to the bad pun. ''Are you sure?''

''Yes, I'm sure. You are definitely fiery and beautiful.''

Jessi shook her head. ''I meant, are you sure I can go on with the story?''

''I'd much rather talk about your fire and beauty, but if you want to go ahead, the floor's yours.''

''You're flirting again.''

''Yes, ma'am, I definitely am.''

"You planning on wearing me down?"

"Nope, just plan to play until you say yes."

"And if I don't?"

"It'll be my loss," he replied without shame.

Jessi searched his eyes and saw that they were serious and unshuttered. What was he really about here? Jessi knew he was flirting, but was uncertain still about the intent behind the words. "What do you want me to say yes to?"

"Whatever you're at ease with. If all you want to do is flirt, I'll go with that. I just like being in your company, Jessi Clayton. One day I hope I get to show you just how fiery and beautiful I think you are."

Griffin wanted nothing more than to kiss those lush, full lips, then magically draw her back into the dream he'd had last night and make slow, sweet love to her. He wondered if her late husband had loved her fully. He knew a gentleman wasn't supposed to ponder such things, but Griff never claimed to be a gentleman.

Jessi forgot all about the story she'd been telling, she was too busy fighting off the effects of Griffin Blake's last words. No man had ever spoken so frankly or so boldly to her before, and because she lacked the experience, she'd no idea how she was supposed to react. "I believe I should go and check on my bread."

"What about the rest of the story?"

"I don't think you're really interested."

"Sure I am."

"Then will you behave, so I can finish?"

"Can't promise you that, but I'll do my best."

Jessi could feel his light slipping into the dark corners of her soul.

Continuing the story, she told him of her grandfather's role in the Texas Revolution. "The Battle of San Jacinto was the battle that finally won Texans their freedom. It was fought on April 21, 1836, and my grandfather was amongst the men there that day. Hendrick Arnold was another freedman at that battle, and he too was rewarded with land for his bravery.''

Griff had never heard of Arnold, nor of a Black man Jessi called Dick the Drummer.

"No one knew Dick's last name," Jessi explained, "but he was a freeman and already old and gray by the time the war came. The old-timers say he was as valuable as the fighting men because his drumming kept Santa Anna's forces confused and off their stride. After the revolution he and his drum helped the U.S. Army at Monterrey and Buena Vista during the Mexican War. Are you sure you're interested in all this?"

"Sure am." Griff loved the sound of her smoky voice.

Jessi went on to talk about other Black heroes of the Texas Revolution, particularly those who'd fought at the Alamo, the most revered war site in the state's history. "Even though all of the White male combatants were killed, some of the Blacks, like Joe Travis, who was a slave of Col. William B. Travis, were spared by General Santa Anna after the Alamo fell. Joe Travis was one of the first people to report the capture of the Alamo to the Texas provisional government.''

Griff found her accounts fascinating. Listening to her he learned that a slave named John, who was owned by Francis De Sauque, fought to his death alongside Crockett, Bowie, and Travis at the Alamo, and to this day lay buried with them in an unmarked common grave. He heard about Jim Bowie's slave Sam, and how he, like the De Sauque slave John, was also captured and released after the battle. Griff had no idea there were women at the Alamo, but according to Jessi, Bowie also had with him a Black female cook named Betty.

Griff said, "But with all the turmoil between the races

in Texas, I can't believe they let your grandfather keep his land."

"He almost didn't. After the revolution, one of the first items undertaken by the new Texas government was to banish all free Blacks from the Republic of Texas who did not have Congressional permission to stay. Those allowed to stay could not vote or own land, but because of the pressure applied by some of the more powerful White veterans, Black men like my grandfather and others were made exceptions."

"What about that Hendrick Arnold fellow? Did they give him permission to stay?"

"Supposedly, Mr. Arnold neither asked for nor received permission to stay. He simply resided on the 1,920 acres given to him in reward for his bravery and lived out his years there. He died in a cholera epidemic in '49."

Jessi looked down at Griff and asked, "So, is that enough history for today, Mr. Blake?"

Griff smiled. "I think so, but one last question."

"Okay."

"When are you going to stop calling me Mr. Blake? Being so formal doesn't make a whole lot of sense, especially after last night."

His soft words stroked her like a caress from his hands.

"It's a very easy name to say," he told her pleasantly. "Repeat after me: 'Griffin.' "

Her eyes lit with humor. "Griffin."

"Again."

"Griffin."

"See, that wasn't very painful at all, was it?"

She shook her head no.

"Do you think you can call me that all the time?"

Jessi hesitated. "Yes. I suppose I can."

"Good."

"I'm going in and check on the bread. Any more questions?"

Griff had plenty, like *When will you let me make love to you?* Instead he replied, "Nope."

She stood, only to have hear him say, "I'll never force you to do anything you don't want to do."

Jessi knew what he meant, and even though she'd known him less than a week, she believed him without question. "I know."

He touched his battered hat politely, then watched the tempting sway of hips as she went back inside.

Sitting alone on the porch, Griffin smiled in response to this latest encounter, but thinking back on their conversation, he wondered about the pain he'd seen flit ghostlike across her eyes when Bob's name was mentioned. She made it quite clear that Calico Bob was not a subject she wished to discuss, so Griff could only assume the hurt stemmed from there. If her sister Mildred and Calico Bob were Joth's parents, how in the world had Jessi gotten involved? More important, why? Why would a smart, educated woman with an independent streak wide as the state of Texas hitch herself to a murderer? He couldn't come up with a reason that fit and it was beginning to bother him more and more.

Sitting there, Griff could feel the heat of the late afternoon rising even higher, so he removed the red bandanna from around his neck and wiped at the sweat on his brow. He'd forgotten how hot Texas could be. Retying the scarf loosely, Griff sensed that when the answers to his questions about Jessi Clayton's past were finally laid on the table, he was not going to like them— he could already feel it.

The sight of Joth coming around the house lightened Griff's mood. "Hey, cowboy," he called. "Is that room clean yet?"

Joth gave him a sheepish smile. "Almost."

Griff moved over so the boy could join him on the porch step.

For a moment, Joth simply sat silently. Then he asked, "You ever kill anybody, Griff?"

"Nope."

"Why not?"

"Never had to," he responded, wondering where this conversation might be heading. The boy looked very solemn.

"Under what circumstances would you?"

Griff peered at him closely and said, " 'Circumstances'? That's an awfully big word for an eleven-year-old."

"Blame it on Aunt Jessi," the boy grinned softly.

Griff's grin matched the boy's. Griff became serious once more as he debated how to answer Joth's question. "Let's see. If somebody was seriously threatening to harm my family or a loved one, it might be necessary, but ending a man's life is not something I'd be seeking."

"My pa killed lots of men."

"Yes, he did."

Joth looked up with earnest eyes and asked, "Do you think I'll grow up and be like him?"

"Nope."

"Why not?"

"Well, let's see? One, your Aunt Jessi wouldn't allow it. Two, *I* wouldn't allow it, and three, you're nothing like your pa, Joth. The two of you are about as alike as Buttercup and Reed Darcy."

That put the smile back on Joth's face.

Griffin then inquired, "The other day, when I asked you what you wanted to be, you said you did want to be an outlaw. You were probably very young then, weren't you?"

Joth nodded.

"So what do you want to be now? And don't say a train robber."

Joth's eyes twinkled behind his spectacles. "A writer, maybe, or maybe one of those folks who go to Egypt and dig up pyramids."

"An archaeologist."

"*Now* who's using big words?" Joth asked.

"I am."

Joth's eyes were shining.

Griff turned serious once more. "I wouldn't worry about you growing up to be like your pa, Joth. Any boy who throws around big words like 'circumstances' has way too many brains to pick something as stupid as outlawing for a living."

"But you're not stupid, Griff."

Griff chuckled and said to himself, *Out of the mouths of babes.* "Depends on who you talk to, cowboy. My big brother doesn't think I'm real smart."

"Why not?"

"He was a sheriff and he didn't like me robbing trains."

"Oh."

Griff looked over into Joth's eyes. "You're going to grow up and be you, Joth, nobody else. Okay?"

Joth nodded.

"Now," Griff said, "don't you have a room to clean?"

Joth sighed like an eleven-year-old boy. "Yeah, I do."

"Well?"

"I'm going." He stood.

He gave Griff a small smile. "Thanks, Griff."

"You're welcome. Now, get going before you get both of us in trouble with the governor."

Grinning, Joth went inside, leaving a thoughtful Griff sitting in the silence of the Texas afternoon.

Jessi was in her room going over the ledgers, when

Joth knocked and came in. She looked up with a smile. "What can I do for you, Joth?"

"Do you think Griff will stay if we ask him?"

"He'll be here until September."

"No, I mean after."

Jessi studied her nephew's face and saw her sister Mildred in his eyes. It was easy to see that he was becoming attached to their resident train robber. She tried to pick her words carefully. "Honey, Blake's not the type of man you can saddle. Once he's done here, he's heading to Mexico, remember?"

His voice dropped. "Yes, I know, but can I still ask him?"

The hope in his face tightened her heart. "Why don't you wait until after this Darcy mess is finished, then see, okay?"

Joth didn't appear convinced, but he nodded. "Okay, I'll wait."

"How's the room coming?"

"Almost done."

"Good," she said, smiling.

As soon as Joth closed the door behind him, she told herself she should have anticipated Joth's growing attachment. Joth had no other men in his life, and because of Blake's engaging personality, people were undoubtedly drawn to him like a dowser to water. Her nephew had been through so much in his short life: he'd lost his mother and his grandfather, lived under siege, and put up with the slurs and innuendoes directed at his family by folks in town and his classmates at school. Never once had he been anything but loving and helpful toward Jessi. Granted, in the last few years he'd been suspended from school for fighting more times than Jessi wanted to think about, but so had Jessi as a youngster. She'd meted out her own fair share of black eyes to classmates who'd dared slur her mother out loud, so she understood Joth a whole lot more than he knew. However, she saw little future in becoming attached to a man such as Blake—for either of them. He would not be staying.

Chapter 5

After supper, Griff saddled up the gelding so he could ride into Vale. He needed to start the investigation.

It was mid-evening by the time Griff made the forty-minute ride to town. When he arrived, there weren't many people moving about Vale's main street, and only a few businesses still had their doors open to customers. As he rode he spied a couple of men lounging outside the barbershop. They eyed him. He eyed them back. He nodded. They didn't. He headed the gelding toward the saloon. Experience taught him that local watering holes were often a wellspring of information. Liquor had a way of loosening lips as well as brains. Griff rarely indulged. During his days at the whorehouse he'd been kicked and cuffed by more drunks than he cared to remember. They all served as sterling examples of what he didn't want to grow up and become.

He tied the gelding up at one of the posts a few feet from the saloon. On his way down the plank walk he passed the open door of a milliner's shop. Seeing the hats on display in the front window, he paused to view them for a moment. He wondered if Jessi Clayton was partial to ladies' hats. The battered, brown man's version she favored had seen its best days, but for some reason he couldn't see her wearing the frippery on display here; when Jessi shopped it was probably for cartridges for that Winchester of hers.

"Young man, are you the outlaw everybody's gossiping about?"

Griff's turned his attention to the little old lady leaning on a cane. She might have been of an advanced age, but her dark eyes were clear and direct. Her curly gray hair looked like a bird's nest framing her brown face and she wore a long flowing robe, as if she were someone from a foreign country. "Well, are you?" she asked.

Caught off guard, Griff fumbled for an answer. "I suppose so. Yes, ma'am."

"You suppose so? Are you an outlaw, yes or no?"

He wondered who this elderly ball of fire might be. "I am."

"And you're here to help Jessi Rose Clayton?"

He nodded. He'd never heard Jessi's middle name before now. *Such a delicate name for such a fierce woman*, he thought.

"It's about time somebody took her side," she said. "Come on in. You and I have some things to discuss." She took his arm.

Griff tried to put her off. "I was just on my way over to the saloon."

"Auntie can wait. This can't." Her directness reminded him an awful lot of his boss lady, and the determination in her eyes made him believe she was not going to take no for an answer, so he surrendered and followed her into the millinery shop.

"What's your name?" she asked over her shoulder.

"Blake. Griffin Blake."

Inside the small shop fabric seemed to be everywhere, along with netting, silk flowers, pin cushions, and hat boxes. He had to wait for her to clear off a small chair before he could sit down.

"There now," the woman said, pulling a foot stool over so she could sit near. "Let me see your hands."

Griff stared confused. "My hands?" He was beginning to wonder if coming in here had been a mistake. Would he find out later from Jessi that he'd been visiting with the town's resident fool?

"I read palms and I want to see your lines. They'll tell me what kind of man you are. Hold out your hands."

Griff did as she requested. He thought it best to humor her then make a hasty exit.

She ran her hands very lightly over the surface of his palms. He was surprised to feel how callused her fingers were, but her touch was as soft as velvet.

For a few moments she traced the lines of his palms, then she stopped to say, "You had someone very dear to you die when you were young? Your mother maybe?"

Griff pulled his hands away as if he'd been burned. He stared.

The lady smiled kindly. "It's okay, I've seen all I need to see. I don't need to read further." She then held out her hand. "Welcome to Vale, Mr. Blake."

Griff shook her hand hesitantly.

"Name's Gillian Priest. Pleased to meet you."

Griff nodded.

The woman stood. "Would you like some lemonade?"

Griff didn't want anything other than to leave this decidedly strange woman and get back outside, but something stayed him. "Yes, ma'am."

Moments later, he and Gillian Priest were sitting in the quiet shop sipping lemonade. "What do you think of our Jessi Rose?" she finally asked.

"Miss Clayton is a fine woman."

"That she is. If we had more men in this town with her gumption, Vale wouldn't be in the mess it's in today. She's been standing up to that bounder Darcy for a year now with nobody guarding her back but the boy. It's a damn shame.''

Griff thought so too.

"So how old are you, Mr. Blake?"

"Call me, Griff. I'm twenty-five."

"Then call me Gillie, everybody does. And although twenty-five is a mite young, you'll do."

Griff frowned. "For what?"

"In time you'll know. In time."

Griff was definitely certain now—Gillian Priest was a strange woman. But maybe he could get some information from her. "How long have you known the Claytons?"

"Since before Jessi and her sister Mildred were born. Taught school here in those days. Never had a student smarter than Jessi Rose, never. Just knew she was going to make something of her life and she probably would have if Dexter Clayton hadn't called her home."

"She said she came home to raise Joth after her sister died."

Gillian cocked her head at him. "She told you the story?"

"Some of it, yes. You look surprised."

"I am. Usually Jessi is as tight-mouthed as a spinster in a saloon when it comes to talking about the past. Do you know what a griot is, Griffin?"

"No, ma'am."

"Well, back in Africa there was always one person in the tribe who knew the tribe's history. Some tribes called these historians 'griots.' I'm Vale's griot. Most folks don't like it that I know more about their families than they do, but—" She shrugged.

Griff didn't know whether to be fascinated or afraid. Admittedly he was experiencing a little bit of both.

"So," she stated. "What do you want to know about Darcy?"

''How'd you know I'm after information on Darcy?''

''If you're here to help my Jessi Rose, you'll need to know your enemy. What kind of outlaw are you, Griffin?''

''Train robber.''

''Successful?''

''Pretty much, yes.''

''Good, this town has enough failures. Take that Roscoe Darcy, for example. Been weak since the day he was born. Came home from back east a year ago with that trollop Minerva—'' Gillie stopped. ''I'm sorry, I'm supposed to be talking about the father, not the son.''

Gillie took a moment to observe him, then said in a very earnest voice, ''You're a dreamer, aren't you, Griffin Blake?''

Griff felt amazement come over him again. How had she known? Did she also know that every now and then he even saw bits of the future in his dreams, like when looking into Joth's eyes at the table that morning after his arrival? He now studied her wise old eyes. She seemed too astute, or was it magical, for him to try and deny the truth. ''Yes, I am. My mother was a dreamer. Her grandmother, too.''

Gillie smiled softly. ''You're going to be good for her, I can feel it.''

''For who?''

''Jessi.''

That made Griff *real* curious. He could think of ways he'd like to be good to Jessi Rose Clayton.

''In what way?'' he asked.

''You're going to give her back to herself. She's been waiting for you a long time.''

Griff didn't know what to say to that. Yes, he found Jessi Clayton both attractive and fascinating, but Gillie made it sound as if he were here to fulfill some kind of ancient prophesy.

"You look skeptical, Griffin."

"Let's just say I'm here to do a job. I'm nobody's knight. Miss Clayton can fend for herself."

"You're right. She's been taking care of herself for a long time. No, my Jessi Rose needs a knight of another kind, and the lines on your hand mark you as a champion. You may be an outlaw, but I know you've done a lot of good in your life, too."

He had, but quietly. There were bankers here and there who'd allowed Griff to stash his ill-gotten gains in their vaults, and in exchange the bankers would lend the money, ensuring them both a profit. At last count Griff's money—well, the railroad's money—had built six schools, three hospitals, a family barn or two, and a church. Griff's brother Jack called the philanthropy nothing more than Griff's way of washing his hands clean of his thievery. Griff called it good business sense. The big banks in the big cities weren't going to loan a small Black congregation the funds to build a church, nor a Black school board money to improve their school. For members of the race, the political climate in the country was dark as a Kansas sky holding a twister, and if Griff could help folks while he helped himself, he saw nothing wrong with it. Philosophically, he knew stealing was wrong, but no more so than denying a whole race of people a chance at success simply because of the color of their skin. The last time he'd seen his brother, they'd argued over this very point. Jackson called Griff's reasoning a convenient excuse; Griff told him to mind his own business. That had been over six years ago.

"What can you tell me about Darcy?" He thought it best to sidestep Gillie's talk of champions and get on with the matter at hand.

"That he loved Jessi's mother, Violet—so the gossips say—and that she loved him so deeply in return she left her family to be with him. So they say."

Griff was surprised to say the least. "You make it sound as if there's another side to the story."

"There might be."

"How'd she die?" he asked.

"She was on her way to meet Reed one evening when her carriage overturned and she was thrown and killed. Dexter found her body."

"How old was Jessi then?"

"She'd just turned thirteen summers the day before. Mildred was fifteen."

Griff felt a kindred sadness echo deep inside. He knew how painful it had been to lose his mother at a young age. He'd been healed somewhat by declaring war on the railroads, but what had Jessi turned to in order to bury the heartache? Griff could see Gillie watching him closely and he really wanted to ask her about Jessi and Bob, but he remembered the look in Jessi's eyes when she asked that Bob not be discussed, so he chose to respect her wishes. Maybe one day she would tell him the story and maybe she wouldn't. "This has been a real interesting visit, Miss Gillie."

"Not as interesting as the next few months are going to be, but I'm glad you could stop by. I'll be here when you need me."

Griff stood. She made it sound as if this would not be his only run-in with Vale's griot, and he found it not that alarming. "Take care of yourself, Miss Gillie."

"You too."

Aided by her cane, she walked him to the door and he stepped back out into the Texas evening.

The sign above the saloon's small doorway had the words *Auntie's House* emblazoned on it in red hand-painted letters that had to be a foot high. As he approached the entrance, habit made Griff pull down his hat brim just enough to cover his distinctively colored eyes. In his train-robbing days, a shadowy saloon could hold any number of complications, the least being rail-road police, Pinkertons, or bounty hunters, none of whom were known for being sociable. At worst, it held some kid looking to get his name in the paper for out-drawing you.

Even though Griff told himself he didn't have to look over his shoulder anymore, habit was a hard thing to shake. As he entered the quiet Auntie's, instinct made him mentally record how many exits there were, two, and where they were placed just in case he had to make a hasty escape: one was the door he'd just come through and the other was near a billiard table on the far side of the room. There was a staircase that led upstairs to where he assumed the girls took their customers.

Business was slow. There was one man seated at the polished wood bar, and a few others playing cards at the back of the room. The piano sat silently waiting for its player, it seemed, while at a table near the bar sat three gaudily dressed hostesses. They all watched him eagerly.

Griff gave them a smile but headed for the bar. It was quite obvious that it had been transplanted here from some other establishment. Amid the dim lighting and the sawdust-covered floor, the ornately carved length of wood looked as out of place as an African princess in a border town bordello.

The man behind the bar, a burly caramel-colored man with arms the size of trees, viewed Griff warily as Griff walked up.

"Tequila," Griff ordered.

The price the man quoted for the shot gave Griff pause, but Griff placed the coins on the bar with no fuss. Sometimes information didn't come cheap. He waited for the man to splash the liquor into a glass.

Once the coins were deposited in the strong box, the barkeep's manners seemed to improve. "Haven't seen you around here before."

Griff took a swig of the tequila. It had been a long time since he'd had a drink, but the bite and kick of the liquor was a familiar one. "Working for Miss Clayton."

The man went still. "Why?"

"She asked me to."

"Are you a friend of Bob's?"

Griff eyed the man coolly. "No."

The barkeep picked up a towel and began wiping out glasses. "You know, nobody works for the Claytons?"

"I keep hearing that."

"What's your name?"

"Blake. What's yours?"

"Keel. I'm the blacksmith here, too."

Griff thought Keel certainly looked the part. Griff had always considered himself a big man, but the smith was much broader and taller. In a fight, he could probably crush Griff like a walnut. "How long have you lived here?"

"All of my life."

"Then you've known Miss Clayton a long time."

"Yes. We went to school together."

"Do you think she's the whore folks say she is?"

The man's manner darkened. "Why do you want to know?"

"Because I don't agree."

Keel studied Griff for a moment, then seemed to relax. "Neither do I, and I dare anyone to call her that when I'm around," he growled.

Griff was glad to hear it. "How do you feel about Reed Darcy?"

"I'd like to put that bastard in a gander pull."

Griff smiled. A gander pull was a sport not much seen anymore. The barbaric pastime entailed hanging a gander upside down from a high tree branch. A rider would then ride beneath it and try to twist its head off. Griff thought gander pulling to be a right nice solution to the

Darcy problem. He lifted his drink in toast to the man's idea. "To gander pulling, may Darcy be so lucky."

Keel smiled.

"Hey, cowboy," one of the hostesses beckoned with a smile, "buy a thirsty girl a drink?"

Griff didn't see why not. In fact, he bought a round for all three of the thirsty women: Lottie with the red hair, Camille in the blonde wig, and the cinnamon-skinned Sylvia, whose very ample bosom seemed ready to jump free from the low-cut bodice of her well-worn red satin dress. The other women were clad in equally gaudy but threadbare dresses, typical attire for a back-water saloon such as this.

In questioning them he found that none had worked at Auntie's very long. "Is Auntie a real person, or just the name of the place?" he asked, taking a drink of his tequila.

"Oh, she's real," Camille laughed. "In fact that's her talking to Keel."

Griff turned and saw a plump middle-aged woman with dark eyes and a red wig who even in her youth could not have been described as beautiful. Life had been hard for Auntie; he could see it in the lines and set of her overly painted face, but when she looked up and met Griff's eyes, her answering smile was as bright and warm as the sun.

He watched as she excused herself from the big bartender and walked to where he sat.

"Evening, I'm Auntie. Welcome to my place." She wore a red feather boa around her neck. The color matched her dress.

"Name's Blake. Pleased to meet you."

"Keel says you're working for Jessi Clayton?"

"I am."

"Then welcome to Vale."

She turned to the girls. "Ladies, I need to talk with this young man, if you don't mind."

Lottie pouted. "Even if we did mind, you'd take him anyway."

A smiling Auntie shook her head. "Lottie, one of these days, that lip of yours is going to stick like that, and you'll have to make your living being a dust pan."

The other two girls howled.

Auntie turned to Griff. "This way, Mr. Blake."

Griff was caught a bit off guard by Auntie's request and he couldn't help but wonder what she wanted; even so, he tipped his hat to the ladies at the table and followed Auntie to the stairs.

As they were heading up, she turned back and said, "I don't have any designs on that handsome body of yours, Blake, if that's worrying you. I just want to talk to you about Jessi."

Admittedly, Griff was a bit relieved to hear her say that because he'd been trying to figure out a way to gracefully decline any invitation she might extend. She was a bit older than the women he usually preferred.

Her office was as threadbare as the gaudy dresses on the girls downstairs. The furnishings consisted of a desk and chair, and another chair for guests. There were a couple of lamps and little else.

"Have a seat," Auntie gestured.

"Thanks." Griff sat.

"Drink?" she asked, as she poured herself a small shot of whiskey.

He shook his head. "No. I've had my ration for tonight."

"I like a man who knows when he's had enough," she replied pleasantly. She went around and sat behind the desk. She hoisted the glass for a toast. "To better times."

Griff nodded as she took a small swallow.

"So, how long've you been working for Jessi and Joth?"

"Less than a week, and I already know that nobody works for the Claytons, so please don't make me hear it again."

She grinned. "Been hearing that a lot?"

"Yes."

"Well, they're right. Darcy's got everyone around here so scared, many of them won't breathe without asking his permission first."

"And you? Do you need his permission?"

"If I did, I wouldn't be here talking to you."

Griff like Auntie.

"Reed Darcy is a thieving, murdering bastard of a man whose going to have his own room in hell. Mark my word," she told him, raising her glass again.

"Does anybody else stand up to him?"

"Not since Jessi's daddy Dexter died. Once Dex was cut down, folks around here stopped hoping."

"So there's no one?"

She shook her head.

"What about you? Has Darcy tried to run you out?"

"Tried and won. He owns this place now. Has since the day after Dex was buried. When he called in my note I couldn't pay. The building reverted to the bank. He lets me stay because he knows he'd have a hell of a time trying to find somebody else to run this hellhole and his hands need the saloon open so they can have a good time come pay day."

"But why did you stay?"

"Because one, I've been here almost two decades—I'm too old to just pack up and move on—and two, I want to dance on Reed Darcy's grave some day and I can't do it if I'm not in Vale."

Her tone was as bitter as the whiskey she was drinking. "So, what's this about you being a deputy marshal?"

He couldn't keep the surprise from his face. "I'm going to assume you've been talking to the sheriff?"

"You can assume that, yes. Is it true?"

"If you talked to the sheriff, you already know the answer."

She gave him a knowing smile. "Darcy's not going to help you lock him up. You know that, don't you?"

"Jessi said the same thing."

"She always was smart as a whip," Auntie replied proudly. "How much has she told you about what's been happening here?"

"Most of it. You planning on throwing in on her side?"

"I've always been on her side. When the good churchgoing folks starting calling her a whore, *this* whore gave them all a good piece of her mind. Jessi's no more a whore than I'm Joan of Arc."

"Then why do they call her that?"

"Mainly because of Bob. Her mother and her sister played a part too."

"In what way?"

"A lot of women around here hated Violet Clayton the moment she came to town because of her fine manners and sweet ways. She was from someplace in England, but they thought she was putting on airs. They didn't like her speech, her beautiful clothes, or the fact that Dex picked a bride from somewhere else."

"How'd he meet an Englishwoman?"

"Through the newspaper. She was a mail order bride. When she was killed in the accident, her girls were devastated. Jessi buried herself in books. Mildred chose men."

Once again, Griff felt Jessi's grief. "What about Dexter Clayton, how'd he react to his wife's death?"

"Her liasion with Reed devastated him more than her death, I believe. You do know about this, don't you?"

"Yes, I met Miss Gillie earlier tonight, and she explained it some, but she believes there's more to the story than what the gossips are saying."

"She may be right. Gillie knows everything about everybody here, but I don't think anybody will ever know the full truth."

"So why would Reed Darcy want to take Jessi's land too? I'd think he'd leave her alone out of respect for his feelings for her mother, especially after having her father backshot."

"Greed, pure and simple. He wants all the land in this corner of the county and he doesn't care who he steps on to get it." She took another sip of her whiskey. "Reed also wants Jessi."

Griff stilled. "In what way?"

"In every way. She didn't tell you?"

"No."

"Reed wants her to marry him."

Griffin stared.

Auntie nodded her head. "She looks enough like her mother Violet to be her twin. His hope that she might say yes is probably the only thing that's kept him from burning her out before now. That and the fact that in her own way she's as ornery as her daddy and refuses to be intimidated."

Reed wants her to marry him, kept echoing over and over in his head. "Has she always been so fearless?"

Auntie chuckled. "Dexter wanted a son, so Jessi tried to be one. Could outwhip, outride, and outclimb every boy in town back when she was younger. The girl had more spirit and mischief in her than any child I'd ever met in my life. She was in and out of scrapes all the time."

Griffin found that hard to believe. "Jessi Clayton?"

"Yep. Have my barkeep Keel tell you some of his Jessi stories. She gave those boys fits." Auntie's voice then softened. "After her mama died, I wish she'd been mine, so I could have helped ease all that pain she used to wear on her face. Then when the rumors started about Reed and Miss Violet—well, that finally broke her heart for good. All the brightness went out of her, like somebody had snuffed out a candle. Stayed that way for a long time."

Her voice quieted, then her eyes turned cold. "Dex didn't do anything to protect those girls from all the name calling and slurring after Miss Violet died. All he wanted to do was kill Reed, to hell with those girls, and they suffered because of it."

"Did he try to kill Darcy?"

"Yep. The night after Miss Violet's burial, he got drunk and went gunning for Reed. Swore he was going to kill him. Scared Reed so bad, he left town for two months. They hated each other."

Once again she quieted as if she were recalling memories. "When Jessi got back after being with Bob, the fire in her had returned, but it was a cold, icy kind of fire. Dex had always been able to ride herd over her. Not anymore. She was as tough as a bed of nails. They fought constantly over everything and nothing. Dex wasn't accustomed to being challenged, but she took him by the horns and rode him with spurs. She put as much of her life into that ranch as he did, worked by his side from sunup to sundown, but he treated her like a spittoon."

Griff now understood why Jessi was so rawhide tough—she'd endured much. He found the idea of Reed wanting Jessi angering, though. "So do you think Darcy'll really harm Jessi when it's all said and done?"

"If he's caught between a rock and a hard place, he will, and right now, he is."

"What do you mean?"

"Reed is starting to choke on his own greed. He's going to be going down to Austin in a few days to explain why he hasn't been able to turn over this land. None of his business partners know he's been playing both ends against the middle."

She must have seen the confusion on Griff's face, because she explained.

"He's in cahoots with the railroad, and also representing the folks who think they're going to carve up all the land the railroad won't have any use for."

Griff held up his hand. "Wait—let me get this straight. Darcy wants to sell all of the land around here to the railroad, but the railroad isn't going to need it all."

"Nope. And all they don't need will be bid out to Reed's other friends."

"And what are they going to do with it?"

"Sell it again—only this time not to any of the people who live here, but to big city types looking to start their own towns and ranches. It's happening all over the West. Darcy has investors already lined up."

"But the deal hasn't been finalized yet."

"As far as Reed's concerned it's all over except the shouting. The only person opposing him is Jessi Rose, but right now Jessi is only one of his problems. Not only has he been unable to deliver the Vale land that he promised—he also used the deposits given to him by the speculators who want to divide up the land."

"Used it to do what?"

"Invest in a land scheme down in Mexico that went bust."

"He is choking on his own greed, isn't he?"

"Yes. In order to save himself he needs to deliver the Vale land as soon as possible. That way he can get his cut and cover those losses, because if his cronies find out they've been swindled, they're going to have his hide.''

"How do you know all this?"

"Minerva the Trollop has her spies, I have mine, and I've been doing this a hell of a lot longer than she has."

Griff chuckled. "Gillie called her that, too."

"It suits her. Who else but a trollop would cuckold her husband with her father-in-law?"

Griff's eyes widened.

"And I don't believe Reed's son Roscoe knows. He worships the ground she slithers on. And they call Jessi Rose a whore."

Griff had heard enough for one night. It would take him a while to digest it all, but he was certainly glad he'd come into town.

He stood and stretched. "Thank you for a very informative evening, Auntie."

"You're welcome. Sure you can't stay a while longer? The girls downstairs are going to be disappointed."

"I'll need to get back. I don't want for Darcy to show up and for Jessi have to hold him off alone."

Auntie nodded.

Griff turned back to her. "Oh, one last thing. Clem Davis, the man who shot Dexter Clayton—is he still around?"

"Yes, saw him the other day. Reed sent him down across the border after the murder to keep him away from the law, I'm guessing, but he's back. Why?"

"I have a few questions for him."

"When you find him, tell him I said he can take his business elsewhere."

"Why?"

"Because he's cheap on top of being a backshooter. He never wants to pay the girls what they're owed."

"I'll tell him," Griff said, moving to the door. He smiled. "Auntie, it's been a pleasure."

"Not as much of a pleasure as it *might've* been, had you walked through my door twenty years ago. But at my age, I take what I can get."

Grinning, Griff exited.

When he finally made it back to the Clayton spread, it was past ten. Careful not to make a lot of noise, Griff led the gelding back to the barn. He didn't want Jessi to think he was an intruder and come out firing.

Griff entered the house as quietly as he could. Moving soundlessly down the short hall that led to his room, he happened to glance into the sitting room and there sat Jessi on one of the chairs, nearly invisible in the shadows. "Any visitors while I was gone?" he asked.

Jessi shook her head. "Not so far. How'd things go in town?"

He stood in the doorway and fed his inner desire on the sight and sound of her. "Fine."

"Did you get the chance to talk to anyone?"

"A very odd old woman named Gillie. Do you know her?"

"Everyone knows Gillie. She's been around forever."

"She always so strange?"

Jessi chuckled. "Yep, but that's what makes her special. Back during the Puritan days she'd've probably been burned as a witch, but here she's just Gillie. Meet anyone else?"

"Yes, Auntie."

In the dark, Jessi smiled. "Another very special lady."

"That she is."

"Were it not for her and Gillie sneaking me food and supplies, Joth and I wouldn't've been able to survive this past year."

There was silence then. Griffin wanted to ask her about Reed Darcy's desire to make her his wife, but he held off. Now didn't seem to be the time.

Since putting Joth to bed, Jessi had been sitting here waiting for Griffin's return and wondering what to do about him. Looking over at him now, standing framed against the door, a part of her wanted to demand he pack his gear and go because of the feelings he'd opened inside her, while other parts wished him to sit with her awhile for the very same reason. There was something about him that seemed to be drawing her down a new and uncharted road, a road she had no business traveling, not at this stage in her life. Admittedly, she'd been wondering what it would be like to be with a man who openly confessed his love of women, and even though she wasn't certain what that really meant, Griffin Blake with his teasing ways and sultry eyes had gotten into her blood. The practical no-nonsense parts of herself wanted to find a cure for this growing attraction. If she could satisfy her curiosity about how it might be, would that do it? Would the knowing finally enable her to get on with her life and reclaim the woman she knew herself to be? She wondered what he would think of her if she asked to be kissed.

"You know, Griffin, if this was snakebite, I'd know how to treat it."

Hearing his given name come uncoaxed from her lips gave him more pleasure than he'd ever imagined. "If what was snakebite?"

"Whatever this is you've put in my blood."

Griffin felt himself become aroused by the implications in her smoky voice. Even though she was half-hidden by shadows, he could feel her intensity projecting his way.

"I've been sitting here wondering what it would take to cure me," she said. "Being attracted to you is neither rational nor logical."

"Why not?"

"Because it just isn't. The last thing I need in my life is a man who flirts as easily as he breathes."

"But you are attracted to me."

"Yes . . . I am."

The confession made Griff smile. He crossed the room to where she sat. "You make it sound as if there's something wrong with that."

She looked up at him. "There is. For one, you're an outlaw—what woman in her right mind trusts an outlaw?"

"I see." He wanted to pull her into his arms right then and there, and prove to her how wrong he thought that thinking to be. "Stand up a minute for me, would you?" He held out his hands to assist her in rising.

Jessi hesitated a moment as the questions continued to swirl in her head, but since no answers or solutions to her dilemma were forthcoming, she placed her hands in his and the connecting touch ricocheted through her blood like hot lead.

He pulled her to her feet and they faced each other in the dark. Griff searched her shadow-shrouded eyes. His need to add himself to this woman's life, if only for a little while, seemed to be growing in spite of the complications it might bring. He slowly ran his finger across her soft brown cheek, telling her quietly, "You *can* trust me . . ."

Jessi's eyes slid closed in response to the hushed voice and the caress. She knew she was being seduced and distracted away from the issue at hand, but right now she didn't have the faculties to enter into a debate; right now, she was too busy rippling from his touch.

He closed the space between them and brushed his lips across her cheek. "You really . . . really can trust me."

His mouth left her trembling jaw to journey to the sensitive, parted corners of her mouth, then touched it with a kiss that made her close her eyes again and made her legs feel like pudding. Using the same feather light pressure, he cajoled and soundlessly invited her to taste the passion he wanted her to share. His lips were knowing, a temptation she felt powerless to resist. When he pulled her into his arms and kissed her fully, Jessi's whole world began to spin.

The kiss was dazzling, potent. She ran her hands up his broad back and he fit her in even closer, making her feel the call of his strong body against her own. He whispered hotly against her ear, "Too bad you don't think you can trust me . . . Jessi Rose . . ."

The sound of him using her full name thrilled her almost as much as his masterful kiss.

"Otherwise, I'd do this . . ." He tenderly filled his hands with her small breasts, testing their soft weight, feeling them burn the flesh of his palms. "And this . . ."

He then rubbed at the berry hard nipples with the flats of his thumbs.

Her soft gasps were audible, rising into the shadow-filled room like passion-filled notes of a song.

His lips danced slowly over the edges of her neck. "If you weren't so afraid to trust me, I'd undo these buttons and kiss you here . . ."

Fitting actions to words, he undid the first two buttons of her shirt and brushed a fire-filled finger across the now exposed expanse of her trembling throat.

"Griffin . . ." she breathed.

"Yes, *querida?*"

Jessi forgot what she'd been about to say. He'd called her darling, and now his lips were moving oh so possessively over the skin bared by her opened shirt. His hands were again on her breasts, teasing, seducing, then moving to undo more buttons. Jessi knew she should be protesting the liberties he was taking, but she was too swept up in the spiraling heat. She could do nothing but let him open her shirt and breathlessly wait for more.

Griff couldn't help himself either. Touching her, kissing her, and having her scents fill his senses made his manhood swell with need. "Too bad I don't have your trust, Jessi Rose . . ." He bent his head and placed warm lingering kisses against the skin above the frayed lace of her cotton camisole. "Otherwise, I could love you like this . . ."

He slid one side of the worn camisole aside and when his mustache brushed her now bared nipple, Jessi almost screamed in response. Her knees threatened to buckle as he set her afire with tiny, wanton licks. Her gasps increased from his suckling and the fervent nibbles from his love-gentled teeth.

"Let's see if the other is as sweet . . ." He eased the camisole down her shoulders, unveiling her fully to his glowing eyes and the sweet brazen pull of his lips. A sensuous moment later he raised his head, but continued to tease the damp, throbbing nubbin with a lazily circling finger. "Do you still think I'm not to be trusted?"

Jessi couldn't think, she could hardly stand, and if anyone asked her to spell her name, she wasn't sure she could comply. Never in her life had a man set her so aflame. Never.

"Look at me, Jessi . . ."

Fighting through the haze, she complied. In spite of the shadows between them, she felt imprisoned by his powerful eyes, eyes certain to haunt her for the rest of her days.

"Now, repeat after me . . . I, Jessi Rose Clayton . . ."

Jessi found it very hard to respond due to the splendid distractions caused by his fingers magically plying the berried buds of her breasts. "I . . . Jessi Rose . . . ohhhh . . ."

Hot sparks erupted as he suckled her yet again. The world teetered and her head slipped back as she fought to form speech. "How do you . . . expect me to speak

. . . if you won't let me . . . catch my breath?''

"Not my problem," he chuckled malely as he gave her one last glancing lick before straightening slowly once again. His fingers continued their lazy play, making her nipples blossom and plead. "You're going to have to start again," he told her. "Now say: I, Jessi Rose Clayton, can trust Griffin Blake."

Somehow, she managed to recite the words. "I—Jessi Rose Clayton, can trust Griffin . . . Blake . . ."

"Perfect," he whispered approvingly, and as a reward, he placed a soft kiss against her passion-swollen lips. "I'll always be at your back, Jessi. Always."

Griffin looked down at her shimmering with passion and knew that he was about two seconds away from tumbling them both down onto the smooth wood floor and filling her with the hard depths of his passion. She was both fiery and beautiful, a temptation no man could resist, but it was too soon. Life had left her as spooked as a wild mare; she needed patience and he had plenty, at least for now. He bent to kiss her softly once again, whispering, "Go to bed, Jessi Rose, before I open more than this shirt."

The soft-spoken warning filled her with heat even though she knew he'd given her sound advice. He'd left her nearly incoherent and she'd left him hard as railroad iron.

Still sharing short fiery kisses, they parted reluctantly as Jessi took a small step back. Their charged breathing sounded loud against the room's silence. Under his watching eyes, she redid her buttons with fingers that trembled. Truth be told she wanted more. She knew it was a scandalous thing to admit, but she did.

Once her shirt was righted, she felt a bit awkward facing him.

"Did that cure you?" he asked, still hard with need.

"No," she confessed truthfully. "It didn't."

"Didn't cure me either. Guess we'll have to try harder next time."

Jessi smiled but didn't reply. She wondered if she would miss him as much as she believed she would once he headed off to Mexico. "Good night, Griffin."

"Night, Jessi Rose . . ."

Back in her room, Jessi turned up the lamp and stood looking at herself in the big standing mirror. Had she lost her mind? She must've. Why else would she let a man take such liberties? *Because you enjoyed each and every minute of it,* a small voice retorted knowingly. Even now, her nipples were still damp and singing, her lips hungering for more of his potent kisses. She'd definitely lost a bit of her mind back there and didn't know if she'd ever be able to reclaim it. Undressing fully, she got into bed wondering if Gillie could concoct something for her to take to counteract his spells.

The next morning, Jessi found Griffin on the roof again. When their eyes met, she felt an uncharacteristic shyness well up inside. "Good morning, Griffin."

"Morning, Jessi."

Carrying her coffee cup, she made her way to his side, then settled down beside him. The sunrise was just beginning. They shared a companionable silence for a moment.

He asked, "Sleep well?"

"I did."

When Jessi got out of bed this morning, she'd vowed to deal with Griffin as if nothing had happened last night, but something had, and her breasts seemed to want nothing more than to be bared again to his caress. She doubted well-raised women were supposed to have such yearnings, so she thought it best to turn her mind to less tumultuous thinking. "Was Auntie able to give you any information, last night?"

Griff wanted to ask about Darcy but held back. "Yes, and she told me she saw Clem Davis in town the other day."

"So, he's back." Hearing his name brought back the painful memories spawned by that awful, stormy night. "I hope you plan on visiting him."

"I do."

"Good. In my father's day, there wouldn't've been a trial, Davis would've just been strung up. What else did Auntie have to say?"

Griff told her then about Reed's losing the funds of the investors.

She mulled the information over for a moment. "So, that means he really needs my land now, doesn't it?"

"Yes, it does."

"I'm the last big landowner left. He's getting ready to up the ante, I'll bet."

Griff agreed and hoped his friends were on the way. He and the Claytons were going to need them.

Jessi then voiced something she'd been worrying over for the past few days. "I think I'd feel better if Joth took his lessons at home with me for a while."

"That's probably a good idea."

Jessi knew that if anything happened to her nephew, she'd shoot first and ask questions after the smoke cleared. If Davis were cowardly enough to shoot a man in the back in the dark, who knew the depths to which he'd sink to harm a child? "Joth's not going to like this decision very much, though. He enjoys school."

"I know he does. He's much smarter than I was at his age. Told me he might want to be an archaeologist, of all things, one day."

"Yes, he has big dreams. I just hope the country will give him the opportunity."

Everyone knew how desperate the situation had become for many members of the race in the South. The triumphs of Reconstruction were vanishing like the great herds of buffalo, and Black men were being killed on their way to the polls to vote. Jessi wanted Joth to come of age in a time when his intellect would be valued, but the horizon did not look hopeful. However, the horror and violence of post-reconstruction and the kluxers not-withstanding, Texas had more higher education facilities for the race than many of the states up north. Black Texans were now able to attend Prairie View State Normal and Industrial College near the town of Walker; Wiley College, in Marshal; Paul Quinn College, founded near Waco in '81 by a group of African Methodist ministers; Tillotson College, over near Austin; and Bishop College, another pioneering institution established in Marshal by a Baptist organization back in 1880. Maybe there was a chance for Joth.

"Hey, are you still with me?"

Jessi was brought back to the present by his soft teasing voice. She shook herself free of her brooding thoughts. "I'm sorry. Yes, I'm still here."

"Do we need to talk about last night?"

Her eyes met his gaze. "I don't know, do we?"

"Should I apologize?"

"No, that isn't necessary. But . . . can I ask you something?"

"Sure, shoot."

"Why do I feel like I wasn't supposed to be enjoying what we did last night?"

He searched her eyes and saw nothing but openness and honesty reflected there. He chose his answer carefully. "Because society puts a lot of fences around women, and not enjoying yourself is supposed to be one of them."

"So is enjoying it wrong?"

He shrugged. "I don't think so, but I'm a train robber, not a philosopher or a theologian. I guess every lady has to make up her own mind."

Jessi supposed he was right, but her questions were still unanswered.

"*Did* you enjoy last night?" he asked her then.

"My answer will only swell your head."

"I take it that means you did."

"I'm not answering you, Griffin Blake."

Her smile gave him all the answers he needed. "Good, I'm glad. Maybe we can do it again sometime soon." His manner turned serious then, and he reached out and traced her mouth. "Never apologize for enjoying what you feel." He kissed her softly but soundly, then turned her loose. "So, what do you have planned for today?"

Still feeling the echoes of the kiss, she found it took a moment for her mind to get moving again. "I should probably go to town and speak with Joth's teacher, Mr. Trent, about Joth taking his lessons at home. I'm fairly certain he'll favor the decision. He likes Joth a lot."

"Need an escort?"

"I'd love one."

Chapter 6

A s they prepared to leave, Jessi hoped her concern about leaving the house unguarded didn't show in her face because she didn't want to worry Joth. Hiding her feelings from Griffin turned out to be a bit more difficult.

"Worried about Darcy's men paying the house a visit while we're gone?"

She glanced over at him as she tightened the cinch on her saddle. He'd only been with them a little while but it seemed he was learning her all too well.

"Yes, I am," she admitted. "But since Darcy won't know we're coming into town, I'm counting on there not being enough time for him to send somebody out here before we get back."

Griff agreed with her logic, but he wanted to banish Darcy from her life once and for all. She shouldn't have to worry about whether or not her home would still be standing when she returned from town. He wanted to tell her not to worry, that things around her would be changing soon, but Jessi was the kind of woman who needed to see action, not hear words, so he kept what he had to say inside.

The sight of Joth leading his beloved Buttercup from the barn signaled it was time to go.

"Me and Buttercup are ready, Aunt Jessi."

"Okay, then, let's head out. You and Buttercup lead the way."

The mounted Jessi and Griffin followed Joth out to the road.

When Jessi taught school in Vale nearly a decade ago, there'd been no schoolhouse. All learning had taken place in the field behind Doyle Keel's blacksmith shop. Now the students were taught in the church. A few years back, there'd been talk about building a real school, but with all the uncertainty facing the town's future, the idea had been dropped.

As they rode slowly down the dusty main street, Jessi did her best to ignore the people stopping on the walk and in the doorways of the businesses to stare at the three riders from the Clayton ranch. Because of the ill feelings her presence usually aroused she rarely came to Vale. She was certain that by the time she reached the church everybody in town would be aware of her arrival. Without a doubt the smug-faced women on the walks would be whispering behind their hands, but she kept her eyes focused straight ahead and did not increase her mount's pace.

A woman's loud voice rang out, "Go home, you whore!"

"Yeah, get out of town unless you're coming to sell your land!" a man chimed in.

"Sell your land, whore!"

A furious Griffin turned in his saddle to try and identify the taunters but could not. All of the faces looked the same: hateful, suspicious. He turned back to Jessi to gauge her reaction. She was sitting ramrod straight in the saddle and refused to meet his eyes. Only the defiant raising of her chin let him know she'd felt the barbs.

The anger tightening Joth's mouth and shoulders showed that he'd been affected too, making Griff won-

der if the Claytons were forced to endure this foul-
mouthing every time they came into town. If so, he
thought it about time someone made it stop. Looking
out at the faces lining the walks once more, the fuming
Griff decided he'd follow Jessi's lead in dealing with
the good citizens of Vale for now, but he wouldn't put
up with them slurring her for very much longer.

When they entered the church, Mr. Trent was pleased
to see Jessi and Joth and excused himself from the silent,
staring students to speak with them. Trent was a short,
round man with a ready smile, and he nodded politely
when Jessi introduced him to Griff. While Trent and
Jessi discussed the lessons Joth needed to master while
at home, Griff and Joth waited outside.

"Do the folks around here always treat your aunt this
way?"

"Yep," Joth replied softly. "That's the reason we
don't come to town much. Aunt Jessi says it doesn't
bother her, but I don't think she's telling the truth."

Griff didn't think so either. Regardless of how the
folks around here felt about Jessi Clayton, she had feelings. She'd also endured a mountain of hell in her life
and she deserved better.

"Do you think you can make them leave her alone?"
Joth asked, looking up at Griffin solemnly.

"I'm going to try my best, cowboy," Griff pledged
gravely.

Joth nodded and his voice became distant. "Sometimes, at night, when she thinks I'm asleep, she cries. I
don't like it when she cries."

Griff didn't like hearing that either. It reminded him
of another woman long ago. She too had cried in response to the terrible hand life had dealt her way. Griff
still carried her memory and his grief deep in his heart.
"Well, you did the right thing writing to Marshal Wildhorse for help."

Joth turned and stared. "How'd you know about that?"

"He's the one who sent me."

Joth's eyes widened.

"But you have to keep it a secret for now. Think you can do that?"

"Golly, yeah! Does Aunt Jessi know the marshal sent you?"

"Yes."

Joth smiled and said, "Good."

Her business with Joth's teacher now complete, Jessi said her good-byes and went out to join Griffin and Joth.

As they mounted for the ride home, Joth asked, "Did Mr. Trent say it was okay for me to have school at home?"

"Yes he did, and he gave me enough lessons to take you through the summer."

Joth didn't look happy, so Jessi added, "Joth, I know how much you enjoy coming to school, but I don't want anything to happen to you."

"I know."

Jessi added one more negative mark to Reed Darcy's slate. Although there were some children at the school who gave Joth a hard time, he did have a few friends and she knew he would miss them dearly. "What can I do to cheer you up?"

"Let me beat you at marbles when we get home."

Jessi smiled. "But if I *let* you win, where's the victory in that?"

Joth never got a chance to reply, because as they rode slowly by the Darcy Hotel, they all quieted at the sight of the lone rider who stood waiting for them in the middle of the street. Jessi recognized Clem Davis immediately and her manner turned grim. "Joth, you and Buttercup drop back behind me and Griffin."

Without a word, Joth did as he was told.

Griffin also recognized the man. "What's a yellow belly like Percy West doing here in Vale?"

Never taking her eyes off of her enemy, Jessi said, "Percy West? Here, he's Clem Davis, the man who killed my father."

A shocked Griff stared at her cold eyes for a moment, then turned his attention to the man he knew as Percy West and his anger at this town grew even larger. He'd met West some years back, up in Cooperwater, Montana. Griffin and a few friends had been in the town, resting up after a particularly lucrative robbery, when the nineteen-year-old West and his gang of young outlaws rode in and began terrorizing the local citizens. Griffin and his friends had to convince the gang to prey elsewhere, but not before Percy's seventeen-year-old brother Zeke shot and killed a six-year-old boy. Although Zeke swore the killing had been an accident, he did hang for the deed. Griff doubted the swinging did much to mend the mother's broken heart.

Jessi could see folks on the streets watching with much interest, but she had no plans to give them a show. She'd let Davis say whatever Darcy had sent him out here to say and then she, Griff and Joth would head home.

"Afternoon, Miss Clayton," Davis said, as they brought their horses to a halt. His young, ferret-thin face sneered smugly at Jessi as he sucked on a toothpick. She supposed his blocking the street was another one of his attempts to intimidate her, but since it was daylight and she didn't have her back to him, she was fairly certain she had little to fear.

When she didn't reply to his greeting, he turned his attention to Griffin and gave him a small smile of recognition. "Mr. Darcy told me you were in town."

Griffin's smile did not reach his eyes. "Well, if it isn't *Percy*. Thought you'd've gotten religion by now. Last time I saw you, you were hightailing it out of Montana so fast, you didn't even have time stay for your brother's trial.''

The sneering lip curled. "The name's Davis. Clem Davis."

"No, the name's Percy," Griff corrected him with a dangerous glint in his faceted eyes. "Percy West. Does Darcy know you're not using your real name?"

Clem didn't reply.

"Miss Clayton seems to think you shot her pa in the back. That true?"

Davis put on his most innocent face. "I wasn't there that night."

Griffin didn't believe him for a moment and wanted to drag him behind a horse until he told the truth.

Without taking his eyes off of Davis, Griff told Jessi, "A few years back Percy here and some of his friends were running roughshod over a town up in Montana. Percy's brother Zeke shot a six-year-old boy in the back. He hung for it."

"The boy had no business being on the street that day."

"He was running for cover when you started shooting up that bank."

Davis looked away as if he didn't want to acknowledge the truthfulness of Griff's account. "Zeke was drunk."

"Jury didn't seem to think that was much of an excuse. Neither do I."

Griffin almost relished the thought of going up against West again. In his mind Percy still owed for that boy's death even if he hadn't been the one directly responsible. "Is Darcy paying you enough to tangle with me again, Percy?"

Davis growled, "Quit calling me that, and yeah, he is. Offering me double pay to get rid of you."

"Good. Better start saving it up so you can buy a good casket. I'm sure the undertaker'll be glad to help you pick one out."

"Better pick one out for yourself, Kid. Too bad those redskin friends of yours won't be here to share it with you though."

Griff eyed the young outlaw up and down. West was referring to Two Shafts and Neil July. They had been with Griff during that time in Montana. Two Shafts was part Comanche and Neil was a member of the Black Seminole tribe. Griff hated the word *redskins*. The slur incensed him just as much as the word *nigger*.

In a falsely pleasant voice, Griff replied, "Funny you should mention them. They'll be here in a few days."

The light-skinned West went visibly pale.

"Yep," Griff added watching West fight and fail to regain his composure. "Two Shafts and his twin brother Neil are going to be real glad to see you."

Griff hoped the news put the fear of God in West. Two Shafts and Neil were known as the Terrible Twins, and it was a name well earned. Griff could tell by West's furtive eyes that this scenario was not unfolding as West had planned. West was a mercenary. His services and his gun were hired out to the highest bidder, and only rarely did men like him meet resistance. "You sure Darcy's paying you enough for all this, Percy?"

"Dammit, stop calling me that!" he snapped like a whining child.

Jessi hid her grin. Percy was not the most manly name for a hired gun. It seemed a far more suitable moniker for the son of one of the English barons who'd been buying up Texas's cattle land for the past ten years. Her amusement at his expense only went so far, however. She'd had enough of him for today. "If we're all done chatting, I need to get home."

Griff told her, "I'm ready whenever you are, Miss Clayton."

Jessi then asked West, "Is there anything else?"

"Yeah, Mr. Darcy wants him out of town. The sooner, the better."

"Tell him I don't care what he wants," Jessi responded quietly.

As they turned the reins of their horses to guide them around West, both Jessi and Griff saw West give a quick look up to a window of the hotel. Reed Darcy stood behind the glass. His anger showed plainly.

Griff waved up at him and Darcy snatched the drapes closed in sharp reply. Wondering who would make her smile when he left for Mexico, Jessi shook her head at Griffin's nose-tweaking ways and headed them up the street.

West called out angrily, "Watch your back, Blake!"

Griff didn't even bother turning around. "With you in town, I'd be a fool not to. See you around, Percy!"

Once they left the outskirts of town, everyone seemed to relax. When Joth asked to ride on ahead, Jessi gave him her permission, but only after cautioning him to stay within her sight.

After he galloped off, Jessi looked over at Griffin. "Our friend Percy looked positively ill when you told him about the arrival of your friends."

"And well he should be. They're known as the Terrible Twins, and they live up to the name, but they're good men to have on our side."

"Were they with you when that boy was killed?"

"Yep. They were as mad about it as the jury. The boy was coming home from school when Zeke and a few of his drunken buddies tried to shoot their way into the town's bank. The boy scrambled for cover but he wasn't fast enough. Broke that poor mother's heart."

Jessi's own heart wrenched. It did not surprise her to

learn that the man she'd come to know as Clem Davis was no stranger to the sort of violence that had resulted in her father's death. Knowing that the man responsible for the boy's death had been brought to justice buoyed her somewhat. Now if she could only bring about justice for her father.

When they reached the ranch, Joth ran in to get his marbles. In preparation for their weekly contest, Jessi used a stick to draw an oval in the dirt of the empty corral while she waited for her nephew to return.

Griff, seated on the top rung of the fence, asked, "Do you really play marbles?"

"Do you really rob trains?"

Jessi was walking around the oval she'd drawn to make sure it was evenly rendered. "I've always loved it. There's something about watching a boy's face crumple when I win away his favorites."

Griff grinned. "Cocky little thing, aren't you?"

"Not cocky. Good. Do you play?"

"Haven't in years. I was pretty good, though."

"Then we should play sometime."

"So you can watch my face crumple?"

Jessi's smile was her only answer.

Joth returned with a small cloth sack in hand. He rolled the multicolored contents out onto the ground and began to pick out his choices for today's battle. Jessi went into the house for her own small cache of stones, and upon returning, spent a few moments picking out her choices for the game.

As the game began it was easy to see that Joth faced an uphill battle. His aunt, braced on her hands and knees in the dirt, was just as good as she'd bragged. After Joth's first two tries failed to gain him any of her pieces, she proceeded to claim four of his. Even though Griff was rooting for Joth, he found himself concentrating less on the contest and more on the arousing sight of

Jessi's behind as she bent low to execute her shots. He never knew he could be aroused by a woman playing a child's game, but being around Jessi was beginning to make him rethink many things. Take for example his chosen profession—he knew without a doubt that he'd never rob another train again, mainly because first, after tasting freedom he'd never go to prison again, and second, train robbing had no future. In the old days, gold-carrying express cars had been ripe for the picking.

When the Reno Brothers up in Indiana pulled off the first train robbery in U.S. history back in '66, they'd needed nothing more than a few pasteboard masks and their own strong backs. The agent in the express car had even been accommodating enough to leave the door unlocked so they could help themselves to both safes traveling on the Ohio and Mississippi Railroad that day. Back then, safe manufacturers placed wheels on the bottoms of their models to ensure easier rolling and also provided thick, sturdy straps on the safes to make it easier for men like Griffin to haul them away. Train robbing had been a thinking man's profession; you relied on good planning, good men, and a good helping of luck. Creativity helped, too. He'd once robbed a train by sequestering himself in a casket and posing as a corpse. Once the train left the station, Griffin rose from the dead. His resurrection scared the agent in the car so badly the man fainted.

But now things were changing. Planning no longer seemed to be a factor today. Gangs were simply derailing trains by tearing up lengths of tracks and sending trains and passengers plummeting off mountain passes and bridge spans. Men like the Texan Sam Bass were setting trains on fire. People were dying as a result of such reckless acts and the railroads were retaliating. Security had become the primary concern. The express companies were now protecting their gold with armies of armed agents. The hated but crafty Pinkertons were being employed more and more, making it increasingly hard for men like Griffin to make a living. No, he needed to find something else to do. Modern times had taken all the fun out of robbing a train.

When Griffin's mind drifted back to the present, the contest had just concluded. Jessi was crowing and declaring herself the best little marble player in Texas while a grinning Joth tried to maintain his mock pout. He'd lost to his aunt again.

That evening Jessi sat on Joth's bed and listened while he said his prayers. As always he asked the Good Lord to say hello to his mother, grandmother, and grandfather. He prayed for Buttercup, his aunt Jessi, Griffin, and Marshal Wildhorse. After he said his amen, Jessi helped him into bed. Marshal Wildhorse was a new name on Joth's prayer list, so after he settled in, she asked him about it.

"I'm praying for him because the marshal sent us Griff."

"Griff told you about that?"

"Yes, today while you were inside talking to Mr. Trent. He says I have to keep it a secret for now."

Jessi caressed his brow and he pulled back just a tiny bit. She knew it was his way of tactfully letting her know he was getting too old for her to baby. She understood his reaction, but it was hard to let go. "And can you?" she asked.

"Yep."

She leaned over and lightly kissed his forehead. "Good night, Joth."

He gave her a hug, rolled over and burrowed in. "Night, Aunt Jessi."

She blew out the light and headed out the door.

"Oh, Aunt Jessi?"

She looked back. "Yes?"

"I love you, even if you do beat me at marbles."

Joy filled her heart. "I love you too, Joth."

Jessi found Griffin out on the porch.

"Is he tucked in?" he asked her.

"Yes, and he added Marshal Wildhorse's name to his prayer list tonight."

"Dix'll be glad to hear that. Joth's praying for one of the best."

Jessi had never met Griffin's marshal friend but hoped she would sometime in the near future. "He said you told him about the marshal sending you here."

"I did. Was I wrong to tell him the truth?" Griff sincerely hoped not. He found he liked pleasing her.

She waved off his fears. "No. What you did was fine."

He sighed. "Good, you had me worried for a minute."

"Why?"

"I prefer to stay on your good side. That's the reason I didn't shoot Darcy the other day when I had the chance. I knew you'd throw a fit if his dead carcass wound up on your land."

She laughed. "You know me well."

The first bullet exploded against the porch post only a few inches away from Jessi's head, and sent both her and Griff frantically scrambling for cover. The second volley tore into the door, hitting wood, glass, and screen, the sounds awakening the night. Jessi kept her head down as more blasts hit, one of which shattered the pane in the parlor window. Moving on her belly, Jessi tried to get to the rifle she usually kept on the porch, but the incoming bullets kept her pinned down. She wanted to raise up to see if she could determine the location of the snipers, but because of the hail of lead she could do nothing but hug the floor of the porch and pray she didn't get shot.

Then the firing stopped and the sound of fast-moving horses riding away from the house faded off into the night.

"Jessi are you okay?" Griff asked anxiously.

"I think so," she said, rising slowly, her heart still beating fast. She checked herself to make sure she was still in one piece. The night was now as quiet as it had been before the shooting began.

"I need to check on Joth."

He nodded.

Jessi didn't bother viewing the damage to the parlor's window. Seeing the broken glass would only add more fire to her rising anger. She'd look at it in the morning.

She found Joth at his window with a rifle in his hand. The sight of him all set to defend his home tore at her insides. No eleven-year-old boy should have to grow up this way.

"Are they gone?" he asked.

"Yes. They're gone."

Joth placed the gun back beneath his window and crawled back into bed. "Was it Darcy's men?"

"More than likely."

"Will he ever leave us alone?"

Jessi stared down at the little boy with her sister's eyes and told him the only truth she knew. "I hope so."

When she caressed his forehead this time, he did not pull away. "Go on back to sleep, now, I'll see you in the morning."

He burrowed down beneath his sheets and she quietly withdrew.

Jessi stormed out onto the porch. "This has to stop," she told Griffin. "Joth shouldn't have to live this way!"

"I know," he replied softly. "It'll end soon. I promise you."

Jessi dearly wanted to believe him, but she was by nature a skeptic. Stopping Darcy was going to be akin to stopping a flash flood. Tonight's visit was only the beginning. If Darcy were indeed as desperate as Auntie believed, all hell was about to break loose, and she and Joth would be in the center of the storm.

"How many do you think there were?" Jessi asked. It was impossible to verify anything at this point, but she thought she'd heard at least one rifle and one shotgun.

"No more than two or three, I'm guessing. In the morning, we can take a look at the shot in the wood and see. Auntie told me Darcy asked you to marry him."

Jessi turned and stared. This was yet another subject she didn't wish to discuss. "Yes he did, and once I stopped laughing, I told him no."

Griff could sense that she didn't want to discuss Darcy. "Didn't mean to pry. Just trying to figure out all the angles."

"I understand, but I don't want to talk about him."

Griff nodded, but her continued stubborness made him a bit frustrated. "Are you going on to bed?"

She shook her head. "I can't. After all the excitement, I'm still too wound up. I'm also too angry."

She wanted to go into town and give Darcy a dose of his own medicine. It apparently didn't matter to him that a child slept in her house, but it mattered to her.

"Then come sit awhile. I promise to be on my best behavior."

Jessi didn't believe him for a minute, but went to sit beside him on the porch steps. Being near him made some of her tension drain. This man was good for her, she'd come to realize. Even though she knew he would not be staying, having him around made her feel stronger.

Griff was as angry about the attack as he knew Jessi to be, and in the morning, he planned on going into town and expressing it, but there was nothing they could do about it until then. He looked over at Jessi seated beside him and even though she seemed to have calmed a bit, he could still feel the anger rising off her like waves of heat.

"You ever think about going back to teaching?" he asked, hoping to distract her enough to get her talking about something else.

Jessi knew what he was doing and she blessed him for his efforts. "I think about it, yes, but it'll have to wait until Joth is old enough to run the ranch by himself. The state's established colleges for members of the race, so I believe I may see if I can teach there when the time comes."

Even though Jessi's father had been cool to the idea of her leaving the ranch while he was alive, Jessi never gave up on the idea of returning to the classroom. The race needed teachers in order to counteract the illiteracy mandated by slavery.

"Was your husband a teacher, too?"

The question brought her back. "No. He had dreams of being a politician, but never got the chance."

"It's always hard losing someone you love."

She thought about her mother. "Yes, it is."

"Do you think you'll ever marry again?"

"At my age the offers aren't exactly pouring in, so I doubt it. What about you, will you ever marry?"

He shrugged. "Maybe, if I can find a decent woman who won't mind my past. Not many mamas approve of their daughters bringing home a once wanted man."

Jessi understood that fully. "It isn't easy being an outcast," she said quietly.

Griff knew she was talking about herself. "It has its advantages sometimes, though."

Jessi looked skeptical. "In what way?"

"You find out who your true friends are when you're an outcast."

Jessi had never thought about it in those terms, but she supposed the theory made sense. Very few people had stood up for her during the Calico Bob years. In fact, she could probably count them all on one hand—folks like Gillie and Auntie. They'd loved her her whole life and hadn't deserted her when times got rough.

"What do you plan to do once you get to Mexico?" she asked, turning to look at him.

"Enjoy being free of the life, I suppose. It'll be nice not having to look over my shoulder all the time for cinder dicks and Pinkertons."

Jessi chuckled at the strange word. "What in the world are cinder dicks?"

"Train police."

"Ah."

"They don't have the power to arrest you away from train property, but they can sic a Pinkerton on you."

"Why did you start robbing trains?"

He paused a moment before answering. "Wanted to pay the railroads back for breaking my mother's heart." Slowly, hesitantly, he told her about his mother's dying. He finished by saying, "I still think about her a lot."

"Do you think she's resting easy, knowing you've spent your life on the wrong side of the law?"

It was a question Griff had been asking himself more and more lately, but he knew the answer, always had. "Probably not . . . definitely not. She was a church-going woman who tried to live her life by the Good Book, but the Book didn't feed us and it didn't stop her from dying poor."

Jessi could hear the bitterness in his voice. Griffin Blake also had dark places in his soul. In that way they were very much alike.

"I still have her Bible, though," he confessed. "It's the only thing she owned when she died."

Jessi felt a kindred sadness echo within. "All I have

left of my mother is the clock sitting on my nightstand. After she died, my father burned just about everything she owned. He let Mildred and me pick out one thing of hers to keep to remember her by, and the rest, every picture, her dresses, hairbrushes, combs, shoes, everything went into the bonfire he set in her rose garden behind the house. I hold Darcy responsible for that too.

"He'll pay Jessi, don't worry."

"But even if he does, it won't bring her back. Nothing will."

Griffin dropped his head sadly. Nothing in his life equaled the pain this lady had suffered. A less strong individual would've broken under such weight, but she hadn't. She'd given up much, but she hadn't broken. And because she hadn't, he wanted to take her in his arms and offer her what solace he could, but she wasn't the kind of woman to be coddled or protected. She wanted justice, plain and simple. In that way she was very much like him. "You're a very strong lady, Jessi Rose Clayton," he told her softly.

"I'm just playing the hand I was dealt, Griffin, nothing more."

The next morning Jessi used a knife to pry the bullets out of the porch. She pocketed six that were fired from a rifle and numerous remnants of small black shot that could only have come from a shotgun. The more bullets she pried free, the angrier she became.

When Griffin came down from his rooftop viewing of the sunrise, he found her prying and muttering angrily to herself.

"Missed you up on the roof this morning."

"I wanted to get this done before Joth got up. I'll board up what's left of my window when I'm through here."

She reached into the chest pocket of her shirt and

tossed him the bullets she'd already freed.

"Rifle and scattershot," Griff noted aloud, rolling the evidence around on his palm.

Jessi declared forcefully, "I'd like to make that West, or Davis, or whatever he's calling himself today, eat that shot. I don't mind them shooting at me, but when Joth's in his room sleeping . . ." Her angry voice trailed off.

Griff most certainly agreed. Only a coward would fire on a child. Which was why Griffin planned on going into town today to teach Percy some manners. The sooner Darcy and his hired vermin learned that certain actions were going to be retaliated against, the sooner they'd get the message. "How about I board up the window?"

She looked up. "That would be fine, thanks. There should be some old wood in the barn."

Griffin found it and began nailing the largest pieces to the shattered glass. If he could steal the glass out of the windows of the Darcy Hotel to replace Jessi's broken ones, he would. Glass was expensive and having it shipped way out here must have made the price even higher. By the looks of the window frame the pane had been in here for quite some time, but it had taken only a second for Darcy's men to reduce it to shards. One more thing to hold Darcy accountable for.

All the hammering awakened Joth, and he stepped outside to investigate the goings on.

"Morning, Aunt Jessi."

"Morning, Joth. Breakfast is on the stove."

"Okay. Morning, Griff."

Griff paused in his hammering. "Morning, cowboy. Those varmints wake you up last night?"

"Yeah."

"Are you okay?"

"The shooting scared me at first, but I'm okay."

"Good. When I get back from town, maybe there'll

be time for me to teach you some marble tricks. Can't have you being beaten by your aunt for the rest of your life.''

Jessi shot him a humorous look. ''And you believe you can change that?''

''I believe I can.''

She tossed back, ''The two of you couldn't beat me playing as one. I've been the marble champion of Vale my entire life.''

''She's telling the truth,'' Joth pointed out to Griff. ''She even has marbles she won from Mr. Keel when they were eight.''

''Sure do,'' Jessi chimed in. ''I have marbles from all the Vale boys who were with me in Gillie's old classroom, Roscoe Darcy's too.''

''Well, you don't have any of mine,'' Griff countered, ''and you aren't going to get any.''

''Don't be so sure,'' Jessi told him.

A smiling Joth went back inside to eat, leaving them alone once more.

''I still say you'll never beat me,'' Jessi said. She'd dug out all the bullets. If there were any more hidden, she'd see to them later.

Griffin doubted he'd ever met a woman so sure of herself and her abilities in his whole life. ''You're too cocky for your own good, Jessi Rose Clayton.''

She put her hand to her ear. ''Do I hear the pot calling the kettle black?''

He chuckled. ''You'll be eating crow soon enough. Mark my words.''

''Not from playing marbles I won't.''

''Okay, you keep on sassing me, woman. It's just going to make my revenge that much sweeter.''

His eyes were sparkling with challenge and so were hers.

''Why are you going into town?''

"To improve somebody's manners."

She went still.

He added firmly, "No one fires on a child while I'm around."

Jessi understood his feelings and she wanted to thank him for stepping up as her champion, but how wise was it to try and beard the lion in his own den? "You're not planning to go alone, are you?"

"Sure I am. I just want to talk to Percy, that's all."

Jessi smiled. "Griffin Blake, you are lying."

"Of course I am. I'll be back, though."

He bent and gave her a quick, sweet kiss. "So don't worry and don't give those kisses to anybody else while I'm away."

She smiled. "I won't, and be careful."

"Always."

Griff stopped first at the Darcy Hotel.

The pleasant-looking clerk behind the desk looked up. "May I help you?"

"I'd like to see Mr. Darcy."

"Reed or Roscoe?" Griff heard a female voice behind him ask.

The voice belonged to Minerva Darcy, Roscoe's wife. She was once again dressed in a gown that would have been fine for Denver or Houston but was far too rich for the plain country blood of Vale. "Reed," Griffin responded.

"My father-in-law's in a meeting and can't be disturbed. Is there something I might help you with?" she asked with a seductive smile.

Griff had no problem understanding what she was offering, and it made him wonder if the rumors about her sharing her father-in-law's bed were true. Personally, Griff had no intention of accepting anything from her; even in her fancy clothes she couldn't hold a candle to

Jessi. "Well, it's real important that I see him, meeting or no meeting."

"I told you, he can't be disturbed."

Griff decided he must not've made himself clear enough. "Mrs. Darcy, I'm usually a pretty even-tempered fellow, but when I don't get what I want, the outlaw in me becomes real nasty."

He watched Minerva try and fail to hold on to her superior attitude.

"Either take me to Darcy or I start shooting up this place the way his men shot up the Clayton place last night. Your choice."

Minerva looked up at him and said with a fake smile, "You're a very forceful man, Mr. Blake. I like that. Come this way."

Griffin followed Minerva back into the inner sanctum of the hotel.

"You know," she told him as they walked, "we'd make a good pair, you and I. You're handsome, intelligent."

Griffin didn't bite. "I usually steer clear of married ladies, Mrs. Darcy."

"Pity," she responded brittlely.

When Minerva opened the doors to the study and preceded him inside, Griff saw that she'd lied. Darcy wasn't in a meeting, at least, not one with any other attendees. He was in the room alone, eating breakfast behind a big, fancy desk.

"Just protecting his privacy," Minerva explained in response to Griff's look.

The interruption made Darcy glance up impatiently. Seeing Griff seemed to catch him off guard, but he gathered his composure quickly. His dark eyes flashed as he asked in a cold voice, "What do you want? And make it quick."

Griff walked over to the desk. "Brought you something."

"What?"

Griff reached into his shirt pocket and withdrew a handful of the battered bullets Jessi had given him this morning, then let some of them stream slowly from his hand into Darcy's coffee and over his eggs and potatoes, and dusted the residue from his palms over the marmalade on the two fat pieces of toast. "Thought you might like them back."

Darcy's face twisted with fury. "Have you lost your mind?"

"No, but you have if you think I'm just going to let you shoot up a house while a sleeping child is in it."

That too seemed to catch him off guard. "I don't know what you're talking about. If Jessi's having trouble with nightriders, she should tell the sheriff."

Griffin grabbed him by the lapels of his fancy handmade suit and snatched him across the desk and dishes so that the older man was no more than a few inches from Griffin's wintry face. "If Joth had been killed last night, you'd already be dead, so listen and listen good. Don't you *ever* send anybody out to harass that boy or his aunt again. Do you understand me?"

"Get your hands—"

"Shut up," Griffin growled back. "This isn't a discussion."

Darcy nostrils flared with emotion, but he kept his mouth shut.

"Jessi isn't going to give you her land and she isn't going to marry you, so leave her the hell alone." Griff threw him back in the chair. "Where's West? I know he was the leader last night."

Darcy angrily righted his clothing. "I don't know anyone by that name."

"He's Clem Davis to you. Where is he?"

"No idea. And don't you ever come barging in here again—"

"Or what? If I ever have to come barging in here again, you'd better be armed. Now, where's West?"

"I said, I don't know."

"Fine, I'll find him on my own. In the meantime, stay away from the Claytons."

"This is going to cost you your life, Blake," Darcy promised with a snarl.

"Only if you can hire somebody to do it. We both know you're too yellow to do it yourself."

Griff walked back to the door. Minerva stood there as if rooted. Griff politely touched his hat to her in parting and stalked out. That was for Joth, he told himself angrily. Now for Jessi.

Instead of leaving the hotel, Griffin walked into the semi-filled fancy dining room and announced loudly, "Folks, the dining room is closed. If you'd be so kind as to leave immediately . . ."

A buzz filled the room as folks scurried to comply. Everyone in town knew the red-headed Griffin's face by now and he didn't have to make the announcement twice. Once the room was emptied, Griffin picked up one of the dining room chairs and hefted it for a moment to judge its weight. Satisfied that it met the test, he forcefully hurled it through the big polished plate window that fronted the street. The noise was tremendous but paled in comparison to the amount of satisfaction he received. If Darcy wanted to create havoc, Griff would give him some.

Most of the banished diners had not left the premises and were huddled in the doorway watching him with dropped jaws. You could've heard a pin drop on cotton as Griff passed them by. "Tell Darcy that's payback for Jessi Clayton's parlor window," he drawled, then walked back out into the late morning sunshine.

He was certain Darcy had been lying about not knowing West's whereabouts, so Griff walked down to the saloon to see if he could learn anything from his new friends there.

He hit pay dirt the moment he walked through Auntie's door. West was seated at a table on the far side of the room, playing poker with four men. When he spied Griffin he didn't bother hiding his smug smile. Griff could see that he'd gotten a shave since yesterday. He looked more like a ferret than ever.

"Morning, Percy. Get all shaved up for your funeral?"

The few patrons in the bar looked up, as did big Doyle Keel behind the bar.

West kept his eyes on his cards. "What the hell do you want, Blake?"

"Your hide. You know, you could've killed Joth Clayton last night."

"I got no idea what you're talking about. Go home to your whore."

Griffin's punch hit West with such force, both man and chair went straight to the floor. Once West stopped seeing stars, his lips curled ferally. He launched himself at Griffin and the fight was on.

Percy managed to land a few well-placed punches as tables were knocked over and big Doyle Keel came running from behind the bar. Griff had the supreme satisfaction of beating the tar out of West for a good fifteen seconds or so, until someone busted Griffin across the back of his head with an object large enough and hard enough to knock him senseless and he slid to the floor like a wet sheet.

When he came to, he was groggy. He had a hard time focusing his eyes and his head hurt like hell. He seemed to be lying down, but he wasn't real sure. At first he thought he was dreaming, because he swore he could see Two Shafts and his twin Neil July grinning down at him.

He closed his eyes again against the tilting room and the pain in his head, then fought to wake up fully.

"Welcome back," the Comanche Two Shafts said.

The smile on Shafts's handsome face equaled the one radiating from his darker-skinned brother Neil.

"You really should've waited for us to get here before you started charging around breaking windows and picking fights," Neil scolded Griffin.

Griff tried to sit up, but the ache in his head screamed so loudly he thought he might retch if he didn't ease himself back down, so he did. "What happened?"

"One of Percy's friends hit you over the head with a chair."

Griff remembered now. He looked around. "So where am I?"

"Auntie's room," Neil said. "Very nice lady, that Auntie."

Suddenly, Griffin thought about Jessi. How long had he been knocked out? Were she and Joth starting to worry? "What time is it?"

"Almost four."

Griff cursed. "I have to get back. She's going to worry."

"The doc says you took a pretty good knock on the head. You're not going anywhere until tomorrow," the Comanche pointed out.

"The hell I'm not."

Steeling himself against the pain he knew would come, Griffin forced himself up and bellowed, "Auntie!!"

Ten minutes later, Griff was being helped down the stairs by his two friends. He was more or less dangling between the twins with his arms around their shoulders, but with Auntie and the girls hovering around his descent like mama birds, he made it.

The main room of the saloon looked as if a tornado had gone through it. Broken and splintered chairs and tables were strewn about, as were broken glass and bottles. Griff tried to make some sense out of the destruction, but try as he might, he couldn't seem to remember a thing.

"Did I do all this?"

"No," Auntie told him. "Your friends here did. They came in just as you were going down. Paid me well for all the damage, though. Anytime they want to bust up the place again, they're more than welcome."

Griff was glad to hear it.

Griff rode to the ranch in the bouncing bed of Auntie's buckboard. She'd come to guide the twins to the Clayton ranch and to tend to him, should he need anything on the way.

On the porch, Jessi used her spyglass to watch the approaching riders and buckboard. She didn't recognize the two men on horseback but she could see Auntie holding the reins of the buckboard. Hoping she might have seen Griffin in town, Jessi swept the spyglass over the bed of the wagon and her heart began to pound. Was that him lying there?

She forced herself to stay on the porch, even though her whole being wanted to rush out to the road. She prayed he was all right, but if he wasn't she didn't want to know until the last possible moment.

When they drove up she saw that he was alive: battered, bruised, and still a bit disoriented, but definitely alive. Jessi looked down at him lying in the wagon and felt relief melt away her anxiety.

"Let's get him into the house," she said.

Jessi had no idea who the two men were, but she could've kissed them for bringing Griffin home.

Griff smiled lazily up at her. "Told you I'd be back."

"Yes, you did, but look at you. Did you get run over by a train?"

His handsome face would be a sight in a few days. Swelling had already taken root around his left eye.

"Should see Percy," he tossed back.

The two men gingerly raised him, and half-carried, half-walked him into the house while a wide-eyed Joth looked on.

On the way to the bedroom, Auntie related a condensed version of the story and after hearing it, Jessi didn't know whether to kiss him too, or scold him for placing himself in such danger.

Griff was eased down onto the bed and as the softness of the mattress and the bedding enfolded him, he thought to himself, *Now I can die.* It felt so good to be home he promised himself he'd never leave again. Of course, the thoughts were just products of his addled brain, but the pledge sounded good to him just the same. He drank a bit of the bitter-tasting bark tea Neil swore would heal his aching head and then he drifted off to sleep.

Chapter 7

Auntie drove back to town, leaving Griff to sleep off the aftereffects of his sojourn, and Jessi and Joth to entertain Griffin's friends.

"Thanks for bringing him home," Jessi said genuinely, as she shook each man's hand. "The name's Jessi Clayton."

They returned her shake firmly.

"Our pleasure."

They introduced themselves as Two Shafts and Neil July. Both men were handsome giants, but Two Shafts had more bulk on his mountainous frame than his leaner brother. He had long dark hair that he wore free, and the powerful arrogant air of the Comanche. Neil, on the other hand, had a beard, and eyes as dark as his skin. Although Griffin had described them as twins, Jessi didn't believe she'd have any trouble telling them apart. The two didn't favor each other a bit.

Joth, who'd been watching the men with great interest since their arrival, suddenly burst out, "You're the Terrible Twins!" Their names and faces had finally triggered his memory. "I have your posters on my wall!"

Jessi didn't know how the men felt about exuberant children, but hoped they didn't hold to the philosophy that children should be seen and not heard. "This is my nephew, Joth Clayton."

Both men shook Joth's hand.

Two Shafts asked Joth, "Why would you hang pictures of us? Are you a lawman?"

Joth laughed at the outrageous question. "No, I have a poster collection. Can I show them, Aunt Jessi?"

Jessi didn't want Joth to overwhelm the men in their first hour here. "Sweetheart, why don't you let them sit awhile and catch their breath—"

Neil stood. "I'd like to see it."

Two Shafts grinned. "So would I. Lead the way, Sheriff. I'm impressed that you even know who we are."

As the two followed Joth to his room, Jessi silently blessed them for their kindness.

Griff slept the afternoon away. Jessi tipped in to check on him a few times, and was pleased to find him breathing easily. As she watched him sleep, she surveyed the bruises he'd gotten defending her honor and realized just how much it would've hurt her had he been seriously injured or killed. She decided then and there that she would start embracing the light Griffin Blake brought to her life. At least she'd have the memories once he was gone. Bending down, she kissed his forehead softly.

That evening, Griff awakened. The roaring ache in his head had been reduced to a gentle throb, thanks to the bark tea, but Jessi wouldn't let him out of bed until he promised not to overdo it.

"I promise," he pledged, looking up at her as she sat on the edge of the bed. Seeing her face again gave him more pleasure than he ever imagined. He reached up and stroked her dark cheek. "I'm sorry if I worried you."

She placed her hand over his, relishing his touch. "Apology accepted, but please don't do it again. Or at least let me come next time. I would've loved to have seen Darcy's face when you threw that chair through the hotel window.''

He gave her a lopsided smile. ''That's what champions do when they're defending their lady's honor.''

''Are you my champion?''

He paused a moment to look into her eyes, and then answered truthfully. ''Yes. I think I am. Are you my lady?''

Her response was soft. ''Yes, I think I am.''

''I can't promise I'll stay.''

''I know,'' she replied. ''I've accepted that fact.''

''Are you sure?''

''Yes.''

For a moment silence reigned, then Jessi rose and said, ''Come on out when you're ready. Joth and your friends have been waiting to see you.''

He nodded and she quietly left the room.

When Griffin came into the kitchen, the Twins greeted him with smiles and teasing. ''You look like you've been in a fight, Cheno.''

''Who's Cheno?'' Joth asked.

''That ugly cuss with the red beard.'' Two Shafts explained, pointing at Griffin.

''Why do you call him that?''

''Because sometimes he acts like Juan Cortinas.''

Joth shook his head. ''I've never heard of him. He an outlaw too?''

''Some American lawmen thought he was,'' Neil replied, ''but the Mexicans living on the Texas border thought he was a champion. They called him Cheno.''

''And since our friend here has a habit of doing good deeds, we call him Cheno too,'' Two Shafts explained.

''Oh, now I understand,'' Joth said.

Jessi did too. When she was younger, some of the Mexican hands employed by her father had spoken Juan

Cortinas's name with much reverence. He'd been a champion for the rights of the Mexican people during the land grabbing turmoil of the late fifties, and was also called the Red Robber of the Rio Grande. He had a red beard and gave the American authorities fits. Since Griffin had a red beard and had become her champion, she thought the Twins had nicknamed him very appropriately.

The three men spent the evening laughing, lying, and catching up on the doings of each other. They talked about old haunts, mutual friends still living, and the ones most recently dead. While Joth went out to the barn to say goodnight to Buttercup, Jessi heard outrageous stories of Griff's train robbing adventures and the help the Twins had provided during some of them.

The bearded Neil July said, "His creativity was legendary, Miss Jessi."

"No one could plan a robbery like our Cheno," Two Shafts declared, smiling proudly as he sat in the chair with his arms folded over his massive chest. "One time he robbed a train by posing as a new-hired express agent. Even forged a letter of introduction on Kansas Pacific stationary—"

"Then signed the president's name to it and reported to work," his brother added, laughing.

Jessi asked, "What happened to the regular man? Didn't he question a new agent just appearing out of the blue?"

"Nope. He wasn't there."

Two Shafts explained, "We grabbed the real agent on his way to work that morning, knocked him out, and left him tied up at a little whorehouse outside of town. The girls there promised that when he woke up he'd swear he'd died and gone to heaven, so we knew we didn't have to worry about him showing up and raising the alarm."

Jessi couldn't suppress her laugh.

"Cheno showed up at the train to take his place, gave the conductor his letter of introduction, and all went well."

"Yep, when the train cleared town, Cheno rolled the safe to the door and he and the safe hopped out. We took in almost eight hundred in gold that day, didn't we, Cheno?"

"I don't remember exactly, but that sounds about right."

Griffin's answer had been noncommittal because he had been watching Jessi and wondering how she felt about hearing the Twins' litany of his past life and crimes. Granted, she already knew he was an outlaw, but would this change him in her eyes? Would she now want nothing to do with him? Whether a woman found him acceptable had never worried him before, but it did now.

The evening went on, however, as more lies were told and more laughter accompanied it.

It soon became time for Joth to head off to bed. Once he offered his goodnights, Jessi excused herself and went to hear his prayers and to tuck him in. When she returned, the men were still at it. She noted how much affection they seemed to share. It was as if three brothers had been reunited around a family holiday table. She found their interactions pleasantly surprising. Calico Bob and his gang never exhibited anything but hostility and mistrust toward one another. It was not uncommon to awaken in Bob's camp and find one of the members of the gang dead, killed by a comrade during the night. The thought of Bob made her remind herself that in reality the men laughing around her table were not the harmless siblings of some Texas farm family, but men who made their living outside the law. Even though she was on the verge of inviting Griffin into her bed, the reminder reignited those small inner misgivings she'd had upon his arrival. Once again, she hoped she hadn't made the wrong decision by letting these men into her life.

The discussion then turned to the reasons Griffin had called the Twins to Vale. "Miss Clayton has some varmints that need exterminating, and I need your help."

He filled them in on Darcy's land grab and finished by detailing the events of last night and this morning.

"So that's why you were beating Percy like an old rug," Two Shafts replied with understanding. "He shot up Miss Clayton's house last night."

"And your boy was in bed asleep when they opened fire?" Neil asked Jessi with quiet disbelief.

Jessi nodded, angry all over again.

Neil told her, "It's good we didn't know this earlier. My brother and I would've taken turns kicking Percy's rear up and down the street."

Two Shafts added, "You'd think he'd be smart enough to remember that boy up in Montana."

Griff agreed. "I know, but evidently not."

The Twins had a few more questions. Neil asked, "So, Percy works for this Darcy fellow? And he killed your pa?"

Jessi nodded.

"Well, Miss Clayton, how about me and my brother work for you? That ought to even things up, don't you think, Shafts?"

His brother smiled. "I think so, yes, and I can't wait to tell Percy."

Griff grinned. He then looked to Jessi. "What do you think?"

Jessi replied, "I'd love to have you here, but I've no way to pay you."

"Don't worry about that, Miss Clayton, Cheno's already taken care of that."

"I have?" Griff asked, surprised.

"Yep."

Neil reached down beside him, then placed on top of the table a small weathered carpet bag. He opened it up and showed Griffin and Jessi the contents. Jessi hadn't any idea how Griffin might be reacting, but she was staring as if she'd just seen the birth of a two-headed cow. The gold layered on the bottom of the bag in Neil's hand had to be two inches deep.

Neil left the bag in front of Griffin and explained, "We were in Austin when we got word that you were looking for us. In fact, we were in Rosita's, to be exact. When we told her we were on our way to see you, she gave us that. She said she'd been holding onto it for two years, waiting for you to come back and get it."

Griffin smiled. He had nothing but fond memories of the beautiful, saucy Rosita Wayne. "How is Rosita?"

"Spicy as ever," Two Shafts replied, his eyes shining knowingly, "spicy as ever. She asked about you."

Griffin avoided looking Jessi's way.

Neil added, "She also said to tell you the banker said he added two hundred in interest."

"Did the town get the school built?" Griffin asked.

"Yep, and were able to hire a back east teacher, too."

The gold Rosita had been holding had been loaned by Griffin to a banker almost two and a half years ago, and it pleased him knowing the railroad's money had gone for yet another worthy cause. The fact that he'd made a fat return on his investment only increased his satisfaction. He could tell by the confusion on Jessi's face that she hadn't an inkling as to what they were talking about and he mentally vowed to explain it all to her later.

Griff closed the bag and said, "Thanks for bringing the gold, but I still don't understand how I've taken care of paying you."

"We figured you'd give us the extra two hundred."

A surprised Griff looked over at the smiling Neil, who

said, "We love you, Cheno, and because we do, we will help you chop down this Darcy, but we have to eat."

Neil had always been the blunt one, and Griffin knew that their request amounted to little when compared to the value of having them by his side. And as Neil stated, even old friends had to eat. He reached into the bag and counted out the sum they'd requested, and while doing so, told the Twins, "Oh, by the way, I also invited the Preacher to this party."

"The Preacher?" Neil echoed in a whining voice that reminded Jessi very much of Joth. "Why?"

Two Shafts added, "He always spoils the fun."

Griff grinned, "Now boys, be nice. He'll keep us all in line."

"He certainly won't let us pecos Percy when the time comes."

"No, he won't," Griffin chuckled in full agreement.

Jessi's eyes widened. To "pecos" someone meant tying rocks to their dead body and dropping it into a wide body of water. Jessi certainly thought Percy West deserved a horrible end, but she didn't know whether to applaud the Twins' solution or be appalled. One thing for certain: they were as outrageous as Griffin had led her to believe, and she liked them. "Who's the Preacher?" she asked. Neil was actually pouting.

"Friend of ours," Griffin told her.

"Friend of *his*," Two Shafts corrected.

Griffin grinned and shook his head.

"Friends do not collect bounty on friends," Neil declared sagely.

"He was just doing his job, Neil," Griff told him.

"What's his job?" Jessi asked curiously.

"He's a bounty hunter."

Jessi was more than a bit surprised. "You have a friend who's a bounty hunter?"

"See?" Two Shafts pointed out. "She thinks it's crazy too."

"That bible toter put us in jail, Miss Jessi."

"That was three years ago, and you were only in for two days," Griff reminded them.

"It spoiled our reputation, though. We'd never had a bounty collect on us before—"

"Or since," his brother declared. "I don't know what's scarier, that big scatter gun of his, or those Old Testament verses he's always quoting."

"A bible-carrying bounty hunter," Jessi said. "I don't think I've ever heard of that before. You seem to have very eccentric friends, Griffin."

"You'll like him," Griffin replied.

Neil whispered loud enough for everyone to hear, "No, you won't."

Soon it became easy for all of them to see that Griffin needed to be in bed. The frivolity had sapped the last of his day's energy. He looked tired and wan.

Jessi had no place for the Twins to bed down. She offered them the porch, but they had other ideas.

"We'll stay in town for now. It'll give us a chance to look around, learn the lay of the land. How about we meet you back here the day after tomorrow?"

Griffin had no problem with their plan, and neither did Jessi.

After the Twins departed, Jessi blew out the lights and walked with Griffin to his room. "They're quite a pair."

"Yes, they are. Did you like them?"

"I did," she replied honestly.

"I should have made them stay tonight so they could sit watch."

"I don't think there'll be a need. I'm betting Reed Darcy and his people'll stay close to home tonight. It isn't every day his foreman gets whipped and somebody throws a chair through one of his fancy imported windows.''

They were now standing outside his door.

"Do I get a kiss for all my good deeds?" he asked.

"You most certainly do." She lovingly placed her hand against his bearded cheek, then raised up and kissed him slowly and, she hoped, thoroughly. When she eased away, she asked softly, "How was that?"

He slid a thumb across her bottom lip and whispered, "You're getting real good at this."

"I wasn't before?"

"Not really, no."

She grinned. "Then maybe we should do it again. Practice makes perfect."

When practice ended, Jessi was breathless and light headed; her lips were kiss swollen, and she craved more. "Do you think you'll have time for another practice session tomorrow, maestro?"

"I will always have time for such an *eager* student. Meet me on the roof at dawn and we'll continue your tutoring."

Jessi could say without hesitation that she was on fire for this man. He was the source, the spark to her kindling, and she wanted to be consumed by the blaze even knowing he would not stay. "I'll be there. Sleep well."

The next morning he was already on the roof when she arrived, and as always, his bearded smile warmed her soul even if the bruises on his face were still ugly and red. He poured her a mug of coffee which she accepted gladly, then she settled in to watch the sunrise. Until he'd entered her life, she'd never taken the time to indulge in such frivolous endeavors because life had been too intense and serious. Granted, little had changed, but with him by her side the obstacles seemed less daunting. She was beginning to enjoy the time spent up here, and when he headed out for Mexico she would probably continue alone. The view was beautiful and she would always be grateful to him for giving her such a simple but priceless gift.

She'd just turned to him to ask about the practice session they'd talked about last night when they both spied a wagon coming down the road.

"Looks like Doyle Keel," Jessi remarked, rising to her feet. "That's Gillie on the seat beside him. I wonder where they could be going this time of the morning?"

As Doyle reined the two-horse team off the main road and onto the one that led to her place, she had her answer.

"Guess those lessons you wanted will have to wait," Griff stated.

She offered a mock pout. "I guess you're right."

Smiling, he gave her a potent good-morning kiss. "Let's go see what they want."

They wanted Joth. Once a year, Doyle drove Gillie down to Austin to visit her sister Maude. Maude now had a grandson living with her, and Joth and he had played together during last year's visit. The two boys had had such a great time, Gillie had promised Joth he could go the next time. Well, the next time was today, and Gillie apologized for her lack of notice. "I got up this morning and decided this is what I wanted to do."

Doyle Keel added, "And with Auntie's closing for a week for repairs, it was a perfect time."

Doyle had been in Gillie's old classroom with Jessi, and he loved the old woman as much as Jessi. The part-time barkeep and livery owner also had a soft spot in his heart for Joth. "I left that lazy assistant of mine in charge of the livery; let's hope he manages to keep the place open until we get back."

Doyle had fired three assistants in as many months. None of the young men had been able to meet his exacting standards.

''I'll go and get Joth up,'' Jessi told Gillie and Doyle. ''Luckily, he's cleaned his room and'll be able to find the things he'll need to take with him.''

Griff, Keel, and Gillie waited in the parlor for Jessi's return. It was hard to miss the wood nailed over the big window. Doyle walked over and peered at it, then tested the sturdiness of the repair. ''I'll bring back some wood big enough to cover the whole window.''

''She'll appreciate that,'' Griff told the big man.

''And I appreciated the way you defended her yesterday. Only one problem—after your friends were done with him, there wasn't any left for me.''

Griff grinned. ''Next time I'll tell them to not be so greedy.''

''Much obliged.''

''Where's West now?''

Doyle looked confused.

''Clem Davis's real name's Percy West.''

Doyle's eyes lit with humor. ''Percy, is it? Well, he's licking his wounds somewhere inside the Darcy Hotel. He and his partners were so broke up when they left after the fight, some of them were just about crawling. Of course, I had to wake 'em all up before they could leave, thanks to your friends.'' Doyle smiled.

Griff had a question. He didn't remember a thing after being hit by the chair. ''When did the Twins arrive?''

Doyle looked confused. ''Twins? What twins?''

''My friends. Two Shafts and Neil.''

''Those two are supposed to be twins?''

The astonished look on Doyle's face made Griff chuckle. ''Yep. Same father, different mothers. Born on the same day, believe it or not.''

''Amazing,'' Doyle replied. ''Well, they came in right after you got hit with the chair. They saw you go down and all hell broke loose. Since there were four of Darcy's men and only two of them, I came out from behind the bar, figuring they'd need some help, but nope, they took care of them with no problem at all and seemed to have a good time doing it.''

"They do enjoy a good brawl.''

"I could see that. Tore the place up, and when the dust cleared, they were the only two men still standing. Auntie was real upset about the damage at first, but after they paid her with the gold from that old carpet bag, she was smiling again.''

Griff went still. *Old carpet bag?* They hadn't said anything about covering the damages to the saloon with *his* money.

Gillie asked, "Is there something wrong, Griffin?''

"No, ma'am,'' he replied shaking his head. Those two were the physical embodiment of Coyote, the supreme trickster of Native American lore, and if you weren't careful, they'd bite. Luckily for their friends, their bite was never mean-spirited; Auntie deserved reimbursement for all the damage, yet Griff did wonder how much the carpet bag had originally held and how much it actually contained now.

Jessi returned carrying a large valise. "Joth's wolfing down his breakfast and will be ready directly.''

She walked over and gave Gillie a strong hug. "Thank you for this. With Darcy and everything, it's a good time for him to be away.''

"That's how I feel. He can play with my sister's grandson and not have to worry about anything but being a child. I will make certain he keeps up with his lessons, though.''

"I know you will.''

Gillie then turned to peer at Griffin. "Although I do wish I were here to see what your champion is going to do next.''

Doyle turned sharply. "Whose champion?''

"Jessi's champion. Griffin.''

Jessi felt embarrassment flood her cheeks. Leave it to Gillie to know everything about everyone.

Doyle didn't look pleased as he surveyed Griffin. "Is that who he thinks he's going to be?"

Gillie told her former student quietly, "It isn't about who he thinks he's going to be, Doyle Keel. It's about who he is."

"Him? And Jessi?"

Doyle Keel had always been sweet on Jessi, and everyone knew it. He'd long ago resigned himself to the fact that she'd never return his feelings, but continued to be a good friend nonetheless. He too had defied Darcy's edicts by bringing her food and supplies.

Doyle looked first at Griffin and then at Jessi. "Can he beat you at marbles?" he asked her bluntly.

Jessi fought to keep a straight face. "He says he can."

"Well, saying and doing are two different things." He turned to Griffin and related just as bluntly, "I've been in love with this girl since I was eight years old, but for some reason she won't have me."

Doyle shot Jessi a grin and she smiled.

He turned back to Griffin. "If she's picked you, I can live with that, because you seem like a decent sort. But if you break her heart, or if she so much as tears a fingernail because of you, Blake, I will find you and break you in half. Do you understand me?"

Griffin most certainly did. He'd already noted the barkeep's great strength and had no desire to be introduced to it personally.

Then Doyle's brown eyes lightened. "But if you can beat her at marbles, you can be my champion, too. Hell, I'll even throw in free drinks for as long as I'm behind Auntie's bar. Deal?" he asked, sticking out his boulder-sized hand.

Filled with relief, a grinning Griffin stuck his hand in Doyle's, then tried not to wince from the bone-crushing power of the man's grip. "Deal," he croaked.

"Men," Jessi said shaking her head.

"You *really* think you can whip her at marbles?" Doyle asked Griffin in a noisy aside.

"Yep."

Jessi rolled her eyes. "If the two of you are finished, I'd like to know how the town reacted to Griffin breaking the hotel's window?"

Gillie chuckled. "It put poor Reed in such a rage, he must've jumped up and down in front of that busted window for ten minutes yelling and cussing. Put on quite a show."

"He's never been challenged before," Doyle said. "I don't think he likes it."

"Good," Griffin replied. "Maybe we can inspire a few others to stare him down."

"You've certainly given folks something to talk about, if nothing else," Gillie remarked.

Joth came in. "I'm ready to go." Buttercup would be going too, and Joth had already trailered him to the wagon. It would be the pony's first long trek, and Joth was a bit worried, but when Jessi explained to him that the blood of the great plains horses ran through Buttercup's veins, he seemed reassured that his favorite mount would make it to Austin and back.

Doyle and Griffin loaded Joth's belongings in the wagon and then it was time to say good-bye. On the porch, Jessi gave her nephew a strong hug which he returned tenfold. "I'll tell Miss Maude you said hello," Joth told her.

"You do that, and remember your manners."

"I will, Aunt Jessi."

Griff was waiting by the wagon. "Bye cowboy. You have a good time."

"I will. Tell the Twins I'll see them when I get back."

"I will."

Doyle slapped the reins over the team and the wagon began to roll. Joth and Gillie waved. Jessi waved back until they were out of sight.

Griff came up on the porch and slipped his arm around her waist. "You're already missing him, aren't you?"

"Yes, but as I told Gillie, he needs to be away for a while."

"I agree. So what are your plans for today?"

"Laundry."

"Laundry?"

Jessi turned in the circle of his arms so she could look up into his bearded handsomeness. "Yes, laundry."

"How about you relax instead?"

"I don't have time. Today's the day I do the wash."

He bent and brushed his lips over her ear. "The Twins will be gone for two days—Joth at least a week—and you want to do laundry? No routine today, Jessi Rose. Today's a holiday."

"Griffin," she sighed pleasurably, feeling her desire awakening. "I have to do the wash."

"Who's the maestro here?"

He punctuated the question with a kiss that warmed her to her toes. She didn't have to answer, and he didn't really expect one; they both knew. As the kiss deepened, she wrapped her arms around his neck and he pulled her closer. The wash was the farthest thing from her mind.

When she finally came up for air, she was woozy and it took a moment for her eyes to open. His mustache rose around his smile. "Still want to do the wash?"

"If I say yes, will I get kissed again?"

"Yes or no, it won't much matter. I'm going to kiss you either way."

Desire rose, warming the cool morning air like afternoon heat. Jessi felt bold and filled with a burgeoning sensuality that made her want to ensure he remembered her when he was gone. "Make love to me," she told him, in a voice quiet as a candle's flame.

Griffin's eyes closed and his blood rushed fast as a canyon flood. The heated request, the seriousness in her gaze, let him know this was not some teasing ploy. She wanted him just as much as he wanted her. Looking down, he saw a beautiful dark-skinned beauty he had about as much business pursuing as he had trying to rob a well-guarded express car alone, but he wouldn't trade his place here with her for all the railroad gold in the world. He traced a finger over her lips and asked quietly, "Are you sure about this?"

She nodded.

He leaned to touch his lips to hers. "Then I am too. Did you already start the water heating for the wash?"

He was slowly undoing the buttons of her shirt.

Filled with anticipation, Jessi was finding it hard to concentrate. "Yes."

He trailed kisses down her bare throat. "Do you think it's hot by now?"

She was certain it was and wondered why he cared. "It should be . . . Why?" she whispered.

"We'll need it later."

Jessi had no idea what he was talking about and didn't much care. His hands and lips were roaming ever so lazily. He pulled her frayed camisole down and gave her breasts a long, lingering loving. Raising up, he looked down at her with blazing eyes, then picked her up and carried her into the house.

The kiss he bestowed upon her as he set her on her bed had enough potency to keep a woman satisfied for a week. While she lay there ebbing and flowing, a haze-filled Jessi felt him leave her. She hadn't an inkling as to where he'd gone or what he was doing, she just wanted him to return.

He did only moments later. "Sorry for leaving . . ."

He kissed her deeply and her desire rose higher. He gently stripped away her shirt. The camisole went next and he filled his hands with the soft bare flesh. His thumbs rubbed against them in silent invitation and they hardened on cue.

"You've learned your lessons well . . ."

He gave them each a glancing lick, then gently bit the yearning peaks. He proceeded to divest her of the rest of her clothing slowly and expertly.

"No wonder society doesn't want decent women associating with disreputable men like you," Jessi breathed, as she looked up at him from atop the sheets on her net-shrouded bed. Her breasts were hard as jewels and she seemed to be throbbing everywhere.

Lying beside her, he grinned softly. "I'll take that as a compliment."

His mouth tenderly captured a nipple and she arched and crooned to the dizzying pleasure. Breathing became difficult as his tapered brown fingers meandered and roamed. A sweet lingering heat flared and grew everywhere he touched. Strong hands slid over her like velvet, learning her lines, tracing her shapes, mapping her as if she were an uncharted land he'd come to claim in the name of some erotic kingdom. Although she'd never enjoyed the marriage bed before, Griffin made her want to be his in every way.

"Open your legs, *querida*," he whispered, brushing a kiss against the small dark whorl of her navel.

Jessi shuddered and rippled like heat waves on the horizon. His fingers dallying with the passion-damp hair below her navel made her legs part without thought. The tiny licks he began to place on the trembling inner skin of each thigh were overwhelming. Her ragged breathing became audible as he alternated the flicks of his tongue with humid, lingering touches from his lips.

Bold fingers tutored and cajoled her to widen her legs

even further, and groaning aloud, she shamelessly complied. He was knowing, masterful, brazen. Continuing to tease her blissfully, he warned softly, "Now, don't scream . . ."

Before Jessi could voice her confusion, his tongue moved over her so wantonly no further explanations were needed. The sensations were so seeringly sharp she had to grab a fistful of sheets to keep from screaming loud and long. What was he doing to her? She knew, of course; she just didn't believe it. While she twisted and moaned, he dallied, nibbled, parted her gently, and gave her passionate fits. When her body rippled its powerful release, she swore she'd been flung up to the stars.

Griffin's manhood throbbed with need as he watched her response. He realized he could want this woman twenty-fours hours a day. Who'd've thought she'd be this lush, this magnificent? He couldn't keep his hands from touching her, stroking her, toying with her. While he knew it would take her a few moments to recover, he was ready to continue branding her into his soul. To that end he stood and undressed. When he rejoined her atop the bed, he began again, teasing, inviting, making her heat rise to match his own in this age-old dance of man and woman. His grip on his own passion was steadily eroding. He had to have her now or shame himself like an untried youth.

He entered her a few heated moments later and their mutual sighs of satisfaction mingled in the otherwise silent room. As he began to move slowly within her, he was glad this first time had happened during the day so he could see her take in his pleasure, watch her nipples grow hard as wild blackberries under his kisses, and view the delicious way she arched as she rode his rhythm. Just thinking about it made him increase the tempo of his thrusts. Her hands traveling sensually over his back were hot, the place sheltering his manhood warm and tight. Next time they'd go slower so they could explore each other's passions at length, but right now, as she rose to his strokes, and her lush, lean body drove him over the edge, his hold on his self broke and the world shattered into a thousand shuddering pieces.

Afterward she lay on the bed sated and dewed with sweat. She was lying on her belly, not wanting to move ever again. He lay beside her, languidly stroking the strong column of her spine, marveling once again at her beauty. "Still think you're too old for me?" he asked softly.

"At this moment, yes. I couldn't move even if Darcy came through the front door shooting."

Griffin didn't believe that for a second, but he was glad she felt so satisfied.

"You're very good at this, too, Griffin Blake."

He placed a kiss at the base of her spine. "So are you. Be right back."

Before Jessi could ask anything, he was gone. He returned shortly, dragging the big claw-footed tub that usually sat on the back porch. The tub had been purchased by her father on a trip to Mexico early in her parents' marriage, and it was more than large enough for Jessi to sit and stretch out in, unlike the hip bath she regularly employed.

After positioning the tub on the far side of the room, he left once more. This time, he returned hauling two cauldrons of the water she'd heated for the wash. She couldn't help but admire the red and gold beauty of his muscular nude body. He poured the water into the tub.

"So that's why you asked about the wash water," she said, getting up and walking to where he stood. "I don't think I've ever taken a bath in the middle of the day, but then again," and she ran the tip of her finger down his fur-dappled chest, "I'm doing a lot of things with you I've never done before."

He raised her hand and tenderly kissed the tips of her fingers. "And much more before the day is done, believe me."

She stepped gingerly over the edge and stuck a toe in. The water was hot, but not too hot to enjoy. "What're you going to do while I bathe?"

"Watch."

Jessi's passion flared to life and her gaze became a prisoner to his hot eyes.

Griffin knew that a gentleman would've withdrawn so his lady could bathe privately, but because Griffin had never claimed to be a gentleman, he stretched out on the bed and feasted his eyes on her glorious dark curves.

"You're really going to stay?" she asked.

"Sure, why not? The view's as pretty as a sunrise."

No man had ever seen Jessi bathe before, not even her late husband. Hell, he had never even seen her fully unclothed, if her memory served correctly, yet this train robber seemed to look upon this as a natural aftermath to what they'd just shared, and Jessi supposed he was right.

With his glowing eyes ever present in her mind, Jessi eased down into the water and felt the silkiness envelop her. Her eyes slid closed for a moment and for the first time in a long time, she had no worries. Jessi loved baths, always had, but since her father's death, she'd had no time to spare for indulgences.

"Is the water warm enough?" he asked softly.

"Oh, yes."

The pleasurable purr made Griffin's manhood quicken and he knew he had to have her again soon. What had begun as harmless flirtation with this lady rancher had turned into something so complicated that Mexico seemed very far away. He was in the prime of his life, far too young to be bound to one woman, mainly because there were so many others yet to meet, but his body and mind seemed to be running on opposing tracks. Jessi Rose Clayton was in his blood and he wasn't sure if he wanted a cure.

She looked so peaceful lying there with her head back and her eyes closed, he padded over to the tub and knelt behind her. When she turned up her face, he kissed her possessively.

Soon his hands were wandering beneath the water's clear surface, once again sensually exploring her valleys, hills, and plains. He took her soap and cloth and washed her gently, pampering her, sliding his soap-slick hands over the arching buds of her breasts and the deep, throbbing darkness between her thighs. He was so achingly adept, she knew he'd done this many times before, undoubtedly with a variety of women, but she didn't care; she was just glad they'd taught him so well.

He rinsed her, and using a drying sheet, toweled her off slowly. As he moved his hands over her breasts and down her belly, he asked, "Are you sore?"

Jessi had no idea what he meant until he languidly grazed a bold knuckle over the tip of her heat-filled dampness.

"Are you sore here?" he asked quietly.

"No," she managed to say, but she was very hot there, thanks to him.

He stole a soft kiss from her lips, saying, "It's been so long for you. We need to be sure . . ."

Through the foggy haze of her spiraling desire, Jessi could feel him touching her gently, wickedly, expertly. *Do couples do this more than once a day?* a voice in her mind asked. Jessi had no way of knowing, and it didn't really matter. What did matter was the low, passion-filled purr she gave as he slid a long, tapered finger into the source of her heat.

His eyes were glittering with a need that equaled her own as she tightened and pulsed around him. "I think

you're okay,'' he whispered provocatively. "Let's see if
I can make you bloom, Jessi Rose . . .''

She felt bereft as he freed himself from her softness,
but her longing soon fled. With his hands and mouth,
he feasted his way down her damp body, touching, teasing, making her succumb to his spell all over again. On
his knees he filled his hands with her dark hips and
brought her forward. This time, she didn't muffle her
responses to his glorious plundering. As he parted her
and lingered, her cries and moans rose. In the end, it
took him only a few minutes to make her shatter and
scream loud enough to be heard in Austin.

Declaring her fit, he laid her back on the bed and there
under the sunbeams streaming through the windows,
taught her that yes, there were couples who made love
more than once a day, and how wonderful it was to be
one of those couples. He coaxed her astride him and it
was unlike any riding she'd ever done before. The position gave him access to all of a young man's toys and
she let him play and play until the world exploded again
for them both.

"This was not supposed to happen again,'' she told
him, when she could finally speak again.

"What wasn't supposed to happen?'' he asked, lying
beside her again, stroking her back softly.

"This. You and I.''

"Why not?''

"Because it wasn't. I figured, one time, then I'd be
cured.''

"And you're not.''

She looked over her shoulder at him lying there all
nude and glorious. "No.''

"Is that so bad?''

Jessi turned back. She didn't know.

"You're a passionate, vibrant woman, Jessi Clayton.
You've nothing to be ashamed of.''

"It's not the shame I'm worried about. It's the wanting you that's giving me fits."

He squeezed her behind and grinned. "Maybe it'll go away."

Jessi didn't think so. Even now, as sated and worn out as she was, the thought of him loving her again rekindled her desire. She dampened it, lest she wind up riding until Joth came home. "I'm going to wash, and this time, by myself, Griffin Blake."

"Are you sure you don't need help?"

Jessi wondered when this wanting would stop. Trying to distance herself from the man she'd begun to crave would be next to impossible. When he left, she didn't want him to take her heart too. But she reminded herself that she was supposed to be embracing Griffin's light, not talking herself into running in the opposite direction. "Maybe I do need a bit of help with my back."

His mustache lifted with pleasure. "Then step over to the tub, and I promise to be good."

She leaned over and kissed him softly. "And you are lying, lying, lying."

He just grinned.

This time, they managed to wash without winding up back on the bed. Jessi even got the opportunity to put on her clothes and keep them on. Good thing, too, because when she left the bedroom to head to the kitchen, she found a note on the table. It read: *Back in a while. Preacher.*

When Griffin read the note, he smiled. "It's good to know he's here."

He took a seat at the kitchen table and fed himself on the potatoes and bacon she'd heaped on a plate for him. "Why do you think he left?"

"He probably realized we were a mite too busy to entertain guests."

Jessi's eyes widened. "Do you think he heard us?"

Griff chuckled at the look on her face. "Probably, but he only heard you, not me. Folks probably heard you in Denver."

She swatted him on the arm. "That's not funny."

"I'm just telling you the truth," he said, and ducked away from another swat. "You are one loud woman, Jessi Rose Clayton."

"Be serious. How am I ever going to face him?"

He pulled her down onto his lap. "He's a grown man, Jessi, and he knows what grown men and women do."

"I'm still going to be embarrassed!"

"Well, don't be. He's a preacher and a gentleman. He'd never tell anyone something so private. Now, the Twins, on the other hand—"

She understood. "No need to say more."

They shared a smile.

He then asked, "Did you enjoy your holiday this morning?"

"I did. It was a day of firsts."

"Well, the day isn't over."

"No?" she asked, her eyes filled with mischief.

"Not at all."

The Preacher knocked at the door later that afternoon and Jessi let him in. Luckily, he hadn't arrived in the middle of Griffin seducing her out of her clothes, because she was already embarrassed enough. "You must be the Preacher. My name's Jessi Clayton."

He was dressed in black. propped his big gun by the door and looked around. "Pleased to meet you. Looking for Griffin Blake. Is he still here?"

"Yes, have a seat. I'll get him."

But Griffin was already on his way into the kitchen, and seeing his old friend made him smile. The two men grabbed each other in a manly hug, spent a few minutes smiling and laughing, then Griffin took a seat at the kitchen table as well.

The Preacher was an average-looking man of average height, with light brown skin. His eyes were arresting, however: green as grass and seemingly lit with an unearthly light.

"What happened to your face?" he asked Griffin.

Griffin told him everything, and just as he'd done with the Twins, he began at the beginning, with Darcy's land grab and the murder of Dexter Clayton, then brought him up to the present by ending with the events of the last few days. "I'm glad you got my wire and came so quickly."

"What wire?" Preacher asked, puzzled. "I never received a wire. I'm on my way back from Mexico. Stopped in Austin. Rosita told me you were here and I thought I'd stop by on my way up to Denver and say hello."

"Oh," was all Griffin could say.

"Rosita said the Twins were on their way here too. They arrived yet?"

"Yesterday."

"Are they still mad?"

"I think so. Neil is, at least."

"They know what I do for a living."

"That they do."

The Preacher then looked over at Jessi. "So this Darcy is making your life uneasy?"

"Yes."

"Well, I guess I can stay around for a few weeks or so," he said. "Shouldn't take any longer than that. What do you think, Griffin? Between me, you, and the Twins, we should be able to do this in a short time?"

"I'm not sure. We have to do this by the law."

"Why?"

Griff told him about the job he'd agreed to do for Judge Parker and Dixon Wildhorse.

"Is that how you got out of the penitentiary?"

"Yep, and they made me a deputy marshal to boot."

The Preacher's green eyes widened. "They made *you* a deputy marshal?"

Griffin grinned. "*And* gave me the power to appoint some help if I need it. Do you want to wear a star while you're here?"

"Sure, why not?"

"I'll give you yours when I give the Twins theirs."

Jessi and the Preacher stared.

Jessi asked, "You're going to make the Twins deputies?"

"Sure. It's no more far-fetched than me being one."

Jessi had only met the Twins briefly but knew that it was far more far-fetched. The Preacher didn't respond but he smiled and solemnly shook his head.

Like the Twins, the Preacher decided to head to town. He too wanted to sample the wind and find a room. After Jessi gave him the names of a few boardinghouses he might try, he tipped his black hat to her, shook Griffin's hand in good-bye and rode off.

"Well," Jessi said as they watched him ride off, "so that's the Preacher. He seems a bit more serious than Neil and his brother."

"I've known prairie dogs more serious than those two, but there's nobody better to guard your back. Now that all my pieces are here, we can play a little chess. We have a king, me. A queen, you. A bishop, the Preacher, and two jokers posing as knights. Not bad."

Jessi smiled at her champion king. "Not bad at all."

Chapter 8

After the Preacher's departure, Jessi and Griffin spent the rest of the day making love, talking, and enjoying each other's company. By the time dusk rolled in, he knew that Jessi's favorite food was ice cream and she knew that he had a real fondness for blueberry pie. He learned that she loved the color green; she learned he'd been kicked out of the church youth choir at age fourteen after being caught kissing the deacon's daughter.

"Really?" Jessi asked, laughing.

"Really."

They were out on the porch, enjoying the night's descent. Jessi was seated atop his lap.

"So you've always had this fondness for women?"

"Can't deny it."

Jessi wanted to ask him about this Rosita she'd been hearing about for the past two days but didn't have the nerve, mainly because she had no claims on him and therefore no right to pry. "I enjoyed my holiday, Griffin."

And she had. As she'd noted earlier, it had been a day for firsts and she wouldn't't've missed it for the world. "It was far more fun than doing the wash."

"Told you so."

She reached up and lovingly cupped his strong jaw. "Thank you," she whispered.

He turned her palms to his lips and placed a soft kiss on the palm. "You're welcome."

"Now, can I do the wash in the morning?"

He kissed her softly. "Yes, you may."

The next morning she was up drawing water when Griffin stepped onto the back porch. It was at least an hour before dawn, but she already had two cauldrons heating on the fire in the pit out in the yard.

"Morning, Jessi."

"Morning, Griff, did you sleep well?"

"Yes. How about you?"

"Just fine. I didn't wake you, did I?"

"No, but I wish you had. I had plans for you this morning."

Jessi grinned. "I would've liked that, but this is an all-day chore, even when Joth's here to help. With him gone, it's going to take even longer."

She walked over to the heating cauldrons and held her hand above them to gauge the water's temperature. "So, the sooner I get done, the sooner I get to enjoy your company. Are you going into town to check on your friends?"

"Nope. Staying here and helping you with the wash. The sooner you're done, the sooner we can play."

"That isn't necessary you know."

"It's purely selfish."

She smiled. "Well, grab the coffee and I'll meet you on the roof in a few minutes. We'll take in the sunrise and then get right to work."

As Jessi had predicted, the work took up a large portion of the day. There were sheets, denims, towels, and pillow slips. There was lye, hot water, and Texas heat. Standing over the large tin washboard, Jessi scrubbed the clothes and wiped at the sweat pouring down her neck. She had on her oldest blouse and skirt. Her few pieces of underthings were in the wash, so she had nothing on beneath. As a consequence, the blouse, wet from all the water and heat, clung to her skin, outlining her bare breasts perfectly. The bareness helped, though; if she were fully dressed, she'd've melted like her beloved ice cream.

Griffin found the sight stimulating. The old blouse had lost a few buttons in its time, and every time she bent over the washboard it added even more spice to the tempting display. As he helped her hang the items on the ropes that ran from the house to a pole in the yard, he feasted his eyes, and doubted he'd ever had this much fun on a washday.

But his glee was a tempered as the day went on and he saw how weary she'd become. Though she didn't complain, he knew her shoulders were aching from bending over the washboard, and her arms were tired as well. Her eyes were red from the lye fumes and he suddenly regretted keeping her up so late last night. Until this day, he'd never really thought about what a woman might have to do after he left her bed. Seeing Jessi made him decide to be more aware of that in the future.

At last they were done. Having pinned up the last piece of wash, Jessi came out from between the lines of flowing clothes to find Griffin pumping more water into the cauldrons. She called out, "We're done, Griffin. We don't need any more water."

He continued pumping.

As she approached, he lifted the now full container, placed it on the restoked fire, and began to fill another. "I don't know about you, but I need a bath," he told her.

"We had a bath yesterday."

"And?"

"And, I usually wait until nightfall and wash out here at the pump after washday."

"Why?"

"Because that's what I've always done."

By now the second cauldron was filled and was soon next to its twin on the grate. "Don't you think you deserve to soak off all that lye and sweat in nice hot tub, no worries, no complaints?" Griffin asked plainly.

Jessi thought about it, and yes, she found the scenario very appealing. "But it's a waste of water, Griffin."

He shook his head. Walking over to her, he gently cupped her face with both of his large hands. Staring down at her, he said quietly, "Sometimes you are too practical for your own good, Jessi Rose Clayton. Treat yourself, you've worked hard today. If I knew where I could get you some ice cream, I'd get it for you."

Her answering smile was tender.

"As your maestro, I demand that you do nothing for the rest of the day."

She opened her mouth to protest, but he cut her off.

"Nothing," he repeated. "You are going to into your room and lie down. I'll bring in the water. You will soak, and you will like it. You will then have some supper, and when the time comes you will go to bed and sleep. Do you understand?"

Jessi could see that he was quite serious. He cared about her, she realized, and she'd never had a man in her life who had before, not in the way she sensed Griffin did. Jessi had no idea what to do with the knowledge, but her heart was so full, she could feel the tears stinging her eyes.

He placed a soft kiss on her forehead. "Are we in agreement?"

"Yes, Griffin," she managed to whisper.

So once again, Jessi Rose Clayton did as she was told; she soaked in the tub and she liked it, a whole lot; she had some supper, and when the time came, she went to bed and Griffin held her cradled against him until she fell asleep.

The Twins showed up around midday, arguing over something that had to do with a casket. Jessi wasn't sure what all the fuss was about, but she followed the arguing giants into the kitchen with the hope that Griff could sort it all out.

"I was the one in the casket!"

"No, you weren't!"

As well as Jessi could figure out, one of the Twins had posed as a corpse in a casket during one of their more memorable train robberies, but it wasn't memorable enough, it seemed, because both men kept claiming to have been the corpse.

Griffin let them argue for a few more minutes, then said, "The two of you have told that same lie to so many women over the years, neither of you remembers the real story anymore."

Two Shafts folded his arms across his chest. "Meaning?"

"Meaning, *I* was the corpse in the casket that day. Neil, you don't like closed in places, and Shafts was too large to fit in the box."

Silence.

Then Neil said to Two Shafts, "I think he's right."

His brother conceded, "I think he is, too."

Jessi asked with a laugh, "You pretended to be a dead man so you could rob a train?"

"Yep, and when I pushed up the casket lid after the train left the station, the express agent took one look at me rising from the dead and fainted right there on the spot."

Jessi found the story amazing.

With the casket question now settled, Griffin asked, "Did you see Preacher while you were in town?"

Neil replied, "Yep, he bought us drinks last night. You'll be glad to know we've patched up our differences."

"I'm glad."

Two Shafts added, "He shouldn't be too far behind us on the road. He said he'd meet us here by noon."

The Preacher arrived promptly at noon. Once they were all gathered around the kitchen table, the talk immediately turned to Reed Darcy and how best to neutralize him.

Neil said, "I say we string him up. There isn't a court in the land that'll convict us for making a backshooter swing."

Secretly, a part of Jessi was all for the idea, but in her heart, she knew that tactic would make her no better than Darcy, so she said, "There's already been enough violence. I want him strung up legally."

"A man like Darcy doesn't deserve legalities, Miss Jessi," Neil pointed out.

"She's too nice, Griffin," Two Shafts told him. "How in the world did she meet an hombre like you?"

"Deputy Marshal Wildhorse."

"The Indian Territory marshal?" Two Shafts asked with surprise.

"Yep, he was the one who got me out of prison and sent me here. Made me a deputy marshal, too."

Neil laughed, "You lie so well, Cheno. No marshal in his right mind would give you a star. We weren't born last night."

"Or this morning," Two Shafts added sagely.

"And all of you are going to be deputies, too," Griffin announced, ignoring their sarcasm.

"Not me," said Two Shafts. "My ancestors will spin in their graves."

"So will mine," Neil July chimed in.

Neil leaned over to Jessi and said in a loud whisper,

"Maybe you should take him back to the doc. He was hit harder with that chair than we thought."

Jessi chuckled.

Griffin let them have their fun, then went to his bedroom to retrieve his saddlebag. Upon his return, he pulled out the extra stars. He tossed one to each of his friends, then said, "Preacher, get out your Bible."

Seemingly stunned, the twins stared first at the stars, then at Griffin.

"You're really serious, aren't you?" Two Shafts asked.

Griff nodded.

"I'm not wearing this," Neil stated flatly.

Griff countered, "Yes, you are. If I have to have one, so do you."

"The Comanche do not wear symbols of American authority," Two Shafts said.

Griffin shook his head at their antics, then to Two Shafts he commanded, "Put the damn thing on so the Preacher can read the oath."

"Oh, no," Neil July said, "I'm with Shafts, I'm not taking any oaths. I'm a Black Seminole, remember."

Watching all this, Jessi shook her head too.

The Preacher, Bible in hand, stood. "Gentlemen, stand, please."

The Preacher's stern voice seemed to settle the matter because the Twins reluctantly complied. He made each step forward in turn, place his hand on the Good Book, and repeat the oath after Griffin.

When the short ceremony ended, Two Shafts declared, "I'll wear it, but I won't like it."

"Amen," said Neil. "Amen."

The Preacher spoke up. "We should find out if there are any warrants on Darcy's men. If there are, we can rid ourselves of at least some of them first thing. I wouldn't mind going home to Denver with a little extra gold in my pocket.''

"The sheriff should have all of the latest bulletins, shouldn't he?'' Jessi asked.

Griff answered, "He should, but he's already declared which side of the road he's on. He won't give us any help if he doesn't have to.''

"Did you get to talk to anyone in town?'' Jessi asked the Twins.

"Nope, we're strangers; folks are too scared of Darcy, I'm guessing—at least for now.''

The discussion and the planning went on for most of the afternoon. At one point, Two Shafts said, "The easiest thing to do would be to make Percy confess to killing Miss Jessi's daddy. It'll be real easy to put a noose around Darcy's neck after that.''

"That's providing he did it on Darcy's orders,'' Preacher noted.

"True,'' Griffin said, "but I think we ought to make that our first job.''

"Can we play with him first?'' Neil asked.

Jessi had no idea what that meant, but Griffin laughed and said, "I don't see why not. Preacher, do you oppose our friends having a little fun?''

"As long as it isn't directed my way, I say fine.''

The Twins smiled their satisfaction.

It seemed Neil was quite an accomplished cook, and after the talk came to a close, he and his brother began bringing in barrels and sacks and bags of foodstuffs from a wagon outside. They had potatoes and corn, flour and lard. There were rashers of bacon, what appeared to be half a crate of lemons, spices, rice, sugar, and so many other items Jessi could only stare.

"I like to cook,'' Neil told her matter of factly, as he carried in a butter churn.

"And I like to eat,'' his brother chimed in with a

smile, as he entered the kitchen hauling a crate filled with cooking pans and skillets.

"Where in the world did you get all of this?" Griffin asked. He'd been on the road with the Twins before, so he was accustomed to their eccentricities, but even he was bowled over by the sheer volume of goods they were bringing in.

Neil began unpacking his pots and pans. "We got most of the food between here and Austin, the rest we got in town at the mercantile."

"Abe sold these things to you?" Jessi asked.

Neil looked up. "He wasn't supposed to?"

"Nope. It's against Darcy law to sell to anyone associated with me."

"Maybe he doesn't know yet. Either way, we have just about everything we need."

So the Terrible Twins and the Preacher made themselves at home, and when Neil asked if he could take over the kitchen duties, Jessi didn't balk. They set up a camp outside on the field behind the house with tents to shelter their bedrolls and gear. Jessi's once quiet house was now filled with supplies, booming male laughter, and the sweet, savory smells of Neil's chili cooking on the stove.

Later, a silent Jessi and Griff sat on the steps of the front porch, enjoying the beautiful night. The day had been full of surprises, and thinking back, Jessi chuckled. "I can't believe the fuss they put up over those stars."

"I can," Griff replied knowingly. "When Marshal Wildhorse gave me mine, I whined even louder. Told him boils would break out on my body if I put that star on."

Jessi looked at him. "Boils? You don't have any boils."

"That's because the thing's been in my saddlebag

since he gave it to me, but it's good to know you noticed their absence.''

His flirting answer made her smile and shake her head. ''Do you ever stop?''

The darkness hid his grin. ''Nope, and if I didn't think your screaming would wake up everybody around, I'd show you why, right here, right now . . .''

Her need for him coiled to life. ''You know, with your friends around, we won't have any privacy, and that means no more practicing for a while.''

''I know.''

''So what will we do?''

He began to nibble her ear. ''I don't know. Shoot them while they sleep, maybe?''

She chuckled softly. ''I suppose we can just wait until they're gone.''

His mouth found hers and for a moment speech was forgotten.

When the seal of their lips eased apart, he said, ''That's easier said than done. Can you hold out for a few weeks?''

She knew it was a lie, but she said, ''Yes.''

He began to laugh. ''No, you can't, Jessi Clayton.''

''If you can wait them out, so can I. In fact, it's been proven that women have far more stamina than men.''

He snorted. ''What books have you been reading? I'm willing to bet you won't last a week.''

Jessi's jaw dropped and she chuckled, ''Are you challenging me, Griffin Blake?''

''Yes, darlin', I am. One week and you'll be so full of need, you won't care who hears you screaming.''

Jessi did not believe him. ''You have had too many willing women in your life, Mr. Outlaw.''

''Probably, but I still say you can't last a week. I'm in your blood like snake bite, just like you're in mine.''

''Okay then, you're on. What're you wagering?''

Griff found her fearlessness both humorous and endearing. "Have you ever walked away from a challenge?" he asked wanting to make love to her in spite of the presence of his friends.

"No," she replied. "What's the wager?"

Amused, he shook his head. "It doesn't matter because you're going to lose."

She leaned over and kissed him slowly and passionately. When she eased away she whispered. "No, I'm not."

Grinning, he slid his hand up to her soft, short hair and brought her back to his lips. His lingering fiery kiss filled her with such heat, she melted as if made of wax. When he finally turned her loose, he told her in a hushed voice, "Yes, you are."

A still spiraling Jessi wanted to retort but couldn't find the will.

"I'll see you later," he said rising. The smile on his handsome face said it all. "Let me know what you're planning on wagering."

He left her and disappeared around the side of the house.

In the back, a whistling Griffin found the Preacher sitting outside of his tent reading a Bible by lantern light. The Twins were out scouting the perimeter for varmints.

"Mind if I sit?" Griffin asked. He wondered if Jessi was still sitting on the porch.

"Not a bit." Preacher closed his Bible and gestured for Griffin to take a seat. He studied Griff for a moment. "You really do care about her, don't you?"

Surprised a bit by the question, Griffin asked, "You weren't spying on me, were you, old man?"

"No," Preacher replied with a soft chuckle. In reality, Preacher was less than a decade older than Griff, but Griff always insisted on pointing out the age difference whenever they were together.

Preacher added, "Just noticed the way you been watching her since we got here, is all."

"I do care for her, and I'm as surprised about it as anybody. Never been attracted to an older woman before."

"Sometimes they make the best kind."

"So I'm finding." Griff rubbed the back of his neck. "I always thought that *if* I settled down, it would be with a young one."

"Both life and love are unexplainable."

"Do you think I'm in love?" Griff asked.

"Doesn't matter what I think. What do you think?"

"Maybe. Hell, probably, but I know she thinks she's just another notch on the bedpost."

"And she's not?"

"Nope."

"What do you propose to do?"

"Find out a way to convince her she's wrong."

"I'll lend a hand whenever I can."

"I'd appreciate it. I really would."

There was a brief silence.

"Do you think this Darcy thing can be fixed?" Preacher asked.

"I do."

"Then I'll be here for as long as you need me."

"I appreciate that, too."

As Jessi lay in bed that night, she smiled thinking back on Griffin. Although she'd never admit it, his kiss on the porch had left her senseless. She couldn't last a few days without his lovemaking, let alone a week. In fact, she wished he were here holding her right now. Deciding it might be best to turn her mind elsewhere, her thoughts moved to Joth. Her desires for Griffin notwithstanding, she missed her nephew's smiling face and hoped he was having a grand time. Closing her eyes, she sent him a little prayer, then turned over and tried to go to sleep.

An hour or so later, the sound of her door being slowly opened awakened her. Turning to the sound, she tensed then relaxed upon seeing Griffin tipping into the room. Pleased that he'd answered her call, she sat up in the dark and asked softly, "Did you come to lose the bet?"

"Nope, came to keep you warm," he answered as he closed the door soundlessly. He had on one of her father's robes.

It was warm muggy night and they both knew it, but a delighted Jessi replied, "It is a bit chilly in here."

"You don't mind me wearing this do you?" he asked indicating the robe as he discarded it.

"No, I—"

He stood before her as nude and as beautiful as a Yoruban god. Whatever else she'd been about to say was forgotten as her desire unfurled in heated response.

She moved over so he could join her beneath the thin sheet and Jessi fit herself back against his bare chest and thighs. The feel of him surrounding her made her want to purr.

"I didn't like sleeping alone," he confessed.

"Neither did I." Having him in bed beside her seemed natural, right. Content, she told him, "You know this does mean you lose."

He whispered against her ear, "How so?" He began to slide his hand over the rise of her nightown covered hip. "I just came to sleep."

As the lazy caress began to roam further, she replied, "That doesn't feel like sleep to me. I think you're trying to make *me* lose."

"Me?" he asked innocently.

His hand moved to her breast and slowly began to awaken her nipple. Jessie husked out, "Yes, you."

He kissed the edge of her neck, "I'm here to sleep, nothing more."

He was now undoing the buttons on the front of her gown. When he'd opened them to his satisfaction, his seductive play made her arch sensually.

"I'm just helping you relax. Where's all this stamina you were bragging about?"

He slid her nightgown above her hips, then his warm, strong hands proceeded to relax her until her soft gasps rose in the silence.

Still playing with her, he teased his mustached lips across her ear. "Sleepy yet?"

"You're incorrigible," she pointed out breathlessly.

"And you feel like silk," he replied thickly.

His hands were magic and she was captured by his spell.

"I suppose I'm not playing fair, am I?" he asked.

"No, you're not," came her hushed reply.

"Okay," he said then, "I'll let you go to sleep before you lose the bet."

"I'm not going to lose." It was a lie. In a few more moments she wasn't going to give a damn about a bet.

But true to his word, he righted her clothes, much to her disappointment.

Leaning above her, he looked down into her night shrouded eyes. "Better now?" he asked teasingly.

"Incorrigible man."

He kissed her soundly then held her against him until sleep claimed them both.

The new Clayton clan went into town the next morning, and as they rode down the center of the main street, everyone on the walks and in the shop doorways stopped and stared. In the ensuing silence, only the horses' steps could be heard. No one taunted Jessi with ugly names. No one said a word.

"Awfully quiet," Preacher said, as he rode slowly at Griffin's side.

"That it is," Griffin replied, eyes cold. He wondered where the folks were who'd yelled out whore on the last visit. Were they too afraid now? Griff hoped so because he planned on taking on the first one who had anything vile to say about Jessi, and he doubted the Twins would show any restraint or mercy, either.

The Darcy Hotel came into view and as they rode by the large white structure, Griff was pleased to see the wood nailed over the shattered glass. He spotted Minerva and Roscoe standing out front by their carriage on the edge of the street, but Griffin spared them hardly a glance.

The Clayton party stopped first at the sheriff's office. Hatcher wasn't pleased to see them. "What do you want, Blake?"

"Good morning to you too, Sheriff Hatcher. These are my friends: Neil July, his brother Two Shafts, and Vance Bigelow. You may know Vance as the Preacher."

Hatcher stilled. "The bounty hunter?"

Preacher tipped his black hat. "One and the same. Pleased to meet you, Sheriff."

Watching from the doorway, Jessi thought Hatcher seemed even less pleased now.

"What do you want?"

"To see your Wanted posters," Griffin said, "and before you say no, we are here in an official capacity. All of my friends are deputies, too."

Hatcher's jaw tightened. He yanked open a drawer in his desk, reached in, and pulled out a fat stack of posters. He tossed the stack on the desk top. "Here, help yourself," he told them tightly.

Griffin said, "Jessi, come and take a look, you'd know the faces."

Jessi didn't recognize anyone in the first five or six

that she glanced at. The men were of all races and were wanted for everything from bootlegging to murder. There were a few women, too, and one face vaguely rang a bell. "You know, if this woman weighed about thirty or forty pounds less and changed her hair, this could be Minerva Darcy."

Griffin studied the face. He didn't see the resemblance. "I don't know, Jessi, I think you're grasping at straws on that one."

Jessi shrugged, but went ahead and read the bulletin anyway. The woman's name was Eula Grimes. *Rhymes with crimes,* Jessi thought to herself. Eula was wanted in St. Louis for embezzlement, in Kansas City for counterfeiting, and in Denver for embezzlement and arson. The two embezzlement charges were for marrying men and then disappearing after the wedding. In both cases substantial amounts of money had vanished with her. Jessi still thought she resembled Minerva in an odd sort of way, but Griffin was probably right, she was just grasping at straws.

The faces on the rest of the warrants weren't familiar at all.

"Well, I guess that's that. None of Darcy's men are wanted," Neil noted, his voice tinted with disappointment.

The sheriff chuckled, "Is that what you were looking for?"

Griff nodded gravely.

"Reed Darcy is smart. Do you think he would be stupid enough to hire wanted men?"

"He's stupid enough to hire a scalp-lock like Percy West," Griff tossed back.

"And stupid enough to think I'm going to marry him," Jessi cracked.

By the shocked looks on the faces of the Twins and

the Preacher, Jessi assumed Griffin hadn't told them that part of the story.

Hatcher told Jessi, "If you did, all of these problems would go away."

"No, thank you. I've been to hell once. I promised I'd never go back." She turned to her men. "Are we done here?"

"I think so," Griffin said, noting how hard and cold Jessi's eyes appeared. He knew without asking that the hell she'd referred to had been her time with Calico Bob. "So, Sheriff, are you going to start honoring your badge?"

"What do you know about honor?" he asked caustically. "When you give up everything you have and possess for the one you love and have her die in your arms, then you can judge my character."

Griffin did not back down. "I've already walked in those boots, Hatcher. A woman I loved more than life died in my arms when I was ten years old. I dug her grave with my bare hands. You and I are a lot more alike than you know."

That said, he then followed Jessi and his friends out the door.

Jessi made them stop a moment at Gillie's millinery shop so she could make sure it was still locked up tight. Jessi peered through the windows to see if anything were amiss inside, but everything appeared fine.

"Where to next?" Griffin asked Jessi.

"Since our trip to see Hatcher didn't unearth anything, I suppose we can head back."

Griff polled the Twins and Preacher. Preacher saw no reason to stay, but Two Shafts did. "I need some cartridges. What about the mercantile? Do you think the owner will sell me any, now that everyone knows who we are?"

Jessi said, "I doubt it, but we can always go in and see."

People were still standing and staring as Jessi and her men moved down the walk. Once again, Jessi Rose Clayton had become the talk of the town, but as always, she didn't care.

The knot of people standing in front of Abe's door skittered out of the way as Jessi and the men made their approach.

Neil July cracked sarcastically, "Nothing like scaring a town full of people to start your day."

"Behave yourself, little brother," Two Shafts warned.

"Yes, mother," his brother shot back, grinning.

Inside the store, the obviously terrified Abe Thomas stood behind the counter with a pasted-on smile. "You boys aren't here to rob me, are you?"

"No, Abe, they're not," Jessi said. "They're just here to buy."

He cast a quick look out of the door. "Uh, now, Miss Jessi, you know I can't—"

Griff tossed a box of cartridges on the counter. "Morning, Abe. How are you?"

Abe's eyes widened. He stammered, "Uh—uh—"

Percy West entered the store, flanked by three of his men, and announced, "What he's trying to say is, he doesn't do business with the likes of you. Mr. Darcy's orders."

It was quite obvious that Percy had been in a fight. Although Griffin's face still sported bruises, and the swelling around his left eye had turned a bright, reddish purple, West looked like he'd been wrestling with a bear. His lip was split, both eyes were discolored, and his jaw bore the marks of having been hit by many mighty fists.

Preacher was at the far end of the store, looking at chaps. Ignoring West, he held up a pair, looked them over critically, then walked them over to the counter. "I'll have these. How much?"

Over on the other side of the store Jessi could hear the Terrible Twins engaged in what sounded like an argument. Neil July was saying, "I'll bet you ten dollars you can't do it."

Two Shafts was weighing the heft of a big bullwhip. "I'll take that bet." He then turned to West standing a few feet away and said, "My brother's betting I can't take that gun out of your holster with this. I say I can. Hold still."

Before West or anyone else could react, the whip uncoiled like a blast of lightning and snaked not around Percy's gun but around his right ankle. Shafts gave the snake a hard yank and a blink later Percy was flat on his face on the floor. Jessi stood there stunned as did the onlookers peeking in the doorway.

Two Shafts turned to his brother and volunteered in mock sheepishness, "I guess I'm more out of practice than I thought. Are you okay, Percy?" he asked, recoiling the big whip and placing it back where he'd found it initially.

West, hand against his busted and bleeding nose, looked absolutely furious as he struggled to his feet.

Griffin passed him on his way back to the counter and said, "*That's* why we don't take them out much." He then paused a moment to survey the damage to West's nose and advised him sagely, "You really ought to have a doc look at that."

Jessi stood there trying not to laught out loud. Was this the kind of fun the Twins had been talking about? If so, she certainly enjoyed their brand of humor, although she doubted West would agree.

It's hard to be intimidating when you're bleeding like a stuck pig, but West tried his best. Jessi assumed he was voicing some sort of threat, but due to his injury

and the hand covering it, she couldn't understand a word
he was saying and evidently no one else could either
because Preacher looked back at West and said, "Speak
up, man, we can't understand a word. Two Shafts, apologize again. Maybe that's what he's babbling about."

"I'm sorry, Percy. I'll get it right next time."

West's eyes widened visibly. He didn't look to be
wanting a next time. Shooting them all malevolent looks,
he left, taking his stunned companions with him.

A grinning Griff turned back to Abe. "Now, as I was
saying, how much for the cartridges?"

"Darcy will burn me out."

"No, he won't," Neil July assured the shopkeeper, as
he fished some penny candy out of a glass jar. He
popped a jaw breaker in his mouth and said, "Mr. Darcy
doesn't want to tangle with us. He likes living too
much."

Abe looked to Jessi. She could only shrug in reply.
Abe was going to have to make up his own mind. He
could stand and fight, or he could continue to cower
behind his fear.

"Okay," he finally said, "I'll sell you what you want
today, but that's as far as I go."

Griff nodded.

Abe added, "And you'll have to give me your word
that you boys will back me if Darcy finds out."

Griffin said, "Just let us know."

Their shopping now completed, the Clayton gang
mounted up and headed their horses back up the street.
In town the whispering and the speculating began as
soon as Jessi and her hands rode away.

The next morning, Jessi awakened at dawn to the
smell of bacon frying. In the kitchen she found Neil July
alone at the cast-iron wood-burning stove. As Jessi came
closer to the stove, she saw that there were biscuits al-

ready baked and waiting, coffee brewing, and eggs sitting in a bowl. Since she distinctly remembered him using all the eggs on hand yesterday, she asked him about them.

"My brother found some this morning," he explained, as he began cracking the dozen or so white orbs into the bowl.

Jessi dearly wanted to know if "found" meant the eggs had been purloined from the coops of her neighbors, but she thought it best not to ask.

"Shafts said the lady was real nice."

"Yep, she sure was," Two Shafts concurred, coming in from the back porch. "I bought them with the gold Cheno gave us. She said her name was Mrs. Cornell. She also said to tell you hello."

Jessi stared. "You bought those eggs from Lydia Cornell, and she told you to tell *me* hello?"

Jessi could see the Twins staring at her, but for a moment she was speechless. Griffin's gold notwithstanding, Lydia Cornell would rather be naked in the front pew of the Vale A.M.E. Church than speak to Jessi. "Are you sure she said her name was Cornell?"

"Yes. You look like you don't believe me."

"I believe you, I just don't believe Lydia Cornell. She'd rather eat raw pig's feet than say anything to me."

"Well, she was real cheerful."

"Was she drunk?"

"Didn't smell any liquor on her."

Jessi had no way to explain Lydia's actions and wondered what in the world had come over the gossipy woman.

Jessi was still trying to figure it out when Griff and Preacher entered the kitchen and said their good mornings. Her mind still churning, she gave them a mumbled reply. She didn't notice how quiet the kitchen had become until she heard Griff call to her.

When she looked his way in answer, she saw that all the men were standing around the table waiting, for what she had no idea.

"We're waiting on you, boss," Griff explained. "Neil hates it when his food's served cold."

"Oh, I'm sorry. My apologies, Neil."

She hastened over to the table. "You could've started without me."

"No, we couldn't've." Preacher declared. "Where I was raised, the lady sits first."

Jessi almost told him that she wasn't a lady, but since they were all waiting so patiently for her to take her seat, she kept her sarcasm to herself and sat.

After the Preacher blessed the food, everyone dug in. They were the most polite bunch of outlaws she'd ever shared a meal with. They said please and thank you, didn't curse, and didn't scratch. She was all but certain their manners weren't this stellar all the time, but she found it oddly pleasing, knowing they were on their best behavior just for her.

By the time afternoon rolled around, the pleasure had turned into a serious case of irritation. She hadn't minded them opening the door for her each time she needed to go out or apologizing when a curse flamed the air, or even when Griff volunteered to take on her stable chores, but when Two Shafts refused to let her carry her own saddle the few feet from her mount to the porch, she'd had it. Finding Griffin still in the barn, she told him firmly, "I can carry my own saddle."

Setting aside the pitchfork in response to her whirl-wind entrance, Griffin, having no idea what she was fuming about, asked, "Does this have anything to do with my making love to you?"

"What?" Jessi asked, baffled. "No, Griffin it does not."

"That's too bad. Well, go on, then."

She shook her head, wondering where all of her steam had gone. "Are you sure?"

"I sure as hell do want to make love to you."

Just a look from his eyes could call up her passion. "You are incorrigible, but then, you're well aware of that."

"Yep."

The lie Jessi told about being able to keep a lid on her desire until the Twins and Preacher departed had been just that, a lie. They hadn't made love since his friends moved in and it already felt as though she and Griffin hadn't been intimate for months. It also seemed as if her need for him grew stronger with each new sunrise. Who knew that she would want him every hour of every day or long to sneak into his bed at night and let herself be filled with his passion.

Griff had been spending the last few days wondering if she'd marry him. Not only did he not want to sleep without her, he didn't want to live without her. He decided he most definitely was in love and had a hard time seeing a future that did not contain her and Joth. He didn't know what her response would be, but he needed this rawhide woman to make him complete and hoped she shared his feelings. "Marry me, Jessi."

Confusion spread across her face. She searched his eyes, then thinking this was another of his jokes, she began to laugh.

She laughed so hard she had tears in her eyes before she realized she was laughing alone. The pain on his face stopped her heart. "Oh, Griffin, darling, you're serious? Griffin, I'm sorry."

But it was too late, he was already striding out of the barn door.

"Griffin!"

Shit! She cursed herself soundly as she took off at a run after him, but by the time she got outside and looked around, he'd grabbed the first available mount and was heading up the road. "Griffin!"

He did not look back. Dejected, she sank to the porch step and sighed.

"Where's he going with my horse?" Two Shafts asked, running out of the house.

A desolate Jessi didn't reply because she had no idea where he was going or if he would return.

The Comanche looked out at the fast-moving horse and said, "If he runs that pony into a gopher hole, I'll kill him with my bare hands."

Neil stepped out onto the porch. "Where's Cheno going? He's riding like he's got fifteen Pinkertons on his back."

"No idea," his brother replied irritatedly, "but that's my mount he's on."

Jessi remained silent.

Neil looked down into Jessi's stricken face. "Something wrong, Miss Clayton?"

"Yes," she answered, then got up and went back to the barn to finish up the work still to do.

Preacher and Neil sought her out in the barn an hour or so later. "He isn't back," Neil reported.

Jessi didn't like how that made her feel. She focused herself on pitching hay into Buttercup's empty stall instead.

"You want to tell us what happened?" Preacher asked.

"No."

"Lover's quarrel, I assume," Neil replied.

Silence.

"We know Griffin as well as anyone, so if you need advice, we're the ones to ask."

Jessi dearly wanted to talk to someone about this whole thing, but she didn't know either of them well enough to trust them with her feelings. "Thank you, but it's between me and Griffin."

Neil said softly, "Maybe if he were here it would be, but he isn't."

And it's all your fault, her inner voice scolded angrily.

Jessi stopped her pitching. Both men looked so sincerely concerned she felt compelled to bare her soul. "He asked me to marry him."

Neil's eyes widened. "Griffin Blake?"

"Yes."

"And you said no," the Preacher stated.

"I didn't say no, I was too busy laughing."

Neil's eyes widened even further. "You laughed?"

The despair returned. "I laughed." Coming to her own defense, she added, "But I thought he was just teasing. You know how he is."

"But you laughed?"

Jessi nodded solemnly.

Then Neil began to laugh and laugh and laugh. He laughed so loud and long, Jessi thought he was in the throes of a fit. She should've known better than to confide in him.

As he wiped away the tears, he bowed to her and said, "Miss Jessi, you are truly a rare jewel. Women have fought in the streets over his favors—they've betrayed their husbands—and the very first time he asks a real woman to marry him, she laughs in his face."

"It wasn't intentional."

"I believe you, but this calls for a celebration. Do you have any idea how many women I have lost to him over the years?"

"No, I don't." And she was quite certain she didn't want to know.

"Well, suffice it to say, he has been a thorn in my side for quite some time."

"You'll have to promise me not to say anything to him about it."

This time he balked. "Aw, Miss Clayton—"

"Please."

"He wouldn't be so considerate of me," Neil grumbled.

"Promise me."

She could see by his handsome face that he didn't want to, but she was determined.

"Preacher, do you have your Bible?" she asked.

"It's in my tent."

"Swear to me, Neil," Jessi said firmly.

"What's he swearing on?" Two Shafts asked, as he came into the barn.

Jessi wondered if the day could get any worse.

Neil replied, "I'm swearing not to tell anybody about Griff asking Miss Jessi to marry him."

It could.

An incredulous and outdone Jessi stared at him. He'd betrayed her confidence already, then he actually had the nerve to wink at her.

"Hot damn," Two Shafts yelled. "Give me my money. I told you he was in love with her."

Upon hearing this, a thunderstruck Jessi watched a disappointed Neil slap two gold coins onto his grinning brother's outstretched palm. "Did she say yes?"

"Nope. She laughed at him," Preacher explained.

"It wasn't intentional," Jessi told them all firmly.

"No wonder he rode out of here like a bat out of hell," Shafts said with a chuckle. "Never heard of a woman telling him no like that. Actually, never had a woman tell him no."

"You'll have to swear not to say anything to him about this!"

He looked at Jessi as if she were loco. "And miss

this opportunity to tease Don Juan? I'm sorry, Miss Jessi. Can't do it.''

Jessi looked over at the Preacher. He must've seen the plea in her eyes, because he walked out of the barn only to return moments later with his Bible. All he said was, ''Boys, gather round.''

With the Preacher's help, Jessi swore them all to a reluctant silence.

''So where do you think he went?'' Two Shafts asked, after the Preacher closed the book.

Jessi told them the truth. ''I have no idea.'' But she dearly wished he would return, so the whole incident could be sorted out and she could make amends.

But he didn't return for supper. By nightfall she was both anxious and worried. She knew he could take care of himself, but she wondered if he were gone for good.

Griffin set his bedroll down on the ground and prepared to spend the night under the stars. Jessi's reaction to his proposal still hurt like hell. He'd never had a woman laugh in his face. Ever. As much as he hated to admit it, he still loved her, still wanted her in his life, even though she'd made it quite clear she didn't share his feelings. He had no idea what to do. His friends would probably laugh themselves sick if they ever found out about this, and well they should, he supposed. After all, he had a reputation for being irresistible, and they'd all lost more than a few women to him over the years.

With his arms behind his head, Griff looked up at the stars. Even though the sting in his heart hadn't faded, he wondered how he could convince her to change her mind. Being around her had him thinking about his future, something he'd never done before. An outlaw most of his adult life, he hadn't needed a future—giving the railroads hell had been all he'd needed. Now, something inside of him seemed to want change, roots, stability.

Growing parts of him wanted to be by her side so he could help her get the ranch back on its feet and watch Joth grow into a man. Sampling *señoritas* and robbing trains were no longer the sole focus of his life, and he'd no idea when the change had come about. Yes, he did, he told himself. He began to change the very first night he saw her up on the roof with that rifle, only he hadn't known it until now. Did this mean he was growing up? he wondered.

So, what to do? He could still see the desire in her eyes, there'd been no masking that. How could he woo his rawhide woman and be successful? Had he not been so undone by her laughter, maybe he'd've opted to stay and talk instead of hightailing it out of there. As he replayed the whole scene, he heard her say something that he'd been too angry to hear at the time: she'd called him *darling!* He sat straight up, then went over in his mind those last few seconds with her again, and dammit if he wasn't right. Jessi Rose Clayton had indeed called him darling. That meant she cared. Jessi was not the type to throw around words she didn't mean. It also meant there was hope. His confidence back, Griff smiled and turned over to go to sleep.

That night he dreamt about a big hand-carved bed, and atop that bed, he and Jessi were making love as if neither of them could get enough. There'd been bandages wrapped about his chest for some reason, but he was paying more attention to the sweet, willing Jessi, riding hotly astride his heat, than to the dream-induced injury.

He awakened at dawn, hard with desire and resonating with the memory of her riding him so wantonly atop that big hand-carved bed. Gathering his gear, he mounted the pony and headed back to the ranch. He now knew what to do.

Jessi couldn't lie to herself. The sight of Griffin riding

up to the porch made her heart sing. He dismounted and removed his gear from the saddle.

He nodded at her. "Morning, Jessi."

"Good morning, Griffin."

Jessi felt as if he'd been away for months, instead of overnight. She thought it best to get this over with. She walked over to him. "I laughed because I thought you were teasing."

"I wasn't."

"I know that now," she said, taking in the seriousness in his eyes. What would she do without this man in her life, she wanted to know. Surely he hadn't been around long enough for a sensible woman like herself to become attached so strongly, yet his absence had kept her awake most of the night, worrying and wondering. "I'm sorry."

"Apology accepted," he replied genuinely.

Jessi still found it hard to believe he'd proposed. She was all but certain that in spite of any pledges his heart might make, the urge to move on would call to him one day and he'd be gone with the sunrise, leaving her with a broken heart. "Griffin, I'm flattered by the proposal, but I don't think marriage between us is a good idea."

"Why?"

"You're very easygoing and I'm—" She searched for a word to describe herself.

"Tough? Prickly?"

She narrowed her eyes, not sure if he was poking fun. She said, "I suppose I can accept that, but most men don't want their wives to be tough."

"I'm not most men, Jessi Rose . . ."

The power behind his words singed her senses. "I can't give you children."

"I'm not asking you to marry me for your childbearing. We have Joth."

That made her heart sing.

"Are you afraid?" he asked.

"Yes," she confessed. "I'm afraid of the past and the future."

Griffin could see the truth in her eyes.

He reached out and stroked her cheek. "There is nothing in your life we can't discuss, so when you're ready, I'll be here."

She looked away so he wouldn't see the tears standing in her eyes. He coaxed her chin back around, kissed her on the forehead, then went inside.

Chapter 9

Later that afternoon, Sheriff Hatcher rode up to the Clayton place. Jessi's eyes were emotionless as she stepped out onto the porch. "Yes?" she asked simply.

"I need to talk to you, if I might," he requested quietly.

His tone gave her pause and she looked him over. For the first time in a long while, there was no crabbiness or anger in his face. He had his hat in his hand and he seemed pensive, reflective.

Jessi nodded. "Go ahead."

"Today's Betsy's birthday. Had she lived, my beautiful bride would have been sixty-one."

He went silent for a moment, then turned his gaze on the horizon as if there were something out there only he could see. "She loved you a lot, Jessi Rose."

Jessi couldn't deny that. "She loved you very much too, Cap."

"I miss her."

Jessi did too. His late wife, Betsy Hatcher, had been both a special lady and a treasured family friend. In addition to being one of the few women who'd been kind to Violet Clayton when she first came to Vale to be Dexter's bride, Betsy did her best to step into Jessi's and

Mildred's lives after the accident had claimed Violet's life. When Betsy first became sick a few years back, Jessi had done all she could to help in an effort to show her how much she cared and to repay her for the many kindnesses, but she'd died in pain.

"My Betsy was a fighter," Hatcher was saying now. "In that way you and she were a lot alike. I guess that's why the two of you got on so well."

Silence came between them again, then Hatcher said, "She'd be proud of the way you've been fighting Reed. Dex would be too."

"This land may be the only thing I can pass on to Joth. It has to stand."

He confessed softly, "When they told me Dex was dead and how he died, I felt like my guts had been cut out."

Jessi's pain awakened once more.

"Forgive me for not standing beside you, Jessi Rose," he whispered raggedly. "I was a foolish and scared old man. I let you down, I let Betsy down, and more important, Dex Clayton was my best friend in life and I let him down too."

In spite of the chasm now separating them, Jessi couldn't hate this man. How could she? She'd known him her entire life; he'd helped raise her. Under his easy-going tutelage, she learned to ride, fish, hunt; how to properly pitch horseshoes and to throw a good punch. Her father hadn't come to Violet's funeral, so Cap Hatcher had stood beside Jessi and held her thirteen-year-old hand when they'd lowered her mama into the ground.

"When you were born, Jessi, your pa might've been disappointed, but your mother, Betsy, and me, we were proud. Real proud. Betsy and I couldn't have children, so you were our Baby Jessi Rose, and the bigger you grew the prouder we got. You were smart, brave, beautiful.''

Jessi felt the sting of tears.

He looked out toward the road again as if the memories were there. ''I'm going to get a good cussing when I see Betsy again because of the way I deserted you. I was scared, can you understand that—scared and lonely and alone. When things around here starting going wrong, it all happened so fast, then when Darcy told me if I interfered and tried to arrest someone, he'd replace me, cut me off, I had to look the other way because Betsy needed those treatments and the medicine.''

Jessi knew that watching Betsy die so slowly and in such agony had torn him apart.

He reached into his pocket and withdrew a folded square of paper. ''So here, take this.''

Jessi stepped down and took the offering. ''What is it?''

''Take a look.''

She unfolded the square and saw it was the Wanted poster they'd talked about that day in town, the one featuring Eula Grimes. She looked up, puzzled. ''Why are you giving me this?''

''Because I believe that's Minerva Darcy.''

Jessi's eyes widened.

''I locked up a drifter about a year ago for being drunk and disorderly over at Auntie's. As I was hauling him to the caboose, we passed Minerva and Roscoe going into the hotel. The drunk looked at her and stopped.''

''Did he say anything?''

''Yep. He was drunk, mind you, but he said, 'Eula! Last time I saw you was in Kansas City. What the hell are you doing here? That your new pigeon?' and Jessi Rose, she turned white as a sheet.''

''What did she say?''

"Told him he had her confused with someone else, then told me I should do something about all the drunks in town. Then she and Roscoe went on inside the hotel and I threw the drunk in jail."

Jessi mulled over this startling news for a moment, then asked, "What happened to the drunk?"

"Early that next morning, one of the Darcy hands came in, saying he'd heard his cousin was in town and in jail. He paid the man's fine and the drifter left Vale right after that. I didn't pay much attention to any of it until that bulletin came in about a month later. I believe she was the one who paid that fine."

Jessi looked at the face again. Could this really be Minerva Darcy? "Are you sure about her reaction to him?"

"Granted, it was dark, but when we met up with Minerva and Roscoe, we were right by those big lamps Reed has out on the front of the hotel, so I saw her face real plain. She knew him, and seeing him scared her stiff."

Interesting, Jessi thought to herself. "Why tell me this now?" she asked warily.

"Because I can't live with myself anymore," he confessed plainly. "I want Reed Darcy to fry in his own grease."

Jessi studied him silently.

"I've been holding on to that poster hoping I'd find a way to use it against him somehow, but so far nothing. Maybe you and your man can."

If Eula Grimes were really pretending to be Minerva Darcy, did Reed or Roscoe know about the charade? She'd have to talk this over with Griff and the others when they returned. This might be very important to Hanging Judge Parker's investigation. "Thank you," she told him genuinely.

Hatcher nodded. "You're welcome, and just so you'll

know, I'm leaving Vale for good in a few days. My widowed sister has a place up near Dallas and I think I want to live out my last years up there with her. Too many painful memories here, especially the ones I'm responsible for.''

Now that they were struggling to close the distance between them, he was leaving. Jessi wanted him to stay. "But you've lived your whole life here.''

"And buried my wife here, had my best friend die here, and turned my back on someone I would've loved to have called daughter. It's time.'' He then looked at her and said, "You just keep on fighting him, Jessi Rose; don't ever give up. Not like I did.''

She nodded, saddened because of the memories they shared and by the hands life had dealt them both.

"Is that cocky man of yours here?''

Jessi smiled. "No, and he and the others are out on an errand, said they'd be back before supper.''

"Well, tell him I said thanks for that lecture the other day, and to give Reed a fit or two for me.''

Hatcher reached into his shirt pocket and withdrew his star. "Give him this too, will you? He's right, I shouldn't be wearing it.''

Jessi took the tarnished shield and slid it into the pocket of her skirt.

Having been taught by the Good Book that forgiveness frees the soul, Jessi went to him and let herself be engulfed by the hug of the lonely old man who before he lost his way had given her nothing but patience, guidance, and love. She returned that hug fiercely; she couldn't hate him, not after this. "Good-bye, Uncle Cap.''

Casper Hatcher whispered with tears in his eyes, "Never thought I'd ever hear you call me that again.''

Jessi smiled, her eyes just as full as his.

"We can't bring Dex back, so let's go forward.''

After she watched him ride away, she went into the house and sat in silence. She knew her relationship with Casper Hatcher would never be the same, but deep down in her heart she would miss him because he'd once been an important part of her life.

Griff and his friends came back with a buckboard piled high with new lumber. Curious, Jessi stepped off the porch to investigate. Griffin hopped down off the seat. "Did you miss us?" he asked grinning.

"I'm not sure. I'd forgotten just how quiet my house used to be."

His mustache framed his smile. "I think that's a no, men," he said to the others.

Amused, she gestured at the wagon. "What are you going to do with all of this lumber?"

"Didn't you say you wanted the roof fixed?" he asked, as they began unloading the wagon. "Put it next to the barn," he told the Twins and the Preacher.

"Well, yes, but I didn't expect—"

"Always expect, Jessi Rose. If I can manage it, you can have it."

His words left her speechless.

Jessi just stood there looking at him, his words resonating inside her head like an echo in a canyon.

She stood there so long, he chided gently, "Darlin', either grab some wood or get out of the way."

Jessi shook herself free of his dazzling smile and grabbed a board.

The unloading took a while and during one of the trips to the barn, Jessi asked Griffin, "Where'd you find lumber?"

"Mill owned by a gentleman named Garland Findley."

Jessi stopped. "Garland Findley?"

"Yeah. He was a friendly enough fellow."

Jessi set the armful of wood by the barn with the rest. "Garland Findley is one of Darcy's close friends. You'd have to flip a coin to determine who's the greediest."

Two Shafts echoed Griffin. "Seemed nice enough to me too."

Jessi didn't understand: first Lydia Cornell and her eggs, and now the lumber man Findley. What in the world had come over them? Since when did folks start defying Darcy law? She was certain Findley knew who Griffin and his friends were. "Did you threaten him?" she asked.

"No," Griffin answered, chuckling. "Told him who we were and what we wanted and he seemed eager to help."

No, Jessi certainly didn't understand this.

After the wood and its accompanying paraphernalia, such as nails and hammers, had been unloaded, they all retired to the kitchen. They refreshed themselves with cups of Neil's lemonade and while he went about dinner, she told them about the sheriff's visit. Griff immediately asked to see the Wanted poster. She passed it to him.

Griffin studied it. "He really thinks this might be Minerva?"

"Yep."

Two Shafts took the bulletin from Griffin's hand and scanned the face. "Too bad we don't know who the drifter was."

Preacher added, "Or where he is now."

Jessi said, "I'd like to call her Eula and see if she turns around."

Griffin shrugged. "Might work. Sometimes it's the little things that give people away."

Neil said, "That's true. Remember that greenhorn Pinkerton that tried to pass himself off as an outlaw back when Rosita owned that saloon up near Denver?"

Two Shafts began to laugh, "The one with the Bloomingdale boots!"

"That's him."

Preacher laughed too. "Bloomingdale boots?"

Griffin joined in. "Yeah. We're in the saloon and this kid comes over and says he wants to join the gang. Starts bragging about the outlaws he knows, how many trains he's robbed. We don't believe him of course, because *we* were the ones who'd done one of the jobs he was taking credit for."

Neil slid a pan of biscuits into the oven then took up the tale. "We figured he was either a Pinkerton or a cinder dick not only because of his lies, but because of his boots."

Preacher asked, "What was wrong with his boots?"

"They were brand spanking new, not a speck of dirt on them."

Neil said, "When Shafts admired them and asked him where he got them, the fool boy said, 'Bloomingdale Brothers'."

Two Shafts began to laugh again. "And Miss Jessi, you should've seen his face. The moment those words came out of his mouth he knew the jig was up."

"What happened next?" Jessi asked, thoroughly amused.

"We took him outside, hauled him over to the train depot, and hung him up on the water tower. When he finally managed to get himself down, he took the very next train out of town."

Jessi smiled. Any fool would know that folks out here didn't order boots from the New York–based Bloomingdale Brothers. Abe Thomas's store had one of the big back east store's catalogs and you could order everything from fashions to dry goods to housewares. However, folks out here ordered their boots from places like

Justin's, one of Texas's premier boot makers because they made boots to last.

Neil came and took a seat at the table while he waited for his biscuits to bake. "What I don't understand is why'd the sheriff change his mind?"

Jessi replied, "Guilt, mostly—that, and what Griffin said to him about his mother's dying as we were leaving. It touched a chord in him, I believe."

Preacher quoted, "*In my distress I cried unto the Lord and he heard me.*"

"Psalm one hundred and twenty," Griffin said solemnly.

Preacher smiled. "I'm impressed."

"My mother loved the psalms."

Jessi was also impressed and moved. She remembered that the only keepsake of his mother he possessed was her Bible.

Two Shafts had a question. "Well, let's suppose this really is Minerva Darcy. Do you think her husband knows about her past?"

Jessi shrugged. "It's hard to tell. Everybody in town is whispering about all the drinking he's been doing."

"I'd drink too, if I had Reed for a father and Minerva for my wife," Griff quipped.

Preacher asked, "Miss Jessi, didn't I hear you say that the drifter wanted to know if Roscoe Darcy was her new pigeon?"

"Yes."

"Then that tells me he probably doesn't know."

"But what could she be up to?"

"The Wanted poster says that when she vanishes, so do large sums of money," Neil pointed out. "Maybe she's after Darcy's money clip."

"Well, if this really is her, I can't take her off your hands until we get some proof," Preacher told them.

"Then that's what we'll do," Jessi said.

After dinner, Two Shafts and Neil rode into town to see Auntie's girls and Preacher went to avail himself of the midweek service at the church. Although Jessi had been baptized at Vale's King David A.M.E., she and Joth hadn't attended in many years. Being hissed at while you're praying tends to discourage attendance.

Jessi and Griffin were on the rooftop watching the sunset, each very much aware that they were alone for the first time in what felt like weeks. Griffin looked out at the sun making its slow descent and thought about how he'd slept apart from her last night. He didn't like being separated from her. "I missed you last night."

"I missed you too," she admitted truthfully. It pleased her that they were able to reach an understanding and patch things up without a lot of yelling and recriminations. "Are you really going to repair the roof?"

"Yep."

Jessi thought it time to ask the obvious question. "Have you ever done it before?"

He chuckled. "Quite a few times actually. Reverend Blake was a carpenter by trade. Learned all I know from him." He laughed at her look of amazement. "Bet you thought all I could do was rob trains and chase pretty women."

"Frankly yes."

"Well, now you know different. A man has to be able to provide for his family."

Jessi held his eyes. Was this man really serious about wanting her for his wife? He seemed to be quite serious. "Griff, I'm not marrying you."

"Can't talk about that right now, Jessi Rose. I've got a sunset to watch."

So they watched the sunset, and after the colors were extinguished by the darkness he said, "I had a dream last night."

"What was it about?"

"Me and you making love."

Seated next to him in the dark, she smiled but said nothing.

"We were in a big bed that had carvings all along the headboard."

"What type of carvings?"

"I didn't see them real close because I was too busy watching you."

"And what was I doing?"

"Shouting the house down, of course."

She punched him in the arm.

His voice then turned serious. "I think I'm supposed to make that bed."

For the first time, Jessi turned to him and she searched his night-shrouded eyes. "What do you mean?"

"I believe I'm supposed to build that bed. I don't know why, but it's how I felt when I woke up this morning."

Jessi hadn't an inkling as to how to react to such a statement.

"You're probably wondering if I've been dipping in the tequila."

"A bit."

"I've been a dreamer all of my life, so was my mother. Sometimes, I see little glimpses of things that may be coming my way. Like Joth. I looked into his eyes that first morning I was here and knew I'd seen him before and I had—in one of my dreams."

Jessi shrugged. "You know, if I hadn't been around Gillie all of my life, I *would* think you'd been sneaking tequila, but there are many things in this world we can't explain, and even a skeptic like me can be a believer sometimes. So, if you wish to make a fancy hand-carved bed because you dreamed it, then you have my blessing."

"And after it's done, I'll invite you to a very private

christening ceremony,'' he promised, as he nibbled her
ear.

''I can't wait.''

His caresses journeyed down the soft skin of her neck.
''So, how're you holding up on our little wager? Still
think you can last the rest of the week?''

She turned her head so she could brush her lips across
his mouth. ''Truthfully, no.''

His grin and kiss mingled. ''What happened to all that
stamina you were bragging about?''

Her eyes and voice were filled with a sultry innocence. ''What bragging? I never bragged about anything . . .'' She then gave him a kiss that she hoped
would make him forget all about the bet.

When she slowly eased away, he traced her kiss swollen lips and husked out, ''You're getting *real* good at
this . . . real good . . .''

He dragged her onto his lap and then showed her just
how good he thought her kisses to be. Soon, the buttons
on her blouse were surrendering one by one and he began seductively wooing each newly bared patch of skin.
He bared her breasts next and Jessi could feel the night
air mingling with the heat of his hands as they stroked
her peaks until they hardened and sang. He took one
into his mouth and then the other, driving her wild and
making her arch back over his strong arm.

''I think we'd better go inside,'' he murmured against
her throat. ''The moon's coming up . . .''

Jessi didn't want to go inside; she didn't want to do
anything but ride the bliss-filled sensations he created
inside her.

He wantonly rolled a nipple between gentle fingers
and she crooned just for him.

He pressed his lips to hers. ''Come on.''

He took her by the hand and led her to the hole in
the roof. A hazy and pulsing Jessi climbed down the

ladder after him, but about three quarters of the way down, she felt his presence behind her and then the warm, strong feel of his hands sliding up her bare legs beneath her skirt.

"Hold still a minute . . ."

She could do nothing as his brazen hands began to explore. He raised her skirt and set her slowly and exquisitely afire. Jessi sagged against the ladder as he played. He silently but erotically coaxed her to widen her stance and she did so breathlessly, willingly. Her compliance only made him that much bolder and Jessi knew she'd never be able to climb this ladder again without remembering this sweet seduction. He untied her drawers and eased them down her legs. Firm and possessive hands toured her now bare hips and the treasures they sheltered. Just when she thought she would die from the pleasure, he took her down and carried her to her room. They were so eager for each other, they barely took the time to remove their clothing. All Jessi wanted was to be filled by the hard soft power of him and he was more than ready to oblige. They made love wildly, possessively, magnificently, and when they finally exploded into nirvana, Jessi wasn't the only one shouting the house down.

Afterward, as they lay sated in the dark, quiet room, he held her close and said, "Now that you've lost the bet, how're you planning on paying up?"

Still dressed in her blouse, an outdone Jessi looked up at him. "We both lost the wager. You ambushed me coming down the ladder."

"And you loved it, admit it."

She grinned. "That has nothing to do with this discussion."

"Sure it does. When we were up on the roof, what did you say when I asked if you could really last the rest of the week?"

"I don't remember."

He pulled her on top of him and filled his hands with her silk-skinned behind. "You don't remember?"

Jessi could feel him hard and vibrant against the front of her thighs. "No."

"Then maybe you remember this . . ."

She heralded the slide of his maleness into her softness with a throaty gasp of delight. The dulcet pace of the rhythm he set made her purr. "I remember this . . ."

"I thought you would."

In the end, Jessi surrendered. She admitted losing the wager, and as the passion climbed she agreed to forfeit whatever he desired. Griffin rewarded her for her truthfulness until fulfillment shattered them both.

The return of Joth, Gillie, and Doyle a few days later fueled a celebration. Jessi was so glad to see her nephew, she kept grabbing him close and hugging him. He squirmed of course but didn't balk too much because he was happy to be home. Jessi and Griff introduced Doyle and Gillie to the Twins and Preacher, then invited them to stay for the evening's meal. Neil cooked a grand dinner and everyone ate until they were stuffed.

After dinner, Gillie and Jessi took a walk across the open land behind the house. Gillie needed to stretch her ancient legs after sitting through the day-and-a-half journey to Austin, and Jessi was more than happy to leave the boisterous, wall-rattling atmosphere evoked by the men for a while.

Once the two women were out of earshot, Gillie stopped and said, "Now I can hear myself think. Lord, men are noisy."

Jessi's affection for Gillie showed in her smile, "I keep telling myself I'll adjust to it, but I haven't so far."

Jessi set down the stool she'd been carrying for Gillie to sit upon, in case she got tired during their walk. Gillie sat and Jessi chose a spot in the thick dry grass at her feet.

"Did Joth have a good time?"

Gillie smiled. "Yes, he did. We all did. How about you? Did you and Griffin have a good time?"

Jessi lowered her head, hoping Gillie wouldn't see just how good a time she'd had, but Gillie wasn't fooled. "That wonderful a time, huh?"

Jessi looked up and wondered if her happiness really showed.

"Well, I'm glad. It's about time somebody started showing you some tenderness and care."

Jessi rested her chin on her knees. "He's so unlike any other man I've met. He's caring, funny, strong when he needs to be, gentle too. He wants to marry me."

"And you said?"

"No."

"No? Jessi Rose Clayton, what is wrong with you?"

"He's younger than I am."

"And? A man like that will have energy long after you'll ever need it."

"Gillie!" Jessi giggled with wide eyes.

"I haven't always been this old, little girl."

"Little girl" had always been Gillie's diminutive for Jessi.

"All right, then, what about his profession? He robs trains."

"If he wants you for his wife, I don't think train robbing's going to be much of a priority anymore."

Jessi had to admit he had talked about wanting to change his life. "Gillie, I'm a fairly intelligent woman, and women like me do not go cow eyes over a man in less than two weeks."

"Why not? Some liaisons catch like lightning and burn for a lifetime."

Jessi pulled up some blades of grass. "Not for me. It wouldn't make sense."

"Jessi you've built your whole life on decisions that made sense, and look what it's gotten you. Do you care about him?"

"I do. In fact, I think I'm in love with him."

"Then what is wrong with you? Glorious men like that do not go around courting old women like us everyday unless they have railroad cars crammed with gold, and since we both know you do not—he must be sincere."

"But for how long?"

"What do you mean how long?"

"Will he stay?"

"Who knows? I can't answer that question."

"Neither can I, and I don't want my heart broken. I keep envisioning waking up one morning and finding a note on the kitchen table telling me he's gone."

"No woman wants to be hurt, Jessi, but it comes with the territory sometimes."

"Then why risk it?" Jessi asked, continuing to yank at the blades of grass.

Gillie placed a gentle hand on her arm. "Because you, of all the people I know, deserve some happiness in your life, even if it's only for a little while."

Jessi mulled over her mentor's advice.

Gillie declared, "I was right to come home when I did. You needed me back here to keep you from making a fool of yourself."

Jessi chuckled and shook her head. "What would I do without you?"

"Probably throw away this chance at happiness, and that would be too bad."

Their eyes held, then Gillie placed a tender hand on Jessi's cheek. "He can bring you light, Jessi Rose, embrace it. You've lived in the dark for too long."

Jessi looked up and nodded.

"Good girl. Now let me walk these old bones back. I brought you something from Austin."

The something turned out to be a dress. She and Gillie were behind the closed door of Jessi's bedroom when Jessi lifted it from the box. It was beautiful, fashionable, and blue. Due to the life she led, Jessi didn't dress up very often. In fact she owned very little clothing outside of her everyday wear. She'd no idea when she'd get the opportunity to wear such a lovely garment, but when the time came, she'd be prepared. She walked over and kissed Gillie's soft brown cheek. "Thank you."

"You're welcome."

Jessi hung the dress in her wardrobe as Gillie asked, "Anything of import happen in Vultureville while I've been away?"

Vultureville was the name Gillie had given Vale many years ago.

"They're still calling me whore."

Gillie shook her head. "Have you heard from Bob?"

"Griffin says Bob is dead."

"I know I shouldn't say this, but I'm glad to hear it. You've had enough hell for one lifetime. Have you and Griffin broached those years yet?"

"No."

"You'll have to eventually, you know that?"

"Yes, I do."

It was not a discussion Jessi wanted to have either. She'd no idea how Griffin would react to hearing about the eighteen months she spent riding with Calico Bob and his gang, and truthfully, she dreaded the prospect.

"It might be easier to tell him than you think."

Jessi wanted very much to believe Gillie, but Jessi didn't know. She did know that if she agreed to marry Griffin, he'd have to hear the story beforehand just in case he wished to change his mind.

The men were in the kitchen playing dominoes, and by all the yelling and laughter coming through Jessi's bedroom door, it was quite apparent they were having a good time. "I need to get Joth into bed," Jessi told Gillie. "Oh, by the way, Lydia Cornell sent some eggs over the other day, along with a hello to me."

"Lydia Cornell!" Gillie exclaimed. "Was she drunk?"

Jessi laughed. "I asked the same question. And Garland Findley let Griffin buy enough wood and supplies to fix my roof."

Gillie's old eyes were perplexed. "Does Reed know about this?"

"I'm not sure. And Uncle Cap's quit as sheriff and is leaving town."

"That poor man. He was never the same after Betsy died."

Jessi then told her about the visit Casper Hatcher paid and their attempt at reconciliation.

"That's good, Jessi. Glad to hear that somebody's making peace."

"I doubt we'll ever be as close as we once were, but I will miss him, and he left me something quite remarkable."

Jessi told Gillie about the Wanted poster that might or might not be Minerva.

Gillie's eyes lit up like Christmas morning. "Wouldn't that be something if it did turn out to be true? Embezzlement, huh? It would serve Reed right if she took every cent he has. Well, that is very interesting. When I get home, maybe I'll do a little sniffing around myself. Is it okay if tell Valeria?"

Valeria was Auntie's real name and Gillie was the only person alive allowed to address her as such.

"I don't see why not. We'll need all the help we can muster."

Doyle and Gillie departed soon after, and once Joth finished waving good-bye, Jessi put the already half-asleep boy right to bed. Preacher went to his tent to read his Bible before ending his day, and the Twins mounted up and rode off to patrol the perimeter.

Jessi and Griffin were left alone. They were seated on the front porch enjoying the night and each other, as had become their habit. Jessi laced her arm through his, and after resting her head against his shoulder, thought how wonderful it would be to end each day just like this for the rest of her life. "I told Gillie about Minerva's Wanted poster. She said she'd make some discreet enquiries. Well, actually, she said she'd do some sniffing around herself."

They both smiled.

Griffin said, "I like her."

"So do I. I hope she lives forever. She's meant a lot to me over the years."

He bent over and pressed his lips to her forehead. "I hope you live forever too."

They began working on the roof the next morning. Under Griff's supervision, Jessi and the others spent the next four days sawing, hammering nails and pulling splinters out of their skin. Jessi found herself watching him with a new respect. Griffin Blake was an excellent carpenter and gang boss, and just as he claimed, he knew exactly what he was doing. He built a trap door in the roof so that he and Jessi could continue to watch the sunrise and she was very touched by the gesture.

One of the assignments given to Joth by his teacher involved writing an essay on three famous people or events in Texas history. Joth wandered into Jessi's room the day after the roof was finished and asked for her help in choosing his subjects. Jessi was sweeping the floor and stopped to think a moment. "Do you have anything in mind?"

"Well, I talked to the Twins about it."

Jessi couldn't contain her chuckle. "You talked to the Twins about your school assignment?"

"Yes, was that all right?"

She straightened her face. "Yes, it was. What did they suggest?"

"Neil said I should write about the Black Seminole scouts that were in the Army and Two Shafts suggested the Comanche."

Jessi was impressed. "Those are two very good choices. What about number three?"

"Maybe that man the Twins named Griffin after. Señor Cheno Cortinas."

"That sounds fine, too, but how are you going to find out what you need to know to do the essay? The Twins can probably help you with the Comanche and the Seminole scouts, but Señor Cortinas might be harder to do."

"What about Gillie? She might know. Gillie knows everything."

"You may be right, Joth, that's an excellent idea. How about we ride into town tomorrow or the next day and ask her? In the meantime, you can talk to the Twins about the Comanche and the Seminole scouts."

He was one happy boy when he left her room, and a smiling Jessi went back to her sweeping.

That afternoon Jessi sat with Joth, Griffin, the Twins, and Preacher as Two Shafts told his story. Two Shafts was indeed Comanche, but only on his mother's side; both he and Neil July were fathered by a Black Seminole army scout named Randolph July. In reality the two men were half-brothers, as each had a different mother, but since they were both born on the same day, it also made them twins. Jessi had never met a true Comanche before, and like many other Texans had been raised to fear the fiercely independent warriors. But as she grew older and began to learn the truth about the lies of the government and the broken treaties, she could not help but sympathize with the plight of the country's native nations.

"We were a nomadic people," Two Shafts said to Joth. "And like our friends the Apache, the Kiowa, and the Sioux, we did our best to hold onto our hunting grounds and freedom, but as more and more Anglos came in, it became harder and harder to do."

Jessi knew that everyone in Texas—Indian, Mexican, Black, and White—had lost lives, homes, and loved ones in the battles and raids conducted by and against the native peoples, both before and after Texas independence.

According to Two Shafts, a seminal incident took place in 1840. "Twelve Comanche chiefs and sixty-five of their people came to San Antonio's Council House to negotiate the release of thirteen White captives. As a show of good faith the Comanches brought with them one of the captives. The citizenry was not so generous. They proposed that the chiefs be taken hostage instead, to make sure that all the captives would be returned."

"Did the chiefs agree?" Joth asked.

"No, and a fight started. When the smoke cleared, thirty Comanche and seven Whites were dead."

"What happened to the other Comanche?" Joth asked curiously.

Jessi was glad to hear he'd done the mathematics in his head.

"They were captured. The Texans named the incident the Council House fight, but for the nations of the Comanche, the Kiowas, and our other Plains brethren, it was just one more step down the road to our deaths as a people."

Two Shafts further explained that as more and more

settlers came west, the tribes from Texas to Kansas were hunted down and stuck on reserves that were often over-crowded, ill run, and understaffed. Supplies of food, clothing, and medicine were delivered erratically at best, and the women and elders starved so the children could eat the minimal rations that were available. The chiefs and warriors, faced with the starvation of their people, did the only thing they could: they left the reservations to find food by hunting buffalo. The great buffalo herds had sustained the nations for as long as the People could remember, but like the tribes, they too were being hunted down and extinguished.

As Two Shafts went on, Jessi remembered seeing an article in one of the back east newspapers stating that nearly four million buffalo were killed in the years be-tween 1872 and 1874, but only 150,000 by Indian hands. The Anglo buffalo hunters with their long-range guns slaughtered the rest for the skins. According to the ar-ticle, the stench of dead buffalo rotting in the sun could be smelled for miles, and when a group of White Texas ranchers went to General Phillip Sheridan to complain about the carnage perpetrated by the hunters and skin-ners, they were told, *"Let them kill, skin, and sell them until the buffalo is exterminated, as it is the only way to bring lasting peace and allow civilization to advance."*

Two Shafts added bitterly, "The free Comanche and the warriors who'd escaped the reservations wanted no part of a civilization based on waste and broken treaties, so a young Comanche chief named Quanah Parker pro-posed war to rid the grazing lands of the hunters once and for all."

Jessi knew about the famous Quanah. His mother was a White woman named Cynthia Ann Parker who'd been taken captive as a child in 1836. In 1860 during a skir-mish with the Texas Rangers, her husband, a Comanche war chief named Peta Nocona, was killed, and she and her daughter, Prairie Flower, were captured by the Texans.

Quanah's quest to rid the plains of the hunters began June 27, 1874, at a supply base camp near the Canadian River, a place known as Adobe Walls.

"He had almost seven hundred warriors with him. Kiowas led by the great war chiefs Lone Wolf and Satanta, volunteers from the Arapaho, and a group of Cheyenne led by White Shield. The Cheyenne had come because a group of buffalo hunters had stolen fifty of their best ponies, and they wanted their return or revenge."

"But wasn't it against the law to leave the reservation? That's what Mr. Trent said," Joth told his Comanche friend.

"Yes, it was. Harsh punishments were promised for anyone who left the reservation without permission, but the warriors at Adobe Walls that day had little time for rules. They were fighting for their lives. Quanah planned to start with Adobe Walls, then push across northern Texas into Kansas, destroying the hunters' bases on the plains. The grazing lands of the buffalo had been promised to the tribes in 1867 under the Treaty of Medicine Lodge, and if the Army wouldn't keep the interlopers out, Quanah and his men would."

But it turned out to be a futile endeavor. Even though Quanah and his forces caught the camp by surprise, the thick adobe walls of the settlement and the telescope-equipped long guns of the hunters kept the Indians at bay. The attack which had begun at dawn under the waning Summer Moon waged on into the afternoon, at which time the Indians finally withdrew.

"The retreating warriors were angry and blamed the Comanche prophet and medicine man named Isatai for their failure. He'd promised victory and Quanah had to intervene to save Isatai from a flogging by a Cheyenne warrior. Quanah never put his faith in another medicine man.''

There were a few more skirmishes after that but after being defeated by the bluecoats at the great Palo Duro village, Lone Wolf and the Kiowas surrendered at Fort Sill on February 25, 1875. Quanah Parker and the last of the free Comanches followed the Kiowas in three months later.

''What happened to them? Were they punished for leaving the reservation?'' Joth asked with a childlike concern.

Shafts nodded sadly. ''Everyone who surrendered was put into a corral and disarmed. If the warrior had any property, it was burned. All of their horses and mules were shot. Those who'd left the reservation were either put into cells or kept in the icehouse. The bluecoats tossed them meals of raw meat as if they were caged animals.''

The memories were obviously too much for Two Shafts. He stood and told his brother, ''I'm going riding. I'll be back later.''

No one tried to stop him as he strode outside.

Preacher, who'd come in during the middle of the story, said, ''Maybe if the country had respected the native races, there might not have been such bloodshed and heartache.''

''Or if the United States had kept their word, instead of changing it every time the sun rose,'' Neil July added as he stood at the back door watching his brother ride away.

Later that night after hearing Joth's prayers, she sat on the edge of his bed and asked, ''Did you get a chance to hear about the Seminole scouts from Neil?''

''Yep, when I helped him do up the dishes after supper. I already knew that the Black Seminoles were once escaped slaves who went to live with the Seminoles in

Florida, because Mr. Trent told us about it.''

"So what didn't you know?"

Joth paused to think a moment, then said, ''Well, I didn't know that when the tribes were forced to live in Oklahoma, many of the Seminoles wound up leaving because slave catchers kept bothering them.''

"Really?"

He nodded. ''Neil said the Seminole chiefs Wild Cat and John Horse took two hundred of their people and left on what he called the Great Trek and went to Mexico.''

"What did they do there?"

"First they helped the Mexican government protect the border, then when Mr. Lincoln's war ended a man from the army came to the Seminoles and asked them to be scouts.''

"Did they agree?"

"Yep. Their commander was a man named Lieutenant John Bullis and Neil said the Seminoles liked him a lot because he treated them like men. They were called the Seminole Negro Indian Scouts.''

Jesse smiled upon hearing the lofty title. ''I heard the Seminole scouts were very brave.''

"They were. Neil said his pa told him that in twelve big fights they never lost a man and none of them ever got hurt.''

Jessi was impressed.

"And one time, his pa and the other scouts were in the desert and they had nothing to eat but canned peaches and rattlesnakes.''

Jessi wrinkled her nose. ''They must've been really hungry if they had to eat snakes.''

"I think so too. Have you ever eaten a rattlesnake?''

Jessi shook her head and chuckled. ''Not that I remember. So, what else are you putting in your report?''

"That the scouts were so brave, Congress gave four of them Medals of Honor."

"I never knew that."

"I didn't either, but things sort of went bad after that," he added solemnly.

"What do you mean?"

"Well, when the Seminoles agreed to be scouts, the government in Washington promised to give the Seminole families land and food, but they didn't. The families started starving, Aunt Jessi, and the men had to become scavengers and thieves so they could eat."

Jessi found the sad tale moving. "Did anybody try and help?"

"General Sheridan talked to the government and so did some of the other generals but nobody listened to them. Some of the local townspeople even started shooting the Seminoles just for fun, and they almost killed Chief John Horse."

"This doesn't sound like it will end happily."

"It didn't. One of the winners of those congress medals, I think Neil said his name was Adam Paine, got shot in the back by a Texas sheriff. The sheriff shot him at such close range, Aunt Jessi, his clothes caught on fire."

Jessi went stock still. "What did the Seminoles do?"

Joth shrugged. "I don't know, but Neil said that after that happened, some of the scouts left the states and went to live in Mexico and they never came back. He said that by 1881, there were no more Seminole scouts."

Another tragic episode in America's history, Jessi thought to herself. She hoped that the bravery of the scouts would not be lost over time, because without their help the West would not've been settled.

Joth looked up at her and said, "Do you think Señor Cortinas's story will have a happy ending?"

Jessi shrugged. "I hope so, Joth."

"Me too."

Chapter 10

⁓ ◯◯ ⁓

The saloon's repairs were completed a few days later, and Auntie decided to throw a party to celebrate the re-opening. Because of her aversion to Vale's social events, Jessi hadn't planned on attending, but when the Twins told her that Auntie had specifically asked that she be brought along, Jessi decided to rethink her position. After all, she doubted if any of her detractors would attend; helping a fallen woman like Auntie toast the opening of her new saloon might keep them from entering heaven, so Jessi decided she would go.

When the day rolled around, the men went to town early to get their hair cut and while they were away, Jessi hauled in heated water for a bath. Preacher had kindly offered to stay with Joth for the evening and the two were now out hunting rabbits.

After her bath, Jessi took out her new dress and then sat on her bed to open the box she'd received the day after Joth's return from Austin. It too had come from Gillie and had been brought out to the ranch by Doyle. The note on the large box read: *I forgot to give this to you. To be opened* only *when you wear the dress.*

Of course, Jessi wanted to open the box right then, but she was afraid the all-seeing, all-knowing Gillie would somehow find out, so she'd put it away. As she opened it now, she stared. Placing her hand over her mouth, she laughed with both delight and shock. Inside was a short, very seductive black corset. Jessi lifted it out and scanned the flared high-cut bottom and the tiny gray roses that decorated the bodice. These were no everyday underthings, they'd been designed to tempt a man's eye. There was a pair of new black stockings, two fancy little garters, a finely made camisole, and a pair of drawers. Gillie had even included new black slippers. A bit stunned by the gift, Jessi found a note on the box's bottom which read:

Tell Griffin there's no need to thank me.
Love to you both.
G.

A shocked Jessi laughed out loud.

Jessi dressed, and once she was done, walked over to view herself in the mirror. She was amazed by her reflection. In the glass stood the woman she used to be, the woman who was fashionable, articulate, and confident—the woman who'd taught sciences at the Miss Paris LaMarr's School for Young Women of Color, and the woman who'd married Evan. In the decade since coming home, this woman had been buried beneath the person she had had to become in order to survive. That woman had had no place on a ranch run by her iron-willed father, or on the road with Bob Winston and his gang. That woman had to be put away in order to preserve her sanity. In its place grew a woman much stronger, more resilient, and far more tenacious than before. Though she might look the same in the mirror, Jessi knew that in reality that woman of a decade ago existed no more.

Jessi turned to view the back of the stylish navy dress.

With its dainty row of buttons down the back and its stovepipe lines, it would be absolutely useless on a cattle drive, but perfect for a social event like Auntie's party. Seeing her all gussied up would undoubtedly give the gossips plenty to talk about, but as always, Jessi didn't care.

"Well, how do I look?" Jessi asked, as she walked into the parlor where the men were waiting. Her short-cropped hair had been dressed and brushed until it shone. In her ears were the gold circlets she always wore. Jessi tried not to smile at the stunned look on Griffin's face.

Joth was staring at her as if he'd never seen her before. "Wow, Aunt Jessi, is that you?"

"No, it's Sam Houston," Neil cracked with a smile. "You look lovely, Miss Clayton."

Jessi gave him a pleasant smile. "Thank you, Neil."

Griff could see Jessi's mouth moving, but he hadn't heard a word she'd said since she'd stepped into the room. He was far too busy staring at her in that dress. She'd always been beautiful in his eyes, even if she did wear nothing but ranch hand attire, but like this, all dressed up, she seemed like another woman altogether. It was as if she'd been transformed into a prim and proper back east lady who carried a reticule instead of a loaded Winchester, a woman he wanted to hustle into the nearest closet and see how long it took him to undo those little jet buttons down the back of her dress. The thought of undressing her and freeing her warm skin to his kisses and his touch made him instantaneously harden with desire.

Looking into her eyes, he announced, "I need to talk to Miss Jessi alone, if I can."

Surprisingly enough, no one balked. They even took Joth with them, leaving Jessi and Griff alone in the parlor.

"What did you wish to speak with me about?"

"Nothing, really, just wanted to get a good, long look at you up close."

Jessi now understood what it meant to drown in a man's eyes. She was so far underwater she could hardly breathe. "Is there something wrong with the way I look?"

"Oh, hell no, you look fine—so fine, I should probably warn you to watch your back for the rest of the night."

"Why?"

"Ambush."

Jessi's senses flared to life. "You'd ambush a woman in a dress?"

"In a minute."

"Then I guess I'll have to be careful . . ."

"Yes, you will . . ."

"Thanks for the warning," she said smiling up at him.

"My pleasure."

Shaken by the force of her own desire, Jessi touched his face softly, briefly, then left the room to join the others.

Griffin went to the door and called Joth.

When the boy entered, he said, "Did you want me for something?"

"Yep, have a seat."

Joth sat on the big overstuffed sofa and asked, "Am I in trouble?"

Griff chuckled. "No, son. Just need to talk with you about something I'm planning."

"If it's a train robbery, I don't think my aunt will let me come along."

Griffin's mustache lifted with his grin. "It's not a train robbery. I want to marry your Aunt Jessi."

Joth's eyes went wide. "You do?"

"Yep, but I need your permission to court her."

"Why?"

"Because you're the only male Clayton around here."

"Oh."

Griffin thought it time Joth knew how he felt about Jessi, and because Griff had come to care for Joth, the boy's approval meant a lot. "So, what do you think?"

Joth seemed to think a minute, then with very serious eyes asked, "Will you be nice to her?"

Griffin nodded. He knew how much pain Joth carried inside because of the way the townspeople treated Jessi. If Joth had his way, Jessi would never know hurt again, and Griffin wanted that hope to come true too. "Always."

Joth smiled softly. "Then you have my permission."

"Thanks, Jotham."

"You're welcome."

When it was time to depart, Jessi gave Joth a short lecture on how he was to conduct himself with Preacher while she was away, and then kissed the Preacher's cheek for his generosity.

It embarrassed him and he ducked away, but the gesture seemed to make Neil jealous. "I slave over a hot stove every day, and nobody gives me kisses."

Jessi went over and kissed the handsome Seminole's dark, bearded cheek. "Better?"

He nodded, pleased.

She swung her attention to his brother. "Do you need one, too?"

"No, ma'am," he replied, his eyes shining with amusement.

Griff began waving his hand frantically, saying, "I do. I do."

Jessi rolled her eyes. "I'll meet you gentlemen outside."

As Griffin slapped the reins across the backs of the

two-horse team, the old wagon began to roll and Jessi waved good-bye to Joth and Preacher. The Twins were on horseback and flanked the old buckboard like an official escort. Jessi could just about imagine the stir they would cause once they arrived. Then she reminded herself that she was coming to town help Auntie open up her newly refurbished place, not to be judged by a bunch of gossips and hypocrites.

She looked over at Griff, decked out so handsomely in a new blue shirt and vest; the trousers looked new, too, as did the string tie. Jessi was of the opinion that Griffin Blake would look handsome wearing a flour sack, and she had to admit, she was looking forward to being ambushed later on.

When they reached town, Neil and Two Shafts rode on ahead, while Griff headed the team toward the livery. Jessi couldn't believe the number and the variety of vehicles clogging the streets: buckboards, carriages, wagons, buggies. She saw some carriages so fancy she knew they couldn't belong to any of her neighbors. As Griff drove slowly through the busy streets, Jessi thought it looked like an old-fashioned Juneteenth celebration. Jessi's assumption that only a handful of folks would come out for this late afternoon event had been a faulty one. With all the goings on, one would think they were celebrating the opening of the new opera house Minerva Darcy kept insisting the town council build.

As the wagon moved past the crowds, Jessi saw the faces of women who'd spat on the walk as she passed, men who had snickered at her mother's funeral. She saw the upright Christian Mary McCoy, who'd told her son Ross that it was perfectly all right to address Joth as a "son of a whore." These people hadn't been kind to her or her family. Only her love for Auntie could bring her into this nest of vipers.

"Are you ready?" Griffin asked her, after he finally

found a space behind the livery to put the buckboard and pulled back on the brake.

Jessi confessed truthfully, "No, but the sooner I go in, the sooner I can leave and get out of these uncomfortable clothes."

Jessi had become accustomed to the freedom offered by the denims she usually wore, and this dress, although costly and fashionable, made her feel bound and constricted.

"You don't look uncomfortable."

"Well, I am. Gillie sent me this damn French underwear. At least the label says it's French, and—"

"French underwear?" Griffin asked, interrupting. "What type of French underwear?"

His eager questioning made her look up. She should've known better than to tell him something so provocative. She smiled. "Never mind. Forget I mentioned it."

"Aw, Jessi, don't be cruel. What kind?"

Silence.

"At least tell me what color it is."

"No, Griffin," she laughed.

"Jessi?"

She silently mouthed the word no, then said aloud, "If you're supposed to be gentleman to my lady, now's the time for you to come around here and help me out of this elegant Texas carriage."

"I'm going to give you all the help you can stand later, and you can bet the ranch."

He got down and came around to her side of the board. She placed her hand in his and he assisted her down with all the grace of a Haitian count. "So you aren't going to answer my question?"

"No, Griffin, I am not." But grinning saucily at up at him, she crooked a finger at him. He leaned down and she whispered into his ear, "I guess you'll just have to find out for yourself, later."

She left him standing there with his mouth open as she walked up the street.

He caught up with her immediately and they both laughed. As they approached Auntie's, Jessi could hear the lively piano playing and the loud voices of the celebrants wafting out to the street from inside. Except for the bunting across the door and the newly painted letters on the sign, the facade still looked the same. Inside, however, things had changed. Auntie'd apparently knocked out a wall and expanded the place. The downstairs room appeared to be much larger. Good thing, because the saloon was packed. Jessi, with Griffin right behind her, waded into the press in an effort to find Auntie. Knowing that her neighbors would not be happy to see her, Jessi was determined not to make eye contact with anyone. However, they seemed to have other ideas.

More than a few men and women who hadn't spoken to her in years came up and greeted her as if she'd been magically transformed into someone else. They asked after Joth, her health, and if she thought the area would ever get any rain. One young mother gushed on and on about her son being in Joth's classroom, while another came up and asked if she'd like to have tea sometime next week. Women who'd pointed and whispered at her were now acting nice as pie. Jessi wondered if someone had slipped whiskey into the ladies' punch, because that had to be the only explanation for such amazing behavior.

Someone placed a hold on her arm as she passed one of the new, highly polished tables and she looked down into the dark brooding eyes of Reed Darcy. "Good evening, Jessi. You look lovely. I'd like to introduce you to some friends of mine."

Jessi scanned the table. Along with Percy West, who

still sported fading bruises, were two White men and one Black. All of the strangers were finely dressed, but Jessi had no desire to meet any friends of Darcy's. ''No thanks.''

She moved to step away only to have Reed's hold tighten on her arm.

He told his friends proudly, ''See why I want her as my bride? She's a fiery little thing, isn't she?''

Griff told him coolly, ''Unless you want to leave this party as a one-armed man, I'd advise you to drop your hand and let her go.''

Reed glanced up at Griffin disdainfully. ''Ah yes, the new suitor.'' He released his hold. ''How're you, Blake?''

''Fine, Darcy, and you?''

''You know you owe me for that window you busted,'' he said pleasantly.

''Soon as you pay Jessi for the one your men shot up, I'll pay for yours.''

Darcy looked away. ''I have no idea what you're talking about.'' Darcy then turned to the men at the table. ''This is the man trying to steal away my bride. What she see sees in him is beyond me, but,'' and he lifted his glass in a mock toast, ''she'll see the light in a few days.''

Jessi saw Percy smile evilly. She had no idea what Reed meant, and at this point, she didn't much care. Ignoring him further, she and Griffin moved on. ''Why can't he just be struck by lightning?'' she asked tightly.

''If I could arrange it, believe me, I would.'' Griffin had no idea what Darcy had meant either, but he planned to watch his back.

Doyle waved as they finally made it to the bar. Jessi didn't imbibe, but Griffin ordered himself a small shot of tequila.

"So what do you think of the new place?" Doyle shouted proudly over the din.

"It's very—red," Jessi shouted back, and it was. The walls were covered with red flocked paper, and the old sawdust and dirt floor had been replaced with one made of wood. The cloths on all the tables were red and trimmed with gold, as was the new carpet on the steps leading upstairs. Everywhere Jessi looked she saw red and gold. She didn't particularly care for the garish new interior, but it certainly looked fabulous when compared with the drab and tired place it had been before.

"Have you seen Auntie?" Jessi yelled.

"She's out back, escaping the crowd and the heat."

They found Auntie and the girls holding court on chairs set out in the field behind the saloon. They were surrounded by men, some familiar, others not. The pungent, mouth-watering smell of meat cooking rose from the hogs and sides of beef turning on spits manned by barbershop owner Wilson Cornell and the shopkeeper Abe Thomas. Jessi looked around for Cornell's wife Lydia, but did not see her.

Jessi and Griff threaded their way to Auntie's side, and upon seeing them, Auntie threw up her hands and jumped to her feet. She gave them both a strong hug. "I'm so glad you two came. How do you like my new place? Can you tell red is my favorite color?"

"Yes, we could. It's so much larger than before," Jessi replied.

"That it is, and I have the Twins to thank. If they hadn't destroyed the place, I would never have been able to fix it up like I always wanted."

Griffin still wondered how much the Twins had given her, but it was far too late to ask.

"Griffin, there's a poker game going on upstairs, go play while Jessi and I talk."

Griffin looked down at Jessi. "How can I refuse a direct order?"

"Guess you can't. I'll find you later."

He touched her cheek and headed back to the door.

"Jessi Rose, that is one gorgeous man," Auntie said, staring after Griff appreciatively. "And he sure looks like he knows how to take the long way around a woman's body. If I were twenty years younger I'd give you a run for your money."

Jessi and the girls laughed. Jessi could see the folks around her watching and listening, but she ignored them. "Auntie, come take a walk with me for a few moments."

"Sure."

As they moved away from the crowd, Jessi mentioned how she'd been greeted by the townspeople upon arrival and asked, "Why is everybody being so nice? You didn't put tequila in the punch again, did you?"

Auntie's black eyes glittered with amusement. "No, though some of them could use a good stiff drink. Did the Twins come?"

"They are stalking the town daughters even as we speak."

"Good, they'll liven up the place." She beamed at Jessi. "Look at you, all prettied up. You should dress this way more often."

"Thank you for the compliment, but I can't ride fences or brand cows dressed this way."

"Of course not, dear, but every now and then you should. It'll help you remember why the Good Lord made you a female."

Jessi knew better than to argue, so she grinned and said, "Yes, Auntie."

"Now, what was your question?"

"Why is everyone smiling at me like I'm the Second Coming?"

"Hard to stomach, isn't it?"

Jessi nodded.

"Damn bunch of hypocrites."

"Watch your language, now," Jessi warned, smiling.

"I'm sorry. *Fool* bunch of hypocrites."

Jessi shook her head. Auntie's speech had been peppered with invectives for as long as Jessi could remember, and Jessi had gotten in big trouble when she was young for emulating her. "So what's the reason?"

"They're acting like you're the Second Coming because they think you are."

Jessi's face mirrored her confusion. "I don't understand."

"They think Griffin and his friends are here to do away with Reed Darcy once and for all."

"Really?"

"Yep, folks are saying you're calling in desperadoes from as far away as California to help you make a final stand."

"Sounds like a marvelous plan. Too bad it isn't the truth."

"I know. They figure if they're nice to you, you'll protect them too."

Jessi was speechless for a moment, then she began to laugh so hard her sides started to ache. When she was able to gather herself she wiped the tears from her eyes. "Oh, Auntie, that's the funniest thing I've heard in years. They want protection from the whore!"

"Some are even saying that when your men are done with Darcy, you're going to start in on everybody who was ever mean to you."

"That'll cover just about everyone here."

"Except for me and Gillie."

"Except for you and Gillie," Jessi replied affectionately.

Auntie looked up at her and said, "It's good to see you smiling again, little girl."

"I've had precious little to smile about."

"Amen," Auntie chimed softly. "It's still good to see though, then again, what female wouldn't be smiling, having those handsome men around the house? Especially that Griffin Blake."

"Auntie—" Jessi warned.

"Don't Auntie me, little girl, you could do worse."

Jessi couldn't argue with that.

Jessi walked Auntie back to the saloon. "There'll be eats in a little while. Stay as long as you like."

Jessi nodded. "Thanks, I will."

Jessi went back inside and was immediately assaulted by the heat of too many bodies in too small a space. Outdoors was much cooler but she doubted Griffin wanted to be pulled away from his poker game so soon just to escort her outside, so she thought she'd go see if Gillie was in her shop. To her disappointment, the shop was closed. Gillie was probably at her home outside of town. Faced with nothing else to do but go back to the saloon, Jessi turned around to do so. As she passed the alley running alongside Gillie's shop, she stopped; she thought she heard someone singing. When the soft, mournful tune resumed, Jessi walked down the alley to investigate.

The singing came from Roscoe Darcy. He was seated on the ground with his back against Gillie's wall, and he appeared to be very drunk. When he looked up and saw Jessi standing over him, he gave her a lopsided grin and said in a friendly but slurred voice, "Hey, Jessi girl. Haven't seen you in a month of Sundays."

She couldn't stop her smile from forming in reply. At one time, she and Ros had been the closest of friends, but they hadn't spoken as friends in years, and since her father's murder, she hadn't spoken to him at all. "Hello, Ros. How are you?"

He'd always been very fastidious about his dress and manner, but today his suit looked as if it had been slept in. His eyes were red from drink, and his hair hadn't been dressed in quite a while. "Well, as you can see, I'm drunk. Drunk, drunk, drunk, drunk, drunk. Plan to stay this way, too."

"Why, if you don't mind me asking?"

"I like it, and it makes Reed furious." He began to giggle like a child. "Nothing he can do about it, though. Not a *damn* thing." He placed his hand over his mouth. "Sorry, shouldn't cuss when a lady's around."

Looking up at her again, he said, "You know, Jessi girl, if you stay drunk, you don't have to see what's right in front of your face. They think I'm blind, and the drink helps me pretend I am."

"Who thinks you're blind?"

"Reed and that whore known as my wife. She's the real whore, Jessi girl, not you."

Jessi wondered if that meant he knew about Minerva opening her bed to his father. It certainly sounded that way. Was that what had started Roscoe drinking?

"You know," he said drunkenly, "she actually thought I'd believe she was a virgin. Can you believe that?"

"No, Ros, I can't."

"Me neither," he replied. "Reed had her before I did. Told her he couldn't marry her because he was going to marry you. He must be blind too."

"He must be."

"Keep telling him, 'Jessi girl ain't gonna marry you, Pa.' He won't believe me. Thinks he's too powerful and rich for you to say no. Keep telling him, 'Jessi girl ain't going to marry you, Pa,' but he don't believe me." He peered up at her. "Did you tell him?"

"Yes, Ros, I did, many times."

"He don't believe you, though."

"No."

"See?" He then took another draw from the bottle that had been resting in his lap. "Arrogant man, my pa, but I hear that Blake's got him on the run. Anybody that'll throw a chair through Pa's window is a good man, to my thinking. Is he a good man, Jessi girl?"

Jessi nodded.

"Glad to hear it. Hope he gives Pa hell."

He took another healthy draw on the bottle. "Now, go on back to the party. I got more drinking to do."

"Ros—"

"Go on. You shouldn't be seen with the likes of me. Not when I'm like this."

She tried one last time. "Do you want me to find someone to walk you back to the hotel?"

"Nope. Find my own way on my own. Eventually."

"All right then." She headed back up the alley.

"Jessi Rose?"

She turned back.

He said, "I'm sorry about what happened to Dex. If I could've stopped it, I would've."

"So he was shot on Reed's orders?"

"Yep."

"Would you be willing to say that to a jury?"

"Maybe, but not today. Today, I got a lot more drinking to do."

"Ros?"

"Yeah?"

"Thank you."

He nodded at her, and then, as if he were alone, began to sing softly once more.

Jessi stepped out of the alley and back onto the walk to find Two Shafts leaning against the front of Gillie's shop with his arms folded across his chest. He looked to be waiting for her. She wondered if he'd been following her. She was just about to quiz him when Minerva Darcy and a group of her harpies came up the walk. They began whispering and raising their noses as soon as they got within wind of her, and as they walked by, the overdressed Minerva looked from Two Shafts to Jessie and quipped, ''I didn't know whores were allowed to ply their wares on the same streets where decent women walk.''

Some of the women tittered.

Jessi felt anger course through her veins.

They were only a few steps past Jessi when she walked up behind them and called out, ''Hey, Eula!''

When Minerva turned, the solid punch Jessi gave her sent her sprawling to the walk where decent women walk. Minerva lay on the ground with her eyes wide and her hand to her jaw. As Minerva looked down at the enamel in her hand, she cried, ''You've broken one of my teeth!''

Two Shafts began laughing so hard Jessi thought he was going to roll on the walk too. Jessi hand hurt like the dickens, but she felt good. ''Sorry,'' Jessi told her coldly, ''I was gunning for three.''

Two Shafts howled. By now the altercation had drawn a small crowd. Minerva's harpies were cowering like a bunch of scared chickens, and only after they seemed certain Jessi was done throwing punches did they rush to Minerva's side.

Jessi turned her attention to the still chuckling Comanche. ''Shall we go?''

''Certainly. By the way, hell of a punch, Jessita, hell of a punch.''

''Thank you.''

''If you decide not to marry Cheno, will you marry me?''

Watching Minerva struggle to her feet, Jessi cracked in parting, ''See you around, Eula.''

Minerva's eyes were filled with fire.

As they walked back to the saloon Shafts asked, "Hand still hurting?"

Jessi cradled her sore hand with the other. She grimaced. "A lot."

"We'll see if Doyle has any ice. Cheno's going to tie me behind a horse when he finds out I let you brawl in the streets. I was under orders to watch you."

"He doesn't have to know."

The Comanche shook his head. "It's going to be all over town by the time we get back to the saloon. He'll know. All he'll have to do is look at that hand."

Jessi could feel pain radiating up her wrist. "Who knew the woman had such a hard jaw?"

"But she dropped like a stone." And Two Shafts began laughing all over again.

When they got to Auntie's, Doyle immediately stuck Jessi's hand down inside a big barrel filled with ice and he held it there until she swore her fingers would pop off like New York icicles. "That's enough, Doyle! My hand's frozen like a pond."

He released her wrist and Jessi slowly pulled her frigid hand free of the barrel. She gingerly flexed her knuckles. The pain had lessened somewhat, but if the hand wasn't broken, it sure felt as if it were.

Somebody found the doc and brought him into the storeroom where Jessi sat with her aching hand. Dr. Lazarus Salt had known Jessi all her life. When he came in, he shook his white head and said, "Well, little girl, what have you broken now?"

"My hand, I believe."

He bent over her hand and examined it slowly. "Aren't you a bit old to still be falling out of trees?"

She grinned. While growing up she'd broken her right arm and her left wrist in two separate tree falls: the arm when she was seven, the wrist at age ten. "Ouch!" Jessi yelled, as he moved her fingers this way and that.

"Not broken. Bruised."

He straightened. "It's going to hurt for a few days. Try to keep ice on it if you have any at the ranch. Either way it's gonna swell, but you'll be right as rain, eventually."

After he wrapped up her hand, he then looked to Doyle. "Where's that man of hers? He know she's out brawling in the streets?"

Doyle grinned. "I don't think so, Laz."

"Well, find him and tell him."

And he left.

Doyle and Two Shafts began to laugh. Jessi rolled her eyes.

Upstairs, Griffin was engaged in a different kind of brawl, and ironically enough, the victim was also a Darcy. It seemed Reed was not as expert at poker as he believed himself to be, at least not when playing against Griffin. Stacked in front of the train robber were numerous piles of bills, gold eagles, double eagles, and octagonal-shaped slugs, most of which came out of the pockets of Darcy and his friends. Stacked in front of Reed, nothing. Word had it that when Reed had begun losing heavily, he'd sent somebody over to the bank to get more money to cover his last bets, but it hadn't mattered, Griffin had taken that too.

Jessi and Two Shafts entered the smoky silent room where the poker was being played and Jessi felt the tension immediately. Neil tipped over and very quietly related what was going on.

"Is Griffin really that good?" Jessi asked, looking at the gold stacked in front of her favorite train robber.

"Darcy and his friends will be lucky to still have their drawers on when Cheno is done with them."

Jessi scanned the room. There were many familiar faces among the men ringing the room, like the glowering Percy West, but many that were not. She assumed that the few well-dressed White men looking on intently were investor friends of Darcy's. By some of the accents she could hear as they whispered back and forth, it was quite obvious that most were from England. Englishmen and other foreigners began flocking to Texas and buying up ranches back in '82, but they didn't seem to know a lot about cattle ranching. Rustlers preyed upon them mercilessly and most went broke during the hard winter of '84 and the drought of '85. She'd heard that many of the English had returned home because of the losses, leaving behind towns with names like Shamrock, Wellington, and Clarendon.

Jessi wondered if the Englishmen were throwing in with Reed Darcy on the railroad scheme in an attempt to offset those losses. The land around Vale would be lucrative if the railroad and Darcy were successful in their attempts to gain control, but they'd have to go through her first.

Neil's prophecy proved correct. Griffin fleeced Reed and his guests like spring sheep, and as the game lengthened and the stakes soared higher, more and more people began squeezing into the room to watch.

Jessi noted that Griffin played decisively, and that his cards never showed on his handsome face. A few of the Englishmen left the table, enraged not only by their losing, but by the former outlaw's expertise. His prowess at poker far exceeded their own and he had a pile of gold and notes stacked in front of him to prove it.

It was quite obvious to the onlookers that none of the men at the table had any business cutting cards with Griffin, especially Reed. The more he lost, the angrier he became and the more recklessly he played. During the late stages of the game, the third-to-last player folded, leaving Griffin and Reed to play on alone. Reed had lost a substantial amount of money, money Jessi hoped he had because Griffin played poker like a man with a gift.

To aid Reed, some of his friends began staking him as the calls went higher and higher. They smugly assumed Griffin would not be able to match the amounts, but he had more than enough winnings to keep himself afloat, especially after Neil slapped the old carpet bag on the table. Auntie slapped some gold on the table for Griffin too, as did Doyle and the old doctor.

As it turned out, Griffin didn't need the support of his friends. When the last hand ended, you could hear a pin drop.

Griffin gathered up the cards and set them aside. "Well, Mr. Darcy. I believe you owe me roughly fifteen thousand dollars."

The sum was astronomical, even for someone as wealthy as Reed. He looked stunned. Not only had he lost his own funds, but he'd squandered the hundreds he'd borrowed from his well-heeled friends. Jessi didn't believe any of them could afford to loose that much money.

"Deal another hand," Darcy demanded angrily. "You owe me a chance to make good."

"I gave you that chance an hour ago, remember?"

He had, and everyone in the room knew it. He'd owed Griffin ten thousand then, but instead of bowing out gracefully, Reed's pride had kept him playing and he'd gone another five thousand in the hole.

"There's no way I'm going to pay you fifteen thousand dollars."

"Why not?" Griffin asked coolly. "Can't you back your bets?"

It was a double-edged question. Any answer Reed gave would land him in hot water.

Griffin waited, as did everyone else gathered around.

Jessi watched Reed glance around the room, and when

his eyes settled on hers, she met his gaze without emotion.

"Pay the man his money or your word won't be worth a dime anywhere," one of the Englishmen warned.

"Shut up!" Reed's replied angrily. "Stay out of this."

Was he going to have to admit he couldn't cover the bets? Jessi wondered.

"All right," Darcy finally relented. "I'm a bit short of cash right now. What else will you accept?"

The crowd began to buzz.

Griffin said, "Well, let's see. How about this? You turn over all the mortgages you've called in for the last, oh let's say, two years, and I'll consider the debt paid."

Reed's jaw dropped, and so did Jessi's. Those in town who'd lost their mortgages had been leasing their land from the Darcy bank at prices so high, the payments left them little money for much else. Some of them were also in the room, and seemed as bowled over as Reed.

"That's out of the question!" Reed stormed.

"Then I want my money. Now."

"You can't expect me to pay it to you right at this moment!"

"Why not? Had I lost, you would be demanding the same."

He was right, and Reed and everyone else knew it.

Jessi eyed Reed's friends. They too were watching the tense situation unfold. Some looked genuinely displeased with this turn of events, but she couldn't determine whether their displeasure was aimed at Reed's handling of their stakes or at his waffling on paying the debt.

Then she heard one of the Englishmen mutter, "I should've known better than to invest in a bloody coon," and she had her answer.

As if someone had given the foreigners a silent signal, they all began saying their good-byes.

"Hey, wait," Reed exclaimed, rising from his chair. "Aren't we still meeting later?"

"No," one of the Englishmen replied pointedly. "It's obvious that you've problems here, Darcy. My investment group will let you know what we decide later on in the week."

Darcy tried to charm them. "Now, hold on, you aren't going to pull up stakes over a little poker game, are you? I can cover the amount, believe me, I can."

The men did not seem convinced. "We'll be in touch. Oh, and when we do, we expect you to have *all* your ducks in a row."

And they filed out.

Darcy dropped back into his chair like a sack of meal. One of the men who clerked in the bank made a move as if to say something, but Reed barked, "I don't need or want your opinion. Go to the bank and get the deeds."

The clerk's jaw tightened, but he did as he was told.

When the man departed, Reed stood and said to Griffin, "I'm sure you'll understand why I don't want to sit here and look at you until he returns. I'll be at my hotel."

Without uttering another word, he forcefully pushed past the folks gathered around and left the room. Percy and his men exited right behind their boss. For a moment there was silence, and then a man in the back asked hesitantly, "What are you going to do with the deeds, Blake?"

Griffin grinned. "Why, turn them back over to their owners, of course."

The room erupted with cheers. Jessi went to his side, and couldn't remember ever being so pleased.

Reed's clerk returned less than an hour later and

handed the deeds over to Griffin. With the glowering Percy West at his side, the clerk then announced, "Mr. Darcy wants everyone out of *his* saloon immediately. Any stragglers will be shot on sight for trespassing."

He stormed out.

Auntie came over and shook Griffin's hand. "Thanks, Griffin. Even though Darcy's closing down my party, I can't complain. The look on his face when you asked him to pay up is something I'll take to my grave."

People began leaving and a grinning Neil July told Griffin, "You know, you ruined Darcy's evening."

"Can't take you anywhere," Two Shafts kidded.

With Jessi by his side, Griffin ignored his friends for a moment and announced to the departing crowd, "You folks can see about these deeds tomorrow at the Clayton ranch."

Many of those in the room paused and looked warily over at Jessi, who returned their looks without comment.

"This ain't over Blake," Percy promised as the Clayton clan passed him by.

"No, it isn't, Percy," Griff replied. "We'll see you soon."

"What a game!" Jessi exclaimed as they stepped out into cool night air and struck out toward the buckboard. They noticed that everyone seemed to be taking Reed's threats seriously. Folks were not tarrying.

"Yes, it was."

"I told you Cheno would take their drawers, Miss Jessi," Neil declared. "He even got a deed to some old Scottish castle as part of the winnings from one of those barons."

"What a Black train robber's going to do with a castle in Scotland is anyone's guess," Griffin cracked. He noticed Jessi's bandaged hand for the first time. He frowned as he cradled the hand. "What happened to you?"

"Well, Minerva was being rude, so I taught her some manners."

A concerned Griffin looked at the hand then up into her eyes. "You know ladies don't brawl in the street."

"I think Minerva knows that now."

He chuckled. "Are you all right?"

"It still throbs a bit, but Dr. Salt says it isn't broken."

Two Shafts put in, "She did us proud, Cheno. Dropped Minerva like a sack of rocks. Too bad you missed it."

"Yes, it is. Are you ready to go home?" Griffin asked. He knew how tough she was; her hand could be aching like hell and she'd never say a word.

"Yes. Oh by the way—" Jessi said to Griffin.

She quickly related the details of her talk with the drunken Roscoe Darcy, adding, "He's says he might be willing to talk to the authorities about Reed's hand in my father's death."

"That's good news," Griffin told her. "Now, if we can just convince at least one more person to get on the stand and tell the truth about that night, we might just have us a cooked Reed."

"Poor Percy," Neil spoke mockingly. "Looks like his time has come."

"Yes, it does," his brother voiced in agreement. "Yes, it does."

Jessi and Griffin left the Twins to their own devices and then headed out of town.

"Sleepy?" he asked.

"Not really. Too much excitement, I think."

"Care for a ride in the moonlight?"

"Yes, I would," she said, smiling up at him.

"Then let's go."

Chapter 11

~~~~~~∞∞∞~~~~~~

While Griff handled the reins, Jessi linked her arm with his and rested her head lovingly against his strong shoulder. "That first night you rode up to the house, I had no idea we'd end up this way."

"Neither did I. You weren't real neighborly, as I remember."

Her soft chuckle blended with the night. "I had a reason not to be, don't you think?"

"Yeah, I do. If I'd had Darcy on my back, I'd've been ornery too."

Her thoughts turned to her nemesis. "Do you think he's finished now? His friends didn't appear very pleased tonight."

"I think there are cracks growing in his walls even as we speak."

"I hope you're right. I'm tired of fighting."

"Well, let's not talk about him anymore. You'll spoil the mood."

Jessi smiled. "Okay, what shall we talk about?" Then it came to her. "I know. Let's stop for a moment before we go home."

"Where?"

Jessi gave him directions to a spot on Clayton land

that had a large stand of trees. "I've something to show you."

He drove them to the patch of trees, then stopped. "What is it?"

She turned so that her back was to him. "Can you see well enough to undo my buttons?"

He laughed. "What?"

"Undo my buttons. Or don't you wish to see my fancy French underwear anymore?"

His smile was a mixture of surprise and delight. "You are getting more outrageous every day, Jessi Rose Clayton."

She smiled at him provocatively over her shoulder. "It's all your fault. I never acted this way until you came riding into my life."

He undid her buttons slowly, and as he progressed, Jessi shivered deliciously to the soft brush of his lips against her skin.

"Do you think we'll still be doing this when we're both old and gray?" he murmured.

Jessi didn't respond, she was too busy melting. She'd never thought she'd harbor such intense feelings for one man, or that those feelings would make her do something as outrageous as having him undress her in the moonlight, but here there wasn't another person for miles so she was free to be as outrageous as she wished. When all the buttons were freed, she stood and he carefully removed the costly dress. Moments later she was clad in nothing but shoes, hose, and her corset.

Griff could feel his manhood rising to the occasion. Over the years he'd undressed his share of beautiful women, but nothing compared to this heat-filled exchange. The corset was small and black. He couldn't decide which bewitched him more, the swell of her breasts above the bodice, or the sweet flair of her hips below the garment. The frilly black garters anchoring the hose on her beautiful dark thighs only added to his excitement.

"Gillie says it's French sateen," Jessi told him, turning slowly so he could see. It was trimmed with Russian lace and the tiny gray ribbons that centered the top of the bodice had been fashioned of silk. Noting the hot interest in his vividly colored eyes, she asked, "Was it worth the wait?"

"Oh, yes."

He leaned forward and touched his lips to the soft, rounded swell of each dark breast, while his hand lovingly caressed the yielding flesh of her tempting bottom. Fired by the sensuous sight and feel of her, he dragged the black silk drawers down and off, rendering her deliciously bare from the middle of her hips down. She could already feel herself beginning to flow in response to his wandering hands and decided she enjoyed being outrageous very much.

He undid the silk ribbon and the two buttons directly beneath it and used his hands to brush open the halves of the boned corset. Her breasts were now free to be pleasured and he went about it slowly, using both his hands and his mouth until she arched and groaned.

He brushed his cheek against a berry hard nipple, whispering, "You're mine, Jessi Rose ... my sweet night rose ..."

He covered the nipple with his warm mouth, then bit her with love-gentled teeth. Jessi ran her hand over his soft red gold hair while he feasted, and as his ardor increased she found it hard to stand. His hand strayed to her bottom and urged her closer so he could explore the source of her desire: teasing, dallying, filling her blood with the soaring magic she'd come to crave.

"Bloom for me, Jessi ..." he said thickly, and the wanton slide of his seeking fingers made her do just that. She widened her stance, her body on fire. He plied her expertly, sweetly until passion dewed her like rain.

Next she knew, his big hands were on her waist and she was being placed on the top edge of the seat's back. She braced herself with her hands and legs as he lowered himself to his knees. "I always wanted to see what you tasted like on a wagon seat . . . open your legs for me, Jessi . . ."

She did, without hesitation, unable to deny him or herself the wicked delight sure to follow. Using a bold finger, he played with her in the moonlight, then leaned forward and brought the shining prize to his mouth. He ravished her slowly, tenderly teasing and plying that vulnerable jewel until her hips rose in greedy, welcoming response. She was kindling and he was flame. Her whole world seemed centered on the erotic sensations. When the explosion ripped through her, she screamed his name into the night.

He brought her back to herself with a gentle touch, but the echoes continued to ripple inside her like flames in a breeze, making her shudder and pulse. Boneless, she slid down the seat.

Griff's own desire raged. He stood and divested himself of his clothing. "Let me show you another use for a wagon seat . . ."

The hot timbre of his voice and the cajoling movement of his knuckle over her swollen damp nipples raised her passions once more. She slid herself aside so he could sit, and as she looked down at him she felt desire fuel her with a glowing power.

The promise in her eyes as she moved sensually to his side was as bold and as brazen as any gaze Griffin had ever seen. She gave him a sly smile and then it was his turn to gasp as her warm hand covered him possessively and began to move. His head rolled back against the seat and his eyes closed. She worked her way down to the floor at his feet and gave him a taste of his own medicine. He groaned in reaction and could barely string two breaths together, so sweet was the pain.

"Is this a good use of a wagon seat . . . ?" she asked him, in a voice as hot as her outrageous little mouth.

Griffin couldn't answer; he could barely remember his own name.

When Jessi thought she'd tortured him enough, she slowly kissed her way up his autumn-colored body, pausing to flick her tongue against the whorl of his navel, then the flat sandy nipples. When she finally touched her mouth to his, he dragged her closer and kissed her deeply. He silently intimated the position he wished for her to take and she straddled his seated body with a wanton grace. He eased her down onto his pulsing need and she went weak feeling him slide slowly inside.

She was still moist from his earlier pleasuring and the warm tight feel of her enclosing him almost made his first thrust his last. He wanted nothing more than to let go and send his soul soaring high into the starry sky, but he wanted her to make the journey with him.

Holding her hips, he began a slow erotic rhythm that closed her eyes. In tandem with the seductive heat within, he placed roving kisses against the damp but night-cooled skin of her neck and the planes of her breasts.

Griffin knew he had little mental stamina left. Her uninhibited response to each vivid thrust he gave only increased his need. The enticing bounce of her breasts and the soft purrs she gave as she rode him brought on his first initial quakes of completion. He gripped her hips below the gaping black corset and shuddered as the intense orgasm washed over him. She followed a heartbeat later and they clung to each other, soaring in a world that held only their love.

It took a while for him to convince Jessi to put on her clothes so they could return to the ranch. Her desire for more tempted him so mightily, it resulted in him brazenly making love to her again on a blanket atop the grass, and again on the wagon seat. Finally, they were both too sated for anything else but the ride home; and even then, they kissed and caressed each other every step of the way.

The next day, Jessi dealt with a steady stream of visitors. Darcy had turned over the deeds for most of the ranches and businesses in the area, and the owners all came to the Clayton ranch to see about their return.

The folks who were new in the area and hadn't been infected by the gossip surrounding Jessi's past came to the Clayton ranch humbly. A man named Faragut drove over with his wife and his three boys and told how he'd been reduced to sharecropping because the Darcy bank had prematurely foreclosed on his small patch of farmland. Like many folks snared by the vicious circle of sharecropping, the bank had taken most of his profits since the foreclosure, forcing him and his small family to borrow against the profits of the next year's crop in order to buy food, seed, and supplies. At year's end, they had little to show for their back-breaking work except a few dollars and more debt. When Jessi handed him back the deed, he and his wife had tears in their eyes.

His wife whispered thickly, "May the Good Lord bless you always, Miss Jessi. Now my children can go back to school instead of the fields."

As the Faraguts rode away in their rusted, battered buckboard, they waved, and Jessi waved back. She had tears in her eyes, too—Mrs. Faragut had given her the first blessing she'd received in many many years.

The owner of the Vale Barbershop, Wilson Cornell, and his wife Lydia, arrived shortly after the departing Faraguts. Unlike the Faraguts, Jessi knew the Cornells very well—so well that Jessi supposed hell must be freezing over. Lydia Cornell had been one of Jessi's biggest detractors. In spite of the eggs, Jessi knew it was undoubtedly killing the woman to have to come with her husband to the Clayton ranch and ask for their mortgage back.

"Morning, Miss Jessi," Wilson called as they came up the gravel walk. "Think we're going to get any rain soon?" Wilson had been one of her father's good friends and one the few men to come to Dexter Clayton's funeral. Jessi respected him for that.

"Hope so, Wilson, we could surely use some."

Last summer's drought had been bad and this year seemed no better. All over the state, livestock and crops were dying from the extreme heat.

Lydia stepped up onto the porch. She was dressed in her best church dress and hat. "Morning, Jessi," she said shortly.

"Morning, Lydia."

"I suppose you're going to make us get down on our knees and thank you," she accused haughtily.

"No, Lydia, I'm not, but if you feel the urge, be my guest."

The barber glared at his wife before saying, "My apologies, Miss Jessi."

"None needed. I know where I stand with Lydia and her friends. Here's your deed. Oh, and thanks for the eggs. Now, Wilson, get her off of my land."

"You should have made her eat crow," Griffin cracked, as he and the others came out onto the porch.

"I should've made her eat arsenic, the old bat."

The next buckboard arriving carried visitors who brightened Jessi's mood. It was Auntie and her girls.

Dressed in her flashiest red dress, the heavyset, light-skinned woman jumped from the board and ran to the porch to engulf Jessi in a big hug. "The girls and I don't know how to thank you."

Camille, Lottie, and Sylvia were decked out in their gaudy finery too. They smiled up at the Twins.

"Your boys can have free services anytime you want," Sylvia promised.

"You too, Preacher," Lottie said, with a grin and a sultry wink.

In response, he began to cough so violently, Jessi became worried.

Griff slapped his friend on the back. "Did you swallow something, old man?"

"Drinks will be on the house, too," Auntie pledged, "and now that my new place is *my* place again, I'm going to enjoy it even more."

When Jessi handed the saloon owner her mortgage, Auntie pulled Jessi to her ample bosom and gave her another smothering hug. "God bless you, little girl. Even if I never said so directly, you have been in my prayers for many, many years."

Jessi returned the embrace. "I know, and it looks as if they're being answered. Thanks, Auntie."

"You're welcome." She finally released Jessi. "Boys, tonight I'm having a mortgage-burning party, and you are the guests of honor. Are you coming?"

Neil bowed. "We'd be honored."

Auntie clapped her hands. "Good. Well, me and the girls are going to head back. You keep your rifle close, little girl, and if you or that handsome devil ever need us for *anything*, just holler."

"We will," Jessi replied genuinely.

"That's some woman," Griffin declared, as they rode away.

Jessi agreed. "She's been a fixture here since I was young. The women in town don't respect her and her girls one bit, but they gladly accepted the money Auntie gave the town to buy new school books last year."

Two Shafts spoke up. "Can I ask why everybody around calls you 'little girl'?"

Jessi grinned. "Because I was such a handful growing up. It began with Gillie in school. She'd be teaching and I'd be causing mischief and she would say, 'I've had just about enough out of you, little girl.'"

"How old were you?" Griffin asked, chuckling.

"Six. Then, as I reached eight and nine, I got into even more trouble. Folks would come stomping to the door and say to my mother, 'That little girl of yours threw eggs at my cows,' or, 'That little girl of yours just fell out of my tree.' I was a terror. Pretty soon, anytime anyone said, 'That little girl did this or that,' everyone around knew it was me they were describing. Finally, it became a nickname."

Griffin had a hard time squaring that mischievous girl child with the rawhide woman who knew her to be today. She held herself on such a tight rein, he couldn't imagine her running wild. What made her change? Had it been her mother's death or the time with Bob Winston? Griff wondered if he'd ever find out.

"What are you gentlemen planning for this already hot day?" Jessi asked, looking around at them. Even though it was still early morning, the heat had gotten out of bed early too.

Griff answered, "Soon as Joth is done with his lesson, the four of us are going to ride out to the range. Joth said you wanted to take a look at the cows today and see how they're faring with the drought."

She did, but the injury to her hand prevented her from holding reins. She'd have to stay behind.

"Preacher, what are you doing today?" she aked.

The green-eyed man in black told her, "I'm going to Austin. Maybe the sheriff there can give me some more information on that Eula Grimes. I'll be back in a few days."

He went off to pack.

All the men left shortly afterward, and once they were gone, Jessi went back into the house and reveled in the silence.

She was in the kitchen reading the newspaper when Griff's contingent returned later that afternoon. Setting aside the edition of the *Freeman*, published in New York by the great Black newspaper man T. Thomas Fortune, Jessi went to hear the report on her cows.

"They're doing fine, Aunt Jessi," Joth said, as the men trooped in. "Some of the big cows are a little scrawny, but they still have enough grass and water."

"Good. How're the new calves holding up?"

"Two were with their mamas and we found one dead."

Jessi sighed with resignation. She couldn't afford any deaths in her small herd, not if she wanted to rebuild the numbers. With the price of beef falling every day, the future did not look bright. Last year's drought had already wiped out many of the small ranchers, and Jessi did not want the Claytons to be next.

The Twins rode off for town to visit the bath house so they could get all spruced up for Auntie's mortgage-burning party. They'd be back tomorrow. Joth went out to see to Buttercup, which left Jessi and Griffin alone in the kitchen.

"That Joth knows an awful lot about cows," Griffin told Jessi as he poured himself a glass of lemonade and took a seat at the kitchen table. "Told me all about Coronado bringing the first cattle to Texas."

"Yep, around 1541, if I remember Gillie's lessons correctly. He and his men didn't want to starve while they were exploring, so they brought livestock. Some of the cattle escaped and that gave birth to the great wild herds of longhorns."

"He talked about cattle drives and imported Brahma

bulls from India. I knew about yearlings, but I'd never heard cows called longs, shorts, tail ends, or scabs. The Twins and I learned a lot from that boy today."

"He's been around cattle all his life. He's bound to have picked up some knowledge."

"Well, thanks to Joth, I now know that shorts are calves over one year old, but short of two. Longs are two years old, but not yet three, and Tails and Scabs are about the same."

"Yes. They're all the calves who aren't yearlings yet."

"I was very impressed." Griff declared again. "Very impressed, and I told him so."

Jessi was pleased to hear Griff sing Joth's praises; her nephew was very special to her also.

Griffin spied the paper on the table. He picked it up and began glancing through it. "Anything new back in the States?"

"Back in the States" was the phrase most Texans used when referring to the states back east.

Jessi began placing dishes in the sink for washing. "The *Freeman*'s publisher, Mr. Fortune, is wanting to form what he's calling an Afro-American League. He says we Black folks need an agency to protect us from all the violence going on, especially the people in the South."

"Sounds like a good idea to me," Griffin replied, as he continued to leaf through the newspaper. "I don't think the men of the race fought in the war just so they could be killed on the way to the polls by a bunch of illiterate Democrats dressed in sheets."

Jessi didn't think so either.

He went silent a moment as he read on. "Did you see this notice about the new colleges?"

"No. Where are they?"

"It doesn't say exactly, but they're named: Kentucky

State College, Florida A & M, and Central State College. That's good news.''

"It certainly is. The race needs schools of higher education. Anything else I missed in there?''

"Some kluxers paid a visit to a Black church up in Denison. When the church folks refused to be intimidated, the kluxers left. It seems that the White citizens were just as outraged as the Blacks were.''

"There are some good people out there.''

"Yes, there are.'' He set the paper down and said, "Those colleges aren't the only good news. You gave some people some pretty good news yourself today by returning those mortgages.''

"Yes, but it was your idea. You deserve all the credit.''

"Just trying to impress a certain lady I know.''

Jessi walked over and kissed him on the cheek. "You have succeeded.''

Griff stood and wrapped his arms around her. "I've been real proud of you.''

She savored how good it felt to have him hold her close this way. "And why is that?''

"Because of the way you handled those deeds. Some of those folks haven't been nice to you.''

"*Most* of those folks haven't been nice to me,'' she cracked.

"I know, but you were gracious and kind.''

"I'll bet you didn't think I had it in me.''

He looked down into her eyes. "They might've thought that, but I know better. You *are* gracious and kind, not to mention magnificent and beautiful.''

"You're prejudiced.''

"I am that.''

Later, after supper, Jessi stood in the door and watched Griffin and Joth play marbles out in the corral. They were too far away for their conversation to be heard, but Jessi could see Griffin giving her nephew pointers on shooting angles and the positioning of his body. Griff may have learned some things about cows from Joth today, but Joth was learning from Griffin, too—like how to be a good man, and the many ways to look adversity in the eye and not blink. If Jessi had her way, Joth would also learn how to be a caring husband, because she'd decided she would marry Griffin Blake, she just hadn't told him so yet. How could she not love a man who'd given her sunsets?

That evening, after hearing Joth recite his prayers, Jessi sat on the edge of his bed, listening to his last words of the day. She told him, "Griffin and the Twins were pretty bowled over by how much you knew about cattle."

"Were they?" His eyes were shining.

"Yes, they were. You're going to be a fine rancher someday."

He just grinned.

Jessi touched his face tenderly. "Can I ask you something?"

"Yep."

"How would you feel if Griffin and I got married?"

"Will I have to live somewhere else?"

Confused by the question, Jessi replied, "No. Why would you think that?"

"Because when Reggie Becker got a new pa, his mama made Reggie go live with his grandmother up in Dallas."

Jessi knew that Reggie was one of Joth's classmates, but knew nothing about his family or their situation. "You won't have to move away, I promise. Griff and I both would miss you dearly if you weren't here."

"Would you?"

"Extremely."

He went silent a moment, then said softly, "I've been real lonely since Gramps died."

"I know, sweetheart."

"But Griff's starting to fix that."

"I'm glad."

"He's a lot of fun, Aunt Jessi. He calls you the Governor."

Jessi laughed. "Does he, now?"

"Yep, and he asked my permission to court you."

Jessi went still. "He did?"

"He said since I was the only Clayton male, he had to ask me."

That Griffin would be so caring as to seek permission from Joth made Jessi's heart full indeed. "And what did you say?" she asked him softly.

"I asked him would he be nice to you, and when he said yes, I said yes, too. Did I say the right thing?"

"Yes, darling, you did, and you asked a real fine question, too."

"Are you crying, Aunt Jessi?"

She nodded. "A little bit, but they're happy tears."

"Does this mean you and Griff will have to kiss?"

"Yep, we *have* to, it's part of the rules."

"Ugh! Mollie tried to kiss me at school one day, and I told her I'd make her eat a lizard if she ever tried it again."

Jessi's tears spilled onto her cheeks as she laughed at that, and she wiped them away. "It's time for you to get to sleep."

She leaned down and gave him a tender kiss on the brow. "Good night, Jotham Clayton. May all your dreams be good ones."

He gave her a strong hug and said, "Good night, Aunt Jessi."

Jessi found Griffin out on the front porch watching the first act of the evening's sunset. "So, I'm known as the Governor, am I?" she asked, standing above him with a hand on her hip and a smile on her face.

He looked up and laughed. "He told you? Wait until I see that boy. Doesn't he know that when you talk man to man you don't tell the womenfolk?"

"Guess not," she chuckled, as she took a seat beside him.

"What other beans did he spill?"

"That you asked his permission to court me."

Her serious tone made him turn to look into her eyes.

"Yes, I did. This will affect his life too. I wanted to make sure it was all right. Does he approve? I know he told me he did, but he'd tell you the real truth."

"He does, as long as we don't make him move away."

"What?"

After Jessi explained she said, "I reassured him that we couldn't live without him and he seemed much more at ease after that. He said you're a lot of fun, and that you're fixing the parts of him that have been sad since my father's death."

Griffin was touched by the words, Jessi could see it in his face and hear it in his voice as he said, "He's a fine boy. It'll be my honor to watch him grow up and be a fine man."

"You're a very fine man yourself, Griffin Blake."

"But not fine enough to marry?"

"Finer."

He searched her eyes. "What's that mean?"

"It means, will you marry me? And don't you dare laugh," she added quickly.

He studied her closely. "Are you sure?"

"Yes."

"When?"

"I'd like to wait until Darcy's out of our lives. We shouldn't have to split the watch on our wedding night."

He fought hard to contain his excitement. "I'd really prefer it be sooner, but you're right. Let's get rid of Darcy first."

Jessi also needed time to gather her courage; the story of Bob Winston had yet to be told.

He put his arm around her waist and drew her close. "I'm glad you said yes."

"So am I. I love you, Griffin."

He kissed her softly. "I love you too, boss lady."

They cuddled close and sat that way in silence until the sun went down and the night crept in.

A few days later, Jessi's hand had healed enough to handle reins, so she and Joth went to town that morning to see Gillie. Joth needed to see her about getting information on Juan Cortinas for his school essay, and Jessi needed her talented mentor to make her a wedding dress.

Gillie was surprised, to say the least, not by the news of the marriage but by Jessi's request. "*You* want a dress? You, who will probably go to your grave in a pair of denims?"

"Yes, Gillie, I do. Granted, I've not been real partial to dresses lately, but Griffin and I are getting married. I have to do what's appropriate."

"Since when? Jotham, your aunt was such a mischief maker she used to put snakes in my handbag."

Joth had a tale to beat that. "Ross McCoy painted Mr. Trent's chair one morning and when Mr. Trent sat down the whole bottom of his trousers were bright red. When Ross's daddy got through with him, he couldn't sit in school for three whole days."

Jessi, who was in the process of leafing through some of Gillie's dress sketches, shook her head at the story.

"So, Joth, what do you need to know about Señor Cortinas? You and I can talk while your Aunt Jessi looks at the sketches."

"Who was he?"

"Well, his full name was Juan Nepomunceno Cortinas and he was the son of a very wealthy Mexican family. His friends called him Cheno."

Joth nodded. "I know that part. The Twins call Griffin Cheno. They said they named him after Señor Cortinas."

"Really?"

"Yep. They said it was because Griffin has a red beard and likes to help people too."

"Well, that certainly describes Señor Cortinas. Some folks called him the Mexican Robin Hood. Now, let's see if I remember the story. It began back in '59, if my memory is correct, and as I said before, the Cortinases were large landholders down on the border. They were ranchers just like the Claytons."

Joth smiled.

"One day, Cheno went into Brownsville for his morning coffee and saw the sheriff trying to arrest one of the Cortinases' former servants."

"Why?"

"The servant was drunk."

"Oh."

"Cheno didn't mind that the sheriff was trying to arrest the drunk, but he thought the sheriff was being a little abusive."

"What's abusive?"

"It means the sheriff was being too rough."

"I understand. So what did Cheno do?"

"He tried to talk to the sheriff, but the sheriff cursed him."

"That wasn't very nice," Jessi offered, looking up.

"Cheno didn't think so either, and he got mad and shot the sheriff in the arm and dragged the servant up behind him on his horse and galloped away."

"I'll bet the sheriff was really mad then," Joth declared.

"He sure was."

"What happened next?" Joth asked.

"Well, like Quanah Parker and the Comanche, he declared war."

"Over a drunk servant?" Jessi asked.

"No, the servant was just one more incident in a series that had the Mexicans as outraged as the Indians over the way they were being treated by the Anglos."

Gillie looked at Joth and said, "Just like Reed Darcy is trying to steal your land, the Anglos were stealing the land from the Mexicans. They didn't care about the Spanish grants that proved the Mexicans owned the land; they wanted all the land on the northern side of the Rio Grande, so they set out to get it. Granted, some Anglos purchased the land legally, but others didn't, and that's why Cheno declared war."

Gillie then told of how Cheno rode into Brownsville in September of 1859 and terrorized the town. "The residents of Brownsville were all sleeping late because they'd all been to a party in Matamoros the night before, so when Cheno rode in with about a hundred men, there was chaos. They sacked stores, turned prisoners out of jail, and shot five men who were either brave enough or loco enough to try and defend the town."

Cortinas and his men held the town for some time while the frightened citizens stayed locked in their homes. Only after receiving pleas from the Mexican authorities did the Mexican Robin Hood and his men leave Brownsville. He then rode back to his Santa Rita ranch and issued a proclamation declaring war on those persecuting the Mexican landholders. As a result, many Mexicans came to Santa Rita to aid Cortinas in his fight to defend their legal rights.

"Meanwhile," Gillie said, continuing, "the Anglos in

Brownsville organized a local militia called the Brownsville Tigers and decided they were going to march on Cheno and his men over in Santa Rita.''

''And?'' Jessi asked.

''And they got their butts whipped. It took them a week to march the seven miles upriver in their uniforms, but they may as well have stayed home. Cheno and his men were hiding in the chaparral and as soon as the Mexicans opened fire, the Brownsville Tigers took off running so fast they left their cannon behind.''

Joth laughed.

''That had to be the quickest retreat on record,'' Jessi said grinning.

''I don't know, but if it isn't it has to be fairly close.''

''What happened next?''

''They sent in the Texas Rangers and got the same result. The Rangers did manage to escape with their cannon, though, and after that, Cheno sent out another proclamation. This time he called on the Mexicans in the Valley to join him in the fight. He said he only wanted to protect Mexican land and rights.''

''Did the authorities believe him?'' Jessi asked.

''Of course not; they called him a bandit and a horse thief and in December sent in the Army.''

''Did they have to retreat too?'' Joth wanted to know.

''No. Cheno and his men were the ones in retreat that day, but they made it safely into Mexico.''

Though the Texas Rangers and the Army did their best to capture him, Cortinas, now based in Mexico, became even more of a thorn in the side of the Texas authorities. He burned the ranches of non-Latins, attacked Rio Grande steamboats, raided border towns, and then slipped away time and time again, frustrating the Rangers and the Army no end. Cortinas's campaign soon drew the attention of the government in Washington and Lt. Col. Robert E. Lee was sent to investigate. His reports to the War Department, Texas officials, and the Mexican government brought about a cooperative agreement that settled the issues Cortinas had championed.

"What happened to him after that?"

"He stayed in Mexico and became a general in the Mexican army. Later he was the governor of the Mexican state of Tamaulipas."

Joth went over to Gillie and gave her a hug. "Thanks, Gillie. I'm betting I'll have the best essay in Mr. Trent's class."

"I'm betting too," she replied.

Jessi spent a few more moments looking through the sketches.

"Did you see anything that caught your eye?" Gillie asked.

"Not really."

"Then let me pick out something. I'll just need to measure you."

Jessi didn't argue. Gillie had been making clothes for Jessi most of her life and she trusted her judgment, so while Joth took out his paper and pen and started in on his assignment, Gillie and Jessi went to the back room to do the measurements.

"Have you and Griffin set a date?" Gillie asked, as she moved around Jessi's body with her tapes.

Heeding Gillie's silent command, Jessi raised her arms so the tape could measure her bosom. "No, we want to get Darcy out of the way first.

"I'm real glad you decided to say yes, Jessi. He'll be a good partner for you."

Jessi smiled. "I think so too."

"But speaking of Darcy, any more news on the Grimes woman?"

"Not so far. Griffin's friend Preacher went to Austin to talk to the sheriff there, but I saw Roscoe the other day and he says he may be willing to testify about Dex's death. He said Reed did order the killing.''

"That's promising. Now, if he can only be convinced to stop his drinking.''

"He looked awful,'' Jessi confessed.

"Smells worse.''

"Gillie,'' Jessi said warningly.

"I know, and I'm sorry, but I've never had much patience with Roscoe. I just wish he would stand up to Reed one time. That's all it will take.''

"Easier said than done sometimes.''

"I know. I know.''

Jessi paused a moment while she thought back. "When mama died and all of the gossip started about her and Reed, Ros would come over and ride with me. We never talked about anything, just rode. It made me feel like someone in the world cared. I'll never forget that, or the trees we climbed, or the lizards we were always hunting. He was a good friend, but that was a long time ago.''

"Yes, it was.''

Silence reigned a moment as they both mused on the past, then Gillie asked, "And what is this about you brawling with Minerva?''

Jessi hoped she wasn't in line for a scolding. "It wasn't a brawl, it was more like a punch.''

"Was it a good one?''

"Broke one of her teeth.''

"Good for you!'' Gillie clapped her hands. Jessi laughed.

When Gillie was done, Jessi had Joth gather up his things and they left the shop for the journey back to the ranch.

That evening, as Jessi and Griffin were drying the last of the supper dishes and putting them in the sideboard she asked, "Where do you suppose Preacher's gotten to, Griffin? He's been gone almost a week now."

"Chasing leads no doubt. He'll be back, he always is."

The dishes were now done and they went out to the porch with the hopes of finding a cool breeze. The ever present daily heat had not abated, nor had there been any rain. The nights now were almost as unbearable as the days.

As they sat, Jessi still had the Preacher on her mind. She was worried about him and missed his blessings at the supper table. "How'd you meet the Preacher?"

"Tracking the man who killed his wife."

Jessi's heart turned over. "Really?"

"Yep, an outlaw named Bivens."

"Was he someone Preacher had turned in for a bounty?"

"No, he and Preacher were in the same gang."

She found that answer surprising. "The Preacher was an outlaw?"

"Back then he was, yes. Robbed banks, hired out his gun—you name it. Even robbed trains for a while."

Jessi shook her head. "I would never have believed it."

"Everybody has a past."

His serious manner made her look into his eyes and then gave rise to thoughts about her own past. What would he say when it was revealed? "So, why did Bivens kill her?"

"Because he took a shine to her and couldn't have her. Her name was Tilda and she was a spinster seamstress when she and the Preacher first met. In fact, she was one of the customers in a bank that the gang robbed, and to hear Preacher tell it, it was love at first sight. He came back to the town a few weeks later and tried to court her but she wouldn't have him. She told him he'd have to walk on the right side of the law.''

"So he did?"

"Yep. Quit the life. Started going to church and everything. A year later some of the old gang members came back to town. Bivens knew she was Preacher's wife, but he didn't care. One night while Preacher was in town, Bivens goes out to the house, forces himself on her . . . cut her throat. She bled to death.''

Jessi was appalled. "How did he know it was Bivens?''

"He got a letter from one of his former outlaw friends saying a drunken Bivens had bragged about the deed in a saloon up in Laramie.''

Jessi shook her head sadly. Who knew Preacher carried such tragic memories inside?

"Out of respect for his dead wife, he knew he couldn't just go and hunt Bivens down and kill him like he wanted, so he became a bounty hunter. That way he could do it within the law.''

"Did he ever find him?"

Griff nodded. "In Nevada, right after he and I met. He'd tracked him for almost a year.''

"How'd you meet him?"

"I was cooking a rabbit in the middle of the night in upstate Nevada and he walked up to the fire. One minute I was by myself and the next minute he was standing there. Scared me so bad, I almost shot him.''

An amused Jessi linked her arm with his and rested her head against his shoulder. "Did he tell you his story?''

"He did. It was easy to see he was still grieving for her, and those green eyes had a glow in them that made me glad he wasn't hunting me. He said he was headed downstate and since I was going that way too, we rode together. We found Bivens in a whorehouse outside of Reno and Preacher marched him out of there at gunpoint. Didn't even let him put on his clothes. It was the last time anyone saw him alive.''

"Did he kill him?"

Griffin shrugged. "Can't really say for sure, but Bivens' buddies found him on the trail outside of town. He'd been castrated. He bled to death, just like Preacher's wife.''

"I hope he's found peace since then.''

"He rarely speaks about her now, but I guess he loved her very much.''

Jessi now had a new understanding of Griffin's solemn green-eyed friend. She could only hope that one day a new love would enter his life to heal the hole in his heart.

The next night an unknown arsonist set fire to the Darcy Hotel and burned it to the ground. Doyle rode out to the Clayton spread to relate the news the following morning.

"Was anyone hurt?" Jessi asked, as she stood with him and the others on the front porch.

"No, everybody got out safely, but folks in town are saying you ordered it done, Jessi.''

"I would've liked to, but I had nothing to do with it.''

Jessi looked over at the Twins.

They shook their heads. "We had nothing to do with it either. Wish we'd thought of it, though.'' Shafts spoke with a light in his dark eyes. "Darcy's living on the street, I hope.''

"Naw, he's moved in with Roscoe for now.''

Roscoe and Minerva lived in a large house not too far from Gillie. Jessi was fairly certain Ros had not been given a choice.

"Do they have any idea who might've set the fire?'' Griffin asked.

"Not a clue," Doyle replied, "and since there's no sheriff now that Cap's gone, Reed doesn't have anyone to look into the matter. I hear he's fit to be tied."

It pleased Jessi to know that Reed's world was tumbling down. First, he'd lost his financial hold on Vale, and now his hotel had been reduced to rubble. She thought it couldn't've happened to a better man.

Griffin asked, "Is there going to be an election for a new sheriff?"

"Yep, early next week. Supposedly your friend Percy West is Reed's hand-picked choice this time and will probably win since no one is loco enough to run against him."

"Percy as a sheriff?" Jessi asked incredulously.

"What do you have to do to be a candidate?" Griff wanted to know.

"Just go to the bank and place your name on the ballot, as far as I know."

"I wonder if you can be a marshal and a sheriff?" Griff asked speculatively.

Jessi could see the light in his eyes. "Why?"

"I think I might want to run against Percy. That'd give Darcy a fit or two."

"Or three," Neil said, grinning.

Doyle had trouble holding in his smile. "Are you serious?"

"I think I am. What do you think, Jessi? Do you want to be married to a sheriff?"

She didn't hesitate. "Griffin, if you want to be sheriff, you have my blessing."

He turned his attention back to Doyle. "Do you think I can be elected?"

The big barkeep shrugged. "Darcy bought a lot of votes last time around and folks were real scared. This time, though, his pockets are lighter, and you did fix it so folks were able to get their land and homes back. So who knows, maybe they'll be less afraid now. I know I'd vote for you.''

''That's one,'' Two Shafts cracked.

So Griffin and Jessi accompanied Doyle back to town. The sight of still smoldering rubble on the spot where the Darcy Hotel once stood brought them up short. The scorched and blackened remains bore little resemblance to what once had been Vale's fanciest landmark. A crowd of curious townspeople were gathered around the ruins, peering and pointing at the piles of debris and ash.

As Jessi and Griffin rode on, the onlookers turned their way. A few met Jessi's gaze and gave her an almost imperceptible nod of greeting, which she returned.

The bank was quiet and shadowy. The two small windows in the front wall let in as much light as they could, but it wasn't enough. The only person inside was the clerk who'd delivered the deeds to Griffin the night of the poker game. His name was Alfred Cooper and he was a short thin-boned man. When they walked up to his desk, he gave them a disdainful glance and went back to the ledger he was viewing.

Griffin turned to Jessi Rose. ''The first thing I'm going to do when I get elected sheriff is teach this town some manners.''

Hearing that, the clerk looked up and his eyes were wide. ''You're going to run for sheriff?''

''Yep, that's why I'm here. Where do I sign up?''

The clerk became very agitated. ''Why, you can't do that! Mr. Darcy has already decided who the sheriff is going to be.''

Jessi retorted quietly, ''In an election the *people* decide.''

The clerk looked from Jessi to Griffin and then from Griffin to Jessi, then stood nervously. ''Wait here.''

A few moments later, Darcy came out from behind a

closed door. His opinion of them showed plainly on his face. "Did you come to gloat?"

Jessi met his gaze squarely, "About what?"

"Burning down my hotel." Darcy looked disheveled. His suit was rumpled and it appeared that he hadn't shaved in days. He seemed to be paying a heavy toll for his sins.

"We had nothing to do with it."

"I'm supposed to believe that, but you won't believe I had nothing to do with your father's death."

"It isn't the same, Reed, and you know it."

"Jessi, I'm in love with you," he told her pleadingly. "Why won't you marry me?"

Jessi didn't believe this. "Why in the world do you keep asking me that? There isn't a chance in hell that I'll say yes—you know it and I know it."

"But to marry someone like him?" he said disdainfully, pointing at Griff. "That doesn't make sense, when I can offer you so much more."

"You caused the deaths of both of my parents. You've given me more than enough."

"How can I convince you that I had nothing to do with their deaths? I loved your mother. Violet was the most beautiful and precious thing to me in the whole world. Her death left me devastated."

"And my father's?"

"Dex and I didn't get along, I admit that. I think we came out of the womb hating each other, but I never wanted him to die like that."

Jessi wondered how many lies one man's soul could hold.

"Jessi, let me give you all the things I couldn't give your mother. Please."

"And what about Minerva?" Jessi asked, wanting this conversation to stop once and for all. "I doubt she'd take kindly to being replaced by the likes of me, even if I were of a mind to agree.''

His eyes grew wide with outrage.

Jessi continued, ''Ros may be a drunkard, but he isn't blind. He knows that you and Minerva are lovers.''

His face turned ugly. ''How dare you accuse me of such a thing?''

''I'll dare anything I damn well please, including fighting you with my last breath. I may look like my mother, but I am not her.''

''You'll regret this,'' he promised with cold eyes. ''I won't ask again, Jessi.''

Griffin drawled, ''I know you like to pretend I'm not here, Darcy, but before you stomp off, I want my name placed on the ballot for sheriff.''

''I don't care what you want, Blake. This is my town,'' he snarled.

''Not anymore.''

''The sheriff will be who *I* say it will be,'' he said pointing at his own chest for emphasis.

''Okay, Darcy. I guess I'll just have to be a write-in candidate.''

''No one's loco enough to vote for you. They know better than to buck me.''

''Tell that to the person who torched your hotel.''

Jessi smiled. ''Are we done here, darling?''

''Yep.''

Griff then turned to the steaming Darcy. ''After I get elected, I'll look into that fire for you. So don't worry.''

''Get out!''

So they did.

Chapter 12

Back out on the street now, Jessi and Griffin split up. He'd promised to pick up a new razor for Neil, so he had to go by Abe Thomas's store; she wanted to stop by Gillie's to check on the progress of her wedding dress. They pledged to meet up when their errands were done.

Jessi found Gillie inside, working on a new hat. The old woman smiled as Jessi entered.

"I didn't know you were in town."

"Griff and I rode in so he could place his name on the ballot for next week's sheriff's election."

"Griffin's going to run for sheriff?"

"He says he is. Darcy refused to give him any of the papers to sign, though, so Griffin's going to have to be a write-in candidate." She was quiet as she thought about her exchange with Darcy. "How could my mother have turned to such a snake?"

"Things are not always as black and white as they seem," Gillie voiced sagely. "Your mother was lonely and Reed took advantage of that. Violet had no business coming out here from England. She was too delicate and fragile for life here. When she married Dex, I'm certain she'd no idea he couldn't love anything but the land or that she'd spend most of her time alone while he went on drives for months at a time, or rode fences at night. Once you and your sister were born, she had the two of you to love, but she never had the love of her husband.''

Jessi found the story sad yet enlightening. ''I knew my mother came to Texas as a mail order bride, but was she truly that unhappy? It doesn't seem that she was. I remember how beautiful she was and all the lovely clothes she wore, and how wonderful she smelled.''

''You were young, Jessi. Children don't often see the true light of things. As I said, I believe she turned to Reed out of pure loneliness.''

''But why Reed?''

''Reed had charm and back east manners and he knew how to treat a lady like your mother, but he and your father always seemed to hate each other, even before Violet.''

''Why?''

''Because your father was everything Reed's father Vale wanted Reed to be, and he threw it in Reed's face every chance he got. Your father could ride, shoot, brand. He was a true son of Texas and Reed was never any good at any of it. Do you know why Reed always travels by carriage?''

''Because he thinks he's a Caesar?''

Gillie grinned. ''No. It's because he's afraid of horses.''

''Really?'' Jessi chuckled with disbelief. ''Reed Darcy, afraid of horses?''

''Yep, one day when he was young, oh, he couldn't've been more than six or seven, your pa and some other boys tied him in his saddle, stuck some firecrackers under it, and set them afire. That horse must've bucked for ten minutes with Reed holding on, screaming and crying the whole time. The horse came right up Main Street. Everybody in town saw it and started laughing. My late husband Virgil was the one who finally grabbed the horse and put poor Reed out of his misery, but his pa never forgave him for embarrassing him that way, and Reed never got on another horse.''

''I never knew that.''

''Yep,'' Gillie nodded. ''His pa wanted Reed to be rough and tough like your father, but Reed wasn't cut from that kind of cloth, so he sent him back east to live with his mother's kin in Pennsylvania, until he was oh, fourteen, fifteen.''

''What was he like when he came back?''

''Bookish, learned, charming, everything your father was not. Drove his father crazy, and the women around here too. Women like that Lydia Cornell worshipped the ground he walked on back then.''

''Lydia Cornell?''

''Well, suffice it to say, she wasn't as chaste then as she claims to be now. She hated your mother for catching Reed's eye.''

''Is that the reason she's been so especially hateful all these years?''

''No doubt.''

When Jessi had come back to town after her time with Calico Bob Winston, she'd been unable to return to her position as Vale's schoolteacher due to what the school-board described as Jessi's lack of good moral standing. Lydia, president of the board at that time, had been one of the loudest voices raised against her.

Gillie peered at Jessi. ''Are you okay, little girl?''

Jessi came back. ''Yes, Gillie, I'm fine.'' The story had given her food for thought, though.

They then spent a few more moments looking at the three sketches Gillie had chosen as finalists. Jessi studied each closely. Her decision made, she handed Gillie sketch number three.

''I like that one, too,'' Gillie declared. ''So I will get started. When I need you for fittings, I'll send word.''

Jessi gave her former teacher a kiss on the brow and left the shop to meet Griffin. She found him peering through the glass of the now vacant sheriff's office. "What're you doing?" she asked.

"Just window shopping."

"Are you really going to run for sheriff?"

"Yep. I've a wife and a nephew to provide for. I'll need something steady. Besides who would know more about catching criminals than a former criminal?"

Jessi supposed he had a point.

There was only one thing standing in the way of Jessi's happiness—her past. The need to tell Griffin everything had begun to weigh on her heavily. She very much wanted to rid herself of the burden once and for all, but she was afraid, afraid that it would change her in his eyes and in the end alter his feelings for her. She didn't want to lose him, not after all he'd given her. Joth would be heartbroken too, should Griffin decide he didn't want to marry her after learning the truth, but she knew she couldn't put it off any longer. He loved her and she loved him, she'd just have to rely on faith and hope everything would come out all right.

To that end, she walked over to the barn and knocked on the closed door. "Griffin, are you in there?" she called.

Since they'd agreed to marry, he'd been spending most of his free time working on the bed he'd seen in his dream. He promised she'd get a look at it but not until it was finished because he wanted it to be a surprise.

He came out and closed the door behind him. She stood silent while he dusted the sawdust and wood shavings off of his shirt and trousers then asked, "Can you walk with me a moment? There's something I need to tell you."

Griffin thought she looked unusually serious, even for her, so he said, "Sure, Jessi."

As they began to walk, she spoke. "They came here in the middle of the night. There were six of them, including Bob Winston."

He realized what story she was about to tell. "Jessi, you don't have—"

"Yes, I do, Griffin, because now is the time. If after I'm done you no longer wish to continue as we've been, you are free to stay, finish the work with Darcy, and then move on. If you decide to stay, we will face the future together."

Griffin loved her more at that moment than he'd ever thought possible. "Then continue."

"They were drunk, all of them, and they rode up to the house yelling and shooting. When I came out of my room they were holding my father at gunpoint. Neither my father nor I had ever seen Winston before, so he introduced himself. He said he'd come to claim his son and for me to get him or he'd send my father to hell. I asked him if he knew anything about raising a three-year-old child. He admitted he didn't, but said it didn't matter, he wanted his son."

The awfulness of that night came back to Jessi like a bad dream. "My father offered him everything: money, land, cattle. He kept saying no. The other men were urging Bob to go ahead and shoot so they could ride on."

She stopped walking and turned to Griffin. "My father then offered him something he did want. Me."

His eyes widened. "You? Jessi, no."

"Yes. He told Winston that I could be his for as long as he wished, if he'd let Joth remain."

"You didn't protest?"

"What was there to protest? There were six of them, my father's hands had been given the night off so they could go to the Juneteenth celebration in town. Had Winston wanted to he could've just taken Joth and killed us both and no one would've been the wiser.''

She quieted.

Griffin wanted to pull her into his arms and hold her until the memories of that night no longer brought her pain. He fully understood the dilemma Dexter Clayton must've faced, but Griffin was still appalled that he'd sacrificed his own daughter.

Jessi went on in a toneless voice. ''You have to understand, Joth was the first male child born in the family in many years. When Mama was alive, my father often berated her for giving birth to two useless girls. A man needed sons to keep the land, he would say, so he absolutely adored Joth.''

''Surely your father loved you and your sister.''

''My father loved this land—he didn't have room in his heart or time in his day for much else, but I tried to win his love anyway. As a young girl I learned to hunt, trap, brand cattle, even went on the cattle drives north. I did my best to be as good as the son he always wanted, but after Mama's death, he was so filled up with anger and rage, I guess I gave up. I turned to my books. Mildred turned to men, the more unsuitable the better. She left home a few months before I went east to school, and she vowed never to live under my father's roof again, but she must not have had anyplace else to go because she did return, carrying her unborn child.''

When Griffin first began falling in love with Jessi he knew that this would be a story he wouldn't enjoy hearing, and he'd been right. He wanted to dig up Calico Bob and kill him again.

''I rode with Winston and his gang for eighteen months. I cooked for them, washed their clothes. I learned to make a smokeless fire, a dozen ways to prepare beans, and how to disguise myself as a man.''

"Did they take you on robberies?"

"A few. I was usually the lookout and held the horses out front. Blessedly, no one was killed when I was along."

Griffin could feel his anger rising at the people in town. They called her whore, but did they know what she'd done to keep her nephew safe? The sacrifice she'd made? Did they have any idea how terrified she must have been, especially at first?

Her voice trembling, she finally confessed, "He took me only twice, Griffin. I swear."

He pulled her into his arms and held onto her fiercely. "Do you think I care about that?" he asked in a voice thick with emotion. "I love you, Jessi Rose, more than anything in this world, and nothing will ever *ever* change that." He pulled back and gazed down into her teary eyes. "Do you understand that?"

She couldn't speak.

"There is nothing that'll make me stop. Nothing."

For a few long moments they held onto each other while Jessi cried out a decade of hurt and fear. He kissed her tears and mentally pledged to spend the rest of his life making sure no one ever hurt her again.

After a while he said, "Let's sit a minute."

He took a seat in the open field and eased her down onto his lap. He kissed the top of her soft dark hair. "You okay?"

Jessi savored the solid feel of him surrounding her and she thanked the heavens for sending her such a wonderful and loving man. Wiping at her eyes, she gladly accepted the clean handkerchief he offered and she blew her nose. "Gillie's the only other person I've told this story to. She thinks another reason my father might've offered me up was because I look so much like my mother." She sniffed. "When I came back here from

New York to help my father raise Joth after Mildred's death, he let me know how he felt. He picked me up at the train, took one look at me, and his exact words were, 'You look just like that whore of a mother of yours. Maybe calling you back wasn't such a good idea.' I'll never forget it.''

Griff held her tight. ''Darlin', you can't be faulted for having your mother's face.''

''I know, but he found great fault with it.''

Griffin wanted to dig up her father too. ''So what did he have to say when you came back after leaving Winston?''

''Nothing, but I found out from Gillie and Auntie that he'd told the folks in town that I'd gone with Winston willingly. He made no mention of having struck the deal on Joth's behalf.''

His jaw tightened once again with emotion. ''So that's where it all began. Why didn't he tell the truth?''

''I don't know. Maybe he was ashamed of what he'd done. Maybe he thought I'd never come back, or maybe he enjoyed the idea of my being labeled a whore because I looked so much like Mama. I'll never know the truth.''

Jessi looked up at him and her voice and eyes were serious. ''So, you still want to marry me?''

He leaned down and touched his lips to hers. ''Only if it's until death do us part . . .''

A happy and tearful Jessi hugged him tight and relished the hug he gave her in return. She'd finally found the light and no longer needed to be afraid.

Later, Preacher rode up and Jessi and the others went to the porch to welcome him back.

Preacher fished into this shirt pocket and withdrew a folded square of paper, then handed it to Griffin. ''Thought you'd want to see this.''

Griffin scanned the paper a moment and then grinned. "I most certainly do."

Griffin handed it over to Jessi. Neil and his brother peered over Jessi's shoulder to see what she held and they smiled too. It was a more recent sketch of the wanted woman Eula Grimes, and it left no doubt that Eula and Minerva were the same person.

"She has a nine-hundred-dollar bounty on her?" Jessi asked with amazement.

Preacher nodded. "That's what it says. It seems she has a habit of marrying old men and then absconding with their funds on the wedding night. She's done it at least three times and the families involved want her brought back to stand trial."

Jessi handed the bulletin back to Griffin. As he pocketed it, he asked, "Do you think Minerva would turn on Darcy to keep from going to prison?"

"Faster than she can say her real name, I'll bet," Jessi cracked.

"Jessita's probably right," Two Shafts replied. "A woman like that has few loyalties."

"Then let's wait a few days before we confront her; we don't want to spook her, but maybe after I win the election next week, we'll sit her down and have a nice long chat."

That night as Griffin and Jessi patrolled the outer boundaries of the Clayton land, they were supposed to be on the lookout for suspicious activity, but their thoughts were focused on each other instead.

When they reached the river, Jessi reined Snake Eyes to a halt and Griffin stopped his gelding right beside her. She dismounted and let the horse drink a moment. "The last few days have been something, huh?"

Griffin dismounted as well. "No kidding."

Jessi looked out over the ribbon of black water and the night-shrouded range beyond. "They've been good for us, though. Don't you think?'' She looked back to study him.

He nodded. ''Yes. It took a lot of strength and courage to tell me the story.''

She was glad she had. She'd been so afraid to confess the truth to him, so afraid it would alter his love for her. ''Some men wouldn't be as understanding.''

''Some men are fools. You didn't have a choice.''

Her voice was as quiet as the night. ''No.''

It still tore Griffin up inside, knowing that she'd gone through the ordeal alone and had been stoically and silently carrying the experience around all these years. What strength she had, and now he knew what had made her so rawhide tough: life.

''Are you ready to ride on?'' he asked.

It was a question that covered many things. She told the truth. ''Yes.''

Doyle had appointed himself Griffin's campaign manager and had tacked up broadsides all over town. It didn't matter that Percy and his men tore them all down, the notices were up long enough for everyone to know that Griffin Blake was running for sheriff. The declaration caused quite a stir. Folks all over the area talked about the coming election and many a bet was laid on the outcome. Some were predicting there would be a record-breaking number of people going to the polls, while others predicted no one would vote at all out of fear of retaliation from Reed Darcy. In a blatant attempt to buy votes, Reed was handing out crisp, new one-dollar bills. He even gave Jessi one, saying she and Griffin would probably need it to buy food once the election was held and Griffin went down to defeat. When Jessi got home, she looked at the new bill and thought there was something odd about the dollar's face, but it had been so long since she'd held a freshly printed bill, she shrugged it off.

Election day, Jessi and the Clayton contingent accompanied Griffin into town. In the past, the polls were located inside the barbershop, but today, because there were so many men wanting to cast their vote, the venue had been changed to Auntie's where there was more room.

Jessi saw folks in town she hadn't seen in years and others she'd never seen before. Percy and his minions had taken up position outside the saloon and appeared to be there for the sole purpose of intimidation. He gave Jessi and the others a surly stare as they passed, but said nothing.

Inside, a line of men snaked up the steps to the room where they'd put the voting station. A few people were seated at the tables conversing quietly, while others were up walking around and helping themselves to the free eats and lemonade. The subdued atmosphere befitted the occasion.

As Jessi, Griffin, and the Twins entered, they saw Doyle seated at a table and headed his way. A few men and women inside offered Jessi a tight nod, which she returned in kind. No one made any overt displays of welcome or acknowledgment and it soon became apparent why. Reed Darcy and his family were ensconced at a table in the center of room as if Reed wanted everyone to know he was there as they waited in line to vote.

He glared at her as she passed, but she ignored him. Roscoe sat at the table looking surly and displeased. Jessi wondered if Reed had forced him to be here this morning because she couldn't imagine Roscoe wanting to be here on his own. If Reed had indeed forced his son to be at his side, he'd had less control in other areas. Roscoe was obviously drunk, and he met Jessi's eyes with a bitter grin and toasted her with the drink in his hand.

The poll closed at seven that evening. Barbershop owner Wilson Cornell and Abe Thomas were locked in the voting room, tallying votes. Two Shafts had gone up to represent Griffin, and Minerva to represent Reed's side.

Auntie's was packed by now. People had been filtering in all afternoon to await the final results. Reed was still holding court in the center of the place, but Roscoe had left the premises hours ago.

The room quieted as Wilson and the others appeared on the stairs. Jessi gave Griffin a big smile, then turned her attention back to the stairs. When Wilson Cornell announced the results, cheers erupted and hats and bonnets filled the air. Griffin had won by a landslide.

Jessi leaned over and gave him a huge kiss. "Congratulations, darling!"

"Thanks," he said grinning.

It was the only moment they got to share, because the newly elected sheriff was immediately mobbed by well wishers wanting to shake his hand.

Reed was livid. If looks could've killed, Griffin would've been dead on the floor. Reed had been rebuked publicly and resoundingly. Fueled by the repossession of their lives and their properties, the citizens had chosen light over darkness, and Reed knew he was out on his ass! As the celebration swirled around him and someone began banging out a tune on the piano, he met Jessi's eyes malevolently. She didn't blink or look away. She held his gaze with the same courage she always had, and it felt wonderful. He swung his glare from her to the celebration, gave it one last look, then forcefully pushed his way to the door. An angry Minerva followed in his wake.

The happy Clayton clan didn't make it home until

very late that night. Griffin carried the sleeping Joth inside and helped Jessi put him to bed.

In the hallway Griffin stood with his arms linked around Jessi's waist and feasted his eyes on the woman he loved. "You know something?" he asked in a slightly slurred voice.

"What?" she asked, looking up at him contentedly.

"I'm the new sheriff."

Her smile peeked out. "Yes, you are."

"I also had a little too much to drink."

She chuckled. "I think so, too, but you deserved to celebrate."

"How many kisses did I give you on the way home?"

"Last count, hundreds."

"Wish I could give you more, but I have to go to sleep now."

"That sounds like a very good idea."

He gave her a sweet kiss on her forehead. "Night, Jessi Rose."

"Good night, Sheriff."

Jessi waited to make certain he made it to the bed, then softly closed his door. She walked to her own room with a smile on her face.

Over the next few days, Griffin, the Twins, and the Preacher spent most of their time in town fixing up the sheriff's office and opening the mail that had been piling up since Casper Hatcher's departure. Gillie took time away from the sewing of Jessi's wedding dress to come over and measure the office for new window curtains. Abe Thomas and the men from the church made Griffin a new Vale Sheriff sign, and painted the place inside and out. Folks donated furniture, lamps, and cots and bedding for the lock-up when word got out that Darcy had stripped the place clean after losing the election.

"I'm impressed," Jessi said, as she looked up at the new sign and the fresh whitewash on the building's exterior. "And they did this all on their own?"

"Never asked for a thing."

The love shone in her eyes as she said, "The town has really taken to you, Griffin."

And it had. People seemed friendlier and more at ease everywhere Jessi went. There were still strained feelings between Jessi and a lot of folks, but she was more than willing to meet them halfway, and that too could be attributed to Griffin.

"Lots of ladies have been dropping by too," he told her.

"So Gillie's been saying. Should I come and remind them where you park your boots at night? I can and I will you know." She raised one eyebrow.

Griff smiled at the spark in her eye.

"No, for now, they're just coming in and introducing themselves. If any get out of line, you'll be first person I'll call on."

"Good. Now kiss me, and I'll let you get back to work."

So he did.

Three days later, Griffin was wired a warrant for Minerva's arrest from the sheriff in Austin. At the dinner table that evening, Jessi and the men decided they'd go after her first, then Percy. They needed all the information she could give them on Reed's shady business dealings, and they needed Percy to confess Darcy's role in the murder of Jessi's father. With Minerva and Percy out of the picture, Darcy would have no one at his back, and hopefully by then it would all be over.

It was now the first week of June and it was Griffin's two-week anniversary as the new Vale lawman. He wore the star left by Casper Hatcher, and the shield had been buffed and polished before being presented to Griffin by Wilson Cornell on behalf of the town and the newly reformed town council.

The week also held two other anniversaries: Jessi's birth and her mother's death.

Jessi usually did not celebrate her birthday because of the bittersweet memories the day evoked. Griffin, having been told this by Gillie and Auntie, hoped to change her thinking about celebrating it.

Doyle's nephew was in town for a three-day visit, and since he and Joth had known each other for years, Doyle invited Joth to the house so the two boys could have some fun. Preacher had been spending most nights in the sheriff's office and the Twins at Auntie's, so Griffin had a clear deck upon which to work.

Jessi got up the morning of her birthday, watched Joth ride off with Doyle and then as always joined Griffin on the roof.

"Good morning," he called, as she walked over to join him.

She leaned down and gave him a kiss. "Good morning to you too."

She took the offered cup of coffee and settled in beside him.

Sitting content and silent, they watched the sun rise.

Jessi had reclaimed the breakfast duties since Neil and his brother had taken to waking up in the soft new beds of Auntie's girls instead of their bedrolls behind Jessi's house, and although she didn't mind the duties, Neil had a way with omelets that she'd never be able to match.

But she and Griffin ate her attempt and it was surprisingly good. At the conclusion of the meal, Griffin grabbed his hat to head to town.

Jessi walked with him out onto the porch. He looked down at her and then laced his hands around her waist. Without a word, he dragged her closer and kissed her until her knees melted into her boots. When he finally turned her loose, her eyes were closed and the sweet warm echoes of his kiss played over her insides like spring sunshine.

"That's going to have to hold you until I get back from town," he said, smiling softly. "Oh, and I'll be bringing you something, too."

"More kisses, I hope. You know, we'll have the house all to ourselves this evening."

"Definitely more kisses, but something else, too."

"What?"

"Your birthday present."

Jessi backed out of his arms. "I—I don't celebrate my birthday."

"I know," he said softly. "And I know why."

Jessi held his eyes. "Having your mother die the day after your thirteenth birthday is not something you easily forget. I haven't celebrated it since because it always reminds me of her."

"I understand."

He walked over and took her back into his arms. She placed her cheek against his chest and they held each other tight as he whispered, "But you are very very precious to me, and the day of your birth is something I want to celebrate, if only a little. Who would've changed my life if you hadn't been born?"

She eased back a bit and looked up at him, "Probably some sweet young thing with a trunk full of money."

"Possibly," he answered, smiling down, "but I doubt it. I prefer my women seasoned, mature."

"Oh, 'old,' in other words?"

"Very old." He slowly traced the tempting lines of her bottom lip, then touched his lips to hers, murmuring, "Very very old . . ."

The kiss swept them away, and as time stood still for that tiny moment, they both felt love grow deeper.

"So do I have permission to celebrate the birth of the

woman who'll soon be my wife?'' he asked, holding her close once more.

She nodded yes.

He gently raised her chin so he could see her eyes. ''Are you sure?'' he asked softly. ''You've been in the dark too long . . . let me be your light.''

Jessi's eyes closed as sharp poignant emotions welled up inside. She loved this man more than life. ''You are my light, Griffin, more than you'll ever know.''

''And I want you to make me a promise.''

''What is it?''

''That you will not do a lick of work today. No fence mending, no stable mucking. Nothing. It's your birthday, and as your maestro and your sheriff, I'm declaring this day a holiday.''

''Griffin—''

''Don't whine. Just say, 'Yes, Griffin.' ''

Her voice was as sultry as her smiling eyes. ''And if I do say yes, what do I get as a reward?''

''All you can handle, little girl. All you can handle.''

Chapter 13

After Griff rode off to town, Jessi moved about the silent house. Bantering with him had lifted her mood, but deep down inside she was still a bit melancholy. Although Griffin hadn't made the time of his return specific, she knew it wouldn't be until much later, and she contemplated how to occupy herself until then. She thought about going ahead and cleaning out the stables in the barn but she ignored the thought, mainly because she'd promised Griffin she would not do any chores in his absence. She located the newspaper she'd picked up in town and sat down with it, hoping it might hold her interest, but it didn't. After glancing over a report on Democratic President Grover Cleveland's recent appointment of Black Bostonian James M. Trotter as recorder of deeds, Jessi set the paper aside.

She went to the barn, saddled Snake Eyes, and rode off to a place she hadn't visited in months.

Jessi stood before her mother's grave and as always felt the sadness well up in her heart. Her parents were buried side by side. Jessi was certain the placing annoyed her father no end. He'd gone to his own judgment never having forgiven his wife for her adulterous liaison with Reed Darcy. After her death, Dexter Clayton had adamantly refused to order a stone to mark Violet's

grave, so Jessi had had one made upon her return from
back east. He'd been very angry over the purchase and
had berated Jessi for days about it, but she hadn't cared.
Violet Clayton might've been an adulterous whore to
him, but to Jessi and her sister, she'd been a loving
mother. Jessi ran her hand lightly over the marker, then
knelt to free the site of the weeds threatening to obscure
the spot. When she was done, she stood and said,
"Mama, I love you, but I'm not going to cling to the
shadows anymore. Griff says it's time for me to start
walking in the light, and he's right."

Jessi used to come here often to talk to her mother
about the goings-on in her life, and she doubted that
would ever change. Although her father had been convinced Violet would be burning in hell for eternity, Jessi
never believed that. Violet had had her hell on earth,
being married to Dexter Clayton. Jessi hoped the Lord
would've seen fit not to punish her twice.

She wondered what her mother would've thought of
Griffin. Would she have loved him as much as Jessi?
The question would remain forever unanswered, but
Jessi was truly thankful to have him and his love in her
life. She ran her hand over the stone to say good-bye,
then went back up to the house.

She wrote a long letter to her friend Paris LaMarr to
catch her up on the goings-on in her life and of course
included many pages on Griffin. She then laid out her
best skirt and blouse and the new camisole Gillie had
sewn for her. The former teacher had taken it upon herself to fatten up Jessi's meager wardrobe with garments
she termed far more suitable for a woman with a man
in her life, and although Jessi had protested, Gillie had
ignored her and started picking out fabrics and patterns
anyway. Even though she was still working on the wedding dress she'd somehow found the time to make Jessi
a beautiful nightgown out of a length of gold silk. Jessi

had no idea when she'd wear it, but Gillie promised it would tempt Griffin just as much as the fancy French underwear.

It was early evening when the sounds of a buckboard pulling up to the house came through the open windows. She hurried to the door, hoping it was Griffin and hoping he wouldn't notice she'd gone ahead and mopped the kitchen floor. It was Griff, and as she stepped out onto the porch, he greeted her with a smile. "I'm back. Sorry it took so long. Can you help me bring these things inside?"

"Sure can."

Jessi left the porch and Griff handed her a wooden crate whose towel-shrouded contents smelled like food. "Whatever is in here?" The tempting scents were heavenly.

"Your birthday dinner, courtesy of Neil, Auntie, and her girls."

Jessi stopped and stared at him. "You're jesting?"

"Nope, so take it on in, then come back and help me unload the rest."

When they finished unloading, a curious Jessi looked at the crates now sitting on the kitchen table. There were three of them. Griff set one aside with a warning that she couldn't peek at the contents of that particular one until later, but he gave her permission to take the towels off the tops of the two that remained. Inside one was a ham studded with cloves and dripping with maple sugar. There were also pots holding still warm yams, collards, and fat yellow cornmeal rolls. The other crate held a large bag of Chase and Sanborn coffee, a plate filled with molasses cookies, some apple dumplings, pretzels, four long tapering candles, a candelabra to nest them in, and a very fancy lace-edged tablecloth. Beneath the tablecloth were two sparkling china plates and two sets of tableware. Jessi was so outdone by the display she'd no idea what to say.

"Speechless?" he asked, as he encircled her in his arms.

"Yes!" Jessi exclaimed, turning to face him. "Why did they send all of this?"

"Because it's your birthday, Jessi, and they wanted it to be special."

"Well, they've certainly given it a start. Do you wish to eat now?"

"Let me go wash up first and then we can. If that's okay?"

She leaned up and kissed him softly. "That sounds perfect."

While he went out to the pump to clean up, she set the table. By the time he returned, she had everything ready. The light from the candelabra centering the food-laden table gave the kitchen a warm romantic glow.

"After you," he said, gesturing her to her seat. He assisted her with her chair, then sat down too.

They helped themselves to the ham, vegetables, and bread, then began to eat.

Griff looked across at her bathed in the glow of the candlelight, and decided they would celebrate her birthday this way every year. A woman as majestic and lovely as his Jessi deserved a bit of softness in her life now and again, and he'd make certain she received her share from now on. He still found it hard to believe that she shared his love or that she'd agreed to be his wife. Hands down, he had to be the luckiest man in all the world.

"This ham just melts in your mouth," Jessi purred.

"That's what took me so long," he told her, smiling in satisfaction. "I had to wait for Neil to say it was just right. I'm glad I did."

"So am I. Everything is simply wonderful." She then

looked over at him and said, "Thank you, Griffin."

"My pleasure."

For a moment the food was forgotten as they gazed at each other through the wavering points of flame atop the candles. He wanted to reach over and touch her, kiss her, undress her; push everything off the table and take her right here under the candles' glow.

"What are you thinking?" she asked softly.

"That I'd like to undress you and make you do shameless things."

The thick timbre of his voice touched her like a potent caress from his hands.

"Neil and Auntie wouldn't be happy if we wasted the food . . ." she said, her eyes sultry.

"No, they wouldn't."

Jessi could feel desire thickening the air in the room, and unable to resist becoming the siren that he sometimes made her be, moved her hands to the top button of her shirtwaist and slowly worked it free. "So how about a compromise . . ." Under the full attention of his vibrant eyes, her fingers freed the second button and then the third. ". . . We'll eat now, and play when we're done."

Enough buttons had been opened to reveal the low-cut camisole underneath.

"You're getting more outrageous by the day, Jessi Rose Clayton."

"If I'm being too forward, I can always close my shirt again." Her fingers moved toward the buttons.

"Don't you dare touch those buttons."

Their smiles mingled through the flames. Griff found her actions stimulating, to say the least. "Eat," he told her, pointing at her plate.

In direct contradiction of his command, she undid the remaining buttons, then slipped off the shirtwaist. Only then did she pick up her fork and return to her meal.

Griffin tried his best to concentrate on the food, but the distracting lady seated across the table fueled his appetite for something else entirely. The lacy edges of the low-cut camisole kept drawing his eyes to the glow-kissed planes of her breasts and the bare expanse of her shoulders and throat. Each time she moved or reached, the garment fluttered open just enough to give him a teasing glimpse of the dark beauties within. Who knew she could be so bewitchingly playful? During the sensual opening of her blouse, he'd had to force himself to stay on his side of the table. It was a display he'd remember for quite some time. He was enjoying the meal, but his eyes were feasting, too.

When they were done eating, they both put down their tableware and silence reclaimed the shadowy kitchen.

"I should store the rest of this food for tomorrow," Jessi told him, even though her rising desire made it hard to remain focused on something as mundane as preserving the remnants of the meal. All she wanted to think about was Griffin's bone-melting loving.

"I'll help."

She stood and leaned across the table for the plate holding the last four rolls. The camisole fluttered down and gave him an unhindered view of her breasts. Unable to resist such a blood-firing sight, he slid his finger over the soft-as-satin swell, then traced the skin down inside until he found the dark-tipped nipple. The nubbin ripened just as it had been trained to do, and so did his manhood. For a few heat-filled moments he teased her silently, lazily moving his touch from one to the other until she purred in the flickering candlelight.

"I thought you were going to help . . ." she gasped, as the sensations climbed.

"I am helping . . ."

"No, you're not . . ."

He eased the bodice down and filled his hands with

her twin delights. "Yes . . . I am." When he had her ripened to his satisfaction, he gently eased the camisole back into position. "Now, you can finish."

For a few seconds Jessi had a hard time remembering what she'd been about to do, because his fondling had left her mind in such a haze.

It shouldn't've taken long to clear the table, but it did, because Griffin couldn't resist the urge to *help*. His assistance consisted mainly of freeing her breasts once more so he could play as he wished, and the slow, sensual raising of her black skirt so he could play there too. Sometime during the interlude her drawers were stripped away, but she couldn't remember when because she was too busy purring in response to his fingers dallying so magnificently. She did remember that they never made it to the bedroom—he took her right there on the clean kitchen floor that she'd mopped and waxed this afternoon. Her camisole was down below her breasts and her skirt rucked up above her hips, but she didn't care about how shameless she might appear. Her whole world centered on Griffin and the glorious, rhythmic thrusting that sent her screaming into paradise.

When she came back to herself, he was stretched out on the cool floor beside her, propped on one elbow. She returned his soft smile. He slid a finger over one of her still hard nipples. "You're pretty loud for an old lady."

She punched him playfully. "It's all your fault."

"Yes it is, yes it is," he answered, his voice filled with satisfaction.

"Do you have *any* humble bones in that red and gold body?"

"Not a one."

She never got the chance to retort because his warm mouth had begun a slow stalking her of breasts; his hands were meandering and exploring.

"I'm going to bathe your beautiful body and have you

again . . ." he murmured in a voice thick with promise. "So come with me."

Encased in the familiar haze of desire, Jessi let herself be led outside to the pump. There was a fire going in the pit near the pump. On the pit's grate sat two large cauldrons.

"The water should be warm by now."

"When did you start the fire?"

"When I came out to wash up. Are you ready for your bath?"

Still throbbing from his touch, she nodded and watched as he pulled the tarp from the big bathing tub. It was soon filled her with the warm water and Jessi ventured in.

Her love for baths rose again as she sank down into the velvety liquid. Griff went back inside for a moment, then returned with wash cloths, drying towels, and a bar of soap wrapped in tissue paper.

"One of the girls gave this to me. She said it's rose scented. Stand up for me," he coaxed softly.

As she complied, the water cascaded down her body, leaving a damp sheen on her skin that caught the Texas moonlight. Jessi vividly remembered the last time they'd done this, and feeling Griff's warm hands sliding the soapy cloth over her filled her with shimmering anticipation. She could smell the scent of roses rising on the night air. The languid movement of the cloth teased her body in all the places he'd loved so thoroughly only a little while ago. By the time she'd been rinsed and wrapped in the large drying towel, Jessi was once again floating on clouds of desire.

"Are you ready for dessert?" he asked, drying her slowly.

"Yes."

"Then go slip something on, and after I wash, I'll get it ready."

A still hazy Jessi padded nude into the house and went to her bedroom. She donned the muted gold gown from Gillie. The sleeveless garment had been designed for a man's pleasure. There were lacy open seams up the front and down the sides and they offered a lover easy access to a woman's charms. One tiny ribbon held each of the sides together and a matching tie positioned between her breasts did the same for the front. It was the most beautiful garment she'd ever worn and it flowed over her bareness like a cloud.

She took a moment to look around her room in anticipation of Griffin spending the night. The space was as neat as always. Smiling, Jessi left the room to rejoin Griffin.

When she walked back into the kitchen wearing a gown that undulated and opened with each step she took, Griffin could only stare. Speechless, he feasted his eyes on the teasing glimpses the gown gave of the sides of her legs and the sweet black triangle at the apex of her thighs. Even in the candlelit shadows the fabric was so sensually transparent he had no difficulty at all viewing the curves and hollows of her dark beauty. "I thought *I* was the one preparing dessert."

She spun around so he could take in the gown's full effect and the edges splayed out and whirled with her. "Do you like it?"

One again he got a teasing glimpse of navel and thighs and the underside of each breast before the gown resettled itself. Griff wondered if too much of this could make him blind. He shook himself free, then remembered that she'd asked him a question, he just couldn't remember what it had been. "What did you say?"

She chuckled at the confusion he seemed to be suffering from. "If you liked the gown?"

Very certain of his answer, he nodded. "Like a little

boy likes Christmas. The way you look makes me feel like it's *my* birthday.''

''When *is* your birthday?''

''March twenty-sixth.''

She made a mental note of the date so she could make his birthday just as memorable when the day came. ''So where is this dessert you promised me?''

''Oh, I almost forgot about that. Close your eyes.''

''Why?''

''For once, indulge me and do what I ask, please.''

''Okay, but you have to promise me that this ordering around won't become a habit.''

''The only thing I'm going to promise is that you and that gown are going to do some mighty shameless things in a few minutes. Now, close your eyes, woman. Wives are supposed to be obedient.''

Jessi grinned and placed her hands over her eyes. ''I'm the most obedient wife you'll ever have.''

''You're the *only* wife I'll ever have.''

Jessi savored the sound of that.

''Are you peeking?'' he asked.

''Nope,'' she responded truthfully. He sounded as if he'd gone across the room. She then heard sizzling noises. The smell of something burning wafted across her nose.

''You can open your eyes now.''

When she complied, her eyes widened with excitement and delight.

He was walking towards her with a beautifully decorated chocolate cake. Atop the cake were lit sparklers.

''Happy birthday, Jessi.''

Filled with wonder, she brought her hands to her cheeks. ''Oh, Griffin.''

''It's from Neil and Two Shafts. Gillie sent along some ice cream. I'll bring out the freezer in a minute.''

She had him set the cake on the linen covered table.

The sparklers spewed and spit little bits of light while Jessi watched with happiness etched all over her face. "This has been a very special birthday. Thank you, Griffin."

"Glad you're having a good time."

Her love for him swelled her heart three times its size and she cupped her palm against his bearded cheek. "Will you always be my light?"

He turned her palm to his lips and brushed them gently against its warmth. "Always."

She blew out the sparklers, then cut them both a wedge of cake. After he served up the ice cream, they sat to enjoy the treats.

When they were done, Jessi pushed her plate away and groaned, "I cannot eat another bite."

"No?"

"Not a crumb."

"Then come here."

Jessi stood and walked around to his side of the table. He eased her down onto his lap and she leaned back against the solid strength of his chest as he circled her with his arms. "You look awfully fetching in this gown, boss lady."

"I hoped it would get your attention. At my age, I need all the help I can get."

"You're not old and you don't need any help. When we're both old and gray, I'll still want you."

"Do you promise?"

"With all my heart."

He kissed her to seal the pact, and she wrapped her arms around the pillar of his neck to bring them closer. The kiss deepened and she could feel him sliding the gown over the skin of her back. "Let's try to make it to the bed this time," he murmured against her ear.

But neither of them wanted to part because their passions were just beginning to rise.

"Stand up, Jessi."

She slid the tip of her tongue over the sensitive corner of his mouth. She didn't want to stand, she wanted him.

He gifted her with a series of short, sweet kisses as he ran his hand up the outside of her thigh through the wide split of her gown. "I thought you said you were an obedient wife . . ."

"I am obedient . . ." she whispered, savoring his caresses and his kiss, ". . . when obedience is called for."

He chuckled and stood up with her still cradled in his arms. "Let's see you prove it."

Before their departure, he dipped her low so she could blow out the candles on the table.

The night songs of the crickets played against the silence of her room as he laid her gently atop the bed. The clean sheets felt sensual against her back; almost as sensual as the kiss he brushed against her exposed navel. Because of the gown's disarray, it veiled some portions of her body but left others deliciously bare: like the corner of her hip and the tender inside of one thigh. He kissed a lazy, meandering trail up to her breasts, then brushed his lips against the rose-scented skin of her throat. He undid the tiny bow which held the front of the gown together and widened the now unconnected halves. She lay there nude and ripe for whatever games they wished to play.

By the time he finished taking the long way around her body, she was fairly bursting with need, but he wasn't done. He made her gown a co-conspirator and used the soft fabric to tease and tantalize all the places he'd already prepared. She moaned as he glanced it blissfully over the undercurve of her breasts, then moved it like a whisper down to her waist. Gold silk stroked her hips, the skin of her legs, and the shadow-filled darkness between her thighs. Her hips rose as the touches intensified and her legs parted from the pleasuring.

When he leaned down to pay her the ultimate tribute, a purr of satisfaction slid from her throat. He parted her gently, then conquered her with such magnificent expertise, she had to fight to keep from soaring away. His mouth was wanton, his fingers brazen; she had no defenses, not against this, so a few hot moments later, as the sensations converged, she cried out and shattered like a pane of glass.

"Happy birthday . . ." he murmured.

It was a birthday Jessi would not soon forget.

The next morning, Griff thought about his future as he lay in bed beside the still sleeping Jessi. For the very first time, he seemed to have a purpose in his life. There'd be no more train robbing, stealing, or running around with women. He had Jessi now, and because he did, he had the potential to have a life even his brother Jackson would approve of. Last night he'd made love to her more times than he could count in a variety of places and positions that made him hard just thinking back on them. She'd been vibrant, thrilling, and very very outrageous. Back on the first night they'd met, you couldn't've paid him to believe she'd wind up being the woman he wanted to marry. He also would've had a hard time believing that her love for him would exceed any other feelings he'd experienced before. His Jessi was magnificent, strong, and shaped by all the heartbreak and pain in her life. There were many dark places in the woman he loved, places that sheltered pain, tears, and betrayal, but not even his ego was large enough to think he could just whisk them away. It would take time for him to show her that the light of his love would never fail and that she now had someone to help shoulder her fears. He knew she'd become accustomed to bearing her burdens alone, but he wanted to change that.

So that was now his purpose; to love Jessi and to walk beside her so she'd never have to walk alone. Ever.

He reached out and ran a worshipping finger up her bare spine. She shifted a bit then turned over and slowly opened her eyes. She smiled sleepily. "Good morning."

He bent and kissed her brow. "Good morning, love. Did you sleep well?"

"No, I had a man in my bed last night who kept stripping me naked and making me do shameless things."

"Did you like it?"

"Extremely."

"Good."

She dragged herself to a sitting position. "We really need to get married."

He kissed her on the collarbone, then brushed his lips over the sleep damp skin. "Why?"

"Because I enjoy waking up with you by my side."

"I enjoy making love to you when you wake up by my side."

His hands were roaming and she was melting. "That sounds like an invitation. Do you think we'll have time before you have to go play sheriff?"

"We'll make the time . . ."

The next night, Two Shafts and Neil slipped into Roscoe's house as soundlessly as twin shadows and kidnapped his wife. With Reed out of town and Roscoe passed out on the porch, they had no trouble.

They brought her, bound and gagged, back to Jessi's kitchen, and Minerva was of course quite furious.

"What is the meaning of this?" she demanded in an outraged voice after Neil removed the gag. She was dressed in a nightgown and the blanket the Twins had taken from her bed.

"We just want to talk," Jessi said. "Nothing more."

"Well, it had better be good."

"Oh, don't worry, it will be."

Griffin pulled up a chair and took a seat before her.

There was a wariness in her eyes as she waited for the next shoe to drop, but she was doing her best to show the outrage instead.

"So, Eula, how've you been?" Griffin asked her casually.

"My name is Minerva Darcy, are you all drunk?" she asked, looking around at them all.

Griffin reached into his pocket and withdrew the most recent of her warrants. He held it up for her to see. "Says here your name is Eula Grimes."

She looked away.

"It also says here that you're wanted in Kansas City, Denver, and Reno for swindling old men out of their savings."

Her manner turned cool. "So what? Just because you're the new sheriff doesn't mean I should quake in my boots just because you *think* I'm someone else. You men are very very small-time."

"She's right, you know," Griffin replied agreeably. "No one really pays a lot of attention to a local sheriff, so boys, let's show her who we really are and maybe she'll respect us a bit more."

One by one, Griffin, the Twins, and Preacher pinned on their marshal badges and Minerva's eyes widened very large indeed. She stared over at Jessi as if she expected her to produce one too. "Sorry," Jessi said with a shrug. "I wish I had one, but I don't—but you do look impressed now, if I must say so myself."

A speechless Minerva continued to stare at the marshals surrounding her.

"Now," Griffin said, "since it's obvious you recognize the badge of a U.S. Deputy Marshal when you see one, let's start again. So, Eula, how've you been?"

She'd been bested and knew it. "I've been better, believe me. Are those real?"

"Yep."

"What do you want?" she asked, sounding defeated.

"Reed Darcy."

She raised an eyebrow. "Fricasseed or fried?"

Griff hid his smile. "Preferably fried."

"And in exchange?"

"You don't go to prison for being Eula Grimes and you get to leave town as soon as you'd like."

"Sounds reasonable."

Jessi had been right, Minerva had turned on Darcy as fast as she could say her own name and showed not one ounce of guilt over it. "You're tossing your father-in-law over mighty quick, wouldn't you say?"

"Would you rather I stay loyal, Jessi? I'm a realist, and like you, a survivor. If marshals are after Reed, that means it's time for me to move on. I've been to prison once, and I swore I would never enter another. So, what do you want me to do?"

"We need to know about his shady business deals and whether he ordered his men to murder Jessi's father," Griff responded.

She didn't hesitate. "He did. Said he was tired of Dexter being a thorn in his side and he wanted it taken out. Told the man you've been calling Percy that he didn't care how it was done."

"If we asked you to write that down and sign it, would you?"

"Do I have a choice?"

Griffin's reply was blunt. "No."

He looked to Jessi, who went to her room to retrieve a sheet of writing paper and a pen.

As Jessi retrieved the items she paused a moment before going back. Even though Minerva had just verified what Jessi had always believed, it saddened her to hear the truth nonetheless. Dexter Clayton, in spite of all his faults, had died because of his strength, his courage, and his belief in standing up for what was right. Yes, Jessi wanted Reed fried—in the hottest grease possible. She took a deep breath and went back into the kitchen.

Minerva took a moment to write down the events of that night and what she'd heard Reed Darcy say. That done, she affixed her signature and the date and Griff set the paper aside to dry.

"Is the government after Reed because of the counterfeiting, too?" Minerva asked then, "because I swear I had nothing to do with it."

"Yes," Griffin lied. He'd no idea Reed had ties to such an operation, but Minerva didn't need to know that. "What can you tell us about that?"

"He has a press in the barn behind Ros's house. Reed's been short on funds lately so he's been printing his own."

Griffin fought to keep his surprise masked, but was certain everyone else in the room had been caught off guard too. "Where'd he get the equipment?"

"Purchased it, I suppose. He said he was a printer's devil when he lived back east, so I assume that's where he acquired the skills."

"Who's he been giving this money to?"

"Everybody: his hands, town merchants, the doc."

Jessi thought back to the dollars Reed had given out during the election. "Were the dollars he passed out during the election bad bills too?"

"Printed hundreds of them."

Preacher asked, "Do you know where he keeps the plates?"

"In the safe."

"Can you get your hands on them?"

She shook her head. "No, Reed shared many things with me, but not the combinations to his safes. Ros might have them, but I never did. I did try though."

Jessi bet she did. "So, Minerva, if you don't mind

me asking, what exactly is your line of work?''

"I'm a confidence woman. I win their confidence and I take their money. Simple.''

"So, was this job a successful one?'' Neil wanted to know.

"No. They bought me clothes and took me on trips, but Reed is a miserly son of a bitch. I never got access to any of the money. Now he doesn't have any, of course, so I was planning on leaving soon anyway.''

Two Shafts said, "Explain.''

"The poker game wiped him out. He was only a few days away from selling the mortgages he had in hand, but at the end of the game he had two choices, both bad. He could not cover his bet and be known as a welsher to those English investors, or he could pay up and lose the mortgages.''

"How badly did he need that money?'' Griffin asked.

"Real bad. In two weeks time, everybody he does business with on both sides of the border's going to know the true state of his finances, and then all hell is probably going to break loose. He took in a lot of funds that he's not going to be able to account for. He was taking Peter's money and investing it with Paul—Paul went belly-up six weeks ago, and Reed was hoping the profits from the mortgages would cover it, but you came to town, Blake—you and your friends, and turned over the table.''

"So, you're leaving,'' Griff stated.

"Yep, I never stay on a sinking ship, and Reed's bailing fast. He's in Austin now, trying to raise more cash.''

Preacher quoted, *"Let the wicked fall into their own nets."*

Griffin nodded. "Psalm 142.''

Preacher looked pleased. "I'm impressed, again.''

Minerva viewed both of them with an odd look before

turning her attention to the Twins. "So, can one of you handsome marshals see me home?"

Neil asked, "Are we done?"

Griffin couldn't think of anything else. He looked around at his small war council, but everyone appeared satisfied, at least for now, so Griff nodded. "We're done. Escort her back."

"Be glad to."

Minerva stood and smiled up invitingly at the tall handsome Seminole. "Will you carry me, like you did last time?"

Neil grinned. "Sweetheart, you should know that I don't have a dime."

She looked disappointed. "Pity. In that case, I'll walk."

Jessi smiled and shook her head.

Both Neil and his brother escorted Minerva home, and after their departure, Jessi, Preacher, and Griff remained in the kitchen to talk further.

Griff said, "You were right, Jessi. Minerva dropped Darcy like a hot coal."

"I'm almost sorry I broke her tooth now," Jessi said. "Almost."

Preacher looked up a moment as if thinking. "Let's see. Murder *and* counterfeiting. How many years do you think Judge Parker will give Darcy?"

"We can't can count that high."

Jessi said, "Even if he's there for an eternity, it won't bring my father back, but at least I know the truth."

When the Twins returned the discussion turned to the next nail in Reed Darcy's casket, Percy West. "I think we should bring him over to the sheriff's office and see if we can't persuade him to tell the truth," Griff proposed.

"We're not letting him leave town afterward, are we?" Two Shafts asked.

"Nope, Preacher can have him when we're through. I'm sure Percy's wanted somewhere by somebody," Griff told him.

So it was decided Percy would be next.

The next night, Griffin, the Twins, and Preacher rode into town. Since Percy had a habit of patronizing Auntie's, that was where they decided to begin the search. He was there all right, playing cards as always, and when he saw the four lawmen stride in, his jaw dropped.

"Yes, Percy, we've come for you," Neil declared easily in response.

"You knew we would," Shafts added.

"You're the law now," Percy shot back, his bravado returning. "You can't just take me out and shoot me."

Standing over the seated Percy, Griff said pleasantly, "Who said anything about shooting? We just want to talk."

"About what?"

Neil reached over and slowly began turning over Percy's cards. "We think you might know something about Dexter Clayton's death that might help us find the killer."

The turned-over cards showed Percy was on his way to a straight. Upon seeing this, the three other players hastily scraped their wagers out of the pot.

"What do you think?" Neil asked into his face.

Percy was staring forlornly at his now useless cards.

Two Shafts grinned. "I think he's thinking he wished you hadn't done that."

Neil patted him sympathetically on the back. "Old Percy here plays cards like a professional, I'm sure he gets straights all the time, don't you Perce?"

"Get your hands off me," he snapped.

Neil looked outdone. "You give a man a compliment, and what do you get in return? Bad manners."

"I think he should come with us," Shafts replied.

"The hell I will."

Neil looked at his brother and said, "Whatever are we going to do with him?"

Before Percy could blink, Neil grabbed him by the front of his shirt and dragged the seated man across the table top. Money and cards went everywhere and the other players scrambled out of the way. Neil held the shorter Percy up at eye level. "Now, we tried to be nice about this, but I don't think you realize that you don't have a choice."

Percy looked like a prairie dog staring into the eyes of a snake. Griffin walked over and relieved Percy of his firearm.

"You can put him down now, Neil," Griff said.

Neil "tossed" instead of "put" and Percy landed with a stumble.

"Mr. Darcy ain't going to like this," Percy said, eyes angry. "When he gets back day after tomorrow, there's going to be hell to pay."

Griff waved Percy to the door with his own gun and gave both the onlooking Doyle and Auntie a wave and a smile as he and his friends marched Percy out into the night.

Jessi waited up for their return, and when they did, she stepped out onto the porch. Percy West's hands were tied to the pommel of his mount's saddle. She was pleased to see they'd returned with their prey. Aided by the light cast by the lanterns on the porch, Jessi watched them help West off his horse and head him up the gravel walk. "Welcome to the Clayton ranch, West. Looking forward to your stay."

As the men neared, Jessi could see that he did not appear to share her sentiments.

Griffin slipped his arm around her waist. "I don't think Percy has too much to say right now, do you, Percy?"

"No."

"See?" Griff told her.

"What'll we do with him?" Preacher asked.

"Well, let's truss him up for now and he can play with the Twins in the morning," Griff replied.

Percy did have something to say now. "You can't just keep me here. Mr. Darcy's not going to stand for this."

"Mr. Darcy has bigger problems. Did you know he's been paying you with counterfeit money?" Preacher asked.

Percy stared around. "That's a lie," he declared firmly.

Shafts replied, "See? I told you all he'd be too smart to fall for that one."

"Yeah, I'm too smart for that one."

Neil shook his head. "Yeah, you're real smart. Let's go."

Neil and his brother led Percy around to the back of the house, and once there, retied his hands behind his back, looped a rope around his ankles, and tied it with a sturdy and intricate knot. They pushed him over on the ground and left him there. When he began yelling about being freed and cursing about the ancestry of the people involved, he was summarily gagged and everyone went to bed.

When Jessi awakened the next morning, she got dressed and went outside to see how the guest had fared. She found the men behind the house and the irate Percy seated on the ground still gagged. "Good morning, everyone. Percy."

Percy's angry eyes showed that he found nothing

good about the morning at all, but the others greeted her with a smile.

"Morning, Jessi," Griff called.

"Morning. What are you planning for our guest?"

Two Shafts replied, "Well, we've asked him about your daddy's death, but he keeps saying he doesn't know anything, so after breakfast we're going to play a little game."

"What kind of game?"

"It's a secret."

Jessi grinned and Percy began protesting vehemently through the gag.

"Anybody know what he's saying?" Preacher asked, his green eyes shining.

"I think he's saying he'd love to play. Aren't you, Percy?" Griffin asked.

Percy had said no such thing, and again tried to make his true opinion known, but since no one could understand a word he was saying, they left him there and went inside to eat breakfast.

Later that morning, Jessi pulled the old rocker to the edge of the back porch so she'd have an unhindered view of the proceedings. She wondered why the Twins were digging a hole in the field behind the house. When Griffin came over and took a seat at her feet, she asked, "What are the Twins up to?"

Hs smiled and shrugged. "Your guess is as good as mine."

Percy's gag had been removed and he yelled, "If you kill me, you all'll hang!"

"Who said anything about killing you?" Two Shafts asked, still digging from within the now knee-deep hole.

Neil chimed in, "We'd love to send you to hell, but Miss Jessi won't allow it, so we had to come up with something else."

"You'll like this," Two Shafts promised. "You really will."

Preacher walked up and asked Griffin, "Do you have any idea what they're doing?"

"Nope, but I'm glad they're on our side."

After about forty minutes of digging, Neil came over to Percy. "Stand up."

"Why?" Percy asked warily.

"Do you want to play or not?" Percy refused to budge.

"Cheno, help our playmate up."

Griffin assisted the sullen Percy to his feet, then Neil came over and stood beside Percy. "How much shorter do you think he is?"

Everybody decided Neil topped Percy by a good four or five inches.

"Then we're just about ready," Neil stated, giving Percy a cold smile.

Two Shafts was still inside the hole, tossing dirt out of the top like a burrowing prairie dog. Jessi walked over and looked down inside. It was pretty deep, so deep in fact, Two Shafts had to lent be a hand in order to climb out. "Okay," he said, once he was on firm ground again. "Untie him. It's time to play. Get in the hole, Percy."

"No."

Two Shafts unholstered his Colt and pointed it at Percy. "You have to."

Percy had a look of panic on his face. He turned to Jessi.

She shook her head. "Don't look at me. This is their game."

Griff grabbed one of Percy's arms and Preacher latched on to the other. Percy struggled, but they forced him to the rim of the hole just the same.

"Get in," Neil ordered.

The still balking Percy yelled, "No!"

Jessi snapped, "Oh, stop yowling like a baby and get in the hole. You're holding things up."

It took the men a few more moments, but they succeeded in forcing Percy into the deep, but narrow hole. Once there, he could not get out, not without help. The only part of his body above ground was his head.

"Now," Two Shafts said with a grin, "the game begins."

Neil picked up the shovel, dug into the large mound of dirt that had come out of the hole, and began to toss it back in.

"What the hell are you doing?!" Percy demanded.

Neil kept tossing dirt down into the hole. "Playing a game my brother and I just invented. It's called Bury Percy To His Neck."

"You can't do this!" he yelled frantically.

"Sure we can."

The filling of the hole continued while Percy cursed and threatened. To shut him up, Neil tossed a shovel full of the dirt in his face. "Oh, sorry," Neil pleaded contritely. "Thought that mouth of yours was part of the hole."

He kept shoveling. When Neil tired, he gave the shovel to his brother. Jessi now understood why they were called the Terrible Twins. As Griffin stated earlier, she was glad they were on her side.

A little while later, the hole was filled. They'd buried him from the neck down. The furious Percy West looked like a severed head.

Two Shafts used the flat part of the shovel to pat the dirt down nice and even around him. Percy flinched every time the shovel came down near his face. Two Shafts stepped back to view his handiwork. "What do you think?" he asked his brother.

"Not bad," Neil replied as he walked around Percy's

head. "Not bad. But I still think we should've skinned him first."

"I know, but Jessita wouldn't've allowed that."

Neil then looked to his companions. "Well, folks, what do you think?"

Everybody chuckled.

Percy spent the balance of the morning playing the Twins' game. No one fed him or offered him anything to drink. Every time someone asked if he remembered what happened the night of the murder, he continued to deny he knew anything, so they left him buried. When he yelled out his hunger, he was ignored; when he yelled for a trip to the facilities, he was again ignored.

Griff hunkered down beside the young outlaw's head. "The sooner you tell the truth, the sooner this will all be over."

"I'm not saying shit," Percy spat.

Griff shrugged. "Suit yourself."

By afternoon, the sun had risen high in the sky and it was hot as Hades. To keep Percy from dying in the sun, Neil went out and offered him a drink, then poured the rest of the bucket over Percy's head. He sputtered and cursed but clung to his avowed innocence, so Neil left him and went back into the house.

Later, Jessi heard a commotion. Fanning herself with a newspaper in an attempt to beat back the oppressive heat, she stepped out to the back porch to investigate. Neil and Shafts were standing over Percy, arguing over who was the better shot. Neil bragged that he could take the wings off a fly at fifty paces and his brother bet him he couldn't. Preacher and Griffin were seated on the shady porch watching them as if they were attending a theater show. Percy, on the other hand, had more panic in his eyes, as if this argument would somehow wind up with him becoming involved, and Jessi thought he was probably correct.

Neil stormed into the house and returned with an apple. He set the apple on top of Percy's head. ''Since we don't have any flies available, let's use this.''

''Nooo!'' Percy yelled, but they ignored him.

Neil took fifty steps, turned, and fired.

Percy's scream mingled with the sound of the Colt. The apple exploded in a hail of pulp, skin, and seeds. Percy's head was still intact, but he'd fainted dead away.

Chapter 14

❦

After the sun started to go down and the heat abated a bit, Jessi left the men to go into town. She wanted to see how Joth was faring with Doyle and his nephew and to see if she could find Roscoe Darcy.

Joth greeted her with a hug and a plea to stay another few days. It seemed Doyle's nephew's visit had been extended. Since Doyle had been the one to encourage Joth's plea, Jessi surrendered and agreed. Both boys jumped for joy.

When it came time for her to leave, Doyle walked her back out to the front of the livery. "What did Griffin and his friends do with Percy?"

When Jessi told him the story, he began to laugh. "Really?"

An amused Jessi replied, "They say they're going to keep him that way until he tells the truth."

"Those Twins are something," a still chuckling Doyle declared.

Jessi agreed. "They are that. Oh, and Doyle, don't do any more business with Darcy until this mess is over."

"Why?"

"He's been printing his own money."

Doyle's eyes grew wide.

Jessi nodded and then told him the information Minerva had given them.

"Well, I'll be damned," Doyle exclaimed. "Does anyone else know?"

"Probably not. Go ahead and tell Auntie, but no one else. We don't want to spook him before we get what we need from Percy. He says Reed won't be back until tomorrow and that should give the Twins plenty of time to extract the truth. Have you seen Ros in town today?"

"Saw him weave by here earlier. He might still be around somewhere."

"I need to find him."

"Good luck," the big man told her.

He watched her unhitch Snake Eyes and asked with amusement in his voice, "When are you going to replace that spawn of Satan?"

Jessi smiled. The name Snake Eyes was often given to horses with a mean streak, and in his colt days, Jessi's mount had had a very large one. He'd mellowed a bit over the years, and he hadn't shown his temper in quite some time, but he still only tolerated one rider—Jessi.

She mounted and patted his sleek head. "Don't listen to him. I'm not going to replace you. You can even bite him next time he says that."

The horse turned a baleful eye on Doyle that looked so humanlike, Jessi could not contain her laugh. "Better watch what you say, Doyle. I think Snake Eyes is on to you."

He grinned and she rode on down the street.

She found Roscoe Darcy sitting in the middle of the wide open range behind Auntie's saloon. He and his bottled companion were alone. She dismounted. "Hello, Ros. What are you doing out here all by yourself?"

"Well, hello there, Jessi girl," he exclaimed happily. "I'm celebrating."

"What's the occasion?"

"The running off of my wife." He raised the half empty bottle in toast. "It is a *very* good day."

He took a drink, wiped his lips on the stained cuff of his dirty suit coat and said, "Got up this morning and she was gone. Gone. No more dresses, hats, shoes, trunks, everything gone. Just like that." He tried to snap his fingers but failed.

Jessi sat down across from him in the grass. "How do you know she won't be coming back?"

"Left me a note. First decent thing she's done since I married her."

"What did it say?"

"That she was leaving. For good. Hallelujah!" and he took another drink. "Only married her in the first place because Reed made me."

Jessi began idly pulling grass. "Ros, you have to stop drinking."

"Don't want to. Like being drunk."

"But why?"

"I'm not strong like you."

He looked over at Jessi and asked, "Did you know that your mother was riding back to your father the night she had the accident?"

Jessi stilled. "No, Ros, I didn't."

"She *was* going to run away with my father, but she got to our place about an hour earlier than the agreed upon time. She found Reed in bed with Lydia Cornell."

Jessi stared.

"It's true, Jess. I was there, and do you know why I was there?" he asked quietly.

"No."

"Because Reed said it was about time for me to learn what a man needs to learn, so he made me sit at the foot of the bed and watch."

Jessi's heart turned over. Roscoe had been only twelve at the time, just like Jessi. How could Reed have done something so perverse to someone as sensitive as Ros? "What did my mother do?"

"Didn't say a word. Just turned and left."

So her mother had been returning home, not because she loved her husband but because she'd seen Reed's true colors. As distraught as she must have been, she probably hadn't been paying very close attention to her driving, thus the accident. More than likely, getting away from Reed had been uppermost in her mind. And all these years, Lydia Cornell had known the truth.

"Do you know what it's like waking up each and every day knowing no matter what you do, it won't be good enough?" he asked her then.

She did. In many respects their fathers had been cut from the same cloth. "According to Gillie, Reed's father treated him much the same way."

"All the more reason for him to have treated me better, don't you think?"

Jessi agreed. "Ros, do you know that Reed's printing counterfeit money in your barn?"

"I know. Your man going to bring him before a judge?"

"If he can."

"I like that man of yours, Jessi girl. Just the kind you've been needing."

"You think so?"

He nodded and took another drink. "Yep."

Ros then began to search the pockets of his coat, for what, Jessi didn't know. "Give him something for me."

The search continued as the inebriated Ros stuck his hands into the pockets of his trousers, and then into the inner pocket of his coat. When he looked her way and smiled, she knew he'd found what he'd been after. He handed her two keys. "I thought I still had them. This one opens the bank. That one opens Reed's office. The counterfeit plates are in the safe."

Jessi was so bowled over she didn't know what to say.

Ros asked, "Do you think you can remember the numbers to the safe if I tell you?"

Jessi nodded, so he gave them to her.

"But why would you do this?"

"Because we were friends once many moons ago, and because my family owes you. For many things."

Jessi was moved by his confession. "How can I thank you?"

"Put Reed in jail and invite me to the wedding."

"You have a deal."

He nodded. "Well, think I'll go home and take a nap. Maybe after I get up, I'll take a hammer to his printing press. Can't print money without a printing press. Can't own a hotel if it burns down, either," and he began to laugh.

Jessi stared. "Did you burn the hotel?"

"Yep, then I sat in the alley and watched. Reed was mad as a Democrat in a Black Republican parade."

"But why?"

"Why not? How else was I going to pay him back for all the years he's had his foot on my neck? If your man can send him away for good, I'd be much obliged."

Jessi did understand. Ros had not had an easy life growing up as Reed's son. "All right, thanks for your help. Will you do one thing for me?"

"What is it?"

"Stop drinking."

He gave her a drunken salute. "I'll think about it."

Jessi sighed her frustration, then mounted Snake Eyes once more. She hoped Ros would pull himself together; being drunk would not exorcise the demons he carried inside.

She stopped in to see Gillie before leaving town; she needed to talk with her about her mother's death.

While she waited for Gillie to finish helping a customer, Jessi spent a few minutes eyeing her nearly completed wedding dress. It was truly lovely. The green brocaded silk suit was trimmed with deep flounces of lace. The overdress, also of brocaded silk, fell in heavy folds in front and looped at the side. It had a pointed waist and vee-cut bodice under which would be worn a black velvet vest. Jessi lifted up the full skirt to view the beautiful green silk, only to have Gillie walk up behind her and ask very politely, "Are your hands clean?"

Jessi dropped the fabric immediately. No, they weren't.

A chagrined Jessi turned and took the offering of a glass of lemonade from her old teacher's hand.

"Have a seat and tell me all that's happened in the past few days."

Gillie laughed at the fate of Percy West, then listened as Jessi told her Minerva's story about the counterfeit plates.

"Well, I'm glad you told me," Gillie pronounced. "He'll do no business here."

They spent a few more moments discussing Minerva's leaving and Jessi's conversation with Ros, then Gillie asked, "Did you tell Roscoe why she left?"

"No, I didn't have the heart to. He said he married her only because Reed forced him to, but you never know how he truly feels underneath all that whiskey." She then added somberly, "Ros told me what really happened to my mother the night she died. She had decided to leave my father, but she walked in on Reed and Lydia Cornell. Mama was headed back home when she had the accident."

Jessi chose not to dwell on how a mother could've turned her back on her daughters because Jessi had no idea of the depths of her mother's misery, and because it hurt too much to think about.

Gillie's voice was as quiet as the little shop. "She did love you and your sister very much, Jessi, believe me, she did."

"I'm sure she did, but from where I stand now, it must not have been enough."

"You shouldn't judge. We all make mistakes."

Jessi nodded. "I know, but since that day, I always hung onto the hope that she really hadn't planned to leave my sister and me—that all the gossips were wrong. This summer has opened my eyes, and I'm not sure I like what I see."

"You can't change the past. That's why the Good Lord gives us the future. Look forward, little girl, not back. You've got a man who really loves you. Let that fill your heart, not the pain of something over which you had no control."

It was sound advice, Jessi knew; she just hoped she'd be able to apply it to her own life someday. Right now, she wasn't so sure.

"So when are you going to come for your next fitting?"

The question lightened Jessi's mood a bit and she gave Gillie a small smile. "Just as soon as you like. I told myself I'd let you make me as many dresses as you wished because Griffin seems to like them."

Gillie snorted. "As if I believe that. Like I said before, if you had your choice, you'd go to your grave wearing nothing but denims."

"It's the truth."

"Well then, come in tomorrow or the day after and prove it."

Jessi went over and gave Gillie a parting hug. "I will. Thank you, Gillie, for everything."

"You're welcome. Now go and get back to that handsome train robber of yours."

Griff was ecstatic over Ros's gifts and he and his

friends decided not to waste time. As soon as night fell, they planned to ride into town to remove the counterfeit plates from Reed's safe.

In the meantime, they still had to extract the truth from Percy. Jessi arrived just in time to see the newest twist in the game. Neil was sitting on the ground in front of Percy eating a very sumptuous meal. On the plate were collards, rice and beans, fat, succulent slices of ham, and big squares of corn bread running with butter. Percy stared longingly as Neil ate. It was quite obvious they'd not fed him.

"How's Joth doing?" Griffin asked, after Jessi went in and came back with a full plate of her own.

"Fine. He's going to stay another few days. Doyle said he'd bring him home once his nephew leaves. How's the game going?"

Preacher chuckled. "Percy is losing badly. Let's see, he's had all manner of fruits and vegetables shot off the top of his head. They've poured buckets of water on him, refused to feed him, and they had ants crawling on him just before you got back. I don't think he's going to last much longer."

Griff added, "I take my hat off to him, he's played the game a lot longer than I thought he would."

Preacher shook his head. "But he's losing points for all that screaming he's been doing. When they dumped that ant nest on him, you could hear him clear to Austin."

Jessi was amazed. "Where on earth did they find an ant's nest?"

"By the barn. Shafts is still out there seeing what else he can find."

Jessi didn't think Percy would last much longer, either. He looked beat, desolate, and just plain done. He had scraps of vegetables, fruit, and Lord knows what else on his face and littering his hair. His ferret face looked as if the ants had bitten him a time or two. She almost felt sorry for him. Almost.

Two Shafts came back from the barn, and after greeting Jessi said, "I found a skunk."

Percy began to moan fearfully.

Neil looked up from his plate with bright eyes. "Where?"

"In Jessita's barn. Looked to be full grown."

A smiling Neil looked at Percy. "Isn't that something? Would you like to play with the skunk?"

Percy started yelling for help.

Neil chided him pleasantly, "You won't need help to play with the skunk, Percy."

Percy's head began twisting and turning as if he could somehow screw himself out of the ground. He couldn't, of course, but he put up a damn good try. "Get me out of this damn hole!"

"But you don't remember anything about the murder," Neil reminded him.

"I do!" Percy yelled, as his wide eyes spied Two Shafts walking back toward the barn. "I remember it clear! Good and clear!"

Griff walked over and took a seat by Neil. "So tell us what you remember."

"Darcy wanted her pa killed. Told me to do it and paid me fifty dollars."

He kept trying to turn his head to see if Two Shafts were on his way back with the skunk.

"Will you write all that down and sign it?" Griff asked.

"Yes!" he cried, "yes!" Percy sounded as if he were about to start blubbering like a child. "Dig me out, please! I've had enough!"

Griffin stood and picked up a shovel. As he lifted out the first of the dirt, he swore Percy had tears in his eyes.

Jessi went back in the house once the hole had been

partially emptied. She'd no desire to witness Percy being freed because she was certain it would not be a pretty sight. He'd been in that hole all day.

The men let Percy wash up at the pump and between them found a full set of clothes for him to wear as replacements for the fouled set he'd come out of the hole wearing. After he was fed, Percy wrote out his version of what happened the night Dexter Clayton was gunned down, and that Darcy paid him to handle the murderous deed.

When he was done, everyone appeared satisfied, except for Percy, of course, who snarled, "I hope to high hell you people get what you deserve."

Neil and Shafts hustled him back outdoors, trussed him up like a steer again, and left him lying on the back porch.

After dark, confident that Percy would be fine until they returned, Jessi and the others rode into town for the plates. The town was quiet, and as they hitched their horses to the post outside the bank, Jessi realized that they probably looked like a gang of outlaws who'd come to rob the place.

Ros's keys worked like magic. The inside of the bank was as dark and quiet as outdoors. Preacher struck a match and brought a lamp to life. They used its light to guide the way to Reed's office door. The big floor safe was up under his desk, and as the men snaked it out, Griffin said, "Feels like old times."

They grinned in response.

Jessi recited the combination of numbers Ros said would open the safe. The plates were inside, just as he and Minerva had said they'd be. Because of the dim lighting, no one could tell whether the piles of money stacked inside were real or counterfeit. It didn't much matter. They were after the plates.

Jessi tucked the plates in the pillow slip she'd brought

along, then watched as the men struggled to fit the heavy iron safe back underneath the desk. When that was accomplished, they made their way quickly back to the door. They were riding back to the Clayton ranch a blink of an eye later.

"So Roscoe burned down the hotel?" Griffin asked Jessi, as they sat on the porch after their return. The Twins and Preacher had gone on to bed. They'd had quite a full day.

"Yep, and said he intended to take a hammer to Reed's printing press."

"Why would he burn down his own father's hotel?"

"He saw it as a way of getting back at him."

"Why doesn't he just move away? It isn't as if he were a child anymore. Didn't you say you, he, and Doyle are all about the same age?"

"Yes, we are."

"If he moves away and starts life somewhere else, he can become whoever he wants to be. Call himself Abe Lincoln, if he wants. Life is too short to be unhappy."

"Maybe you can talk with him."

"Nope. The last thing a drunk wants to hear is a lecture on being drunk. If he wants to turn his life around, he will."

Jessi didn't know if she agreed with him not talking to Ros, but she did agree that in order for Ros's life to change, he had to change it himself. No one else could do it for him. "Now that we have the plates, what's next?"

"I figure Reed's going to come stomping into my office as soon as he's back in town and we'll play it by ear. This will be his last day of freedom though. Between the plates and the signed statements by Minerva and Percy, he'll be lucky to see another sunrise."

"Are you going to take him in?"

"Yep. After I lock him up, I'll wire Dix up in Indian

Territory. Hope he's back from California by now. If not, I'll hand him over to Preacher and he can escort both he and Percy up to Judge Parker at Fort Smith.''

''You wouldn't want to turn them in yourself?''

''I would, but I'd have to leave you to do that, and I don't want to.''

She searched his face. ''You can go. Joth and I will be here when you get back.''

''Nope. I'm staying put. I kind of like being a family man.''

Jessi cupped his bearded cheek. ''I kinda like you.''

''Good, because when I say, 'Until death do us part,' I'll mean every word.''

He kissed her then, softy and sweetly, and sent her on in to bed.

Griffin was right. Reed Darcy came storming into the sheriff's office the next morning with steam rolling out of his ears. He looked around at the Twins, Griffin, and the Preacher, then barked, ''What the hell is this about you jailing my foreman Clem Davis?''

''Who told you that?'' Griffin asked calmly.

''It doesn't matter. Is it true?''

''The deputies and I questioned him about some things, then let him go.'' In many ways, that was true.

''What did you question him about, because he's missing.''

''This and that, but mostly about Dexter Clayton's killing.''

Darcy went still. ''Sheriff Hatcher said it was an accident, and I agreed.''

''Jessi and Joth didn't.''

For the first time since entering, he did not seem to have a ready reply. Finally he asked, ''And what did he have to say?''

"Nothing that concerns you right now. Did you say he was missing?"

"Him and my daughter-in-law."

Two Shafts replied, "Maybe they ran off together."

Reed shot him a look that normally quelled lesser men, but Two Shafts held the gaze easily.

"Minerva wouldn't just run off."

"We'll ask around. Maybe someone's seen her." Darcy would know everything he needed to know at the appropriate time.

Darcy wasn't through, it seemed. "You should've never won that election. We've got people missing, and where were you and your deputies when that gang broke into my bank last night?"

"No one reported a robbery to us," Neil spoke up in their defense. "How much money did they get?"

"They didn't steal money."

"Well, what else is there in a bank to steal?"

"They took some personal items," he amended hastily."

Griffin had a decidedly puzzled look on his face. "What kind of personal items? I can't conduct an investigation if I don't what I'm trying to recover."

"They're family items, heirlooms from my grandfather."

"Oh, really? I thought you might be looking for these." Griffin opened the pillow slip on his desk and took out the two plates.

Reed's eyes went wide as a harvest moon. "How'd you get those?"

"So they are yours, then?"

"No, no," he denied hastily. "They belong to a friend of mine."

"You do know these are plates for printing counterfeit bills?"

"No, really?"

"Aw, Cheno," Neil declared, "Just lock him up before he makes us all sick."

Two Shafts told Darcy, "Do we really look that stupid to you? I agree with Neil, lock him up and save our delicate sensibilities."

Griffin grinned. "Well, Mr. Darcy, what do you think?"

"You can't arrest me. I have friends in high places who wouldn't stand for it."

"Do they know you've been paying your debts with money you're printing in your son's barn?"

Darcy's eyes widened further.

"Yep, we know all about that, too. Your son's been real helpful these past few days."

"What do you mean?"

Preacher said, "He's the one who gave us the key to the bank and the numbers for your safe."

"What?"

"He even told us who burned down your hotel."

"Who?"

"He did."

This time he yelled even louder. *"What?"*

"Yep, he's been real helpful."

"So, are you going into the lock-up peacefully, or are you going to need assistance?" Griff asked.

"I'm not going to jail, to hell with all of you. You don't have the authority to arrest me or to confiscate my property."

"I thought you said the plates weren't yours?"

Darcy went silent.

Griffin came from behind the desk and walked over to where Darcy stood. "Now, Mr. Darcy, I know you can count money, but let's see if you can read."

"Read what?"

"My badge. What's it say?"

"Why in the world do I need to do that? It's a tin plated sheriff's star."

"Humor me, Mr. Darcy. Read the words aloud."

An exasperated Reed said, "United States Deputy . . ." His voice trailed off and he stared at the men in the office as if he'd never seen them before.

Griff said, "I think this star gives me all the authority I need, don't you? Take him away, boys."

The grinning Twins escorted the still stunned Darcy to the back room that held the office's lone cell.

Once word got out that Reed Darcy had been jailed, so many people stopped by to ogle him, Griff thought he was a circus attraction. Griffin let them look. After Darcy's arrogant and violence-filled reign, being stared at like a dog-faced boy would go a long way in deflating his superior opinion of himself. Griffin thought the people Darcy had tried to swindle and burn out of their homes deserved to know that justice had prevailed. He let them look their fill, but he drew the line at letting the Twins sell popcorn to add further excitement to the event.

Jessi spent her day keeping an eye on the trussed-up Percy and wondering what was going on in town. She knew this was supposed to be the day that Darcy went to jail and she'd dearly wanted to go into town and watch the scene unfold, but someone had to stay with Percy and she supposed she'd been the logical choice. However, the waiting and not knowing if Griff had been successful or not made for a long day.

Later, a man Jessi did not know rode up to the ranch. He introduced himself as Deputy Marshal Dixon Wildhorse.

"Pleased to meet you," a surprised Jessi said as she invited him in. "Griffin's in town. Thank you so much for sending him to us. He's been a godsend."

The tall, dark-skinned marshal nodded. "He's been helpful, then?"

"Very."

"I'm glad. How's my young friend Joth?"

"He's in town, visiting. I hope you'll stay long enough for him to see you. He'd be quite disappointed if he didn't get to thank you personally for answering his letter."

"I will be. So what has happened since Griffin's arrival?"

They sat in the kitchen and Jessi told him the story.

When she ended, the marshal said, "Griffin has been busy, hasn't he? And he was elected sheriff?"

"Yes, fair and square."

Dix seemed amazed. "Well, I can't wait to see him and offer my congratulations for a job well done."

"He didn't do it alone, he had help."

"From whom?"

"Preacher Vance Bigelow and the Twins."

He went still. "You aren't talking about Neil July and his Comanche brother, Two Shafts, are you?"

"Yes, I am. Do you know them?"

The marshal gave her a pointed look as he responded, "As a matter of fact, I do. They're wanted up in Indian Territory for a list of offenses a mile long and two miles wide."

"Oops," Jessi said.

"Are they here?"

Jessi shook her head. "No, they're in town. They're Griffin's deputies."

"The Twins are wearing stars?" he shouted.

Jessi nodded hesitantly. "They've been most helpful, too. Most helpful."

The marshal looked genuinely upset. "Take me to them."

"I can't. I'm watching a prisoner."

''What prisoner?''

Not certain of the marshal's mood, now that he knew the Twins were involved, she took him to the back porch to see Percy.

The trussed-up criminal took one look at the marshal and his eyes went wide as saucers. ''Marshal Wildhorse?''

''Well, hello, Percy.''

''You two know each other?''

''Yes, we do. Percy's wanted up in Indian Territory for bootlegging. Aren't you?''

''Yes, I am, so please take me with you when you go back. I'll stand trial, do whatever you want, just get me away from here.''

The marshal turned to Jessi and he appeared very confused, so Jessi explained, ''He had to play with the Twins yesterday.''

''Ah. What did he do?''

''Gunned down my father, on Darcy's orders. The Twins got him to confess.''

''I'd've confessed to killing Ol' Abe to get out of that hole,'' Percy exclaimed.

Jessi then explained the game. When she finished, the marshal chuckled.

For Jessi, just thinking back on how comical Percy had looked with only his head above ground made her smile all over again. She'd never seen anything like that in her whole life. The Terrible Twins were terrible indeed.

''So that's why he's so anxious to leave here. Can't much blame him,'' Dix said.

He looked down at Percy and said, ''Miss Clayton and I have to go to town. I want your word that you'll be here when we return.''

''Don't worry, Marshal. Just don't hand me over to those lunatics!''

"Be here when we return and I promise I won't. If you go back on your word, I'll have the Twins track you down."

Percy shivered as if that fate chilled his bones.

Jessi and the marshal rode off for town.

There was so much activity and people milling around, you'd've thought it was Juneteenth. A long line of folks stretched from the sheriff's office and down the street, but Jessi couldn't imagine why.

"What's going on here?" Wildhorse asked Jessi.

She shrugged. "I've no idea. Maybe we'll find out once we're inside."

They hitched their mounts to the post, then waded through the crowd to the door. Jessi noticed the Faraguts standing in line. "What's going on here?"

"Afternoon, Miss Clayton, didn't you hear? Sheriff Blake arrested Reed Darcy and we're all here to take a gander at him."

Marshal Wildhorse did not appear pleased. Jessi thanked the couple, then excused herself and followed the marshal inside.

The interior of the Vale sheriff's office was as crowded as the walk outside. Griff was pleased that people weren't lingering. It appeared half the town had shown up. When he looked and saw Dixon Wildhorse step through the door with Jessi trailing him, a grin spread across his face. "Well, welcome, Marshal. I thought you and your wife were in California?"

"We were. Katherine went on back to the Territory, but I made a detour here so I could find out how you were faring. Miss Clayton says you have everything under control."

"Sure do."

Just then, the Twins came out of the back. They took one look at the big Seminole lawman and both said in unison, "Uh oh," and immediately tried to tip their way back out.

"Hold it!" Dixon yelled.

They froze.

"Get back here," he growled.

They came back looking like guilty children.

Neil said, "Hello, Marshal."

"Hello, boys. How are you?"

"Fine," Two Shafts said. He looked hopeful. "Griff tell you he made us marshals?"

"No, but those stars look real familiar."

Wildhorse turned to Griffin and said pointedly, "I need to talk to you, privately."

Like a child headed for the woodshed, Griffin led the marshal to the back door.

Once Griff and Dix were alone, Dix requested calmly, or as calmly as he could, "Start from the beginning."

Griff told him the story from the beginning, emphasizing why he needed the help of two of the most wanted men in the territory.

Dix's jaw tightened.

"Look, Dix, you sent me down here to do a job, and I did the best I knew how. Of course my friends are going to be outlaws. I was an outlaw, too, remember?"

"What do you mean, *was?*"

"I'm giving up the life. I plan to spend the rest of my days walking on the right side of the law."

"And what brought about this miraculous conversion?"

"The lady in there. Jessi Clayton. We're going to be married as soon as things settle down."

Dix stared. "I sent you down here to help her, not help yourself to her bed. Dammit, Griff!"

"It's not like that. I truly do love her. Amazing enough, she loves me."

Dix studied him for a long time. "You realize this is very hard for me to believe."

"Yes, but how do you think I feel? I had plans for Mexico and the *señoritas*, remember."

"I do. So this isn't just another conquest?"

"No. I plan on being faithful, too."

Dix chuckled and shook his head. "I don't believe this."

"I'm serious about her, Dix. She's honest, fiery, and can shoot the wings off a fly at fifty paces."

"Then it's probably in your best interests to be faithful."

Griff laughed. "No kidding."

Dix surveyed Griffin for another few moments. "So you're through with train robbing?"

"And anything else that might bring shame to her and Joth."

"Okay, then maybe I won't be so mad about those two being here."

Griff was grateful. "Thanks. If it hadn't been for them, I doubt Darcy would be behind bars."

"I saw Percy back at the ranch."

"Yes, good old Percy. The Twins were able to get him to confess to murdering Jessi's father, and we have his confession on paper. Got another one from Darcy's daughter-in-law."

"Good. Sounds like having the Twins' help wasn't such a harebrained idea after all."

"No, it wasn't, and they've been real respectful of the badge. A sheriff couldn't ask for better deputies."

"Miss Clayton said Preacher Bigelow is here also?"

"Yeah, he's down at the saloon, getting something to eat. He'll be back shortly."

Dixon looked at Griffin and said genuinely, "I'm real proud of you. Judge Parker's going to be glad this has been resolved."

"Not as glad as I am, because as soon as you take Reed and Percy off our hands, Jessi and I can get married."

"Congratulations on that, too."

"Thanks. You aren't going to take the Twins in, are you?"

"No, not this time. I think the judge will consider their help valuable enough to look the other way. Are you going to stay on as sheriff here?"

"Yep. I have a family to provide for and this is a decent way to make a living, don't you think?"

Dix nodded. "I sure do." He then said genuinely, "You've done yourself proud here, Griffin, and to know that you've turned your life around makes it even better."

Griffin felt good about his job here, too, and about the life he sensed waiting for him just over the horizon. "If it weren't for you, I'd be rotting away in that prison. Thanks for having faith in me, because in the beginning I did have my doubts."

Dixon gave Griffin one of his rare smiles. "I knew you could do it. Now, let's get back in. I want to meet this Darcy."

Inside the cell, Darcy took one look at Wildhorse and asked Griffin, "Who the hell is this, another rube come to gawk?"

"Nice man," Dixon told Griffin. To Darcy he replied, "No, I'm not just another rube come to gawk. I'm U.S. Deputy Marshal Dixon Wildhorse, and I'm here to take you to Judge Parker's court up at Fort Smith."

"I'm not going anywhere. My friends will be here any minute to get me out of here and then I'll have your star, marshal, and your job. Don't you know who I am?"

"Yep, you're Reed Darcy, and you're wanted for counterfeiting, murder, embezzlement, and a laundry list of other offenses."

Darcy turned away from the marshal's wintry face and demanded, ''Blake, did you send that wire like I told you to?''

''Sure did,'' Griff told him, ''but we never got a reply. Looks like your cavalry has a prior engagement.''

Darcy'd had Griff send wires to his so-called highly placed friends but so far no one had shown up or wired back to pledge their support.

''They'll be here, don't worry,'' Darcy promised.

''I won't.''

When Griffin and Dix returned to the front office, they were both laughing about something and Jessi felt relief wash over her. The marshal had appeared very angry when he initially asked to speak with Griffin in private and she'd been afraid something bad would come of it as a result. Now it appeared as if everything would be all right.

Wildhorse looked her way. ''I hear you and Griffin are planning to marry. Congratulations.''

''Thank you,'' Jessi replied. She swung her gaze to Griffin and saw that he appeared as happy as she felt inside. ''Will you be staying for the wedding?''

''I'm afraid not. The sooner I get Darcy and Percy to Fort Smith, the sooner I can get back home to my Kate.''

''Is that your wife?''

''Yes.''

''Then you and Mrs. Wildhorse must come and visit us when you can stay longer.''

''We will.''

The Twins had been standing quietly as if they were trying not to draw the lawman's attention. It didn't work. Dixon zeroed in on them.

''And as for you two, I heard you've been exemplary deputies.''

''You did?''

''Yes, and for your help, I'll see if I can't convince

Judge Parker to suspend the warrants you've been accumulating for the past three years.''

The Twins looked at each other with glee.

''Would you consider staying on as deputies?'' he asked.

The brothers shook their heads. ''Nope. We're here to help Cheno, and once that's finished, we're turning in our stars.''

Just then, Joth came tearing into the office and looked around excitedly. When his spectacled eyes settled on Marshal Wildhorse, a big grin filled his face. ''Marshal Wildhorse!''

''How are you, Joth?''

It was as if Joth couldn't believe his eyes. ''I'm fine, sir. What are you doing here?''

Looking down at his young friend, Dix said, ''Oh, thought I'd come down and pay you and your aunt a visit. I wanted to see how things were faring.''

''It's been real exciting, *real* exciting. Thanks for sending Griff to help.''

''You're welcome. Thanks for sending me that letter.''

''You're welcome. When I heard you were here, I had to come. Had to.''

Jessi smiled. ''Joth, honey, take a breath.''

He quieted for a moment, but the brightness of his grin continued to shine.

The folks in line to see Darcy in the back room cell had heard and seen all of this and were looking on with smiles—all of them except Lydia Cornell. She came in looking anxious and nervous. She stood in the line impatiently clutching her handbag. Jessi wanted to confront her about the death of her mother, but decided she would take Gillie's advice and leave the past in the past.

When Lydia came out after seeing Darcy, Jessi noted that she had tears in her eyes and that she rushed out as if she were terribly distraught. Jessi wondered what Lydia's husband Wilson would've had to say about his wife's display, but she moved past the thoughts as she returned her attention to Griffin and the others.

A few moments later, one of the women in the back let out a scream and a gun-wielding and angry Darcy appeared at the door. Before anyone could react, he snatched Joth in front of him to use as a shield. "I want everybody on the other side of the room. Now!"

Dixon pledged stonily, "Darcy, harm that boy and I'll string you up right here."

"Shut up and do what you're told."

Everyone in the office moved to the far side of the room. The tension was thick as fog.

"Jessi! Make those rubes outside clear a path, then unhitch me a horse."

Jessi remembered Gillie saying Reed was afraid of horses. If he were that desperate to escape, Joth could be in real danger, so she said, "Okay, Reed, just don't hurt Joth."

With one arm around Joth and the other arm extended to hold the gun on Jessi, Darcy kept a steady eye on the angry faces of Griffin, Wildhorse, and the Twins. Joth appeared terrified.

Jessi went out and quickly cleared him a way. People began scrambling as Darcy and Joth stepped out onto the walk. He maneuvered his way over to the hitching post and snapped at her. "Untie one of those horses."

He was now positioned with his back to the street. By now the lawmen were standing in the doorway, furious but powerless to do anything but watch.

Darcy grinned evilly. "I told you help would come, didn't I? Give me those reins, Jessi!"

Keeping a wary eye on Griff and the others, Reed blindly took the offered reins, pushed Joth aside, and stomped into the stirrup to mount. The moment he did,

Snake Eyes reared violently to register his displeasure. Darcy cried out because his foot was tangled in the stirrup and he tried to grab hold of the saddle, but Snake Eyes didn't care. The horse kept rearing and twisting and Darcy was flung up and down like a rag doll again and again. He was finally thrown free and landed hard against the edge of the wooden walk. His eyes were closed and his body limp. His head appeared to be leaning at an odd angle. The doc rushed out of the crowd. He knelt by the body and then after a few moments looked up and shook his head. Darcy's neck had been broken. He was dead.

"I didn't know Snake Eyes would wind up killing him," Jessi told Griffin solemnly. "I just thought he'd show his hostility *before* Reed stuck his foot in the stirrup and he'd be forced to pick another horse. I was trying to buy some time."

They were back at the ranch now and evening had claimed the day. Griffin held her close and placed a light kiss on her forehead. "I know, it was a good plan. Too bad Snake Eyes didn't get briefed on the details beforehand."

"Well, it's too late now."

"Yes, it is. Now, don't get me wrong, I have as much respect for the dead as the next fellow, but will I mourn Darcy? Not even a little bit. He's shoveling coal for the devil just like he's supposed to be. So, enough about him. When's the wedding?"

Jessi looked up at the man she loved. "If Gillie has the dress finished, we could have it tomorrow."

"Really?"

"Sure, why not? It isn't as if it's going to be a big affair."

The way he quieted made her cock her head. "Why

do I have the feeling that you have something you've been meaning to tell me?''

He gave her a chagrined grin. ''Well, Auntie wanted to give the wedding, and—''

''Auntie?'' Jessi exclaimed. ''Oh, Griffin, please don't tell me I'm going to be married in that whore-red saloon. I love Auntie with all of my heart, but—''

''No, she's having a bower built outside.''

''A bower? I'm going to be married beneath a bower?''

''You certainly have a lot of questions. How about I kiss you and make you forget about them all?''

She chuckled. ''Sounds like a very good idea.''

Chapter 15

Because Gillie still had a few last touches to add to Jessi's dress, they agreed to have the wedding in three days' time. Although Jessi anxiously wanted to be Griffin's wife, there were loose ends to tie up on the Darcy affair and Jessi wanted none of the matters to be hanging over their heads on their wedding day.

The morning after Darcy's death, Marshal Wildhorse rode out to the ranch. He said he had news everyone needed to hear, so they all gathered in the kitchen.

"First of all, the judge sends his regards and his thanks for all your help. He was especially intrigued by the game you two played with Percy, said he might add it to his own options for justice."

The Twins broke out into matching grins until Dix said, "You two don't actually believe that, do you?"

The Twins looked stunned.

"Judge Parker says if you ever pull a stunt like that with a suspect again, he will personally bury the both of you the same way."

The Preacher laughed out loud.

Griff faked a cough to hide his own laugh.

Two Shafts appeared to be amazed. "The marshal has a sense of humor!"

"Sure does," Neil exclaimed. "He didn't have one the last time we met up."

"Must be the new Mrs. Marshal's doing."

"Must be."

Jessi gave up on trying to hide her smile. Whatever would she do around here for entertainment once they left town?

Griff asked, "What about my parole?"

"It's all taken care of."

Griffin felt relief wash over him like a summer rain. A grinning Preacher slapped him on the back.

"The judge wants to know if you'll remain as the deputy marshal here?" Dix asked.

Jessi looked at the man she loved and he stared back at her from his spot on the other side of the porch.

Jessi then heard Neil ask quietly, "Is the marshal trying to be funny again?"

Two Shafts shrugged. "Who knows?"

The marshal then asked Griff, "Well, what's your answer?"

Still holding Jessi's eyes, he offered this heartfelt reply, "Tell him I'll do whatever he wants me to do as long as I can be at her side," and he pointed at Jessi.

Her answering smile radiated her love.

"Good. You can resign your position as sheriff. The town can have two lawmen if it wants, but you're the marshal here. One small detail left: the Twins are going to be your deputies."

The porch echoed with the roar of "What?"

Neil came quickly to his own defense, "Marshal Wildhorse, my brother and I really don't want to keep the stars."

"Too late. I already asked the judge and he's already agreed."

"But you can't possibly believe we'd make good lawmen."

Preacher was now laughing so hard Jessi feared he'd hurt himself. "No, I don't, but Judge Parker thinks it'll be ample punishment for all the havoc you two have caused over the past few years. It's either the jobs, or I take you to Austin with my other prisoners."

Two Shafts asked pointedly, "Doesn't the Constitution have a clause about cruel and unusual punishment?"

"Yes, but the last I looked, it didn't apply to those of us with Native blood," Neil cracked.

Two Shafts thought a minute, then declared, "Well, maybe we should take the job. If Griff is getting married and Dixon Wildhorse is making jokes, either hell is freezing over or the world is about to end."

Everyone laughed.

So the Twins agreed to be Griff's deputies. Griffin didn't believe for a minute that they'd stick around longer than a few weeks, but he didn't say it out loud.

That afternoon, the marshal left town, taking with him a very grateful Percy and Lydia Cornell. She'd been arrested for aiding Darcy's escape. She'd provided the gun and a key to the cell's door. Because of her husband's position as head of the town council, he had a key to every door in town, from the undertaker's office to the key to the jail, and that was how Darcy had gotten out. Wilson Cornell appeared devastated by his wife's collusion when Griff arrested her right after Darcy's death, but he obviously loved her because he'd gone along too, so he could be by her side during her trial.

Jessi knocked on the barn door and opened it just a bit. Griffin was inside working on the dream bed. "Can I come in?"

"Just a moment."

She could hear him moving around, then he called her in.

"Hello, beautiful," he said, smiling as she came in.

She took a look at the tarp covering his project, then replied, "Hello, yourself."

She strolled over so they could share a kiss. When it ended Jessi was left a bit dazed. Still standing in the circle of his arms, she looked up into his sherry-colored eyes and said, "I know your ego is already larger than the state of Texas, but you are one good kisser, Griffin Blake."

"Glad you like them, because for the rest of our lives, they'll be all yours."

"Good thing. I'm a selfish old woman."

His grin warmed her.

"How do you feel about the parole?" she asked softly.

"Wonderful."

"Me too."

"Have you talked to Auntie about the wedding? Any idea what she has in store?" he asked.

"Nope. She won't tell me, and it's probably better that I don't know, because I'd probably veto half of whatever she's cooking up."

"Well, let her enjoy herself."

"I plan to."

Griff still found it hard to believe that this beautiful woman returned his love.

"I had a talk with Gillie the other day about my mother's death."

"And?"

When she didn't respond, he reached down and raised her chin so he could see into her eyes. "It's bothering you, isn't it?"

She didn't want to admit it, but it did. "Gillie told me not to judge, but I keep wondering how my mother could've planned to leave Mildred and me behind."

"That's a natural question. Is that one of the things you and Gillie talked about?"

"Yes, she told me the past is the past and that the Lord gave us the future so we could go on."

"She's a very wise woman, that Gillie."

"I think so, too. She suggested I let your love fill my heart instead of the pain of something I had no control over."

He reached up and stroked her cheek. "She's right again. We both lost our mothers in untimely ways, so those are words of wisdom we can both use."

Jessi placed her head against his chest and heard his heart beating in time with her own. "I believe we're going to do well together, you and I."

He kissed the top of her soft hair. "I believe so, too."

That night, they took the old buckboard out and parked in their special spot hidden among the trees. Because the passion and desire they harbored for each other had been simmering since their last interlude, it didn't take long for the kissing to melt into the game Jessi liked to play most. She called it, A Dozen and One Ways to Use a Buggy Seat. They made up the rules as they went along.

In the days that followed, Griff divided his time between finishing the dream bed and getting his marshal business in order. Dixon had left Griff a mountain of notes on how to handle the job, and another mountain of notes explaining the paperwork. Sheriffs were elected officials, but no one in Vale seemed opposed to having an appointed deputy to keep the peace.

To Griff and the Preacher's surprise, Two Shafts and Neil were extremely attentive to their duties, at least for the present. They even paid close attention to all the notes left by Dixon Wildhorse, and for now, enforced the law in a professional manner. Griff knew that sooner or later mistakes would be made, not only by them but by him too, but he refused to worry over it; if Judge Parker thought it was a good idea to appoint a reformed train robber as an agent of the law, who was Griff to argue?

Griffin finished the bed the morning of the wedding. After Jessi and Joth left for town to pick up their wedding duds, he had Preacher and the Twins help him move his old bed out of the room he and Jessi would be sharing as man and wife so that the new one could take its place. Once he had it positioned, he added the new mattress and the new satin sheets he'd gotten from Auntie. For his last act, he pulled out the new rug he'd purchased at Abe Thomas's store and saw that the big circle he'd had Gillie sew in the center looked just right. He set the rug on the floor, smiled the smile of a plotting man, then went to get ready to get married.

Later, the lady rancher Jessi Rose Clayton stood before Preacher Vance Bigelow and, after placing her hand on Griffin's mother's Bible, became the wife of the former train robber and now U.S. Deputy Marshal Griffin Blake. The Twins, all decked out and duded up, stood up with Griffin, and a smiling Joth gave the bride away. Auntie and Gillie both cried, as did Jessi and every other woman in the packed field behind the saloon.

At the reception, Jessi stood beside her husband and looked out over the amazing crowd. Auntie had certainly outdone herself: there were tents to shelter the guests from the hot afternoon sun, strolling musicians, a harpist over in a quiet portion of the grove, and enough good food to supply six other wedding receptions. There were even jugglers and a trained dancing bear for the amusement of Joth and the other children in attendance.

"You know, Griffin, I have a feeling an old carpet bag filled with railroad gold had a lot to do with all this. I've never seen anything even close to this spread."

Griffin said, "Well, there was a carpet bag involved, but only a little bit."

He pulled her into his arms. "Are you sure we're

going to have the house to ourselves tonight?''

''Absolutely. Joth's spending the night with Gillie.''

She was about to say something else when she noticed Roscoe Darcy making his way over to where she and Griffin stood. He looked tired and worn, but his eyes were clear. Jessi backed out of Griffin's arms to greet him.

He walked up and shook Griffin's hand, then turned to Jessi. ''Congratulations, Jessi girl,'' he said solemnly.

''Thanks, Ros. How are you?''

''As well as could be expected. I buried him yesterday.''

From what she'd heard, Garland Findley had been the only person besides Roscoe at Reed's grave site. ''What are your plans?''

''I think I'll head to California. See if I can't make me a new life.''

''Sounds like a grand idea.''

He then turned to Griffin. ''You take care of her now, Blake. She's a jewel.''

Griff nodded. ''I will. Take care of yourself.''

''Write me when you get settled, Ros,'' Jessi said.

His eyes looked far older than his years. ''Do you mean that?''

''Yes, I do.''

He gave her a small smile. ''Then I will. Bye, Jessi.''

''Bye, Ros.''

As he walked away, she was reminded of the young boy who once went riding with her after her mother's death, and now Jessi wished him godspeed.

Once they were alone again, Griffin asked, ''Did I tell you how beautiful you look today in that emerald-colored dress?''

''Yes, at least a hundred times, and I never tire of hearing it.'' And it was true, she felt like a queen.

After the cake was cut, Preacher came over to say his

good-byes. He was heading back to his home in Denver. Jessi gave him a tight, lingering hug and whispered her thanks for all he'd done. The Twins joined the bittersweet sendoff and the men embraced like the friends they were. Preacher promised to visit again soon and Jessi had tears in her eyes as she watched him ride off. Two Shafts and Neil were on their way back to man the marshal's office for the rest of the day and night. As they departed, they vowed to see both Jessi and Griff sometime tomorrow.

Later that evening, the newlyweds finally came home. As soon as they stepped onto the porch, Griff scooped her up into his arms, and after making her close her eyes, carried her, laughing, inside. He took her straight to their bedroom and laid her down on the new bed encased in the new satin sheets. "Now you can look."

Jessi took her hands away from her eyes and stared transfixed by the beautiful creation. The bed was large, very large, large enough for them to sleep in together comfortably and to do anything else Jessi's outrageous little heart might desire. He'd carved a beautifully entwined gothic "B" for Blake and "C" for Clayton into the headboard, and it was so distinctive looking, she wondered if she could register it as their new brand with the local cattleman association. It was a bed dreams were made of, and it looked as if it would last for many, many years to come.

"Do you like it?"

"Yes. It's truly beautiful. The Reverend Blake taught you well."

"Auntie had the mattress shipped in from San Antonio. It only arrived the other day. She also provided the bedding as a wedding present."

Jessi stood up and walked around the bed. For the first time she noticed the tiny roses and stars decorating the top edge of the headboard.

"Roses for you. And marshal stars for me."

She looked at him. "Do you think you'll take to being a marshal?"

"I think I will. It's an honorable profession, it pays decent, and I get to be here with you."

"That just about covers everything, but you don't like guns."

"No, I don't, and I plan on using mine as little as possible. Justice can be creative, just ask the Twins."

"Do you really believe they're going to stick around?"

He came up behind and wrapped his arms around her. "Nope." He nuzzled her neck. "My money says they'll be gone by this time next week."

Jessi bloomed under his intoxicating nearness. "If you're right, Marshal Wildhorse will not be pleased."

"No, he won't, but he'll have to find them before he can tell them that."

Jessi smiled.

"How about you and me play a little marbles?"

"Right now?" She turned to look up at him.

"Sure, why not? Didn't you set down a challenge a few weeks ago?"

"Well, yes I did, but this is our wedding night. I assumed you'd be more interested in stripping me naked and making me do shameless things?"

"Oh, don't worry, that's coming, but right now, I want to play marbles."

"Where?"

"Right here."

"But marbles won't hold on this smooth wood floor."

"You're right, so we'll use this."

He gestured to the rug under their feet. Jessi looked down at the circle and grinned. "You've thought of everything, haven't you?"

"Just about. So how about it? I figured if we play in

here behind closed doors, we won't have to chance you being seen crawling around half naked.''

She had no idea where he might be headed with this snare, but she took the bait anyway and let herself be reeled in. ''Why am I going to be crawling around half naked?''

''Because, my very sweet wife, that is what we will be playing for—your clothing.''

''My clothing?''

''Yep. Every marble I win, wins me one article of clothing.''

His eyes were ablaze with such brazen promise, her desire blossomed to life. ''And what about your clothes? Will my boon be the same?''

''Yes, but since you aren't going to win *any* marbles, it isn't going to matter.''

''Griffin Blake, you are the most arrogant man I've ever met.''

''And I can't wait to see you crawling around dressed in nothing but your drawers, Mrs. Blake.''

He was right. Jessi didn't win a single marble. She lost her beautiful emerald dress first and then the chemise underneath. As the game continued she forfeited her camisole, stockings, garters, and shoes. Jessi Rose Clayton Blake, who at the age of ten could whip any boy around at marbles, was now crawling around the rug dressed in nothing but her drawers and the new gold circlets in her ears as she tried to set up her very last shot.

Griffin of course was still fully dressed. He'd opened a button on his fancy shirt only because he'd grown so warm watching her add to the growing pile of clothing at his side. When she lost her camisole, he'd consoled her by suckling her softly until her breath stacked up in her throat and then let her take her turn again. Throughout the game, he touched her, stroked her, and kissed her until they were both bursting with need. Griffin had indeed stripped her and now with the last shot about to be played, the time had come to make her do shameless things.

Jessi didn't know why she was trying to concentrate on this last shot. Each and every time she'd lost a marble he'd removed a piece of her clothing with wandering hands and tantalizing kisses. Because of that she couldn't concentrate—hell, she could barely see. He'd left her throbbing everywhere.

Her last shot went wildly astray. The game was over.

"Stand up," he whispered thickly.

She got to her feet slowly and stood in a passion-induced haze while he took her last piece of clothing, her drawers. He then proceeded to boldly show her that maybe losing to him wasn't so bad after all. He carried her to the bed and neither of them went to sleep until dawn.

The next morning, Jessi was still asleep when the nude Griffin came charging into the room yelling, "I'm going to kill them with my bare hands!"

After such a prolonged night of marital passion, Jessi had trouble trying to discern what he was bellowing about.

"Read this!"

Still half asleep, she almost asked if it was really necessary to comply with his request, but she pushed the covers aside and took the piece of paper from his adamant hand.

She read:

> *Dear Griff,*
>
> *Shafts and I got the urge to move on after Preacher left, so we're gone too.*

She looked up from the note and into her husband's blazing eyes. "Well, darling, you said yourself you didn't expect them to stay. I admit, they took off a lot faster than either of us thought, but—''

"Read on."

"Okay." Jessi read on:

> . . . *Oh, by the way, since you now have a regular job, we took your carpet bag with us. We were going to knock on the door last night and ask you about it, but you sounded* real *busy, so we just left.*

Jessi's eyes widened.

> *We hope you and Miss Jessi will be happy. See you soon, we hope.*

It was signed *Neil July and Two Shafts.*

Jessi set the note aside. She could see that her irate husband found no humor in the note at all, but she did and began to laugh.

"This isn't funny, Jessi."

"Oh, it is too, and you know it. They're tricksters, you said so yourself."

"Damn those Twins."

"They are terrible, aren't they?" Jessi added, unable to suppress her chuckling. She'd no idea what Griffin had planned for the money, but now it didn't matter.

Griff grinned and shook his head. "Guess I'll have to wire Dix and tell him they're on the loose again."

Jessi smiled. "Guess so."

She missed the Twins already and hoped they would come back to visit real soon. "You aren't going to town right now, are you?"

The sassy look in her eyes made him ask, "Why, do you have something more interesting in mind?"

Feeling quite brazen after last night, Jessi Rose Blake

slid the covering off her nude, sleep-warmed body and said, "Maybe. If you're up to it."

Griff grinned, "Oh, I'm up to it as you can see."

Jessi gave him a grin in reply.

Later, as completion sent them both soaring into love's heaven, Jessi knew Griffin would always be her light, and that she'd never have to walk in darkness again.

Afterword

~~~~~⌒◝◝◝⌒~~~~~

I do hope you enjoyed reading *The Taming of Jessi Rose* and the historical information surrounding the contributions of pioneering African-American Texans. If all of the mail I received after the 1997 publication of *Topaz,* my fifth book from Avon Books, is any indication, westerns seem to be a particular fan favorite, so thanks for all the feedback and encouragement. One of the most interesting geographical facts I learned while researching this book had to do with the sheer size of the original Republic of Texas. It encompassed over 100,000 square miles, and included parts of what are now New Mexico, Oklahoma, Kansas, Wyoming, and Colorado!

As always, I'm passing along a list of books for those of you wishing more information on the historical aspects highlighted in Jessi and Griffin's story. *Knowledge is power, but shared knowledge empowers us all!*

Patterson, Richard. *Train Robbery*. Johnson Publishing. Boulder, Colorado. 1981.

Durham, Philip, and Everett L. Jones. *Negro Cowboys*. University of Nebraska Press. Lincoln. 1965.

Love, Nat. *The Life and Adventures of Nat Love*. Black Classic Press. Baltimore, Maryland. 1988.

Williams, David A. *Bricks Without Straw: A Comprehensive History of African-Americans in Texas*. Eakin Press. Austin, Texas. 1997.

Texas: A Guide to the Lone Star State. American Guide Series. Hastings House. New York. 1940.

Katz, William Loren. *Black West*. Anchor Books. Garden City, New York. 1973.

Brown, Dee. *Bury My Heart at Wounded Knee*. Henry Holt and Company. New York. 1991.

Burton, Arthur T. *Black Red and Deadly*. Eakin Press. Austin, Texas. 1991.

In closing, let me give a shout out to all of you who've taken the time to write me this past year. If you've not received a reply, please know that due to the volume of mail I'm receiving it's becoming increasingly harder to answer each of you individually, but I do read and keep each and every piece, so keep them coming. I would also like to thank the following individuals for keeping my feet on the path: Lucia Macro; Monique Patterson; N. Yost; Rochelle Hardy, aka The First Fan; Ladies in Line and the members of the Beverly Jenkins Fan Club; Felicia Wintons, owner of Books for Thought and bookseller extraordinaire; all of the bookclubs nationwide who've invited me to their meetings or featured my books on their lists; the ladies of Delta Sigma Theta Sorority, for their support during their national convention in New Orleans; Shirley Covington in Greensboro;

and G.O. in Chicago; and of course, my family. Until next time.

Peace,